THE LAW OF FALLING BODIES

To Ellie, who helps me solve the mysteries.

Epigraph

So now I'm goin' back again,
I got to get to her somehow.
All the people we used to know
They're an illusion to me now.
Some are mathematicians
Some are carpenter's wives.
Don't know how it all got started,
I don't know what they're doin' with their lives.
– From "Tangled Up in Blue" by Bob Dylan
(© Copyright 1974 Ram's Horn Music)

Contents

Foreword

▼

This novel takes place in the seventies. You know what I mean.

Prelude

▼

Falling, the snow was, lightly. From inside the warm university bookstore, he carefully kept his face toward the pages of a magazine while his eyes slid slyly sideways, watching through the window next to him. He turned the pages of the magazine slowly, and moved his head minutely from left to right, from top to bottom, in case anyone was observing him. The article on Ford's defeat by Carter went unread.

Presently, he saw the dark shape of the expected courier appear out of the swirling snow, near the entrance to the university library. The courier pulled the door open and entered. The watcher kept turning pages, waiting.

Within two minutes the courier left the library, glanced self-consciously left and right, then vanished into the snow again.

He continued turning pages for another four minutes.

Then he stood slowly and returned the magazine to the rack. He walked to the door, automatically bundling himself against the weather outside.

It was a short walk from the bookstore to the library. Its blank white walls loomed above him, their slashes of windows leaking warm light. He tugged at the glass door, which slid open silently. He held his identity card out to the inattentive student on duty, and continued walking to the very rear of the library.

From there, he mounted the deserted back staircase to the fourth floor. He walked all the way back to the front, and descended one floor. The aisle he was interested in was on the right, and he passed it. Instead, he found an empty study carrel in the back and watched for two minutes. No one was following him. No one was watching the aisle of books.

He stood up again and moved back toward the aisle. He pulled one book at random off a shelf as he passed, and pretended to be paging through it as he walked. Again, he passed by the aisle. There was no one coming from the opposite direction. He turned down a parallel aisle to the far end, turned again, and finally walked along the aisle of his interest.

It held oversized art history books, dusty from disuse. He stopped halfway down the aisle, lowered himself to a squat, and appeared to be looking for a particular title. He drew a large brown book from the shelf, along with the book next to it. He carried them negligently under one arm, climbed the stairs to the next floor, and then proceeded to another empty carrel isolated in a far corner of the library.

When he was seated, and satisfied that no one was nearby, he began leafing through the large brown book. He got to page 26. The envelope of money that he had left there earlier in the day was gone. When he reached page 52, he found a large manila envelope, which he withdrew and placed under the book.

After waiting several more minutes, during which he turned pages slowly, he put one hand under the brown book and loosened the metal clasp of the envelope. He opened its flap and withdrew a small pile of papers. He placed them on the pages of the brown book. They contained mathematical formulae, and some diagrams of equipment. They were stamped "CONFIDENTIAL" and "SECRET". He smiled slightly.

There were ten pages, no, eleven. Puzzled, he pulled out the last page. Unlike the others, this had no formulae or diagrams. Only a short and simple typed message:

This is the last delivery.

I know your secret.

I'm dropping our arrangement.

He was furious, and automatically clamped down on his rage, so that no one would notice his expression. He continued to turn the pages of the book, oblivious to the colors and forms within.

The last delivery? He smiled crookedly. He would decide when the last delivery would be, if ever.

His secret? His expression sobered. That was more serious. Perhaps merely a threat, a shot in the dark. But if true? The crooked smile returned. He could deal with that too, as he had before. Many times.

Dropping the arrangement?

He collected all the papers and slid them back into the large envelope, which he concealed under his coat. He stood, leaving the books on the desk in the carrel. He tapped them with a finger, once.

He knew all about what – and whom – to drop, and from just how great a height.

Thursday

▼

One

She pulled the trigger.

The gun bucked with a metallic snap. A shiny steel marble arced across the physics lab, struck the floor, and rolled into a corner. Instantly, two sophomore engineering students bounded forward, measured how far from the gun the marble had traveled, and retrieved it. She was already cocking the spring-loaded gun for her next shot.

I wasn't watching. Sitting at the tall table at the front of the lab, a pile of ungraded lab reports in front of me, I was extremely busy pretending to grade them. I was aware of it all, though, and especially of her.

She raised her hand. "Mark?" I didn't mind my students calling me by my first name. It wasn't as if I were a real professor, only a graduate student. At least they didn't attempt to pronounce my last name, always a painful experience.

I looked up from my avoidance of work at her. Stephanie was on her knees, bending slightly over the projectile gun, like some technological Madonna and child. With a great effort of will, I was able to appear as outwardly calm as I ever was when addressing a human adult female. "Um...er...yes...ah...Stephanie?"

"We fired five shots. What do we do now?"

Read the lab manual, was my reflex thought. Instead, I merely recited, for probably the twentieth time this week, "Find the average of the five distances. Then change the angle of elevation of the gun, and shoot and measure five more. You want five shots per angle for each of ten angles."

She frowned. "But that's fifty shots."

Too fast to stop myself I said, "Very good: five times ten *is* fifty." Giggles rippled from around the lab. I spread my hands apologetically. "Sorry. You *will* need fifty shots though. And don't forget, I want everyone's graphs before you all leave today."

She pouted the pout of the oppressed and gave me a look that could have meant several things, mostly unpleasant. Then she stole a glance at the wall clock. I suspected a popular soap opera figured largely in her urgency. She turned on her lab partners savagely. "Come on, you guys. You want to be here all day?"

Her exhortation sparked a dramatic transformation, and her group, and all the other groups in the lab, snapped to their tasks with the zeal and enthusiasm that only the prospect of leaving physics lab early can inspire. Young minds, hungry for knowledge.

According to my estimate, I had given her about 20 to 30 seconds of my attention, so I was careful to make my way around the room and give at least that much attention to each of my other 26 students afterwards. I didn't want anyone to be able to accuse me of favoritism, but it did take time and effort. However, I actually enjoyed watching the metal balls dependably trace their parabolas through space, the translation of the spring's captive energy into the freedom of flight. I never did get back to pretending to grade those reports.

I didn't need the complication of thinking Stephanie—a student— attractive. In fact, I wasn't even sure that I *did* find her attractive. I never let myself get that far along in my thinking before slamming the steel gate down. I wanted very much to keep that Pandora's box shut.

Besides my desire to avoid getting involved with a student, I was rather leery of the whole man-woman thing these days anyway. True, it had been almost a year since I had seen Lee—not counting the nightmares—but I was still far from over her. That painful episode fell like a shadow over anything I avoided feeling for women like Stephanie.

Despite her impatience, she was still one of the last to leave. When she dropped her graph of the graceful curve onto the pile, I deliberately said, "Thanks" as offhandedly as possible, and intentionally looked up absently.

She gave me a smile, and a look that could have meant only one or maybe two things. "See you later." She turned and strolled out the door. I watched the empty doorway for several seconds after she had gone, but could perceive no explanatory echoes with my limited senses.

I directed my gaze back to the lab reports lying patiently in front of me on the table. I never did get around to grading them. What with classes, dinner, studying late, and the murder, there just wasn't time.

Two

After everyone had gone, I straightened the lab rapidly, shoving all the projectile guns onto a cart for later transport to another lab room. Then I dashed up the stairs to my two o'clock class in electromagnetic theory, with the dread Professor Speen.

This Speen was a major thorn in the collective butts of us graduate students. He succeeded in being both demanding and unhelpful, and his handling of this class was typical. Electromagnetic theory is a pretty opaque topic anyway. Even with the best professor possible, it would have been difficult, though I could have gotten *something* out of it.

In many ways, electromagnetic theory is the most important part of physics. Maxwell had ingeniously blended the separate laws of electricity and of magnetism into a single symphonic whole, producing a model we physicists were still trying to emulate with other laws. Einstein's relativity had grown from the roots of Maxwell's equations. Every beam of light, every song on the radio, every TV image danced on waves of electromagnetism. The equations were beautiful, symmetric, and sparkled like a precious gem.

But Speen had crushed all that, rendering understanding absolutely impossible, which was his professorial forte. In short, there was nothing wrong with Professor Speen that six tons of steel dropped from a height couldn't solve.

I rushed to get to the room on time, not because I was so eager for his company, but because he was merciless to stragglers. Of course, he wasn't there yet. He often wandered in fifteen minutes late, expecting us to wait for him. You'd think we wouldn't mind missing fifteen minutes of Speen, but the catch was that if he were fifteen minutes late getting to class, he'd keep us twenty minutes late at the end to make up for it. On the other hand, if he were on time and you arrived after him—not late, mind you, just after him—he would scorch you with a laser glance.

Besides myself in this class, there were the Four Asian Students and Peter Schultz. I thought of them as the Four Asian Students because they were students, they were Asian, there were four of them, always, and neither I nor anyone else knew their actual names. They were always together and, while I knew what their four names *were*, having heard professors call the roll enough times, I had no idea which name belonged to which person. Even the professors didn't know. A name would be called and an acknowledgment would emanate from their midst, but there was no telling who had said what.

The Four Asian Students consisted of two men and two women, and they were utterly inseparable. I wondered what they did when one of them had to go to the bathroom.

When I entered the room, they were all talking quietly in what I took to be Chinese. They stopped talking the moment I entered, waited until I had walked past them, and then began talking again. I didn't know if they thought I could understand Chinese, or if they were being polite, or if they were being hostile. I found this somewhat unnerving, and had for the past two years.

I took a seat in the back, next to Peter, who was dozing lightly.

I cleared my throat. "Excuse me?" I had a plan that I wanted to outline to the class, a plan to extract some clarification, some—dare I say it?—actual teaching, from Speen, and I needed everyone's cooperation to make it work. I couldn't believe that I was the only one in class who had no idea what was going on.

When I spoke, the Four stopped talking and turned toward me. Even Peter briefly stirred from his coma.

"Listen, I'm having trouble with this class, and I don't think I'm alone. It's the beginning of November, and I still don't understand what he covered in September. Does anybody really understand what Speen is talking about?"

The Four looked at one another, conferred telepathically, then turned back to me and shook their heads no. Peter smirked. "Are you kidding?"

"Okay. I'm going to ask him a question about one of the homework problems." The Four looked alarmed and frightened, as if I'd just announced plans to throw Speen out a window. He assigned bales of homework on topics he had never covered. He then collected the homework and returned it weeks later with no comments, corrections, suggestions, or hints except a grade, usually a low one. He had once assigned a homework problem, part of a pile of 30 to turn in by next class, that completely baffled me for many sleepless hours, and which I later learned had first been solved by somebody who got the Nobel Prize for doing so.

I continued, "All you have to do is, if he asks if anyone else would be interested, just nod your heads. That's all. You don't have to say anything. Just nod. Can you do that?"

The Four consulted wordlessly again, then turned back to me and nodded, showing they were at least physically able to do it. Peter shrugged. "It won't work, but I'll do it. Any last words?"

"Thanks for the optimism," I muttered. "Okay, I'll ask him then. Just nod when he asks you." I felt good, as if I had achieved something of a victory just by bringing up the problem and getting the class unified in opposition to Speen. Maybe we could turn this course around after all.

As predicted, Speen appeared fifteen minutes late, snapped his book open on the table in front, turned his back on the class pointedly, and began rapidly covering all available surfaces of the blackboard with illegible equations. I took a deep breath, let it out, commended my soul to God, and raised my hand.

"Excuse me. Professor Speen?"

He whirled around and transfixed me with a look as if I had just popped him with a spitball. "What is it, Napoli? We have a lot to get through today." He mispronounced my name, but I couldn't really hold that against him: everybody did. I forged ahead.

"Professor, I was wondering if you could please possibly show us how to do problem 16? I've already tried it and I'm ready to hand in my solution today, even if it's wrong. But I was just wondering if you could please give us a little idea on how to solve something like that."

Notice how I emphasized the "us" aspect. I was trying to let him know that we were all having trouble, not just me.

Speen gave me a withering look and frowned. "Does anyone else need help with these simple exercises?" he demanded.

This was the moment, that heroic instant that would begin the Revolution. I looked over at the Four. One was copying the equations from the board. One was turning the pages of their notebook. One was studying a page in the textbook. One was staring straight ahead. No one was nodding. Peter was asleep.

I looked down at the floor tiles and shook my head slightly. There would be a slight delay in the Revolution.

Speen was nastily jubilant, "Well, Mr. Napoli, it appears that only you need to have your hand held. I don't think we need to waste any more of the class's time to make up for your lack of preparation."

My face burned. It was somehow no help that I was right. After a last triumphant look, Speen turned back to the board and resumed his high-speed hieroglyphics. I stared angrily at the Four and at Peter, but none of them would meet my gaze.

It was a very long class for me, and not just because he kept us thirty minutes late.

Three

When class ended, I figured that my academic career with Speen was pretty much over too, so I might as well take the opportunity to annoy him as much as possible. Certain doom can be a liberating experience. I went to his office on the fifth floor to wait for him to return.

All the professors are supposed to hold regular office hours, when you can see them privately about any questions that you don't get answered in class. Speen was notorious for missing office hours. He only scheduled one hour each week, at four o'clock on Thursdays. Naturally, not many students wanted to hang around the physics building so late, so no one ever came. But since it was almost four o'clock on Thursday now, I thought I'd call his bluff and make him spend an hour helping me.

When he showed up, he was in a heated discussion with Dr. Wilhelm. These two struck terror in the hearts of graduate students. Speen, as you've already observed in his natural habitat, acted out of pure malevolence. Wilhelm wasn't exactly nasty, he just had impossibly high standards that no one had ever met. Einstein would have earned a "Requires more effort" from Wilhelm. I had had him for an introductory course on atomic physics once—relatively simple stuff—and it had been like something out of Dante's *Inferno*. Wilhelm's nickname was, of course, "Kaiser," while Speen's was "Speen", that being about as derogatory an insult as anyone could come up with.

Seeing them together like this was very unusual. While we referred to them collectively as Scylla and Charybdis—or as the Dynamic Duo, if not classically educated—and while we firmly believed that they coordinated their evil-doing—it being practically an axiom that when one assigned a paper, the other would assign a take-home exam—you never saw them with each other. Wilhelm, older, sixtysish, dwelt in the basement with his superconductor minions and only rarely was to be observed in the upper strata of the physics building.

Indeed, although they were together now, they were far from being together, if you get my drift. Wilhelm was gripping the handrail tightly, urgently trying to get Speen to agree to something, but Speen wasn't having any and continued stomping up the stairs. They hushed when they saw me. Wilhelm said, "We'll talk about this later," and rapidly descended the stairs again, throwing me a look that made me want to change my major to Art History.

When Speen saw me at his office door, he was annoyed. A good start. "What do you want now, Napoli?" he growled. The kindly professor, you see, gently guiding his young charges along the Path of Knowledge.

I indicated the schedule taped to his door. "Office hours," I said innocently. "I had a question about problem 16."

With one swift gesture, he ripped the schedule from his door, crumpled it, and dropped it on the floor. "No office hours today, Napoli. I'm meeting somebody important." He made it clear that that category did not include students.

He turned from me to unlock his door. I shook my head in amazement and fury. A bomb in his car? Or a bucket of acid over his office door? Decisions, decisions. I turned to stomp down the stairs myself, still shaking my head.

"Oh, are you going downstairs?" he asked from behind me. This was typical Speen. Of course I was going downstairs. Did he think I was going to leave the building by dropping out a fifth floor window? He pulled this all the time with students, asking a question to which you had to assent, then making you perform some foul but unrefuseable errand for him.

I turned to face him. Go take a leap, and your little dog, too. "Yes," I said.

"Good." He turned his back on me and disappeared into his office. I looked through his open office door, hoping to pry. The interior was rather luxuriously appointed for a college professor: big oak desk, cushioned high-back chair. Most professors had gray metal navy surplus desks and chairs. And I had never seen a file cabinet with a combination lock before.

Speen was supposedly an expert on how objects fall through the atmosphere, which sounds trivial—they fall down, right?—but is actually very complicated, what with air resistance, friction, flocks of geese, and so forth. The government, being understandably interested in preventing certain foreign countries from dropping certain hostile objects on us through the atmosphere, paid him big bucks to do research for them, or so it was rumored. Hence, the special file cabinet, for holding what I imagined to be Secret Papers.

He emerged again. "Take these books down to Jackson for me. Tell him to keep them for me until I need them."

As predicted. And he omitted the Magic Word, to boot.

He held out a white plastic shopping bag with five or six books in it. I took my sweet time reaching for it, so that he had to wait for me and his extended arm began to tremble. I lifted the bag from him and turned to leave. Behind me his door slammed, the noise echoing up and down the empty stairwell.

"You're welcome," I said.

Four

As I trudged downstairs, debating whether to simply drop his blasted bag in a trash bin, I contemplated this Jackson Katanga, Speen's long-suffering graduate assistant. Why didn't *Jackson* kill Speen as a public service? As Speen's grad student, it was clearly his responsibility, would save us all much grief, and would, on the whole, be good for the species.

Jackson could do it, too. He was enormous, by far the largest and strongest human being I'd ever personally met. He was also the most mild, humble and self-deprecating person I had ever met. Which meant that Speen danced all over him, of course. Speen made him do all kinds of scut work, so Jackson had hardly any time for his own research. It seemed as if he might never finish his degree. The other graduate students and I all felt for him, but there was nothing we could do. He bore his burden (i.e., Speen) with saintly patience. It was all rather like the story of Cinderella, but with physics.

Jackson's office was way down in the basement, conveniently located in the same room as the furnace. He wasn't there, so I dropped the books on his astonishingly tidy desk and left him a note.

In the sincere and fervent hope that I was invading Speen's privacy by doing so, I peeked at the books in the bag. I was deeply disappointed to see that they did not contain any material suitable for blackmail. They seemed to be about World War II. Nothing very incriminating about that. World War II had been a very important war, and my only real complaint about its outcome was that Speen had somehow survived it.

Five

Before leaving the building, I decided to check my mail in the main office. The only one there was Mrs. Arden, our 50s-ish department secretary and an absolute wizard of a typist. This wasn't easy in a physics department where you had to type mimeograph masters for tests full of formulas and terms like dielectric permittivity, and even one mistake meant starting over from scratch. Her In box was always empty. She was like the Bionic Typist. But right now, she was frowning alternately at a key in her hand and two pieces of paper on her desk.

"Anything wrong?" I wondered, as I checked my mail slot in the back room. Empty. Always was.

She looked up at me through large glasses that partly hid a pleasant face. She looked the way you'd like your wife to look when you were getting older. Her graying hair was cut short and she wore sensible rubber-soled shoes. "Hello, Mark. How are you at mysteries?"

"You mean murders? Like Agatha Christie?"

She smiled. "No, although some days I am tempted. More mundane, but still frustrating." She held up the key for inspection. "I found this on the floor in the back. I don't know who it belongs to."

This seemed a disappointing kind of mystery. I would have rolled my eyes at its triviality if I hadn't been afraid of hurting her feelings. "How about posting a notice with the key taped to it?" It seemed obvious.

"Well, the thing is, you don't want a key to fall into the wrong hands."

Made sense. "Okay, post the notice, but keep the key yourself."

"'Myes," she said, in a low confidential voice, "but with something like a key, it might be embarrassing to the person who lost it. You know what keys can open."

"Got you," I replied. "Complications. Can I look at it?" She handed it over. "Door key." She nodded. "Not to this building, though." She shook her head. I frowned. "What's funny is that it's not on a ring or anything. Sometimes students carry their room key loose, because it's the only key they have."

"But only professors and grad students go back there."

"Right, and it doesn't look like a dorm room key anyway. So, it's probably a key that someone just got, but hasn't put on their key ring yet. Anybody in the department move recently, buy a new house, something like that?

At this moment, our tête-à-tête was interrupted by the entrance of Dr. Cheepak Dopra, a new professor, small, young and always smiling. Admittedly, he wasn't smiling now, but he did bow formally to Mrs. Arden—and extended the bow sideways to include me—before disappearing into the back room.

Mrs. Arden bent her head forward conspiratorially and breathed, "Just between us, Dr. Dopra and his wife have separated. He's moved to an apartment."

That explained the lack of smile. "Suspect number 1," I suggested.

Dr. Dopra emerged from the back with a sheaf of mail. Mrs. Arden held the key up. "Excuse me, Dr. Dopra, but do you recognize this key?"

Dr. Dopra bent forward to examine it, then felt in his pocket. "It is mine. Thank you so much," he said, producing the smile.

"You're welcome," said Mrs. Arden, returning his smile. He left and she said, "I'm impressed."

I looked modest. "You said two mysteries. What's the other one?"

She nodded forcefully. "That was only the preliminary, here's the main event." She pointed at one of the papers on her desk. "For one thing, somebody keeps pulling the cable out of the back of the computer terminal upstairs."

Seemed odd. The computer center had only recently installed terminals in buildings around campus and there was just one in the whole physics building, on the third floor. We generally treated it with awe and reverence. "Pulled out the cable?"

She nodded. "Not just once, either. Almost every month, more or less. Somebody comes in, at night I suppose, although I don't see how they can get into that room, because it's locked at night, and only professors have a key. They pull the cable out of the back of the terminal. Most of the time, the computer center can just reconnect it, but this last time the cable had to be replaced. This is the invoice. Thirty eight dollars."

I picked up the invoice for no particular reason and shook my head. It seemed like a totally pointless crime. I could certainly understand someone getting frustrated with the computer, maybe even enough to pull the cable out. But every month?

"Weird. Did you say there was another thing?"

"Yes." She indicated what looked like a phone bill. "Somebody keeps making unauthorized long-distance phone calls to Germany."

"Well, that's not *so* weird." I occasionally made unauthorized calls myself, although not to Germany. By definition, anything I did was okay.

"That's not the weird part. The calls to Germany are always on the same nights as the cable is pulled out. And made from the same room."

That stopped me. I picked up the phone bill too and looked from it to the invoice and back. "You mean somebody pulls the cable out of the terminal and then calls Germany?"

She shrugged. "Or maybe they call Germany first, then pull the cable out of the terminal. Take your pick."

"Either way, it doesn't make sense. Do you know where they're calling in Germany?" I perused the phone bill, where one number was circled in red.

She nodded. "Yes, the phone company said it's the University of Esel."

"A university? Well, maybe it's one of the professors calling a colleague." I began to wonder if I could somehow pin this on Speen. Get him defrocked, or disbarred, or deloused, or whatever it is you do to jerk professors.

"I've asked." She sighed. "They all claim to know nothing about it."

They would, I thought. Or he would.

An idea occurred to me. I handed her back the phone bill. "Hey, what if you called the number yourself? See who answers. See if they know anyone here."

She smiled. "I thought of that, too. I did call it."

"Great. Who answered?"

"Nobody did. The phone was picked up on the other end, I could hear that. But all I could hear was this screeching noise. Like it's out of order."

"Well, that makes a little more sense. Maybe somebody calls that number, it doesn't work, and they get mad and pull the cable out of the computer."

Mrs. Arden gave me a look that made me think that she was probably somebody's mother. "Every month?"

I shrugged and gave her back the invoice, too. "Okay, you win: I'm baffled. It really doesn't make any sense, does it?"

"I'm glad you think so, too. I thought I was missing something."

"Well, I'll think about it," I promised.

She cocked her head at me. "Are you leaving for the day?"

I nodded. "I'm quitting while I'm behind."

She smiled. "See you tomorrow."

"Right. Don't you stay too late, now. It gets dark early these days." She had lost her husband the year before, and I felt sort of protective of her.

"No, I won't. But I can get a lot done when no one's around."

I left her office, pondering. Strange mystery. Or two strange mysteries. There must be a connection—had to be—but what could the connection be?

Six

Out in the hallway, I noticed old Mr. Andersson perusing the bulletin board on the first floor.

Mr. Andersson was a lunatic. Not a professional lunatic, of course, but a very highly ranked amateur. I guessed he was deliberately maintaining his non-pro status in order to compete in the next Lunatic Olympics. With the gold medal his, he could then turn pro, and cash in on lucrative endorsements for lunatic-oriented products.

Mr. Andersson prowled the paths and corridors of the campus, closely scrutinizing every building, person, and tree with his perpetually disapproving scowl. He was dedicated to his chosen vocation and stalked around the university unceasingly. It was *never* a surprise to run into him, literally anywhere at any time. Once I had cut through an unlit and deserted art building well after midnight to reach the parking lot without getting drenched, and had almost tripped over him as he inspected *their* bulletin boards by cloudlight. He lived in a small house that was practically across the street from the physics building, so we were especially lucky to win him as a frequent guest.

He never spoke to anybody, except to mutter half-audible—what? curses? threats? chicken recipes?—at anyone unlucky enough to be in his vicinity at the moment. These pronouncements were simultaneously dark with menace, because of his belligerent tone and accompanying glower, and uproariously funny because of their delivery in the sing-song intonation of his native Denmark. Everything he said sounded like a fiendish version of Jack and Jill.

Lunatic was apparently his second career, rumor having it that he was a former schoolmaster of the Dickens variety, who had retired to America to live with his sister, no doubt inspiring a new national holiday among

Danish schoolchildren at his departure. I could imagine them gleefully donating their kroner for a one-way ticket to Kingston University, USA.

His performance today was typical. He turned from his ferocious appraisal of months-old notices on the bulletin board and gave me a glare that left no doubt he found my continuing existence largely unnecessary, then turned away again with a remark under his breath that may have been, "Bohemian homo", or possibly "Little Jack Horner", but it was hard to tell, and I didn't ask him to elaborate.

I felt an urge to correct him on two points. First, my family origins were not in the hilly regions of northwest Czechoslovakia, as he seemed to believe, but in small towns near Naples and in the Azores. And second, I was not, never had been, and did not plan to be, a homosexual. Not that that wouldn't have been a shrewd move on my part, given what my love life with women was like. But I didn't correct him. I've found empirically that any time spent pointing out logical inconsistencies to lunatics is largely wasted.

I toyed briefly with the idea of sneaking his aluminum cane, but only for a moment, and I let it go. Live and let live. If people want to be annoyingly offensive, they have a constitutional right to do so. Who was I to deprive Speen of a role model?

Seven

Instead, I grabbed my stuff, left the building, and walked down the big stone steps to the sidewalk. Halfway down, I met Emily Whitney coming up. Emily was another physics graduate student, near to getting her doctorate. She was attractive, but so deeply into physics that it was painful speaking with her, so I didn't even make the attempt. At the moment, her head was bowed in deep thought. She was also coming up the steps the wrong way, straight into me.

At the last instant, I sidestepped to the wrong side to avoid a collision. However, she had just noticed that she was about to walk into me, so she sidestepped at the same instant, so we were back where we started. There are probably suave and debonair guys who can make witty remarks to attractive women on such occasions, and even do an impromptu do-si-do on the steps, but I'm not one of them. Instead, I sighed, turned around, climbed back up the steps, stood to the side out of the way, and waved for her to go by. She did so, with only a glance as she passed to acknowledge my existence.

I tramped back down the steps and started across the quad. I pulled my gaze up from the ground. It was already getting dark. A thin cold wind had the feel of snow to come. Fall in New England was definitely over, at least the foliage portion of the program.

The campus was at its most beautiful in the fall and summer. In fall, the trees were a patchwork of sunny yellow, rich orange, and heart-stopping red. In the summer, the whole campus seemed to bloom, the cool green, the drowsy buzz, the spirited chirp of life everywhere. The university snagged many prospective students in the summer, when recent high school grads came to tour the campus. Not many could ignore the magnificent walks lined with budding trees, the impressive cool stone buildings fronting the grassy Quadrangle, and the scantily clad summer students. But summer and fall gave no clue to the winter and spring. In winter, the trees were as bare, hard, and cold as concrete. In spring, the campus hills ran with rivers of mud.

Mrs. Arden's mystery had distracted me from thinking about Speen temporarily, which was all to the good. Why didn't somebody drop a house on that guy? Another pile of problems due by Tuesday. I sighed. I'd better get started on them as soon as possible. Maybe I could get some study time in before dinner.

Dinner. Which reminded me that I hadn't eaten lunch.

I pulled my coat close around me, and turned my face toward the library.

Eight

I set my cafeteria tray down on the dining hall table that we had reserved by draping our coats on seats before getting into line. Ben, Stan, and Lisa were still choosing desserts and drinks. I sat down, lifted my knife and fork, and began trisecting my long-awaited meatloaf.

A young woman with a tray approached the far end of our table. She was pretty and I could feel myself getting flustered. She was also rather well dressed for a student, wearing a plaid skirt, a white shirt with one of those ribbon ties, and a fuzzy pull-over sweater—on a campus where jeans and sweatshirts were the norm.

"Excuse me, are these seats taken?"

This startled me, and a few words about my appearance may be in order here. I look like Rasputin on a bad day. My hair grows way past my shoulders and, since I never comb it, it just falls where it wants. I push it away from my glasses when it's in the way, but otherwise ignore it. Also, the big bushy beard, as popularized by Karl Marx and Samuel F.B. Morse, the late inventors of Communism and the telegraph, respectively. Mind you, I always keep my hair and beard scrupulously clean. I just don't do anything of a cosmetic nature to my appearance. Plus, the dark-framed glasses and clothes that a Salvation Army store would reject. My theory is that people should be able to see past my exterior appearance to the treasures within, blah blah blah. Besides, I simply can't be bothered with it.

Given the above, therefore, I wasn't used to women, especially pretty young women to whom I had not been previously introduced, suddenly initiating conversations with me.

However, I did attempt to answer her question, which was my first mistake. "I…uh…we…er…"

She tilted her head at me helpfully, which didn't help.

"They…uh…you…er…"

She was peering at me intently as if trying to drag the answer out of my brain directly through my forehead, which would probably have been simpler. Pieces of responses were pinging around in my head like a pinball machine.

Since oral communication wasn't going so well, I tried gestures. I nodded, which she imitated, then I realized that that was the wrong answer to her question so I shook my head, which she also imitated. Growing more and more frustrated with my own incoherence, I brought my hands down onto the table with a crash and barked, "Sit!"

She sat hastily, staring at me in apprehension. I didn't dare attempt an apology. I'd probably injure some innocent bystanders and myself. Instead, I turned my face away in embarrassment, blushing hotly.

"This silver-tongued devil sweet-talking you?" asked my alleged friend Stan. He was setting his tray down on the table across from me and giving her his Charming Smile #6. She gave him the smile his dark handsome features deserved, glanced at me and then quickly away again, apparently deciding I was not actually rabid. Then her friends arrived at the table, they started talking, and I was mercifully forgotten.

Stan was still beaming #6 in her general direction when Lisa, his girl-friend, arrived and cleared her throat daintily. He whipped his head toward her with an audible snap. "Hi, honey. How about here?" Kick-save, and a beauty.

Ben joined us and sat beside me. "What's up?"

Stan was gleeful. "Don Juan here was making his move to the hoop." Ben gave a small smile. Stan went on. "You know, you have no right to turn your animal magnetism on this poor helpless girl. It's a lucky thing for both of you I happened along. We'd have been hosing you down by now."

"Yeah. I feel lucky," I replied flatly. I had come out of my stupor somewhat and continued slicing up my meat loaf.

Stan continued. "Thought you weren't going to try that without a net."

Ben said, "Stan" in his always-calming tone. Ben was my best friend, former room-mate from my undergrad days, and a pacifist in the struggles that arose between Stan and me. With red hair and freckles, he was identifiably Irish at a hundred paces.

"I think it's cute," said Lisa.

I was recovering, and for some odd reason felt like ragging on Stan. I noticed his clothes for the first time. "You're quite the fashion plate tonight."

Stan looked down at himself. Lisa giggled. Stan scowled. "I've got hockey practice after dinner," he said defensively.

I had seen Stan play hockey, and he was amazing to watch. Some of his moves flat-out defied certain well-regarded laws of physical motion. He was tall, well-built, and had dark and vaguely exotic good looks that I had come to assume must be common in Lithuania, where all four of his grandparents had come from. His last name was Simson, a homogenized version of some extraordinary collection of consonants that immigration officials had pruned back severely. He had so frequently introduced himself with the phrase, "Simpson, no P," that Lisa often called him "No-P" for a nickname.

Lisa herself was tall, slender, blonde, beautiful, and often the subject of interest of any males in her general vicinity, until Stan's hulking glower zeroed in on them and scared them off. She was also breathtakingly intelligent, juggling two majors and a handful of minors with ease. She had a wonderful sense of humor besides, judging by her appreciation of my remarks. In short, she was the kind of woman I dreamed of meeting myself. I mean, I had met her, of course, but, well, you know what I mean. Except for Lee, I had never known anyone like her. She was practically the only woman my own age I could speak to without getting totally tongue-tied, and I attributed that to the fact that she was safe, i.e., not available, she and Stan being very much a couple.

Their couplehood seemed, no offense to either of them, utterly incomprehensible. I could discern almost nothing that they had in common, for example. Stan was in engineering, being most interested in building bridges and things, while Lisa majored in both French literature and textiles, a combination I always felt would be most useful in studying the Bayeux tapestry, but which seemed not to have a lot to do with engineering. Stan, as I have described, was an athlete and avid sports fan, while the most demanding physical activity Lisa ever undertook was flipping over a Mozart album or turning a page of Rimbaud. Even given my extreme ignorance in the ways of romantic relationships, I still could not get it.

Besides, it seemed that Lisa was ever-ready to enjoy a joke at Stan's expense, like now.

He turned to Lisa. "What's so funny?" Lisa instantly assumed a serious expression, which was even funnier than her giggling.

With nothing outward to complain about, Stan turned back to his meal. Lisa's shoulders shook gently with suppressed laughter.

I myself was quiet for a count of five. "Hey, Stan, I saw a buddy of yours today."

Stan looked up warily, but said nothing.

"Speen."

Stan made a gagging noise, dropping his fork onto the tray and turning his head in disgust.

"All right, Mark," Ben said.

Stan hated and feared Speen. All engineering students had to take at least two required physics courses: Stan had already drawn the black spot and landed Speen for the first one, and had barely survived the experience. He lived in mortal dread of encountering Speen for the second, much harder, course.

"He was asking for you. He said, 'Where's my friend Stan been hiding? I can't wait to see him again.'"

Stan's face was grim. He looked as if he might either get sick or stab me. Lisa broke in on us.

"Truce," she commanded. She was serious.

Stan and I eyed each other warily.

"Okay," I agreed meekly. "I'll be good."

Stan only nodded and retrieved his fork.

"So, when's the game?" Ben wondered theatrically.

Stan looked at Ben, then at Lisa, then me. He cleared his throat. "Saturday. We're a little nervous about them. They're Division A."

"You'll clean their clocks," I stated. "Just like Carlisle."

Stan smiled crookedly. He had scored three goals against Carlisle. "Yeah. Maybe. We've been watching their game films." He launched into an account of goalies, defensemen, and blue lines.

As he talked, Lisa gave me a warm look Stan couldn't see. My insides glowed in response.

Nine

After dinner, Lisa accompanied Stan to hockey practice. She enjoyed watching the practices, but almost never went to his games, finding the mayhem, and the possibilities for his being involved in it, too disturbing to observe firsthand. I never went to the practice sessions, but I could imagine how distracting Lisa's presence in the stands would be. Just a guess.

I was on my way to the library to do a little preliminary machete work on Speen's latest assignment. Ben walked with me part of the way, headed to what I considered the ultimate horror of college courses—and this to a guy who currently had Speen—an evening course in business. I regarded all business courses as pure sedatives. Such a course at night would have to involve pillows for me, which the professor would probably frown on. Ben didn't mind it though. His major was finance, which to me only meant that he had sold his soul to the god of tedium. It takes all kinds to make a species.

We were walking along a poorly lit walkway in the gathering darkness, just shooting the breeze until our paths diverged. Ben took the high road to Snoreland, while I trudged to the library.

Suddenly I was rooted to the spot, unable to move, speak, or hear. Walking toward me from Ben's path was Lee.

It hit me like a blow: she had left her fiancé.

I had been stupid to fall in love with a woman already engaged. Discovering the closeness of our minds and thoughts had been bizarre. Denying the physical intimacy she desired had been wrenching, and left me feeling foolish. Her leaving had been a wound. The time since had stretched cold and desolate, like a lunar crater after a long-ago meteor impact.

Yet, all of that now seemed vindicated, even ennobled. She had returned to me after all. I had been right to fall in love with her.

She was walking toward me now with the same willowy wobble I had never been able to decide was due to shoes, gait, or femininity. It did not matter. Nothing else mattered now. My life was now made right and whole again.

She passed Ben, giving him a polite smile. She ignored me completely and walked on past. Because it was not Lee.

I felt like dropping to the ground and never rising again. For long minutes I just stood, the cold night wind pouring through me, glacial and hard.

Finally, I moved one leaden foot and set it down again. Lifting my head was like lifting a boulder. The lights of the library shone through the trees. I moved toward them like an advancing glacier, pointless and persistent, a man of ice and solitude. I didn't look back.

Ten

At the library I sat alone facing a large window, books and papers spread across the surface of the table before me, ignored. Beyond the window was darkness, with occasional lights along the sidewalk. People suddenly appeared in the regions of light, then abruptly vanished back into darkness again.

She was out there in the world somewhere. We had shared an almost telepathic bond, and at this moment I thought I could feel her, her location on the surface of the earth, like the epicenter of some far-off tremor.

She was not in New England, or even on the east coast. I could tell. She would not be in the south or midwest. The west coast then. Not California. Not her. Oregon? Possibly. But. No. Not Oregon. Washington. Yes. Seattle. The feeling a near-certainty to me. Her fiancé would be an intern by now, at a hospital there. In Seattle. A three-hour time difference. Call after eleven, eight her time. Directory assistance. "Hello, Lee…"

Stop it, I commanded myself. Stop it. But it was so hard to stop.

And then I used my solution, my only solution, not perfect, not the best, but the only one I had, the only one that had worked for the past year.

With a will, with an effort, I took possession of my sight.

I moved my gaze down the window of darkness.

To the silvery metal window frame near the floor.

Back along the floor, tile by tile.

To the far edge of the wooden table.

Then back along the surface of the table.

To the white page of the textbook.

To the neat rows of black ink. Text. Equations. Diagrams.

I read, word by word, "The dielectric field strength equals the electric field strength only in a vacuum."

Now just what did they mean by that?

Eleven

I left the library just before midnight. This was a purely arbitrary decision on my part, since Speen's homework was nowhere near being done. I'd be slogging through it all weekend.

Graduate Village was a goodly distance from the main campus, on unlit slippery paths through woods and across the main road. I mainly watched my footing, then finally trudged up the three flights to the apartment door.

Unlocking and opening the door, I realized my apartment-mate Eli was mercifully not home. Presumably, he was at her apartment, whichever her it was tonight. He hadn't been around this morning when I had left either. Any day without Eli was, by definition, a good day, I guess, Speens and pseudo-Lees notwithstanding.

I had missed Hawaii Five-O, and Johnny Carson's opening monologue. I washed, undressed, pulled on an old torn sweatshirt, and flopped into bed. Alone. Very much so.

Twelve

I was having a nightmare that was simultaneously frightening and depressing, in that I had had the same nightmare almost every night for the last year. Even in the dream, I could feel a resigned tedium that I was about to be scared witless again.

I was falling.

I was falling down a well or a deep hole that had no bottom. I kept trying to grab hold of the sides, the walls, whatever. Whenever I touched the wall, I would get slashed by some razor-sharp projection. Sometimes I would collide with things as I fell, going oof as I hit, and then tumbling off again, spinning from the impact, spiraling helplessly, head over heels, out of control.

With no bottom. No end at all.

And always accelerating, speeding downwards at 32 feet per second per second, faster and faster until air and thought and walls and time were a screaming blur.

I could see people and objects along the walls of the hole, and in the maddening illogic of dreams they would speed down the wall alongside me, barely creeping, speaking in slow-motion until I thought my brain would burst from the sheer shrieking insanity, the frightening unphysicality of it all.

And it would build and build like this and get worse and worse, narrower and narrower, more and more buffets, faster and faster until I would jerk downwards in my bed, actually bounce, and wake up heaving for air, and look at the clock and see that there were still hours to get through before dawn. And knowing I had to sleep, just had to. And the well waiting for me in my sleep.

With no bottom. No end at all.

I had had this dream many times before. And in the strange way that you know things in dreams, things you could not possibly know, I knew the name of the well with no bottom, the hole with no end.

The name of the well was Lee.

Friday

▼

Thirteen

I was still tired when I woke up on Friday morning, and it took me a long time to get myself back in gear after spending the night hurtling down bottomless holes. I was even late getting to class, except I wasn't.

Being late wasn't an unusual experience on Fridays. I was used to plodding the long walk up the hill to the physics building, taking the stairs two at a time to the fourth floor, easing the door open quietly, and smoothly slipping into a seat in the back of Soper's class. He would usually note me with a neutral look, then continue without a pause in whatever he was saying in his deep weighty voice. I liked Soper's teaching style, thorough, and presented in a logical progression of concepts, and I liked listening to his voice, but I had learned never to take a class with him before 11 in the morning. The deep sonorities of his voice too early put me right to sleep.

But he wasn't there. None of the dozen or so students in the class was there either. I had one of those bewildering moments you get sometimes, when you don't know what day it is or what time it is, and you're sure you've just blown something important in a major way.

But wait. Yesterday was Thursday. I had taught the usual lab and enjoyed the usual pleasant interlude with Dr. Speen. This was the next day. Ergo, it was Friday morning, around 11.

I looked up at the wall clock. It was in fact nearly quarter past eleven. Could they have gone to one of the labs for a demonstration? Seemed unlikely. Statistical mechanics dealt with nearly invisibly tiny objects. It was hard to imagine any demonstration that would be relevant. Besides, Soper wasn't a demo kind of guy, strictly a stand-up lecturer, no show biz involved.

But where was everybody?

I stepped back out in the hall. Where was anybody, for that matter? Not that the physics building was ever a rollicking hangout, but there was almost always some student or some professor—or some lunatic like Mr. Andersson—in the halls. But there was nobody.

Except a cop who walked down the stairs past me, completing that what's-wrong-with-this-picture feeling.

I decided to go down and see Mrs. Arden. If *she* wasn't there…Well, I couldn't even imagine an outcome outrageous enough to think after so unlikely an event as that.

On my way down the stairs, I passed another policeman coming up. Unusual. In fact, unprecedented. You never saw real cops on campus. Campus cops, sure, giving out tickets and so forth. But the real cops seemed to instinctively avoid the place.

I passed still another cop on the first floor landing. I began to get very nervous and it was with tremendous relief that I saw Mrs. Arden sitting at her desk. If she hadn't been there, I would not have been surprised to see Rod Serling step out of a doorway and start introducing another episode of the Twilight Zone.

I walked into the office and she looked up. Her eyes were red from crying.

"Hi." I spoke hesitantly, not wanting to intrude on an emotional moment. "Where is everybody? There's nobody in my 11 o'clock class."

Her mouth opened a little. "Haven't you heard?" She was dumb-founded.

"Heard what?" I was always the last person in the department to hear any piece of news or gossip. In fact, a pretty good definition of "common knowledge" was to see if I knew about it.

"Dr. Speen is dead," she said simply.

"Dead?" I said. This seemed simultaneously so shocking and so too good to be true that I felt she must be pulling my leg. I hate being fooled, and resist believing things like this on mere say-so. Still, I could not accept Mrs. Arden pulling a practical joke at all, much less one in such dubious taste.

"He fell off the roof," she explained. "Or was pushed. Last night sometime. They found him out in the courtyard." She pointed out the window. "Somebody is supposed to have seen it. The police have taken Jackson in for questioning."

Each of her statements had felt like a blow to the head. I tried to grab each one as it came past, with little success. But this last was too much.

"Jackson?" I cried incredulously. This was all clearly impossible. And Jackson's involvement most of all.

I haven't mentioned much about Jackson Katanga, other than his role as Speen's doormat. The first time I ever encountered him, I had been reading a bulletin board in a corridor on the fifth floor when suddenly all the light from the window was blotted out. I looked up, surprised at the sudden eclipse that I hadn't been informed of. Instead of an eclipse, I was surprised to see a gigantic individual looming over me. He was probably twice as wide as me, and a good foot taller. He was so tall, and his shoulders so broad, that he totally blocked the window.

I had said, "Uh," or something equally clever. This was hardly a dark alley, but I feared that my fate would soon be the same as if it had been. And then he spoke.

"Pardon me," he had said, in a smooth British accent I found both startling and comforting. I later learned that he was originally from some former British colony in Africa. "I didn't intend to disturb you. I only wanted to pass by without inconveniencing you."

It was then that I had noticed he was holding a long and heavy piece of lab equipment in one hand, without much effort, and was trying to maneuver it around where I was unintentionally obstructing the corridor. A few weeks earlier, it had taken myself and three other normal-sized persons to carry that piece of equipment into the building, and it had been a tough and grunting bit of work.

I had flattened myself against the wall to get out of his way. "Sorry."

"It is no trouble at all," he had assured me. He looked like Muhammad Ali and sounded like Lawrence Olivier. "Thank you for your help. And again, pardon me for disturbing you." And with that, he was gone around the corner.

When I later introduced myself and got to know him, I realized that Jackson Katanga, despite his imposing physique, was a pussycat. That was why it would be difficult to imagine that Jackson had murdered Speen.

And yet, only yesterday I had been thinking how great it would be if Jackson would kill Speen. Could it be that he actually had? In a moment of horror, I thought that somehow I had caused all this, but the illogic of that possibility evaporated rapidly from my mind. It still left a residue of doubt and guilt, though.

"I can't believe it." I walked to the window and glanced out. Seen from above, the physics building was in the shape of a C. The courtyard, enclosed on three sides, was intended as a place for students to walk and sit and congregate. As with all such designed spaces, no one ever used it. There were cops out there now, milling about officially, apparently assigned to keep away the less official millers.

Mrs. Arden nodded. "I know. I don't know which is harder to believe: that he fell accidentally, that he jumped deliberately, or that he was pushed." She had apparently given this some thought already. Of course, she had known about it longer and had had time to absorb it a little. I was still grappling with the raw facts, and hadn't had time to move on to the theory part of the scientific method yet.

But I could see what she meant. The physics building had a high, pitched roof, just like a house. You could get out onto the roof at several places where windowed dormers opened out from the attic. But there was no reason for Speen, or anybody else, to be in the attic, much less on the roof. The attic was empty and unused, as far as I knew. It was hard to imagine why he might go up there, or why he would go out on the roof if he did go up there. And even if he did do those extremely unlikely things, it was hard to imagine him falling to his death accidentally. He might have been in his fifties, but it wasn't like he was some feeble old guy. It just didn't make sense.

But neither of the other possibilities made much sense either. Speen kill himself? No way. He wasn't that kind of person. To my way of thinking, only people who were fairly sensitive would commit suicide. Using the words "sensitive" and "Speen" in the same sentence was a major stretch. Half the problem with the world was that not enough jerks did kill themselves.

But murder? Granted that perhaps hundreds of students hated Speen to various degrees at any given moment, myself included, would any of them really kill him because of it? Push him off the roof? I mean, that's not exactly a spur-of-the-moment way to kill somebody either. Not in the guns and lead pipes league, I mean. I might have felt like killing him myself last night at his office, but I couldn't see myself dragging him up onto the roof and shoving him off to accomplish it.

"I see what you mean," I said to Mrs. Arden. "It's hard to imagine him falling off the roof accidentally. But it's even harder to imagine him killing himself, or that someone would kill him by pushing him off the roof."

"I know. Or that Jackson could have anything to do with it. I can't believe that at all."

I shook my head. "Me either. Maybe they just want to ask him about Speen. Personal stuff. Speen was his major professor."

"Maybe."

I tried to imagine Jackson's reaction to all this. If I were him, I would be doing cartwheels. Ding dong, the Speen is dead. Free at last, free at last, thank God almighty, free at last. That kind of thing. But I doubted that's how Jackson would react. He would probably actually mourn the guy. Kind of miss the whips and leg-irons. Jackson would probably set up a scholarship in his honor.

Then I thought about myself. No more Speen. No more cruel and unusual homework. I came pretty near to breaking out in the "Hallelujah" chorus, except that Mrs. Arden was sitting right there.

Then another thought occurred to me, the reason I had actually come in here.

"So, where is everybody?" I wondered.

"Oh, Dr. Axalt has canceled all physics classes for today. Out of respect for Dr. Speen." Dr. Axalt was the chair of the physics department. Quiet guy, but with a commanding presence. When he spake unto you, you listened.

"Wow." This was yet another unprecedented act. The closest the physics department ever got to canceling classes was on Isaac Newton's birthday, which happened to be on Christmas.

"I guess I'll be going," I said lamely.

"I'll see you later." She was dabbing at her eyes when I left.

Fourteen

In the hallway, I thought of going around to the courtyard, but the place was crawling with police. And I was beginning to feel a little queasy about the whole thing. I walked along, automatically headed toward the library to work on Speen's homework. Then I turned back again.

While there were police around, the courtyard wasn't crawling with them. They stayed behind a length of yellow tape that spanned the mouth of the courtyard, hanging in a catenary curve I had once sketched in calculus 3. I looked down at the carefully-avoided place on the sidewalk, then up at the roof. Feeling that I had discharged some kind of duty, I started for the library again.

Speen. What a legacy he had left. Such a wide repertoire of skills for impeding learning. The ability to careen through material at the speed of light. Impatient during questions, impervious to requests for clarification. More than willing to go off on tangents interesting only to him and completely irrelevant to the course, which would show up in excruciating detail on the next exam. I kind of wished I could have a hand in writing his eulogy.

I was halfway to the library when it hit me. Speen was dead. Speen was gone. Speen had ceased to be part of my life. And without Speen's homework, I had almost nothing to do.

I looked up at the library and a brief internal struggle ensued. Bag that, I thought, and headed to the dining hall for an early lunch.

Fifteen

Stan was jubilant.

"I guess you've already heard." I set my tray down across the table from him. He was beaming a smile so bright he was blinding passersby.

"Good news travels fast." I had never seen him so happy. And I had seen him happy.

"Just let me get this straight." I gestured with my fork. "A man is dead, and you're happy."

"Correction," he replied. "*Speen* is dead—big difference—and I'm *real* happy. Yes."

"Well," I said huffily. "I guess I'm a little…"

"You don't approve." Stan made a little stab of his head.

"No, I guess not."

"I," Stan stated, "don't care."

"Oh, I can see that."

Stan waved his fork. "You're not going to tell me you're all broken up over this."

"No. Broken up, no. But still, the man is dead."

"So you probably feel like I do, but you don't think you should show it."

"I guess."

"So I'm being honest and you're being, what, maybe a little hypocritical?"

That sounded about right, although "hypocritical" didn't seem a Stan-type expression. "Yeah. Maybe."

"Well, at least we got that straight."

We resumed the eating portion of the luncheon activities.

Then Stan held up a small cardboard box. "Oh, by the way, would you like to contribute?" On the side of the box, he had written in magic marker, "Speen Reward Fund".

"You think he was murdered then."

"Gosh, let me think," Stan said sarcastically. "He didn't just fall off the roof, and no way he'd ever kill himself. What does that leave?"

"I guess you're right. It's hard to imagine anybody hating him that much."

Stan snorted. "*That's* not hard to imagine. What's hard to imagine is how he lasted so long."

I laughed in spite of myself. I dug a buck out of my pocket and stuffed it into the slit in the top of his box.

"So that's to reward anybody with information about his murderer?"

Stan smirked. "Of course not. It's for the murderer."

Sixteen

Sparrow was playing Yes in the Lambs' Den.

Allow me to explain.

Due to its origins as an agricultural college, Kingston University has a number of unfortunate associations with sheep. For example, its male sports teams are called the 'Herders, leading to cheers like, "Heard of the 'Herders? Oh-yeah!" While this sounds like a wimpy team name, it's actually a vast improvement over the original team name, the Shepherds.

As if that weren't bad enough, the alumni group is known as the "Sheep's Kin", and various places on campus are called the Lamb Shop and the Mutton Jeff Playhouse. In the Memorial Union is a spacious room with a ceiling three stories high and floor-to-ceiling windows that offer spectacular views of the mudflows that dominate the campus scenery for nine months out of the year. This is the Lambs' Den. In the daytime, a coffee shop and snack bar. On Friday nights, a dance floor.

You see, the student government figured that if they could keep students on campus Friday nights, they would stay all weekend. A student at rest tends to remain at rest kind of thing. And if there were a critical mass of students around, then more interesting things could be planned for the weekends. So, to keep students on campus on Friday nights, they started sponsoring dances in the Lambs' Den. For a buck, you could dance to whatever band was desperate enough to accept the pittance that the student government was paying. This usually meant bands like Toast Your Tooties or The Drills, groups who had played together maybe twice and who tried to stretch a five-song repertoire over three hours, with predictably dire results.

However, on this Friday night it meant Sparrow. Sparrow was different. The five K.U. students in Sparrow were each excellent, and collectively incredible. They had a few original songs, but they mostly played covers.

Their Beatles set had to be heard to be believed. That they even attempted to play Yes songs was impressive. That they played Yes well was amazing.

So, Sparrow was playing Yes in the Lambs' Den.

My friends and I were regulars at these Friday night dances. We had very little money—except Lisa, whose family was loaded—and the price was right. We even derived some enjoyment from the lousy groups. In a kind of symbiotic relationship, they pretended they were making music, we pretended we were having a good time: it worked out. Naturally, we idolized Sparrow.

For this was during an epoch in history when a fierce battle was being waged between the forces of good and the forces of evil, between right and wrong, between light and darkness, between, in short, rock music and disco. Disco seemed to possess some people, even people we had known and trusted, suddenly and inexplicably. Sometimes my friends and I felt we were the last outposts of reason and civilization in a world delirious with Saturday Night Fever. If there was anything you could count on at these Friday night dances, it was that you were, for too brief a time, safe from the BeeGees.

In this titanic struggle, Sparrow was a force for goodness and right. They played canonical rock. The Beatles. The Who. Yes. Led Zeppelin. The Stones. And, my personal favorites, Steely Dan. And they played well, hard, and long.

I was dancing with Lisa. Stan did not like to dance or, as he put it, "jump around like a spastic moron," but Lisa loved to dance. I was still ignorant enough about relations between men and women to believe that such a conflict would inevitably cause a breakup between them. It never did.

I loved to dance, too, but for me finding a willing partner was problematic. If I did manage to summon up my courage enough to make my way across the room to ask a woman to dance, I would usually get a swift up-and-down look, lingering at my hair and beard, and an incredulous stare for my trouble. Of course, the *right* woman would see beyond my hair and beard to the inner me and dance. I hadn't found a right woman yet. At least not since Lee. And she had definitely been the wrong right woman.

Thus it was that Lisa and I were dancing, with Stan's enthusiastic approval. Again, my naiveté would have led me to predict that any guy with a beautiful girlfriend like Lisa would be unwilling to share her with any other guy, even a friend. On the contrary, Stan seemed glad to give Lisa an acceptable outlet for her incomprehensible desire to dance, as long as it didn't involve him and was with someone safe, namely me.

For my part, I couldn't help wondering what people made of lithe, beautiful Lisa dancing with, well, me.

You're probably thinking it somewhat inappropriate that I was out dancing on the night after the murder of Professor Speen, an instructor and a physics colleague. All I can say is that, despite the death of a person I hated and despised, and despite the fact that I would not have to spend the entire weekend slaving to finish a pile of homework for Tuesday's class, I was in a good mood.

After a few songs, Lisa and I took a breather to sit down and cool off. It got pretty steamy from people dancing, even in that large room. As we neared our table, I happened to look up at another table nearby. A group of young women was just sitting down, my student Stephanie among them. I looked away quickly, but not quickly enough. She saw me, saw that I saw her, smiled at me, and waved. My chest thumped. Now what? I could not socialize or fraternize or anythingize with a student. That would be over the edge. Yet, I couldn't be impolite either. All she had done was wave to me.

I nodded to her.

She turned away and sat down. Good. I sat down too, a little shaken, but feeling it was okay. Nothing wrong with nodding at someone I know, even a student. Students are people too, or so I'd been given to understand. Besides, no one had even noticed.

"So who's that?" Stan asked.

"Who?"

"The hoop that you, the above-named Mark, were j ist nodding to, unquote," he explained with mock patience.

"Student of mine."

"Really? You going to ask her to dance?"

"That would not be a good idea."

Stan nodded seriously. Lisa was drinking her drink. Ben was looking over my shoulder with a strange expression on his face. The band started playing again, a slow and romantic song.

Suddenly, I felt a tap on my shoulder. I hoped it was not some drunk picking a fight with me over my hair and beard. I usually didn't have to deal with that on campus much. I tipped my head slightly to see past my dangling hair and saw a finger resting lightly on my shoulder. Turning my head further, I saw a hand—identifiably female—then a wrist, a lacy blouse cuff, sleeve, shoulder and face.

Stephanie was standing behind my chair, tapping me lightly on the shoulder. I leaped to my feet, knocking my chair over.

She smiled at me brightly and crooked her finger at me. I widened my eyes questioningly. She pointed at the dance floor.

Now what? This was several furlongs beyond the edge. This could not be done. And yet. She had initiated this, not me. And I knew she could not be doing this to try to get a grade from me, because her grades were already the best in the class. This really was just a neutral social encounter. This was a public place. Everyone could see there was no intimate contact or anything like that. Just people dancing. I saw nothing wrong. In fact, I saw a lot that was right. I had a momentary experience, imagining dancing with her, looking into her smiling eyes.

Right.

"I…er…I'm sorry." I struggled to get the words out. "Not a good idea."

She smiled and wrinkled her nose at me. She was looking up at me like a quizzical puppy dog. "Just one dance?"

I spread my hands in a helpless gesture. How to say no without her feeling badly about it? This was not something I had a lot of experience with. Or any.

"I'm sorry. Maybe under different circumstances. But I...er...you...uh..."

She nodded, embarrassed. I knew that feeling. "Okay. I thought it would be fun." She smiled a little sadly and moved away.

It would have been. That was the whole problem. I looked out at the dance floor, people dancing to the slow song. I watched the couples in their close embraces. I could not remember the last time I had held a woman, and I tried to recall the sensations. The brush of soft hair against my face. The touch of her clothes. The warmth of her. I wanted to hoard her warmth against the coming winter. I was like a freezing man desperately trying to kindle a life.

I turned away.

I righted my chair and sat down again. Stan was staring at me. Ben was watching sympathetically. Lisa appeared to be studying me, trying to solve some mental problem.

"Who was that?" Stan asked.

"I told you, a student of mine."

"She asked *you* to dance?" He seemed both impressed and dumbfounded.

"Yes." I tried to be off-hand about it, but I was pretty dumbfounded, too. And something else. A rising sadness.

"Well, why didn't you dance with her?" Stan wanted to know.

I looked at him, trying to disguise my sadness with horror. "I can't dance with her. She's a student."

"So are you."

"But she's *my* student."

"It's not like *you* asked *her*. She asked you."

"That doesn't make any difference. It would be wrong."

"Why? Would you boost her grade because she danced with you?" He was getting frustrated. So was I. It was hard to defend myself against him, especially since a lot of me was on his side.

"No. She already gets the best grades in class."

"So one innocent dance, in a public place, where everyone could see there was nothing going on." His voice was rising in exasperation. "For heaven's sake, you dance with Lisa, and that's okay."

I felt tired. I couldn't come up with any new reasons to defend myself. "It would have been wrong."

"You're crazy," he stated slowly. "Here this good-looking girl comes to ask *you* to dance, and for no good reason you say no." Stan shook his head. "If I knew a good-looking girl like that, student or not, and she asked *me* to dance, I know what *I'd* do."

"What would *you* do?" Lisa asked mildly.

Stan snapped his head around, realizing what he'd just said. I could feel the breeze. He recovered smoothly.

"I'd introduce her to one of my single friends, like Mark." He stood up. "Want to dance, honey?"

Lisa rose demurely and they moved to the dance floor.

"Saved by the belle," I commented. Ben laughed and I smiled. It helped ease the tension.

"Part of me thinks I just made a big mistake," I said dejectedly. "But I know what I did was right."

Ben shrugged. "You know, just because Stan thinks it would have been all right doesn't mean it would have been wrong."

I smiled. "Too bad. He's usually a pretty reliable reverse barometer."

"This really bothers you, doesn't it?" he asked.

"Yeah. Sounds stupid, but it really does."

He smiled. "Then you're all right. If it didn't bother you, *then* I'd start to worry."

Seventeen

I needed something to distract myself, clear my head. "I'm going to waste some aliens. Want to come?"

Ben shook his head.

"My treat," I offered. We were both equally broke.

"No, thanks." I waved and moved off to the game room.

There was a small room with video games off one end of the Lambs' Den. I pushed a quarter into Alien Intruders and began to play. You remember Alien Intruders. At the bottom of the screen, you have a cannon that you can move from side to side and shoot upwards. A whole screenful of aliens is dropping inexorably downward in rows, dodging from side to side. They are raining bombs down on the flimsy fortifications that protect your cannon. The more aliens you shoot, the faster they move, until the last one is whizzing across the screen. If you manage to shoot the last one, a whole new screenful of aliens appears, this time even lower and faster than before. It requires strict concentration, and forces extraneous thoughts out of your mind. Just what I needed right then.

After a few minutes of frenzied alien butt kicking, I had topped the HIGH SCORE on the machine, and racked up three free games to boot, so I could relax a little. It occurred to me that I could study this game as a physicist and examine how things behaved in this little universe. My eyes naturally noticed the little aliens dithering back and forth across the screen while chugging relentlessly downwards. My immediate thought was: *Real things don't fall like that.*

I froze. Light exploded in my head. I stopped playing because I couldn't see the screen anymore. I stepped stiffly away from the machine. Around me, onlookers howled in dismay. A small crowd had gathered, watching me play, cheering me on, but I hadn't seen or heard them, so oblivious to the real world did I become while playing. One of the crowd uttered a little cry and leaped to the controls to rescue my poor cannon from the peril I had left it in.

I wandered away, out of the game room, back into the Lambs' Den. I didn't hear the music. I didn't see the people. My mind was totally filled with that thought: *Real things don't fall like that.*

Through hazy vision, I saw Stephanie, now dancing with some guy. I was vaguely happy for her, but looking at her, I saw another image: Stephanie kneeling over the spring-loaded gun. The experiment I had taught to four lab sections this week. Projectile motion.

The law of falling bodies.

I felt my whole body chill and an electric tickle went up my spine. Two thoughts collided. Real things don't fall like that. The law of falling bodies.

And then, like I was hearing some far-off call, I turned, and looked out through the tall glass windows, out into the night. Between two dark buildings, I could see a slice of the Quadrangle. At the far end of the Quadrangle was the physics building, its ivy-covered walls lit by spot-lights. And at the top of the physics building, the roof from which Professor Speen had somehow tumbled to his death. Fallen.

Real things don't fall like that.

A picture was forming in my mind, trying to come into being out of three disconnected jigsaw pieces: the alien intruders, the lab experiment, the fall. I had to fit the pieces together. I felt them tumbling about in my mind like socks in a dryer, linked by some force that kept them in orbit about each other. It was a compulsion, an overwhelming desire to simply know. I was on the brink of some discovery. I had to go finish the research.

I stepped around people and chairs until I reached our table. Lisa and Stan were just returning from the dance floor. I pulled my jacket from the chair.

"I have to go," I said urgently.

"What is it?" said Ben, concerned. He'd be thinking of the Stephanie incident. It wasn't like this was his first encounter with my weirdness around women.

"Something at the physics building I have to do." I sounded strange even to me.

"Oh, wait, no way," Stan protested. "It's Friday night, for heaven's sake, you're not doing homework on Friday night." He spoke as if I intended to violate one of humankind's most sacred tenets.

I turned to him with vacant eyes. "I have to."

"No," Stan howled, appealing to Ben by looking at him.

Ben raised a hand to quiet Stan. To me he said, "Are you okay?"

I nodded. "I just have to find out something." Stan was outraged. Lisa was curious. Ben was tolerant.

I turned and left. Speechless, they watched me go.

Eighteen

It was cold as hell outside—whatever that means—and I pulled my thin coat on and zipped it up tightly. The winter night was ethereally still after the pounding of the band. The streetlight illumination pouring onto the sidewalk seemed solid and eternal. The stars were white ice above.

What the hell was I doing?

I stopped and looked back at the Lambs' Den. Condensed moisture from the warmth of bodies distorted the view through the large windows. The music was muffled behind the glass. The laughter, the talk, the singing was muted. There was life and warmth sealed inside there. I was separated from it by an invisible wall. I was apart, not a part.

I looked away to the stars in the darkness. Stars are immense spheres of burning gas, but to me they were cold white pinpoints in the night, uncaring and infinitely far away.

I headed for the physics building.

Nineteen

Once there I walked around to the side where Speen had fallen, my queasiness now replaced by an urgent need to know. The spot was actually marked in chalk on the cement walk. I thought they only did that in the movies, but maybe cops watched movies, too. I looked at the chalk out-line, then up at the overhanging roof. Then back at the outline and back at the roof. I felt that electric tickle again. I wondered what it was I was looking for. And then I saw it.

Real things don't fall like that. The law of falling bodies.

I knew now what I had to do.

I used my keys to let myself into the physics building. With my fear of heights there was no way I was going out on that roof, so I headed for the floor closest to the roof, the fifth floor. On the way, I unlocked a lab room and removed a long bamboo pole and a meter stick, then locked it again.

On the fifth floor, I found the room with a window closest above where the body had fallen. I had to go by Speen's office to get there, which gave me a creepy feeling in the empty building. This involved a dead person, I realized.

I flipped on the lights in the room—an ordinary classroom—and set the pole and stick down. I pulled down the top of the window and looked down. The five-story view was dizzying to me, and I backed away from the window, breathing hard.

This has to be done, I told myself. I have to know. I clamped my jaw shut and turned back to the window. I looked straight down. The chalk outline was directly below me. I looked up. I could see the overhang of the roof above.

I picked up the pole and stuck it out the window. I maneuvered it with both hands until the far end of it was just touching the outermost edge of the roof, and the shaft was resting up against the top of the window. I held it there with one hand while my other hand fumbled a pen out of my pocket and I marked on the pole where it touched the window.

I hauled the pole in and laid it on the floor. I used the meter stick to measure the distance along the pole from the mark I had made to the far end. This was the distance from the outer edge of the roof to the window. I wrote that number on the blackboard with chalk.

I took the pole and shoved it out the window again, this time straight up, until it hit the underside of the roof directly above the window. Again I marked where the shaft touched the window, hauled it in, and measured the distance. This was the distance from the window straight up to the roof. I wrote this on the board under the first number.

From the window straight up to the roof, from there out to the edge of the roof, then from there back to the window was a right triangle. I wanted to know the second distance, the amount the roof overhung the wall. So I used the Pythagorean Theorem: the sum of the squares of the sides equals the square of the hypotenuse. The first number I had written was the hypotenuse. I squared it by multiplying it by itself on the blackboard. The second number was one of the sides. I squared it, too. The difference between these two was the square of the other side, which I wanted. I subtracted the two, then mentally estimated the square root.

About two and a half meters, or seven and a half feet.

I shut the window, picked up the pole and meter stick, flipped the light off, and left the room. I put the pole back in the lab and went back outside with the meter stick.

There's probably nothing here. I'm doing all this for nothing. Freezing my butt off. Missing the dance. I sighed. Might as well make sure, as long as I'm here.

I bent over the chalk outline. The head was nearest the building. I measured the distance. Half a meter, about a foot and a half. I measured the distance from the building to the center of the outline. A little more than a meter, about three and a half feet.

I stood up. What did that tell me? I looked up at the roof, then down at the outline. Then I felt that electric tickle again. I stared straight ahead. I dropped the meter stick. I stepped back until I was leaning against the building.

"My God."

I once read an account about a famous scientist, Hans Bethe—okay, at least he's famous to other scientists—the first person to discover where the sun got the energy to shine. He got the Nobel Prize for his discovery. He said that when he had finished his calculations, and knew they were right, he was suddenly struck by the thought that at that moment he was the only person on earth who knew what made the sun shine.

This was what science was all about. That delicious thrill of discovery, of *knowing* an answer, perhaps being the only person on earth to know the answer.

I felt that thrill now. Because I had made a discovery. I knew something that maybe only one other person on earth knew. It was a little thrill for a little discovery. Not like the mainline thrill of discovering why the sun shines, but it was enough for me, for now. I could only imagine what the thrill of a big discovery must be like. It must be wonderful.

I smiled up at the stars. My smile wouldn't reach them for a million years. I was too happy to care. I had made a discovery!

But what had I discovered?

Three things, really.

First, the eyewitness, who claimed to have seen the murder, was lying.

Second, Jackson Katanga could not have killed Professor Speen as they suspected.

And third, Speen had not been thrown from the roof, or pushed from the roof. He hadn't jumped from the roof or fallen from the roof either.

Speen had never been on the roof at all.

Saturday

▼

Twenty

After Friday night's discovery, I had walked home from the physics building to Graduate Village. I made a rough sketch of what I had found, noted
down all the numbers I had measured, and called the police, something I
had never done before.

"I have some information about the murder of Dr. Speen at the college," I told whoever answered the phone at the Kingstown Police station.
"Who should I talk to?"

The phone answerer seemed skeptical. "That would be Lieutenant
Trask or Sergeant McKinnock, but they're not around now."

That seemed reasonable. It was pretty late. "When will they be
around?" I asked.

"I'm pretty sure they'll be here in the morning. They usually come in
on Saturday mornings even if they don't have an investigation going."

"Should I make an appointment?" I wondered.

"Naw, just come by in the morning. Ask for Lieutenant Trask."

"Trask. Okay."

I hung up. I guessed it could wait. I went to bed.

When I woke up and saw the paper with my scribbling on it, I didn't
recognize it. Then when I recognized it, I didn't believe it. Did I really go
to the physics building last night? Did I really investigate a crime scene?
Did I really make that discovery? It couldn't be right.

Before I even took a shower, I checked my calculations again. They
came out the same. I did them again, in a different way. They came out

the same. If I was wrong, at least I was being wrong in a consistent way. Heck, that should count for something. I headed for the shower.

In a way, I wanted to do this and get it over with before I changed my mind. I was soon in my lesson-preparation mode, as if getting ready for my next lab section. I rehearsed the explanation from beginning to end. I tried to make each succeeding step in the logic sound like it followed inevitably from the preceding step. I tested each word, weighing it, measuring it for effect, nuance, and connotation.

While in town, I would stop and do my food shopping for the week. In my pocket, I had six dollars, a five and a one, which was what my budget allowed for food this week. We graduate students received our pay once a month, a real strain on the finances. I used the "envelope method" to make sure I didn't get caught short. Each month I put my half of the rent money in the rent envelope, my estimate of the phone and electric bills in the phone and electric envelopes. Ten dollars per month went into the fun envelope. The rest I divided into four parts, for the four weeks each month I would do food shopping. There was never much in those four envelopes. Months with more than 28 days were a problem.

Maybe I'm making it sound grimmer than it was. I wasn't starving. My weekday lunches and dinners at the cafeteria were covered by my scholarship and loans. The money in the food envelopes had to cover breakfasts on weekdays, and all meals on weekends. If you buy smart, a little can go a long way. Of course, six dollars falls well within the definition of "a little".

Twenty-one

Saturday morning found me tooling along the road from Kingston U. to the police station in the metropolis, Kingstown proper. The big city.

The weather was strange, even for New England. It was frosty out, colder than it had been even last night. And yet, the sun was out. It was also raining lightly. This combination might seem odd, but not if you've lived in New England. The weather can switch from cold to rain to sun in a minute, and sometimes nature isn't fussy about waiting the minute.

My black VW bug had started right up, which was a pleasant surprise. One of the things I liked about the bug was that it was so light I could push it myself, jump in, and start it by popping the clutch, if necessary. Last winter, after a plow had buried it under a hill of snow, six friends and myself had managed to lift it straight up and set it back in the street. Try that with a Buick.

As I turned from the university onto the road to town, I saw someone hitchhiking on the side of the road. I generally picked up hitchhikers, as long as they looked okay. Big burly guys with scars on their face and tattoos on their arms (or vice versa), probably not. People who seemed unlikely to commit violence against my person, more likely. Probably not a smart idea, but there had been plenty of times when I was without a car myself. I knew what it was like to be out there, freezing your tootsies off, walking backwards as fast as physically possible (which is to say, not very), thumb stuck out, smiling, trying to look acceptable to drivers, hoping whoever picked you up wasn't a Charles Manson disciple.

Through a swipe of windshield wiper, I saw that it was a young woman. I really hated to see that. I worried about women getting rides from dangerous people. I often thought there should be some kind of national register of safe hitchhiker-picker-uppers or something, but I had never figured out how to do it. Computers, maybe.

I pulled my ancient Volkswagen over about twenty feet past her and stopped. She turned and ran towards the car, which I found gratifying. I hate it when you pull over to pick up a hiker and they saunter over taking their own sweet time. I like to see that they appreciate my gesture.

She was trotting up to the car. I leaned to the right and opened the door.

"Where are you headed?" I asked, before I could even see her.

She stuck her head in the door and looked in at me. It was a shock to the poor girl, and I couldn't blame her. My appearance is tough to take even when you know it's coming, never mind all at once without any warning, the way she had gotten it.

"Into, uh, into town." She kept looking at me steadily, then slid into the seat and pulled the door shut. I turned my eyes to the road, made sure to put both hands on the wheel, and started the car moving again. She sat looking straight ahead out the window. She was in a good defensive position, her right hand gripping the door handle, her left balled into a fist in the pocket of her jacket, just in case.

To be fair, I was also somewhat taken aback by *her* appearance. She was beautiful. I had noticed that right off. Her blondish-brown hair was pulled back from her face into a knot. It was a little bedewed with drizzle, and pearls of rain here and there were most becoming. She had a creamy complexion sprinkled with freckles—no makeup—and the most luminous green eyes I had ever seen. But there was something else.

I swept a swift glance at her, then concentrated on driving and what I had seen. Her face, jacket, jeans, shoes, and knapsack all added up in my mind to only one conclusion.

I took a while editing and re-editing my question into something I could actually say without my usual embarrassment tying my tongue into knots, then made a throat-clearing sound. "So, did you run away from home in New York or New Jersey?" I asked her mildly.

Her head whipped around toward me, the astonishment on her face supporting my theory nicely. Then her mask snapped shut again and she faced forward.

"I haven't run away from anywhere. Why should you think such a thing?"

Note the syntax, I thought. This is an educated, intelligent young woman. And, to have survived on her own for several months, obviously a resourceful one, too.

I shrugged. "A lot of things. You don't know the name of the town we're heading towards, for example, so you aren't from around here."

She shook her head. "I know the name of the town. It's Kingston. I live there." She jutted her chin out defiantly and stared determinedly out the window.

"Actually, through an accident of spelling and geography, Kings*ton* University is located near the town of Kings*town*."

She was silent.

I went on. Sticking to the facts made it easier to speak. And, for some reason, she was easy to speak to. "You're a little too young to be in college, you don't live around here, so you're passing through. Your face is pale, which could be several things, but you don't seem sick, so I think you haven't been eating well lately. Therefore, you have little money, and no family around to help you. No hat or gloves. Your jacket isn't windproof, waterproof or warm. A summer jacket. If you had another, you'd wear it, especially on a day like this. So, it must be all you have and you've been wearing it since the summer. Therefore, you probably left home in the summer. Your jeans are very worn. I know that's the style these days, but yours look like real wear, not fashion. Also, I can see another pair in your knapsack. Since you'd probably wear your warmest on a cold day, the others must be worse. Your sneakers are worn smooth, so you've been doing a lot of walking in them. So," I concluded, "you ran away from home in the summer and I'm curious about where you're from. I'm not very good with accents, but you're obviously not from the south or Midwest or the more Yankee parts of New England. So, I'm thinking it's either New York or New Jersey."

I could feel her staring at me. "Who the hell are you? Sherlock Holmes?"

In view of where I was headed, and why, I thought that was a very perceptive comment.

And a literary allusion besides. She has done some reading, possibly a good student in school, before whatever trouble it was.

I shook my head. "Nope. Which is it?"

She looked down, looked out the side window, looked straight ahead, sighed heavily. "New Jersey." She sounded tired, not defiant.

I tried another angle. "I know it's none of my business, but you really shouldn't hitchhike. There are some dangerous people around. The bus only costs a quarter around here."

She was furious now. I could feel her glaring at me as she spoke through clenched teeth. "I don't *have* a quarter."

I drove with my right hand and dug my money out of my pocket with my left. Six dollars: my food shopping money for the week. I pulled the one free of the five, sighed, and stuck it back in my pocket. I held the five out to her.

She sneered. "What do you think five dollars is going to get you?"

I felt sick and sad. "Don't do it for money."

She stared straight ahead again. "What do you know about it?"

"I know it's not good for you."

"Yeah? And how did you come by that experience?"

"You don't have to murder somebody to know that murder isn't a good idea. It's not a good idea. And it can lead to the kind of life you don't deserve."

"How do you know what I deserve?"

"I know. You're a smart person, probably good in school. A nice girl. You ran away from something to protect yourself. Keep protecting yourself. You left in a hurry, but my guess is something had been building for a long time. Your mother and father?"

"Step," she said with an edge on it. "Father."

Step-father. With a beautiful teenaged step-daughter. Who ran away. I clenched my teeth to stem a sudden distaste. "I'm sorry," I said softly.

And we were silent together for a while.

Finally, she said, "Okay, Sherlock. You seem to know everything. Maybe you can tell me what I'm supposed to do now. Instead."

"You didn't finish high school."

She shook her head no. "I would have been a senior," she said, as if describing something very far away.

Homecoming game. Applying to colleges. Cutting class when the weather got nice. Parties. Gowns and tuxes. Graduation.

Not this girl. Not this life. Not this way.

An idea came to me. A stone in a pond. It expanded, it grew. Pieces fell into place. In about three seconds, I had it all, and I started talking.

"Where I'm going to drop you off is in front of the state employment service," I began. "They're open on Saturday mornings, so people can get their unemployment checks. They like helping people who are actually looking for work. You're looking for work. You tell them you're over 18." I looked at her to see if she would object.

She didn't. She looked straight at me and she looked scared. Hope can be frightening. "I actually am," she said in a low voice. I gave a minute shrug and smile.

I went on. "Look for anything you can do. Get creative if they ask about experience. My guess is, if you've survived on your own with no money since summer, you must be pretty sharp and can learn anything they show you. Waitress, clerk, stuff like that. Use their free phone and call all the local jobs, starting with the best ones. Take the bus or walk, don't hitch." I shook the five insistently and she took it gently and looked at it in her hand.

I stopped and thought, then shook my head. "I know they don't need any help in the physics department, or I'd ask there. Anyway, keep looking until you find something. Job."

"Tonight, you take the bus back to the university, but go to the first stop *past* the campus. The youth hostel is there, a little house for students coming and going. It's clean and safe, run by a married couple. Costs 50 cents a night to stay there, but if you do some of their chores, maybe you'll save the 50 cents. Stay there until you get an apartment. Lodging."

"When you get hungry today, go across the street from the unemployment office. Day-old bakery. Buy the leftover donuts. They go stale fastest, so they're cheapest. They also come in assorted flavors. Food." I spoke from experience. I had bought a lot of stale donuts recently. Sometimes that six dollars didn't cover a whole week. Like maybe this week, for instance.

"When you get your job, do good work, show them they were right to hire you. See if you can get paid daily, or a little in advance. Find an apartment in the paper, clean, safe, doesn't have to be fancy.

"This is a good area, lots of cheap and free things to do at the college. Do you have a religion?"

She was startled by the question. "Presbyterian," she said, as if suddenly finding something she thought she had lost.

I nodded. "One of their churches in Kingstown. Go tomorrow. Maybe you don't believe it all right now, but you can meet people there, make some contacts, maybe find a better job, a better apartment. Faith can come later."

I took a breath and went on. "You're pretty. That'll help, but I'm sure you know it goes both ways. For all the people who'll want to help you, there'll be some who want something from you. Be careful and take care of yourself. I bet you already know how."

I pulled off the road into the parking lot. "Here we are." I stopped the car—another pleasant surprise, because the brakes were iffy—and turned to face her. I had been looking out the windshield all the time I had been talking. Too embarrassing to look at her while I was saying all that stuff. She was holding the five in her hand as if it were a fragile glass butterfly, afraid that the slightest movement might shatter it or make it fly away. She looked fragile herself in that moment, but I knew she must be smart and tough to survive on her own as she had.

She was looking at me strangely. Part like she wanted to smile, and part like she wanted to cry, and part just mystified. Finally, she said, "Who *are* you?"

I laughed. "I'm nobody. I'm just some guy. The last person you ever hitchhiked with. Right?"

"Right," she said, a little shyly. I think I caught a glimpse then of what she might have been like. Before August. Kind of shy, kind of quiet, kind of unsure.

"I'm gonna leave now, and you're going to be okay. You're going to take care of yourself, right?"

She nodded. She opened the door, gathered her stuff and stepped out. She turned and looked at me through the door. She was bending slightly to look in, and her hair framed her face and eyes. She was young and beautiful and smart and strong. I felt things stirring in me, and I ignored them.

"Why are you doing this? Why are you helping me?"

I shrugged and looked into her eyes. "When I stopped the car you looked in at me."

She shook her head and smiled, puzzled. "Yes. So?"

"You got in anyway."

She gave me a look I can't describe, a look that made me want to keep her with me forever. So I said good-bye, and she walked away toward the unemployment office. I drove away and left her there.

Oddly, the first thought I had when I left her was: I can never tell Stan about what I just did. Why would I let a beautiful, intelligent young woman just walk away, without even getting her name, without even giving her my number, when I obviously felt something toward her, and maybe she did a little for me? Oddly, though, I thought Stan might understand—if not accept—the real answer. It had to do with last night, the dance, temptation, and wanting something so badly that you were willing to do something you knew was wrong to get it. They taught you all about it in Catholic school.

Penance.

Twenty-two

The Kingstown Police Station was called, against all odds, Maybelle.

Allow me to explain.

It had been donated to the town, just given to them, by a wealthy local real estate developer named Russell Mercer. A large and rambling building like an oversized suburban ranch house, it was easier to imagine it holding a basement rumpus room with a ping-pong table than jail cells.

This Mercer was a local legend, and something of a hero to me, a category that not many real-estate developers fall into. But Mercer was special. He had started out as a humble builder's helper, had quickly picked up the skills of house construction, and struck out on his own. Not having any money, he specialized in finding ramshackle abandoned property, fixing it up, and reselling it. Soon he had made enough money to start building houses to order. There was always something special about his houses. They weren't the ordinary four walls and a roof. Not that they were bizarre or outlandish, which builders tend to produce when given free rein. You could just look at some houses and tell they were special. They were Russell Mercer houses.

Once he built these beautiful condominiums on a bluff overlooking the ocean, intended, of course, for very wealthy people, and they sold like hotcakes. It was very successful financially, and even aesthetically: they looked wonderful all gleaming in the sun on what had theretofore been a sort of unofficial town dump. But this led to a concern that the town might be forgetting its poorer citizens in its haste to lure richer ones. In fact, the only low-income housing in town had been built just after World War II and was embarrassingly run-down. Mercer contracted with the town to improve this run-down property. Apparently remembering his own father-less and impoverished childhood, Mercer instead built an entirely new sys-

tem of low-income housing, identical in basic design to the expensive con-
dominium complex. And for the same money as the fix-up job.

This is a guy who, far from forgetting his own start in construction, still
actually worked most mornings alongside his employees. And you can bet
he bought the doughnuts. Still only in his thirties, wealthy, good-looking
and popular, he was linked romantically to rich and beautiful women all
over the world. As it turns out, he married some local woman only a few
years ago.

I like to think that I would act like that if I ever became rich. Given the
discouraging statistics about physicists becoming millionaires, it seemed
unlikely. But it was nice to know there were some Russell Mercers around
in the world.

All of which is a roundabout way of explaining why Kingstown had a
police station called Maybelle. It had been christened the Maybelle Mercer
Police Station, in memory of Mercer's mother.

Twenty-three

I took a deep breath of cold air to clear my mind of—well, I didn't actually know her name, did I?—then pushed open the glass and metal door. With my hair, beard and clothes I felt vividly out of place entering the police station.

The officer at the desk did not look particularly askance at me, though, and, when I asked to see Lt. Trask, waved me down a corridor to the back and returned to his morning newspaper.

The interior looked more like an insurance office than a police station. Rows of desks with typewriters. Little partitions. Bulletin boards. Where were all the criminals? Maybe they slept late on Saturday mornings.

I stopped in front of a door with a black nameplate, "Lt. Trask", on it. I suddenly felt uncomfortable. What was I doing here? Then I reminded myself that I did have some information, facts, that they should at least be made aware of. I knocked twice, medium loud.

The door was opened by the largest policeman I had ever seen. He was a good head taller than me, and wide in proportion. He was in his fifties, if not his sixties, judging by his gray and balding head, but he looked plenty solid and powerful to me. This threw me. Somehow, I'd been expecting Lt. Trask to be a moderately sized human, with grizzled hair and a rumpled dark suit, if not an actual fedora. This specimen wore a uniform, and the name above his breast pocket, at a level with my eyes, said "Sgt. McKinnock." This threw me some more. I had had Sgt. McKinnock penciled in as Trask's young, wisecracking assistant.

From far above me I heard him say in a moderate voice, "May I help you?" He reminded me of Jackson Katanga, and I wondered if all these enormous people were so placid and courteous. Maybe, being enormous, they could afford to be.

I cleared my throat and said, "My name is Mark Napoli. I was a student of Dr. Speen's at the university. I wanted to see Lt. Trask."

He nodded and said, "Would you mind waiting just a moment, please?" and waved a hand at a bench opposite the door.

I said sure and sat down. He closed the door and I could hear muffled voices within. I tried to steel myself for the coming introduction. If this was McKinnock, Trask, by extrapolation, would be something on the order of King Kong. I checked for the location of exits and tried to remain calm.

Presently Sgt. McKinnock opened the door and said, "Lt. Trask can see you now."

I followed him into a spacious office. Lt. Trask was coming around the side of a desk, hand outstretched toward me for shaking.

Once, when I was eight or ten, I was playing someplace I shouldn't, in the newly-excavated hole for the foundation of a house going up in our neighborhood, when a large rock became dislodged from the side of the hole somehow and bonked me smack on the top of my head. I saw stars— literally—and lights whizzing around and my ears buzzed and the world took on a dreamy far-off slow-motion quality.

This sensation was very similar to what I felt when I met Rachel Trask.

She had stood and come around her desk toward me smiling with her hand outstretched to shake. She, you understand. Very much she.

I had never seen anyone like her in my life.

She was probably five or six years older than me. She was as tall as me, maybe even an inch taller, but I like tall women. She wore one of those suits professional women wear, man-like but with a skirt and frilly at the wrist and neck, with a little ribbon tie. I had always thought those suits kind of silly—I myself hated dressing up in suits, so why would women do it if they didn't have to?—but not now, somehow. Her light light brown hair, almost blonde, swooshed back. She had a smile that seemed full of mischief and delight, as if at any moment she might suggest that we sneak off and play hooky on Sgt. McKinnock. Her deep blue eyes sparkled in accompaniment.

I hoped she would keep her name when we married. I had never heard the name before, but it was obvious that Rachel Trask was perfect. Rachel sounded silly with Napoli anyway. Most names did.

Marriage? My eyes instantly flashed to her left hand, her ring finger. There was no ring. No jewelry on her hands at all. No wedding ring. No engagement ring.

Not yet, anyway.

Shaking hands with her was like shaking hands with the future, with my destiny. Part of me now understood the universe and life. It all made a certain sense now. All the pain and annoyance and fear and worry of life somehow fell into place. I had met Rachel Trask. It had happened. Now I understood. Now I could get on with the rest of my life.

She said, "I'm pleased to meet you, Mr. Napoli. Thank you for coming over."

I said, "Gladda meja," or words to that effect.

"Won't you sit down," she offered graciously, indicating a seat at a table arranged perpendicularly to her desk. She sat and, as she did so, her jacket flapped open, giving me a momentary glimpse of a holster under her right arm.

"Thank you," I managed, and sat. Sgt. McKinnock sat across the table from me. I gazed at him, intrigued. What a lucky man, I thought, to be able to work each day with Rachel Trask.

"I understand that you were a student of Dr. Speen's," Lt. Trask, Rachel, began. She had a folder open in front of her and was penning a note. She was a lefty, I could see. That jibed with the holster under her right arm.

I nodded briskly. "Yes, I had electromagnetic theory with him."

She gave me a dazzled kind of look at this. McKinnock was impassive.

"What did you think of him?" she asked conversationally as she leafed through her file.

"He was a scumbag," I said without hesitation.

Her mouth popped open a little and she stopped leafing. McKinnock looked interested.

"Really?" she said, recovering. She went on, a little formally, "That, er, differs from other reports we've heard about him." She read from some statements in the folder, and phrases like "gifted researcher", "prominent scientist", and, finally, "dedicated teacher" oozed out.

I snorted. "He was a jerk," I maintained. "He was nasty to anyone he could get away with. He hated students and did his best to make their lives miserable."

"I see," she said, apparently trying to mentally reconcile my views with the quarter-pound of thinly-sliced baloney in front of her. "Was this true in your class as well?"

"Especially in my class," I agreed. "Everyone in that class was floundering, and he could not give a damn if he'd had two beavers to help him."

"Uh-huh," she said, then pulled a paper from the file. "I understand that on the day he died you attempted an insurrection in his class, trying to overthrow him with a coup d'état, and assume power yourself."

My own mouth popped open. "Insurrection"? "Coup l'état"? "Assume power"?

Suddenly my face brightened. "I get it. You've been talking with the Four Asian Students." The interpretations of their perhaps over-politicized minds did make a certain sense.

She smiled at me. I wondered I didn't melt onto the floor. "Yes, we have been speaking with…" She struggled courageously over the four names. "They said you tried to enlist their allegiance but that they maintained their loyalty to Dr. Speen."

I smiled. "I asked him to go over a homework problem. In Speen's class, that would pretty much be revolutionary."

"They say that you hated him," she continued.

I considered this and nodded. "Pretty close," I admitted. "I wouldn't count myself among his fans."

"And that he humiliated you in class after your revolution attempt failed," she went on.

"That he did," I said.

"And that you probably killed him for revenge," she concluded.

I sat up straight in my chair. "What?" I didn't know whether to smile or scream. One hates being tricked into confessing to murder by one's beloved.

"You were observed talking to him outside his office on the fifth floor afterwards," she said suggestively.

"Well, yes," I admitted. "I wanted him to show me that homework problem."

"Did you see anyone else in or near his office at that time?" she persisted.

I shook my head. "No. Well, yes, Dr. Wilhelm, but he left. Just him. And me." I felt inadequate that I couldn't help her more. If only I had seen the actual murderer!

She didn't seem disappointed. Far from it. "That makes you the last person to see him alive," she noted meaningfully.

I was beginning to understand how she had become a Lieutenant at such a young age.

"Wait a second," I blurted with my hands out protectively. "You're making it sound as if *I* killed him."

"Well," she sighed in a strangely apologetic way. "You certainly had sufficient motive. You could have pushed him off the roof as easily as anyone else. And you admit to being on the scene at about the time of the murder."

The word "roof" finally dislodged something in my brain. I didn't come here to fall in love (though that had happened), or to be accused of murder (though that had happened too), but to tell them something about the roof.

"I," I said, slipping some folded papers out of my coat pocket, "could not have shoved him off the roof. Because nobody shoved him off the roof."

"Oh?" she said dubiously. Somehow, I had not convinced her yet.

"You have an eyewitness who claims Speen was pushed off the roof."

She looked at Sergeant McKinnock. He met her glance, but said nothing and made no gesture. Yet, something seemed to have been communicated between them. I could see they had learned a thing or two from the Four Asian Students.

"Yes," she said. "A witness claims to have observed the entire incident. There was a struggle which resulted in Dr. Speen being pushed off the roof."

"Well, they're lying," I said flatly.

She sat back in her chair and tapped a pencil lightly on her file once.

"Are they?" she said at length.

"Yes they are, because it's not possible." I spread my diagrams and calculations out on their table.

They both seemed a little affronted by this intrusion in their space, and regarded the papers with distrust.

"The roof overhangs the building by seven and a half feet," I began. "Speen's body, the center of it, was only three and a half feet from the building. The head was even closer, but that may not matter. It is impossible for the body to have fallen inward, toward the building, from the edge of the roof. So any witness who says that's what happened is lying. Speen couldn't have been on that roof at all."

I sat back in my chair, smiling happily. This would be the moment, I thought. She would realize what I had done here. She would be grateful. She would look at me with admiration for having helped them. She would begin to appreciate me, then to love me. It had begun.

She leaned forward and tapped my drawings lightly. "I don't want to give you the wrong impression," she said. "We don't really believe that you murdered Dr. Speen."

"Whew," I said and wiped my brow exaggeratedly.

She smiled again. I didn't think I could take much more of her smiling at me without proposing to her right here in front of Sergeant McKinnock.

She went on. "And we do appreciate your coming here and giving us this information. And I think it's all very interesting."

She smiled a little more and I smiled, too. I was in a fog, so full of her that I could hardly understand what she was telling me. She seemed to be saying that she appreciated what I had done. But I sensed something was wrong.

She sighed. "But on the other hand, it's all pretty much beside the point for us."

"Beside the point?" I repeated, and trailed off. How could physical impossibility be beside the point? I looked down at the drawings, searching for the one that would convince her, help her understand. "But it's...it's..." I sputtered.

She consulted McKinnock again with another unspoken exchange. I looked from her to him and back again. She seemed to make up her mind.

She put her hand down forcefully on the drawings, and I looked up at her.

"You see," she said with utter sincerity. "Jackson Katanga has already confessed to the murder."

Twenty-four

There was a silence of about thirty-seven years. At least, it seemed that long to me. There seemed only one thing to say, so I said it.

"*What?*"

She shrugged. "Katanga said he wanted to talk to us last night. He confessed to the murder. He said it happened just as the witness said it did."

I left the police station shortly thereafter. At least, I suppose that I did: I don't really remember that clearly. After the electrifying meeting of Rachel Trask, the shocking near-arrest of myself, and the final bombshell that *Jackson had confessed to murdering Speen*, my mind had taken a well-deserved vacation.

Suffice it to say that I did not, in fact, regale them with any further presentations on the subject of the dynamics of falling objects. Suffice it also to say that I did not charm Rachel Trask into matrimony, or into any intermediate step thereto. Suffice it finally to say that I suddenly found myself on the road driving back to campus, with only a very hazy memory of how I had gotten there.

Jackson murdered Speen?

I was still reeling from the shock of this confession. To me it was like saying that tomorrow, instead of being a Sunday, was going to be Monday. It made that little sense.

I suddenly snapped back to reality for a brief visit and remembered that, murder or no murder, confession or no confession, dream-woman or no dream-woman, I still had to do food shopping. First things first. I pulled over on the shoulder, and when there was no traffic either way, pulled a U-ey across the road. Bugs are good for that, too.

I headed for Val-U-Village, an ultra-cut-rate market at the edge of town. You could bring your own bags to Val-U-Village, or they would be happy to charge you five cents each for their own. They sold these packages of sub-generic frozen waffles, six packages for a dollar, the packages smelling faintly of fish. I already had some jelly at home in the fridge. They would have to last me until next week. Five weekday breakfasts, and six weekend meals. Simple math shows us that this means about half a package, three waffles, per meal for the next week. Yum.

At the checkout counter, I was glad there was no sales tax on food. I didn't have a nickel.

Twenty-five

At home, I delivered nature's bounty into the freezer, took three aspirin and lay down on the bed. This had been a rotten day already, and it wasn't even nine a.m. yet. At least, I consoled myself, the day could get no worse after a start like this.

Wrong again, peanut brain. An ominous clicking from the doorknob of the other bedroom, a door opening, and a footstep in the hall alerted me that my despised apartment-mate, Eli, was home.

Eli's full name was Elijah Demi Rwande, and I'm not kidding. He was from Nigeria, and we had the goat tails on the living room walls to prove it. We did not get along very well, which I attributed to his being a jerk by any rational and objective standards. His jerkhood manifested itself in ways too numerous to list in a single-volume work such as this.

The footsteps approached my room and I braced for impact. However, it was not Eli at all, but a young woman on the chubby side with a sleepy, if not anesthetized, look on her face. She attempted to smile at me, couldn't seem to quite make it, and proceeded on past my room. I heard the front door open and close softly.

I had no idea who she was. Whoever she might be, she was certainly not Jeanne, Eli's girlfriend, fiancée really. No, this was yet another in the seemingly unending procession of apparently myopic and unquestionably dim-witted females Eli had managed to bed. He would chase virtually any woman who possessed certain rather common anatomical traits. For some reason, he was very successful in reeling in a large number of them, despite the fact that he was no male model himself.

Jeanne, a local girl and one of the sweetest people I'd ever met, had caught him several times in flagrante delicto, as they say in ancient Rome. There would be a big fight, she would leave him forever, he would call her and talk to her in his soft and dreamy voice and, a few days later, she would be back. She kept believing he would change. I was under no such illusion.

Now I heard his door open again and he passed by my room on his way to the bathroom. Poking his head in the door, he shook his head at me and said, "Still in bed! You Americans."

I hated this "You Americans" stuff, which he pulled on me all the time. To hear him talk, America was the most backward country on earth, and its people the stupidest and most unsophisticated imaginable. Which may well have been true. Being stupid and unsophisticated myself, how would I know? Yet, he had already announced his intention never to return to Nigeria, and was pursuing citizenship with every fiber of his being, including the possibility of actually wedding poor Jeanne if he had to. One could only admire his courage and generosity of spirit in trying to make do in the most backward nation on earth.

I got out of bed, since I would no longer be able to relax with my teeth gritted so tightly. I went to the kitchen, filled a cup of water and drank half. I sat at the kitchen table and looked out the window. Snow was now falling lightly. This had originally been Eli's apartment in the Graduate Village. I had answered an ad to become his apartment-mate over a year ago. Another in a series of good decisions on my part. At the time I had thought, how difficult could it be?

When he emerged from the bathroom, I asked him if he knew Jackson Katanga. He shrugged. He knew who he was, and knew some things about him, but wasn't actually chummy with him.

"Oh. He murdered Dr. Speen Thursday night," I remarked with pretended casualness. Eli was a graduate engineering student, and shared Stan's experience, and opinion, of the late physics professor.

"Jackson?" he replied incredulously. It was pleasant to see his usual smugness disturbed, however briefly. "Impossible!" he declared, quickly recovering his smugness. Eli also spoke with a British accent, but his had been softened and blurred by American phrases and pronunciation.

I made a face. Had he been peeking over my shoulder? "Why impossible?" I wondered.

He put on his patiently suffering look, the one that made me want to throttle him. "Jackson is from a country where they revere their teachers. He could never lift a finger against a teacher. He could never even disobey a teacher. Besides, he is too much of a butt-kisser," he declared. I had to admit that I liked the way he pronounced "butt-kisser".

Crudely stated, but pretty much what I thought myself. The cultural angle of his native country was intriguing though.

"That's interesting," I said, preparing to blow him out of the water. "Because he just confessed to the murder to the police."

Instead of being leveled by my information, he gave me a pitying smile that made me sick to look at. "You Americans," he added. "So naïve."

At the cue, "You Americans," I found myself glancing around the kitchen for sharp knives. Not seeing any, I took a calming breath and said, "Oh? And why is that? People lie to get *out* of a murder charge, Eli, not *into* one."

While we had been talking, he had put a skillet on the stove, taken eggs from his supply in the fridge, and started cracking them onto its sizzling surface. He added about a quarter of a pound of bacon around the eggs. "Do you think that the only reason to confess to a crime is out of guilt for committing it?" he asked with a cynical smirk.

I was confused. I felt like he was setting me up for some trap, designed to demonstrate my stupid unsophistication. "You think he might have another reason?"

He spread his hands, dripping bacon grease from the spatula. "Of course. He obviously did not do it. But he has confessed anyway, so you say. So he must have another reason."

He seemed to have an angle on this I hadn't considered, and I didn't mind being stupid and unsophisticated to find out what it was. "Like what?"

He shrugged. "He may be protecting someone else."

"Like who?"

He considered. The snapping of the eggs and bacon in the pan was driving me insane. "That is hard to say. I know he has a sister, but I cannot see why she would kill Speen. And it is hard to imagine Jackson involved with a woman whom he might protect, also."

It sure was. It was almost easier to imagine him killing Speen. "I don't see it," I said.

Eli sighed, and dropped four slices of cinnamon bread into the toaster. "Who knows? Perhaps it is a saving lie."

"A saving lie?" I had never heard the phrase before. "What is that?"

"You don't know much about Jackson's country, do you?"

This was true enough. Like many stupid unsophisticates, my knowledge of non-American geography was pretty shaky. Other than knowing it was in Africa, I didn't know anything about it. I didn't even know where in Africa it was. I wasn't about to admit this to Eli, though. Especially with the smell of bacon and eggs permeating my very being. "What about it?" I asked.

Eli gave me his pity-the-ignorant-American look. "In Jackson's country is the secret police. If *they* arrest you they maybe kill you, or only torture you, or maybe torture then kill you."

Just to annoy him, I felt like asking if they ever did it the other way around, but I didn't.

He went on, with a little shrug as he slathered honey onto his cinnamon toast. "In such a country, if you think the secret police are after you, where can you go? This is where the saving lie comes from. You go to the civil police, the ordinary police, and you confess to some crime. Then the civil police send you to jail, where the secret police can't get you. In such a country, people often read the newspapers and memorize minor crimes, in case they need to confess and escape from the secret police."

I was staring at him, appalled. "You aren't kidding, are you?" Maybe I *was* naïve, but this had enough topspin to shock anybody.

Eli shook his head, shoveling eggs and bacon onto a plate. "So naïve. This lie, this confession can save your life, some times."

"So you think Jackson confessed to the murder just to get away from something else, something worse?"

"It could well be."

I was still appalled by the concept, but I kept up the struggle anyway. "But we don't have secret police here."

"It may be something else he wishes to escape."

I laughed. "But what could be worse than being convicted for murder?"

He looked thoughtful, as he piled toast beside his eggs. "They have death penalty here?"

I thought about it. They had repealed the death penalty in this state back in the 1800s after some poor schmuck was hanged for a murder somebody else later confessed to. Whoops! Lot of red faces then, I'll bet.

"No," I said.

Eli brightened. "Well then, so he may go to prison for a little while if convicted."

"But what's worse than that?" I asked exasperatedly.

Eli looked at me, then shoved a forkful of genuine breakfast into his mouth. "Getting murdered himself, of course."

Twenty-six

Needless to say, I did not hang around the apartment to enjoy Eli's companionship and easy camaraderie. Maybe it's just me, but I have always found it hard to pal around with people I loathe. Personal preference.

I trudged toward the library. And it was a trudge. My six-year-old boots were nearly treadless as of this date, and I slipped around a good deal in the thin layer of wet snow. It wouldn't have been so bad if it had been downhill: I could have slid along. But everything on this campus seemed to be uphill.

As I neared the library, I passed a white clapboard building. It has been a while, I thought.

I clumped around to the front door. Probably locked. No reason to be open on a Saturday. Just try it, then go to the library.

The door opened easily.

Probably something going on inside. Don't bother anybody. Just stick my head in, then go to the library.

There was no one there at all.

I took a seat in the back. Struggling sunshine squeezed through the windows and splashed their colored lessons across the rows.

I cleared my throat.

"Hi," I said. "How are you doing?" There was no answer. Never was. That didn't matter: the book says you talk anyway. Operators are standing by.

"I'm doing pretty okay myself," I continued. "Thanks for the nice job I've got. It's indoors, clean, no heavy lifting. Tuition thrown in. Could pay better. Anything that can be done about more money, I'd sure appreciate it. I'm not complaining. I manage three meals a day, place to live, clothes, a car. I'm doing way better than a lot of people. It's just hard sometimes, that's all.

"Thanks for my friends. They're a comfort. Please help me not to murder Eli. That would make a bad impression on this detective I just met."

I sighed. "You know, of course, about Rachel Trask. As usual, I blew it big time. I don't know what to do anymore. That's hard sometimes, too. This definitely comes under the heading of miracles, but anything that could sort of push things along there, I'd be eternally grateful. It is not good that the man should be alone sort of thing. You know."

I looked around me. "Sorry I don't come here when everybody else does. It's easier for me when it's just us. Thanks for being here. Thanks for listening. Thanks for caring. I appreciate it."

My glance then fell on a Bible in the rack in front of me. I picked it up and it fell open to an old woodcut illustration by some famous artist whose name I should probably know. The illustration showed what I assumed to be Lucifer, falling from heaven. The falling angel.

I didn't get it. It couldn't mean Speen. Sure, he had fallen all right. But I couldn't see him as an angel nor—as much as I disliked him—as a devil either. As usual, whatever the Almighty was transmitting just wasn't registering on the meter.

I got up and walked to the door. A priest entered from the other end, one of those young-looking thirtyish priests they send to college campuses. He looked at me, smiled, and asked, "Can I help you?"

I waved. "I'm all set, thanks. Just visiting."

Twenty-seven

I did actually make it to the library.

Even without Speen, I had some homework due in other courses. And that grading I still hadn't finished. Plus, the library had books and magazines I could never have afforded to buy. People to watch. It was warm and well lit. And the crowning touch was that Eli never went there.

I spent a pleasant few hours doing a little homework, a little grading, a little reading, and a little watching. I went home around two. I wanted to make sure that I was good and hungry before facing those waffles.

I was thrilled to discover that Eli was gone again. I celebrated with a few waffles. The phone rang while I was enjoying a postprandial glass of water.

"Nick's pizza, we deliver," I said. I tried my best to amuse my callers, and confuse and annoy Eli's.

"Oh, I'm sorry." It was a woman's voice that sounded vaguely familiar. "I was trying to reach Mr. Napoli."

"Speaking," I said, embarrassed. "Sorry about that. Little joke."

"Hello, Mr. Napoli. This is Rachel Trask. We met this morning at the…"

I didn't hear the rest of her sentence, because I had dropped the phone. Onto the couch, luckily, so I was able to snatch it up again without her being aware of it.

"…how are you?"

"Fine. Great. Super. Terrific," I recovered suavely. "And yourself?"

"Fine, thanks. I, er," she seemed somewhat embarrassed herself, or hesitant, or something. I was so thrown off by her mere call that, as much as I wished to spare her any awkwardness, I was incapable of smoothing the way for her. "I enjoyed talking with you this morning. I was wondering if you, if we, might be able to get together tonight sometime. If you're not already busy, I mean. I know it's a Saturday night."

I had been trying to say "Yes" or "Sure" or "Yahoo" for the past few seconds, but my larynx had seized up on me. I put my hand over the mouthpiece, turned my head, and gave an enormous cough to dislodge things. I removed my hand and smoothly replied, "Why, yes, that would be great."

"Oh, good," she said with feeling. "I was hoping that would be okay. I was thinking we could meet for coffee somewhere quiet, say around eight."

She had obviously given this some thought, which I found astonishing. Nothing like this had ever happened to me. I tried to remember what I liked women to say when I called them up for dates. "Eight o'clock sounds fine. Where did you have in mind?"

"Is there somewhere on campus? It would be more convenient for you."

How considerate. I was touched. "Well, there's the Lambs' Den, in the Union. They're open until ten."

"That sounds good. And we can just take it from there."

The open-ended nature of her response set my heart fluttering.

"I'm looking forward to it," I said, delivering the understatement of the millennium.

"Then I'll see you there at eight," she said, a smile in her voice.

"At eight."

"Bye."

"Bye."

She clicked off.

I regarded the phone in my hand. What a wonderful object. I had never really noticed its beauty before, never appreciated it fully. I felt like it should be exhibited, on a pedestal perhaps, for all to experience and enjoy. With great reluctance, I hung up.

My mind tried unsuccessfully to encompass what had just occurred. Rachel Trask (okay so far) had called me up (Now Leaving Reality, Come Again Soon) and asked me on a date (off the scale).

I then felt a certain caution overshadowing my thrill, like someone who has just seen their lottery number drawn on TV. Understandably, I wanted some confirmation, and a thorough examination of any possible alternate interpretations.

I sat down on the couch and thought hard.

She was definitely unmarried, right? I nodded. Her hands had been thoroughly free of wedding rings, engagement rings, and any other jewelry, marriage-related or otherwise.

And she was definitely *not* interested in my physics theories, as applied to police work, right? I nodded again. She had certainly not been interested this morning. She had poor Jackson under arrest, and his confession in hand. She definitely didn't need me for that.

And she had called me, right? This was no hallucination. I had not called her, for instance. Reality was still ticking along. Certainly with a new soft golden light on it, but reality nonetheless.

And what exactly had she said? I screwed my eyes shut and tried replaying the conversation in my mind. "Enjoyed talking to me." "Wondering if we might get together tonight." "Meet somewhere quiet." "Take it from there."

I kept turning it over in my mind. I kept coming to the same conclusion. Rachel Trask had called me up and asked me on a date.

Wow.

My serene bliss lasted about three seconds, then I whirled my head to the clock.

Good grief, I thought. I only have five hours to get ready.

Twenty-eight

I entered the Lambs' Den at 7:45 with a confident stride. I was ready. Sort of.

I had spent the time since Rachel's call immersed in the infinity of decisions and details attendant upon an impending first date. I approached a date with the kind of strategic and tactical preparation usually associated with intricate surgery or complex military maneuvers.

Clothing had been my immediate concern. What look did I want to project? A big consideration here was that she was obviously a little older than I, anywhere from three to five years, I guessed. (Why had I not obtained some background biographical information on her while I was at the library, I berated myself. Then I remembered that at that time there was no reason to think that I would ever see her again, so I let myself off with a warning.) I wanted to seem a little older, but not old in a negative sense: not stodgy or formal.

I had finally resolved on a look that was mature but informal. That involved my sole sports jacket (tan, with pale blue stripes), my one wearable dress shirt (light blue, cotton, button-down collar), my most presentable jeans (the ones I used on teaching days), socks (this being a special occasion), and loafers. I had a problem with the sports jacket and loafers: they were not strictly functional in this weather. If I had been choosing clothing merely for my own purposes, I would not have selected them. I sighed. I would just have to compromise my standards of functionality somewhat for this …date. Somehow, in the light of that one word, no compromise mattered.

I washed, dried, and ironed my shirt and jeans. I had never ironed jeans before. Probably no one ever had. I sighed again. More compromise.

Once my clothes were laid out on my bed, I addressed myself to myself. I looked at myself in the bathroom mirror. For a feverish moment, I wanted to rush to the nearest hair stylist and throw myself on their mercy.

Then I settled down and assessed the situation more calmly. She already knew what I looked like, of course. And she had still called. I felt that gave me a certain leeway.

I finally settled on combing out my beard thoroughly, then trimming it back a bit with scissors. I tried to eliminate any weird little projections, and generally give it a more symmetrical appearance. The sink was a mess when I finished, but I cleaned it out thoroughly, unlike certain apartment-mates who shall remain nameless.

I took a long hot shower, during which I washed my hair and beard four times each. After drying off, I combed my hair back away from my face, and again combed out my beard. Facing the mirror once again, I looked like a fairly presentable young hermit from the last century. It was the most I could currently aspire to.

I decided against after-shave, first on the grounds that it seemed some-what inappropriate since I never shaved, and second because it smelled too weird for me to imagine anyone, i.e., Rachel Trask, would like it.

I dressed slowly and carefully. My most recently purchased underwear. Socks rigorously checked for holes. I remembered to wear a belt. I dug a clean handkerchief out of my dresser. I put the sports jacket on last. I checked myself in the mirror again. I looked pretty good. I felt pretty ridiculous.

Finally, I opened up the hitherto sacrosanct envelope containing my half of the rent. I took all the money out and put it in my pocket (I don't use a wallet). I wanted to make sure I could treat her to anything from a cup of coffee to the bridal suite at the local Holiday Inn. The idea of using this money made me very nervous. But then I thought, This date is more important than rent. And it was true. There was nothing more important.

Twenty-nine

I drove, rather than walked, to the Lambs' Den, partly to spare the loafers unnecessary damage from the snow and wet, and partly to have my own wheels available Just In Case. After all, who knew where this date might lead?

Now, let me be candid here. I had no illusions about what might happen. Or rather, I had plenty of illusions, but at least I knew that they were illusions. It seemed outrageously unlikely that Rachel Trask was attracted to me. While I had felt a spark of a few million amps when we had met, I had noticed no similar reaction in her.

My main concern tonight was to avoid saying something grossly inappropriate or stupid. I had a tendency sometimes, out of nervousness on a date with a woman, to make amusing comments that were not very funny. Somewhat appalling, in fact. I had once expressed the opinion to a date that the best way to win a Nobel Prize was to steal someone else's work, for example. Now, I hadn't been thinking that. I had never thought that. But I just found myself saying it, and then wondering who exactly could have made such a blockheaded comment, before realizing with a sickening shock that it had been me.

For example, the day I had met Lee, in a sailing class where I had already skillfully outmaneuvered potential rivals to be her partner in a two-person boat, I had started proving to her in a rather demanding way that Yes was like Wagnerian opera. She had spoken to me afterwards even so, of course, but the jury was still out on whether that was a good thing. I rather wanted to avoid all of that tonight, if possible. Tonight was a long shot, I knew, like from here to downtown Alpha Centauri. But you don't win the lottery if you don't buy a ticket. I had bought my ticket, and my mood was one of optimistic pessimism.

Even if nothing else happened, I would always remember: Rachel Trask had asked me out.

She was not there when I arrived. There were only about a dozen people in the whole place. I scanned the room carefully to plan the best place to be found sitting nonchalantly. I wanted a table from which I could see both entrances, where I could see all or most of the other people in the room, but not too near other people, and not covered with trash and dirty ashtrays. That narrowed it to one table. I sat at it and prepared to wait without seeming to be waiting.

By twenty after eight, I figured that she wasn't coming. I sighed. She would not be the first date to stand me up. Not by a factor of ten. And then there were those dates that had been so grim that being stood up would have been a great improvement. I began wondering if I could still make it to the hockey game in time to see Stan in action when she floated through the main entrance and stopped, looking around uncertainly.

I stood so she could see me. She waved and beamed a smile in my direction. It was all I could do to keep standing until she reached the table.

My first estimate of her had not been exaggerated. She was someone special. And in non-formal clothes she seemed more approachable somehow. Oddly enough, we were wearing nearly identical outfits. She wore a brown blazer over a blue cotton shirt and medium-tight jeans, with female-style loafers. She was also wearing tiny gold earrings, I could see as she got closer, and a slender gold chain around her neck with two metal hoops on it, one of them kind of sparkly on the bottom. Despite our similar fashion choices, she looked better than me.

"Hi," she said, and we shook hands. As we did so, I again caught sight of a holster under her right arm. I'd had very few dates with women who were packing. "Sorry I'm late," she apologized.

"Are you?" I scrutinized the wall clock as though I'd just noticed its presence. In actuality, I could have drawn it from memory.

"Shall we?" she said, glancing at the coffee bar.

"Sure."

"My treat," she offered as we walked over.

"Great. I'll have the lobster."

She laughed appreciatively. Take me now, Lord, I thought.

She ordered her coffee, then turned to me. "How do you like yours?"

"Actually I'll have a hot chocolate. I never developed a taste for coffee. Like the smell though." She ordered my hot chocolate, then looked at me appraisingly. She was probably thinking what a wonderfully secure person I must be to order hot chocolate in a coffee-oriented society. What a free-thinker. What a sincere and straightforward guy.

She graciously handed me my mug when it came, then paid and I thanked her. We sat at our table, and tentatively sipped, then stirred, our too-hot drinks.

"I wanted to apologize about this morning," she said seriously. I looked up, surprised. "I'm afraid I wasn't very patient with your ideas about the murder."

"Oh, that's okay," I said, waving away the incident. "After all, you have a suspect with a signed confession. What do you need complicating details for?

"Well, thanks, but I am sorry if I was abrupt."

"Please, think nothing of it. I was glad to help out."

She gave a small sheepish smile. "You know, I have to admit I don't remember very much of my high school physics. But I do remember it has a lot of laws. Very similar to my job."

I smiled broadly at this clever observation. "You're right. Maybe I should introduce myself as a law student. But in your line of business, you know what the laws are, and only get involved when laws get broken. In my work we have no idea what the laws really are, and they never get broken."

"Really?" She scrunched her face up quizzically. "You don't know what the laws are?"

"Well, there's no way to be sure. Like, for hundreds of years people thought Newton's law of gravity was right. Now we know it's wrong."

She blinked. "It is?"

"Yes. Einstein showed it was only approximately correct, and his own theory is the accepted one now."

"But, when you say that the law of gravity is wrong, things still fall down, right?"

I smiled. "Of course. Two different things are going on. One is what actually happens. Things fall down. That's reality. That never changes. The other thing is our idea about *why* things happen. Our *idea* about why things fall down has changed, that's all. Newton thought it was one thing. His idea explained everything people knew about for a long time. Then people noticed some things that Newton's idea didn't explain. So Einstein thought up a better idea, that explains everything Newton's idea did, plus the new things besides."

"So Einstein's idea is right?" She seemed to be straining to put it all together.

I spread my hands. "No one knows. It might be exactly right. Or maybe in a few centuries people will notice some things that Einstein's idea doesn't explain, and another genius will have to come up with a better one."

"So you're saying that science is really only our best guess about what the laws of nature are."

I nodded in profound agreement. "That is exactly right. Our current best guess about the way things work makes up what we call the laws of physics. Some laws seem exactly right. Other laws we know aren't exactly right, because we already know some things they don't explain. What physicists like myself do is try to come up with better laws."

She shook her head. "My job is easier," she stated. "It almost doesn't matter if I catch the right person. All I have to do is convince twelve jurors I'm right."

My mouth dropped open. This sounded so much like one of those appalling things I wanted to avoid saying that I was very glad to find out I hadn't said it.

Rachel clapped her hand to her mouth with wide eyes. "I can't believe I said that," she said slowly. "You must think I'm terrible. I really don't believe that. I lie awake nights sometimes wondering if I've really arrested the right person. I don't know why that came out."

She had done exactly what I did on dates. Did that mean she was nervous like me? Hard to believe. But she had handled it so much better than I ever had. I always tried to bluff it out, never really retracting what I had said. But she had. She probably felt foolish for a moment, but it was over. And I felt much closer to her as a result. Strange.

I shrugged. "We all say things we don't mean sometimes. For example, this morning I told you I didn't kill Dr. Speen. No harm, no foul."

This brought a chuckle and she seemed to relax. She looked at me. "I like you."

"I like you too," I said from within a dreamy mist.

"You don't talk like a scientist."

"I'll take that as a compliment."

She smiled. "No, I mean it. I interviewed all the professors in the physics department. I found most of them, I don't know, stiff. Formal. Not personable."

I nodded. "I know what you mean. Scientists sometimes give the impression that they don't care much about people."

"Exactly," she agreed animatedly. "That was the feeling I had. That they cared more about their science than about people."

I considered. "I think the problem is that science is much easier for scientists to figure out than people are. Even if you do care about people a lot, they are much more frustrating to deal with than equations or lab equipment."

"Is that how you feel?"

I toyed with my mug. "Well, let's put it this way: no equation ever broke my heart."

She nodded. "Somehow, when I woke up this morning, I never thought I would be sitting talking about physics with a scientist tonight."

"And I never thought I'd be sitting talking about police business. It's a strange planet."

She set her lips together, and then with a let's-bring-this-meeting-to-order kind of tone, said, "Speaking of police business, I wanted to tell you something."

I hunched forward and listened attentively.

"We've released Jackson Katanga."

"You…have?" I was baffled. Then I remembered that I had never thought Jackson was guilty to begin with. That only made me more confused. "I'm glad, but I guess I'm surprised. Now correct me if I've got the details wrong, but isn't he the one who confessed?"

She nodded and sighed. "Yes, but we've received some new evidence. Partly yours, your idea about how it couldn't have happened that way, but mostly, I'm afraid, from the Medical Examiner. We only just received the report today. Apparently Dr. Speen was unconscious when he fell to his death."

"Unconscious." I didn't really see the connection.

"Yes. And there was also evidence of a blow to the head, which would have caused the unconsciousness. But all prior to his falling to his death."

I shook my head, still not getting it. "I'm sorry, but I don't see why that would change anything."

She spread her hands. "Both the witness and Jackson Katanga claimed there was a struggle which resulted in Katanga pushing Dr. Speen off the roof. But if Dr. Speen were unconscious, there could not have been a struggle. That is certain from the M.E.'s report. Your idea makes it clear that Dr. Speen was not on the roof at all."

I got it. "So Jackson and the witness were both lying."

She nodded gravely. "Yes. I don't know why, but they both were lying."

"You know, I have to say, that even without any of this evidence I could not believe Jackson could kill anybody. He is simply not that kind of person." I described in a few words the type of mild individual Jackson was, and the apparent cultural regard he had for teachers and authority, and Rachel frowned and looked perplexed.

"What I don't understand is why he would confess, when it seems as if he may have had no connection with the murder at all."

I cleared my throat. Reluctant as I was to acknowledge Eli's worth in any way, I told Rachel his idea about the saving lie, being sure to give Eli the credit. She listened, and seemed as shocked as I had been.

"But what would Katanga be trying to escape from?" she wondered.

"I don't know, unless he was afraid of being murdered himself."

"But why would he think that he was in danger just because Dr. Speen had been murdered?"

That was something I hadn't considered. "He must know something we don't. Something that would affect both Speen and him. Maybe I could talk to him."

"Would you?" she asked, brightening. "That would be helpful. Anything would be helpful at this point."

"It must be hard for you," I commiserated. "This morning you had an eyewitness and a confessed murderer. Now you don't have either one." I paused. She looked glum. "By the way, who was this eyewitness? Can you tell me now?"

"I don't see why not. A Mr. Vitus Andersson," she said matter-of-factly. "His house is almost directly across the street from…what's so funny?"

I had exploded into involuntary laughter so wild that people were turning to look at me. With a great effort, I managed to stifle myself down to mere giggles.

"But he's a lunatic!" I pointed out, wiping my eyes.

She seemed affronted. "I don't know what you mean."

"Look. Take my word for it. This guy is out to lunch and it's a seven-course meal." I then regaled her with a few choice Mr. Andersson anecdotes.

Slowly, and almost against her will, she began to smile at my stories, finally bursting into laughter herself.

"Oh my gosh! Are you kidding me?"

I cleared my throat. "You don't know the half of it. I would love to be a defense attorney examining him as a witness."

She let out a breath. "I feel as if I've had a narrow escape. He seemed so serious, so sober a witness. He described the scene so clearly."

I took a sip of chocolate. "I find it hard to believe he could see across the street. He's got to be 80 if he's a day."

She shook her head. "No, he's not that old. And we actually did have his eyes tested. His vision is perfect, in fact better than perfect."

I recalled his usual squinting scowl at the bulletin boards. Probably just his natural facial expression. I shrugged. "Well, he may have seen something, but separating what he actually saw from his imagination would take a whole squad of tag-team psychologists. How frustrating to have a witness, someone who may have actually seen what happened, but who is too unstable a character to rely on."

She nodded. "It is frustrating. We're really back to square one."

I hated to see her so dispirited and disappointed. "I'm sorry. I wish there were something I could do to help."

She brightened. "Actually, there is. It's something I wanted to ask you, but I didn't want to impose on you."

I hastened to assure her that any imposition from her was no imposition at all. "Please, tell me what I can do to help."

"Well, this morning you were able to describe very clearly and logically, even scientifically, how the murder could *not* have occurred."

I winced a little. I had obviously caused her difficulty, and even though it had been in a good cause, that was clearly not my goal in my relationship with this woman. "Sorry."

"No, that's fine. Because maybe you can help me now. I want you to tell me how the murder *could* have happened."

I nodded. What a wonderful idea. And not just because I would be helping our local police solve a murder. Because I would also get the chance to spend more time with her.

At least, that was my first thought. However, I confess that I had momentary misgivings almost immediately. It seemed odd to me that the police would be turning for help to a non-policeman—in fact, a confirmed civilian like myself. Something seemed not quite right there. You'd have thought they would have wanted to keep things all in the family, as it were. Still, as I turned it over in my mind, it seemed more plausible. I mean, it wasn't as if they had a colossal force of detectives at their disposal—just Rachel Trask and the immense McKinnock. And I did seem to have specialized knowledge that they could use. Besides, the great thing was that I would be thrown in with Rachel Trask a good bit. That was the prime consideration here, and I dismissed any misgivings from my mind.

"I'd love to, Lt. Trask."

"Please," she said, "Call me Rachel."

Thirty

The air was crisp and cold as we stood near the chalk-marks in the court-yard. The sky was clear except for the occasional hillock of cloud, and the stars and a quarter moon dropped their silver light like icicles around us. I wanted to hug Rachel, not just because of romantic notions and not just because I was freezing my willy off. It occurred to me that, dressed as she was, she was probably as cold as me.

I stood in the center of the chalk figure and shivered. I looked up the side of the building, down again, then up again. A window on the fifth floor was located almost exactly above where the body had fallen. I thought it was the window I had made my measurements from the previous night, but I wasn't sure.

"Let's go inside and check out that window," I said nonchalantly, as if I didn't really care if my behind froze and fell off.

Inside, the building was warm by comparison. The physics department was not exactly hopping on this Saturday night. It seemed utterly silent and empty. When I spoke, my voice echoed weirdly. I felt like a ghost in a deserted house. "Let's use the stairs."

On the fifth floor, I flicked on the lights and realized this actually *was* the same room I had been in last night. I hoped this wasn't becoming a habit, as the classroom furnishings were distinctly dreary. At least I had company this time.

As before, I opened the window and looked down five stories. Rachel stepped up next to me, which made me flinch a bit. I dug in my pocket and pulled out a quarter. I set it down on the window sill, then flicked it out with my finger. It hit the chalk outline dead center, to my amazement.

"Nice shootin', pardner," Rachel commented with a touch of awe.

"Thankee, sheriff," I returned, kind of impressed myself. "I think we can safely conclude that something dropped out this window could hit that area."

Rachel nodded, crossed her arms over her chest and turned to survey the room. I shut the window. I had an irrational fear of somehow getting sucked out the window of a high building.

I surveyed the room myself. "Did you search this room before?"

She shook her head, deep in thought. "No. There seemed no need. We were told this happened on the roof. We went up to the attic. Plenty of recent foot marks up there, although nothing incriminating. We never came in here."

She was pouting, looking at the door to the room. Then she said, "Where is Dr. Speen's office from here?"

"It's right on this floor," I said helpfully, leading the way out the door into the corridor. "Right around here." I led her to the upper arm of the C. His office was on the left.

She pointed to his office door. "That's the outside of the building." I nodded. She turned and pointed at the doors across the hall. "So these must face the courtyard." I nodded again. Then she faced me. "This is where you last saw Dr. Speen?" She was looking around the hallway.

I looked around. "Yes, right about here. He went into his office, slammed the door in fact, and I went down the stairs."

She nodded.

Giving up on my telepathic talents, I asked, "What are you thinking?"

She sighed. Her eyes were still darting around. "Well, given that he started out in his office, and probably went out that window, I'm trying to imagine what happened in between."

I nodded. "He said he was meeting somebody important at 4."

"And he would probably meet them in his office, not in that class-room."

"Probably. More private."

"So let's suppose that whoever he met hits him over the head and knocks him unconscious. We found his office in some disarray. Half his desk things were on the floor."

"What hit him, by the way? Can they tell?"

She nodded. "Sort of. The M.E.'s report said it was a 'semi-rigid blunt instrument'."

"Er, what manner of thing might that be?"

"Their idea was something like a golf club shaft, or a flexible pipe."

I made a face. "Ah, so we're looking for a plumber who golfs?"

She smirked. "Or a golfer who plumbs."

I looked around the hallway theatrically. "That does not ring a bell."

She shrugged. "In any event, the visitor strikes Dr. Speen. Speen is unconscious on the floor. The visitor decides to drop him out a window…"

"Why?" I wondered aloud. It seemed utterly loony.

"Who knows? Why is the toughest part of my job. Let's do the what first."

"Okay." That seemed reasonable. I was regarding her with interest. She was an actual detective. It was neat to be in on this.

She continued. "So the visitor wants to dump the body out a window. Dr. Speen's are on the outside of the building. Too visible. The offices across the hall…"

"They were all shut," I volunteered. "I distinctly remember, because Speen was being a jerk and I wondered if anyone would see him. I don't know if anyone was in them, but they were all shut. In fact, it was so late in the afternoon, everyone had probably gone home and they were locked."

"Okay, that fits. Because the visitor doesn't throw the body out any of those windows. The visitor moves the unconscious body around the corner to that classroom, then out the window."

"Hmmm, I find that hard to believe. They dragged this body along the floor? Wouldn't there be blood stains, or marks from his shoes?"

She was nodding. She walked away, back into the classroom and I followed her. "Not only that. Look at that window sill."

I saw what she meant. The sill was about waist-high. "They would have to lift the body up to the window sill. That might not be easy."

"Let's try it," she said impulsively, and suddenly lay down on the floor. "Pick me up."

I looked down at her and my heart began pounding. I stood for a moment, then crouched and scooped her up in one motion. She was as light as a whisper. Her face was only a few inches from mine. She was smiling mischievously, her eyes gazing up into mine. I could smell her, and feel her in my arms, and it was delicious. I was quite prepared to stay that way for the rest of my life.

"Okay, Samson. You can put me down."

I set her feet gently on the floor.

When I spoke, my voice was husky. "I think Speen probably weighed more than you do."

She was still watching me and smiling. "One eighty seven."

I raised my eyebrows. "That would be a lot harder."

She pursed her lips. "Maybe our visitor was much bigger than you. Someone Katanga's size, now…"

I objected. "Yes. He could do it physically. But not mentally."

"Someone his size, I said. I don't see an alternative."

I looked at the window sill, then at the floor, then at the window sill again. "What if," I said, then stopped because what I was about to say made no sense. Then I said it anyway. Physicists get used to saying things that make no immediate sense: it's the only way you get anywhere. "What if the body were already at the height of the window sill?"

Her eyes narrowed. "You mean they carried him? But they would still have to pick him up off the floor."

I was seeing something in my mind. "Imagine Speen suspended above the floor, at the height of the window sill."

"Suspended? By what?"

I frowned. "Never mind by what. He's this high above the floor. Moving from his office to the window. Moving at that height. He's on something. What is he on?"

She shook her head, baffled.

"Something moving. So, it has wheels. Something with wheels, this high." I got it. I looked at her. "A cart."

She blinked. "A cart? You mean, like with horses?"

I smiled. "I mean a lab cart. You move equipment around on them." I stopped. "In fact, there are some on this floor, near one of the labs I teach in."

Rachel was serious now. "Show me."

I led her around to the lower arm of the C. There were two undergraduate labs here. I taught here sometimes, and did grading here sometimes. There were three carts parked in the hall. Each cart was metal, about waist high, with four black rubber wheels, and two shelves underneath. Rachel was examining each cart carefully, moving them experimentally. She stood up and looked at me. "Could be. I want to get the lab guys down here. They have tests that will show bloodstains."

"Really? Neat."

She looked at me, smiling. "'Neat'?"

"Sorry. I meant 'Keen'."

All the while that we were walking around the fifth floor hallway, something was nagging at the back of my mind. Something that I had forgotten. Something about the classroom? The hallway? The stairs?

The stairs. Dr. Wilhelm arguing with Speen on the stairs. Seriously arguing. What had Wilhelm said? "I'll talk to you about this later."

What if he had come back? What if he had waited until I left, then returned? Could he have been the important visitor, there at four o'clock? Then why leave? Because I had seen them together when I wasn't supposed to? Or, what if he had seen something? Surely, if he had, he would have told the police. Wouldn't he? Probably. Unless Wilhelm was the murderer.

I was brought back to the present by Rachel talking to me.

"I said, what kind of scientist are you, not knowing about bloodstains?"

I gave a little shudder. "Wrong science. That sounds suspiciously like biology. Biology and me don't get along. I prefer inanimate objects."

"I see. So, would these same carts have been here on Thursday night?"

I considered, then shook my head. "Not necessarily. Sometimes you move equipment from one floor to another in the elevator. You usually leave the cart where it ends up. There are maybe a dozen carts in the whole building."

She had pulled out a small notepad and was scribbling on it. "We'll check them all," she said absently. Then she tapped the pad with her pen. "How did the body get from the floor to the cart?"

Something else had occurred to me. "Who says it did?" She looked confused, but I just said, "Come here."

She followed me back to Speen's office. I was excited. I had it now. I pointed to Speen's office. "Visitor comes to see Speen. In Speen's office. Something happens. Visitor hits Speen on the head with something. What, we don't know. This does not seem like a premeditated crime, it's so disjointed, so visitor probably just grabbed something at hand and hit Speen. Speen goes down, but not," I held up a finger, "not on the floor. Onto his desk."

"Ah," she said appreciatively.

"Visitor," I continued, walking down the hall and around the corner, "wants to dump Speen out a window for some reason. How to move the body?" We reached the lab and I grabbed a cart and began pushing it. "Visitor shuts the door, goes and gets a cart." We were back at Speen's office. "Visitor puts cart next to desk, *slides* Speen onto cart, knocking half the desk stuff onto the floor. Visitor checks the corridor, nobody's around, wheels the cart to the classroom." I did so. "Wheels the cart to the window. Opens window. Shoves Speen out. Maybe *that's* what looked like a struggle to Mr. Andersson. If the visitor had some trouble shoving the body out the window. His imagination got the better of him."

Rachel was looking from the hall to the door, to the cart, to the window. Then she looked out the window. You could see Mr. Andersson's house across the street. She turned to me.

"That's it. It has to be. I want to get the lab guys on those carts, but I think you're right. The desk. No blood. The window sill." She was looking at me with something like admiration.

"Now," I mused. "Why?"

Sunday

▼

Thirty-one

Love.

I went to bed in love.

I woke up in love.

And I was still in love—right up until the phone rang.

After leaving the physics building, we had strolled back to the Union to get our cars. We said goodnight in the parking lot. No kiss or anything. No hug or handshake. But, still, it was special, for me, at least. I had driven my same old car back to the same old apartment and slept in the same old bed with my same old self. But everything had changed.

I didn't know what she felt, but I sensed some respect for me, and appreciation, and maybe even some kind of affection.

It was much simpler for me. I was in love.

I felt a thrill every time I thought of her, and I thought of her often. I was filled with her, and each ticking second seemed shaped by her. I remembered holding her in that classroom. I called the memory to mind over and over.

I wanted to be with her, to feel that way, always. It was a wonderful feeling, and it transposed every other thing in my life to the same key. Even the waffles I had for breakfast seemed wonderful.

I had already finished breakfast when the phone rang. I had been sitting looking out the window, wondering what to do on such a wonderful gray and sleeting day. It was so wonderful, it didn't matter what I did, it would be wonderful. It was so wonderful, even doing nothing would be wonderful.

I ambled over and answered the wonderful phone on the seventh wonderful ring.

"Hello," I said, warmly and graciously.

"Mark," said a voice that was strained and urgent. I rather resented this intrusion into my wonderful world, until I realized it was Rachel. My heart began to pound.

"What is it?" I was holding my breath.

"It's Jackson Katanga. The killer struck again. Can you meet me at the hospital?"

My heart hammered in my chest. Jackson too? My God…

"I'll be right there," I said, and hung up.

Within a minute, I was in my car careening to the hospital, my mind awhirl with thoughts.

Jackson Katanga, murdered like Speen. It had to be related. Jackson must have known something after all, known that when Speen had been killed, he too would be in danger. And he had been right. He had been right to try to escape into police custody. I felt a stab when I realized it was partly due to my actions that he had been released from custody, only to be killed as he had feared. Sure, there had been the medical evidence also, but I still felt guilty at what my involvement might have caused.

What had Jackson known? What connection was there between them besides the obvious one? There had to be something else besides the student-teacher link. How would we ever know what? Now that…

Poor Jackson.

Our small local hospital offers a lovely view of the ocean, but I did not notice it now. At this hour, there were few cars in the parking lot. I went in the front door and looked around the main lobby wondering where to go, when Rachel appeared at the far end. She was dressed in her office-type suit. Her face was serious and in control. She was in charge here.

"Thank you for coming," she said shortly, leading me back the way she had entered. "He's in the intensive care unit. He's just recovering from the anesthesia after last night's surgery."

I stopped short and stared at her. She turned and looked back at me, unsure of what I was doing. "I thought he was dead," I blurted.

Her eyes widened in horror and her mouth opened. Then she seemed to be trying to remember something, possibly the exact words she had said to me. "No," she said hastily. "No, no. He's alive. Just. He was attacked, but not killed."

Relief flooded through me in a wave. I felt gratitude and release. We started walking along again. "I must have misunderstood you. I thought he had been killed. What happened?"

She shook her head. "These are the strangest attacks I've ever seen, or even heard about. First, to push Dr. Speen out a window. Now this." She turned to face me. "Katanga was coming out of his apartment in the Graduate Village last night, and someone dropped a cinder-block down on him from a third floor landing. It actually grazed his head, and broke his shoulder and collarbone. One of the doctors said that if it had been an inch to the side it would have killed him for sure. Even missing his head, it would probably have killed an ordinary-sized person. If Katanga weren't such a big powerful guy, he would be dead."

I stared at her, trying to take it all in. "Do you have any clues?" I felt sheepish using the word. Did real detectives talk about clues?

"We have nothing. We interviewed everyone in the area. Nobody saw anything. And you can't get fingerprints from a cinder block."

We had entered the elevator and she pushed 3. "On the other hand, aside from this awful occurrence, last night was great."

I smiled warmly at her. "I thought so, too."

She nodded. "Yes, the lab guys did find traces of blood on one of those carts. Speen's blood type, too. They're still checking the office and the window sill. But I'm pretty confident your idea is right."

"Thanks." Her response was not exactly what I had hoped for. I found it hard to pick up the romantic threads after a discussion of bloodstains. Before I could think of anything to say, the elevator doors opened, and Rachel exited and turned left.

At the end of the hall, a flock of police stood near a closed door. Sgt. McKinnock was among them. He nodded at me, then bent to tell Rachel something in a whisper. I looked away politely. Near the center of the long hallway two nurses were moving around acting busy at their station, throwing occasional curious, and slightly disapproving, glances our way.

As I turned back, Rachel was nodding to Sgt. McKinnock, who made some hand gestures to the other police and gave them some inaudible instructions. One removed his coat and sat alertly in a chair by the door. The other police disappeared into an elevator, except for one who stopped to make small-talk with the two nurses.

I addressed Rachel. "Not that I mind being with you," I began, earning me a sly smile, "But what am I doing here?"

She took my arm, which I liked a lot, and strolled me away from the door. In a low voice she said, "I want you to talk to Jackson Katanga privately. See if he does know more than he's told us so far."

I squirmed a little. "I feel funny about this."

She shrugged. "This may seem sneaky, but I'm not asking you to gather evidence here. His life is obviously in danger. He doesn't trust the police, but I'll be damned if I'm going to let whoever it is get another shot at him without doing something to protect him. Nothing that you find out will be used against him, I promise."

I squirmed more. Then I looked her in the eyes and sighed. How could I say no? I certainly couldn't ignore the danger to Jackson, which he could not escape without help from the police. Moreover, they needed whatever information he had in order to help him. I couldn't refuse Rachel. Could I? And yet, I did feel funny about this. Like a snitch. A police informant.

On the other hand, I was intensely curious about whatever Jackson could tell me about all this.

I sighed. "Okay," I said. I made for the door.

The cop automatically stood up, giving me some eye and chin action. Lt. Trask gave him a look and he sat down again. Were all cops telepathic?

Thirty-two

I pushed through the swinging door and found myself in a little antechamber painted mint green. A woman looked up as I entered. "Hello," I said. "I'm Mark Napoli. I'm here to see Jackson. I'm a friend of his, from the physics department."

"Ah, Mr. Napoli," she said, with the same British accent Jackson had. "I am Lillian Katanga. Jackson is my brother." We shook hands.

Lillian Katanga was tiny—I would be surprised if she were over four and a half feet tall. I towered over her and felt enormous and ungainly in her presence. She wore a somber but polite expression. I could not guess at her age, but thought she must be much younger than Jackson, just from her height.

"I believe we have much to be grateful to you for," she continued. "I understand you endeavored to demonstrate to the police that Jackson could not have committed this shocking murder."

"Oh, thanks," I said, struggling a little to keep up with speech that sounded like a newspaper editorial. "I don't know how much good it may have done, but I tried."

"We are both indebted to you," she stated graciously. She possessed a certain air of decision and of judgment. I had a sudden image of her as a queen, diminutive upon a large throne, but in unquestioned command of all she surveyed.

"Could I see Jackson for just a second?" I asked.

"Yes, of course, let us go in."

She preceded me through the inner door to Jackson's room. Jackson lay in a standard hospital bed with the back tilted up. He seemed far too large for the bed. His head was swathed with bandages, and his neck, shoulder, and right arm were encased in a continuous plaster cast. The right arm was extended stiffly, and I saw it was supported at that unnatural angle by a metal brace buried into the cast at both ends. An IV tube was stuck in his other arm.

When we entered, his eyes swiveled slowly toward us. I could almost see them focus. He must still be doped up.

"Hi, Jackson," I said.

He looked at me for a long moment, and it occurred to me that he did not recognize me. Finally, his face made an effort to smile, in slow motion, but it must have pained him considerably because he winced and his features returned to the expressionless demeanor they had had before. "Hello, Mark," he said, in three ponderous syllables.

I sat by the bed, so that he wouldn't have to look up at me. I looked pointedly at his cast and bandages. "How are you feeling?"

He sighed heavily, stirring the whole bed frame. "Better, now." His tone carried the clear message that "better" was nowhere near "good".

I nodded, looked around some more, then pursed my lips. "You're in a whole lot of trouble, aren't you, Jackson?"

He shut his eyes, opened them, looked blankly at the end of the bed. "I don't want to talk about it," he intoned, his voice as deep as a volcanic rumble. I was stunned. Jackson Katanga refusing to cooperate! I could not believe it.

"You *shall* talk about it!" declared Lillian in a high strong voice that brought me up out of my chair. Jackson turned his head away slightly, like a boy caught stealing a cookie.

"This man has been trying to help you," she continued. She stood at the end of the bed, drawn up to her full height, her arms crossed over her chest. She looked more than ever like some empress keeping the more uppity nobles in line. "You are in serious trouble, and we will need help to get you out. Perhaps he can counsel you on what to do."

Jackson had winced and lowered his eyes as she spoke. There was no doubt in my mind where the power in this family resided.

Finally, he sighed again and gave a slow, minute nod.

"Okay, Jackson, tell me what's been going on with Speen. Start at the beginning. Take your time. I'm not going anywhere."

He swallowed slowly and seemed to be collecting and arranging his thoughts, as if they were errant sheep he was having trouble corralling.

"One day," he finally began, "Dr. Speen gave me a package which he wanted me to deliver. He did not want it mailed. He gave me very detailed instructions as to where I was to place it on campus. He said that a friend of his would collect it."

I felt my skin crawl. What on earth was this? Secret packages left for "friends"? Drugs? Smuggled goods?

"Jackson, what was in this package?"

"I do not know. It was a manila envelope, bound with tape and a metal clasp. It felt as though it might contain papers, but I am not sure."

"And where did you leave it?"

"I placed it behind some books on a specific shelf in the university library."

I shook my head. Man. "Okay, go on."

"When I returned to the physics department, Dr. Speen congratulated me on doing it successfully. Then he gave me money."

My eyebrows went up. "He gave you money?"

"Yes. He gave me ten hundred-dollar bills."

My mouth popped open. "He gave you a thousand dollars?"

"Yes."

I closed my eyes and shook my head. "Jackson, what did you think you were doing?"

He sighed heavily. "I did feel that there might be something wrong. This seemed so irregular. However, I dared not question Dr. Speen about it. I resolved not to spend the money he had given me, just hide it. Then I thought that perhaps it might be something innocent. After all, Dr. Speen was a university professor. I could not imagine that he would be involved in anything illegal. And so I did nothing."

I, on the other hand, could easily imagine Speen as fully capable of the foulest misdeeds. If it had been me, I would have turned him in, and I rather fancy I would have kept the grand, just on principle. Of course, that may be why Speen asked Katanga, not me.

"Okay, then what?"

"About a month later Dr. Speen again asked me to deliver a package on campus. This time I asked to know what it was."

There was an image for you: Jackson confronting Speen. I had never imagined such a thing was possible. Maybe I was wrong about Jackson. Then I had a sick feeling. If I were wrong about Jackson, maybe he really had killed Speen.

"What did he say?"

"He said that it was none of my concern. All that I had to do was deliver the package. He said that the less I knew about it, the better it would be."

"And what did you do?"

He swallowed hard. "I delivered the package."

I did not want to be angry with him. He had obviously suffered for his mistakes. Still, I could not believe he had been so foolish as to deliver the second package.

"Wow," I said.

"Again he paid me a thousand dollars. I put this money with the rest. Then next month he asked me again, and I refused."

This floored me. "You refused?" Oh dear, I thought. I have been very wrong about Jackson. He definitely killed Speen. And had a good motive too, it seemed. My innards grew cold.

"Yes, I refused. And then he told me what it was that I had been delivering."

I was all attention. "What was it?"

"Dr. Speen, as part of his work, has access to certain secret American defense documents. He told me that he had been copying them and selling them."

I felt like I needed to sit down, then realized I already was.

"He was selling government secrets?"

"Yes, and he said that if I did not continue helping him that he would report me, and we—my sister and I—would be deported."

From Eli's description of Jackson's home country, I got the impression that this was not a place one would enjoy being deported to. Speen's threat would be pretty convincing. I didn't doubt for a moment that Speen was capable of delivering, and carrying out, such a threat. What interesting hobbies the admirable professor Speen had: espionage and blackmail. I would have to boost my donation to Stan's fund.

"What did you do?"

"I delivered the package. And he paid me once again."

"Jackson, how long has this been going on for?"

He looked at Lillian, at the bedclothes, at me, and back at the bedclothes again. "Ten months."

I felt frozen in my seat. "Ten months! You've been going through this for ten months!"

He looked at me in appeal. "I have been so afraid, Mark. I have not known what to do. It was wrong. But how could I refuse him without endangering my sister and myself? Who could I tell about this? What could I have done differently?"

I nodded and tried to calm him down. "Okay, Jackson," I said reassuringly. "I don't blame you. I don't know what you could have done differently. Not with a jerk like Speen. You were definitely between a rock and a hard place. That part's done now. But what has been going on lately?"

He took a deep breath. "A few weeks ago, Dr. Speen decided he wanted to stop sending this secret information. But, apparently, Dr. Speen's contact was unwilling to sever their relationship. Dr. Speen told me that his contact threatened to expose him, Dr. Speen, if he stopped sending information. Dr. Speen was furious."

I snorted. "He didn't mind blackmailing you so much, but he didn't like it when someone did it to him."

"I suppose not."

"So what happened then?"

"Dr. Speen said that he thought he could find some information with which he could blackmail his contact. I believe that he found something about a week ago."

"Do you know what he had?"

Jackson shook his head, stopping abruptly at the pain. "No. He did not tell me."

I fumed silently. "Who was this contact? Do you have any idea?"

He shook his head slowly, and seemed to regret it. "No. Dr. Speen always referred to him as "he", though, so it must be a man. And near the end, he called him 'that German bastard'."

"German?" I repeated. "Do you think Speen really meant that? That his contact was German?"

"I don't know. Apparently," Jackson said disconsolately.

This was coming over the net a little too fast for me. Secret packages. Espionage. Payoffs. Blackmail. German spies. I almost began to think Jackson was pulling my leg, except for the anguish these admissions were obviously causing him.

"Okay," I said, somewhat in self-defense against the enormity of it all. "Jackson, what happened on Thursday? Do you know?"

"Dr. Speen told me he was going to confront his contact on that day. He told me to stay away from the physics building all afternoon. He was afraid that I would interfere in his plans in some way."

"So you weren't even around when he was killed?"

"No. I went to Providence to use the library at Brown University."

"So you didn't even know Speen had been killed until you got back?"

"Yes. When I returned to the department around six o'clock, I found police there investigating. After hearing what had occurred, I realized that Dr. Speen must have confronted his contact, and that his contact must have killed him. But I could not tell the police that without revealing my part in the espionage. I feared that if I told them about that, we would be deported, as Dr. Speen had told me. But I also could not but wonder if Dr. Speen had mentioned my involvement to his contact, or indeed if his contact had not observed me making the deliveries himself. I felt that since Dr. Speen had been murdered, my life was in danger also."

"So you confessed to murdering Speen."

"Yes, it seemed my best chance for protection was to be in police custody."

"But then you were released."

"Yes. There was evidence that contradicted my confession." I winced. Part of that had been me. "They released me. I determined to go into hiding then. I was returning to our apartment last night after making some arrangements, when I was struck down."

"And you think whoever attacked you also killed Speen."

"I have no doubt of it."

I slumped back in the chair. "Gosh, what you've gone through," I said to him. I felt like I myself had been through a wringer. "Both of you," I added, regarding Lillian.

"But what are we to do now?" Lillian asked me.

I spread my hands. "Look. Let's think about this logically. You, Jackson, are in danger so long as the murderer is free. Therefore, the police have to capture him. The only way that they can capture him is to get whatever information you have. That means they have to learn about your involvement in all this." Jackson looked defeated and dejected. Lillian looked alarmed on his behalf.

I went on, "As it happens, I am friendly with the police detective lieutenant on this case. Let me talk to her and see what we can do. To me, there sounds like extenuating circumstances to your involvement. In any event, I also want you to get a lawyer. Lillian, what department are you in?"

"History," she replied.

"Perfect," I said. "Ask the chair of your department to recommend a lawyer."

"I will," she stated.

I stood up and smiled at Jackson. "Get better," I told him. "Don't worry. It will work out. You're not in danger anymore: the police are guarding you. You're not going to be deported. I won't let that happen."

"Thank you, Mark," he said. "You are my good friend."

I felt embarrassed that he might think so.

I left the room with Lillian. In the antechamber, she turned to face me.

"It is on my account that he is afraid," she said dejectedly. "If it was only himself, he would have faced deportation rather than submit to this evil man. My brother is very brave. When we fled our country, he helped me cross the barbed wire, and carried me across the river. If it were not for him, I would have died there."

I was certainly seeing a new side of Jackson Katanga today. Whatever he had unwittingly done espionage-wise, he had also earned my respect as a non-doormat.

"I'll do all I can," I assured her.

She turned to re-enter Jackson's room, but I couldn't resist detaining her. "Can I ask you something? Is he your older brother?"

She smiled. "Yes, by twenty minutes. We are twins."

Thirty-three

Rachel was waiting out in the hallway, leaning against the wall. She looked tired, and I realized she had probably been up most of the night about this. I felt like giving her a hug, but I wasn't sure if our relationship was at that stage yet. Besides, there was the cop sitting there. I didn't think my hugging the lieutenant would go down well with the troops.

She looked up as I appeared. "How did it go?" she asked.

I looked around the hallway. "Great. This place have a cafeteria?"

She nodded. "Downstairs."

"Come on," I said. "I'm gonna buy you a coffee and tell you the damnedest story you ever heard." To the cop in the chair I said, "Get you anything?" to which he shook his head.

The cafeteria was a shade of green I would have paid money not to see, and deserted except for the woman who took my money. After we got our respective beverages and sat down, I recounted to her what Jackson had told me. She listened in your basic stunned silence through the whole thing.

When I was finished she looked away, apparently focused on something at mid-infinity, then slowly shook her head and said, "Why me?"

"What?" I said, involuntarily smiling at her remark.

"No, really," she went on, still checking out the unseeable. "Why freaking me, pardon my French. I get a lot of, you know, fisherman hassling another fisherman at a bar, goes out to find his van trashed. Girlfriend makes off with a guy's motorcycle. Some drugs. Break-in at a summer house. Runaways. That kind of thing. I don't get much in the way of espionage. Blackmail. Revenge murders. Spies, for God's sake."

"It's kind of out of my league, too."

"Why couldn't they have done all this in Providence?"

"More scenic here?" I suggested.

She gave me a dangerous look, and I was reminded of the gun under her jacket. I realized I was pushing it with my beloved and had better lay off the humor for the nonce. Then she said, "Errr" irritably, put her face in her hands, rubbed her eyes vigorously, and pushed her hair back from her face. She mumbled something that might have been, "To protect and to serve."

"Okay," she addressed me. "Do you believe this guy? Because I already have one confession of his in the wastebasket. I'm not inclined to tell my captain that I'm switching my theory over to the spy/blackmail/revenge version if Katanga's going to change his mind again in a couple of days."

I pursed my lips and let out a breath. "I don't know. If you had asked me yesterday, I'd have said I believed him implicitly. But after hearing about what he's been up to in secret for the past few months," I shook my head, "I'm not sure I know who he is. I don't think I ever really did."

"And yet he's the one who told you all the stuff that now makes you not believe him," she pointed out. "I suppose he could just be an honest guy who got caught in a bad situation."

"That's true enough. I find that easier to accept than that he's still jerking us around. One thing in his favor is I can't see why he would admit to this espionage if he didn't do it. Believe me, there's nothing he fears more than possible deportation, but that's exactly what he's facing by admitting that. I don't see any reason for him to lie about it. He has nothing to gain if it's not true. But if *that's* true, then most of the rest of it must be true also."

Rachel was making a weird grimace with her mouth. "And we had already come to the conclusion that some third person had some reason to kill Dr. Speen. This tells us what that person's role was, and what their motive might have been. So it fits in with that."

"You know, I would feel a lot better about all this if we could substantiate his alibi for Thursday. A guy like Jackson would probably be pretty obvious to other people in the Brown library. Hell, he would be fairly obvious anywhere but a pro football locker room."

Rachel nodded. "Yes, that's something we can check. I'll get that started."

"Make sure you check out the room with the physics journals," I suggested. "That's where I always head first in an unfamiliar library."

She smiled. "Thanks for the tip."

"Other than that, I don't know where else to go with this. I'll have to think about it."

Rachel nodded. "There is one other thing. He has admitted to espionage, and he's accused Dr. Speen and an unknown third party of being involved also. That's a federal offense. Even if we don't name names, I have to notify the FBI."

I was alarmed. "That's getting pretty serious, isn't it? Do you really need to involve them? The FBI will put Jackson through a meat-grinder."

"I have to do it," she stated.

I raised my eyebrows. "Then Heaven help us all," I mused.

Thirty-four

Rachel left to perform cop-appropriate activities, and I drove home. Parting was such sweet sorrow.

On the way home, it occurred to me that I was now officially done with Rachel Trask. I had shown her how the murder could have been done. I had proven that the suspect had not actually done it. I had demonstrated that the witness could not be relied on, only partly because he was crazy old Mr. Andersson. Plus, I had led her to this whole spy thing, which seemed like the right track.

She didn't need me now. It was just a question of following up with Jackson's information. Verifying his alibi. Looking for witnesses who might have seen someone picking up the papers Jackson dropped off. Maybe tracing the money Jackson had received. Cop stuff. She didn't need me for that.

Somehow, I had to get myself back into this case again. To be near Rachel some more. To score more points with her. To get her, somehow, to be interested in me. But how?

At home, I went into my room, shut the door, put on my headphones, started side one of "Tales from Topographic Oceans", and flopped onto the bed staring at the ceiling.

The whole Speen-Katanga-spy-espionage-blackmail-murder thing was whirling around in my mind. I found listening to loud complicated music helpful. Conducive to thought. When I was an undergraduate, Ben used to marvel at how I could do advanced calculus homework while listening to bone-jarring music through headphones, carrying on a conversation, and playing Jeopardy on TV. And winning. What can I say? It's how my brain likes to work, and I make it a point never to argue with my brain.

During the twenty-minute song, I wrote down whatever words or phrases that occurred to me. At the end, I had a list that read, "Phone. Books. Witness. Money." This was shorthand.

Phone. If there really were a spy, and a German, that might connect with those strange monthly phone calls to Germany that bothered Mrs. Arden. But it was hard to see how. If Speen were delivering packages of papers, what purpose would a phone call serve? On the other hand, I thought that calling from a university phone would be a clever idea, since it would probably be more difficult to trace or tap phones through the university switchboard.

Books. I remembered the bag of books Speen had made me bring to Katanga. They had been about World War II, which, if memory served me correctly, involved Germans. If the phone calls were involved, then maybe the books had some connection.

Witness. Mr. Andersson claimed to have seen Jackson throw Speen off the roof. Now either he had seen something, or he hadn't. If he hadn't, why would he say that he had? To throw suspicion on Jackson? Why? To protect someone else? If he had, why had he lied about the details? Again, to protect someone else? I had a strange suspicion that he had seen someone else, someone he did not want to take the blame, for whatever reason. But if it had been the spy who killed Speen, then Andersson must know who the spy is. What was his reason for protecting this spy?

Money. If Jackson had received one thousand dollars (one thousand dollars!) for each delivery, Speen must have gotten much more. If Rachel and the police could find some evidence for his getting large sums of money each month, that would help substantiate Jackson's story.

So there were four strands that maybe I could use to get back into the investigation again. I thought about each of them. Of these four, there was only one that I personally could do anything about. I left the apartment and drove to the physics building. There were some books I wanted to take a look at.

Thirty-five

The physics building was empty and silent, except for those little building noises that are utterly harmless and that scare the willies out of you. I clumped downstairs to Jackson's office in the basement.

The door to his office is right opposite the door to Dr. Wilhelm's lab, which was ajar. I peeked inside but no one was around, not even Emily Whitney, who practically lived there. At least she and the other denizens of Wilhelm's lab knew how to spend Sunday mornings properly.

The first thing I noticed was that the bag was in a different place on his desk than I had left it. This seemed tremendously significant to me for about sixteen seconds. Then I realized that any of five billion people on the planet could have done it, for any of ten billion reasons. Come, come, I told myself. Surely we can restrict that to only the people in this country, perhaps in this state. After reasoning in this vein for a while I concluded that the bag being moved was probably significant, but there was no way to know what the significance was.

I sat in Jackson's chair. It wasn't very comfortable, which was not a real surprise. I opened the bag and removed all the books. Just to be thorough I turned the bag upside down and shook it. A white sales slip fluttered to the desk. I set the bag aside.

Suddenly I heard footsteps. The acoustics of the room were unfamiliar and the furnace didn't help. I slid the chair back, and it made a loud scraping sound. I rolled my eyes. Last of the Mohicans.

The footsteps had stopped, if they were footsteps. I tiptoed to the door and yanked it open. No one was there. Not that they had been, but they weren't. I shut the door and sat down again.

I picked up the first book. There was a black and white picture on the cover of a German soldier goose-stepping to the left, his head turned away from the camera. I flipped through the first few pages. It was not about

World War II in general, but about the Gestapo. It was mostly black and white photographs, with captions and a little text. Frightened civilians being marched off by uniformed soldiers. The gates of Auschwitz. "Arbeite Macht Frei," and other words to die by. I determined not to read this book—ever—and closed it. I was conscious of my breathing and my heart beating.

I picked up the next book. No picture on the cover. Inside, more pictures of the Gestapo, making arrests, executing people. More text than the first. I closed it and set it on the first one.

I picked up the third book. More pictures. Many more. Horrible things. I shut it hurriedly and set it aside.

I just riffled through the fourth and fifth books and put them down on the pile.

I sat and stared at the pile, breathing heavily.

Good God.

I looked away, saw only the furnace, then hurriedly looked away again.

Okay. Let's think logically about this. Five books. Books mainly of pictures. Pictures of Nazis, the Gestapo. Prisoners. Deaths. Lots of them.

Speen had these books. He had them in a bag in his office. And Speen had wanted these books out of his office and into Jackson's. Why?

The timing seemed significant. Speen gets rid of these books. Speen meets his important visitor, presumably his spy contact. Speen dies.

So, Speen wanted the books out of his office before his important visitor arrived.

Something else occurred to me. Speen was being blackmailed by the spy, and thought that he had found some counter-blackmail to blackmail the blackmailer. And Speen had died. You didn't have to be Albert Einstein—or the detective equivalent—to imagine that the spy had gotten ticked off at being blackmailed, and had killed Speen. Blackmail is one of those things that's only really enjoyable if it's going the right way.

So, what was the connection with the books again? Maybe he didn't want his visitor, the spy, to see them. Suppose this spy had let something slip that suggested to Speen that the spy had been a German soldier. Big deal. No, wait, even better, a Nazi, perhaps Gestapo. Perhaps killing people. Speen gets some books about the Gestapo. Books of pictures. Why?

It was obvious: he was looking for the spy in the pictures. He was looking for proof. Looking for something to break the spy's blackmail of him, Speen. He could say to the spy, Leave me alone or I tell everyone you're—what? I looked at the books. Former Nazi. War criminal. Nazi war criminal. Big leverage with the spy. To counter the espionage charge the spy was threatening him with.

He must have found something, too. Why else would he want to have the books out of the way? Why else meet with the spy? He must have found the proof he wanted.

I looked at the pile of books. The proof was in them. Somewhere.

However, I could not find what Speen had found. Speen knew the spy, knew what the spy looked like. Speen could search these books for a face. I could not. I felt some relief. The thought of going through all those books disturbed me.

So, the books were useless to me. Speen had found something, someone, in them, but I could not. This was a dead end. I sighed heavily, simultaneously relieved and disappointed.

But the good news was that I now had something else to tell Rachel about. This whole German, if not Nazi, angle could be important.

Jackson, surprisingly, had a phone on his desk. I stuck my fingers in the holes and dialed the police station, a number I was a little troubled to find that I knew by heart. Rachel wasn't there, which was not all that surprising for a Sunday morning. The officer on duty wouldn't give me another number where I could call her. Romeo had had the same trouble with Juliet's associates. I left my name, home number, and the message that I had important new information about the identity of the spy. That would get her attention. The officer seemed skeptical, but I didn't care.

After the phone call, I stood up, stretched and left.

Thirty-six

I returned within five seconds.

I stared at the pile of books on the desk. There was something I was not getting in this situation. Why were these books here? Why did Speen want them in Jackson's office, rather than his own, when his spy pal came to visit?

I tried to put myself in Speen's shoes, a creepy feeling no matter how you looked at it. Suppose that I am being blackmailed. Suppose I have some material that I can use on the blackmailer, like a picture that shows them doing something despicable. What do I do? I show the spy the picture, right? So, I have to have the picture handy. I shook my head. If that was his reasoning, there was no reason why I would want any books out of my office. Dead end.

I tried again. Suppose I have the material, but I don't show it to the spy. I just tell the spy that I have the material, someplace safe, and start to apply pressure. Then I might want the material safely out of reach, like in Jackson's office. So, I would send away the material that was damaging to the spy. That was why Speen had asked me to take the books to Jackson. Something in the books that was incriminating, that named or showed the spy.

I looked at the books again. This still didn't help me, though. I still had no idea who, out of all the people mentioned or depicted in those five books, was the bad guy. It was frustrating. The answer was right there on the desk in front of me, but I couldn't find it. So close and yet so far.

I sighed, started picking up the books and putting them back in the bag, just to have something to do while my thoughts chased each other. Then I noticed the sales slip and put that in the bag also. Then I took it out again and looked at it.

It was from Fabulous Beast, a little bookstore in Kingstown. It was dated a few weeks ago. The total for the books was over a hundred fifty dollars, serious change. And six items listed.

Six.

I looked in the bag. There were only five books. I counted them again. Still only five. I counted them one more time, setting them down on the end of the desk to be absolutely sure I wasn't overlooking anything. There were five books. I stood up and walked around the desk to see if I might have dropped one. No. Six books bought, only five in the bag.

I stared at the sales slip in my hand. Then I left the room, ran up the stairs, unlocked the main office and made a photocopy of the sales slip.

Back in Jackson's office, I compared the price on each book to the sales slip. I checked off each price on the copy of the sales slip until there was only one left. $39.95, the most expensive one.

One book missing. What did that mean? My mind was racing, but nothing was coming out. I sat down again. Think, I thought. Speen looks through six books. Speen finds something. What does Speen find? Speen finds a picture. *A* picture. *A picture in a* book. Of course. So five of the books contain nothing useful. Only the sixth book does. And one book is missing. I wanted to believe the spy had taken it. But what if Speen had? No, that made no sense. Even if he only wanted the sixth book to show the spy, why send away the useless others? So, he would either keep them all, or get rid of them all. He had gotten rid of at least five of them. So, he must have gotten rid of all of them. Therefore, the sixth book *had* been among them when I brought the bag down.

I stared at the books, the bag, and the sales slip. There was only one conclusion. The spy had taken the sixth book.

I stood up and backed into a corner of the room. The spy had been here, in this very room. The spy had come in through that door. The spy had gone to Jackson's desk, and seen the note on the bag.

The spy had opened the bag, and taken out the books. He found the one book. He took it with him. He put the others back in the bag, put the bag back on the desk, the note back on the bag.

The note I had left!

I swallowed hard. The spy now knew that I was connected somehow to all this. Speen had been murdered. Jackson had been attacked. I felt a sudden panic.

The note was gone.

I was next.

I closed my eyes and tried to compose myself. There was something I had forgotten in all this. How did the spy know to come to Jackson's office? Speen would not have told him about Jackson on Thursday, since that's where he had sent his books. And he wouldn't have sent the books down to Jackson at all if he'd ever mentioned Jackson to the spy before. So, the spy must have known about Jackson before. And on his own. Therefore, the spy had seen Jackson, and knew who he was. Therefore, the spy was on campus. Possibly even in the physics department.

I suddenly laughed. A few days before, I had been complaining about homework and dining hall meatloaf. Now I had a Nazi war criminal hiding in my department waiting to murder me.

Isn't that always the way?

Thirty-seven

I looked at the clock on the wall. Twelve-fifteen. Late enough for a bookstore to risk the Puritan wrath of the state's blue laws by opening on the Sabbath. I sat down in Jackson's chair again and dialed off-campus information, got the number, and called Fabulous Beast.

I liked Fabulous Beast. It was a small bookstore, in a house converted for that purpose. It had smooth wood shelves, plants, attractive lighting, rainbow-scattering prisms hanging in the windows, and usually some soothing and other-worldly music playing softly in the background. It didn't have a lot of books, but the books it had all seemed fascinating. I loved browsing there, although I rarely had any money for actual purchases.

The woman who owned and ran it didn't seem to mind. She was pretty other-worldly herself, of some indeterminable age. I did occasionally buy used paperbacks for fifty cents or a dollar from the racks on the front porch. I felt like that was more like paying dues to a club than buying anything.

I don't know where the name of the store came from. Maybe the store itself was one of those fabulous beasts—part one thing, part another. Maybe the books were the fabulous beasts. Sometimes, I even thought it was the woman who was the fabulous beast.

"Hello. Fabulous Beast," she said when she answered.

"Hi. I have a weird problem about a book," I said apologetically.

"Great!" she enthused. "I love weird problems about books."

"Okay. About a month ago, Dr. Speen, from the university, bought a bunch of books about, er, World War II. I would like to get one of those books, too."

"Fine," she said. "Do you have the title or the author?"

"No, I don't remember. That's the problem."

"Hmmm," she paused. "Wait, I think I remember them. They were all special-order as I recall. Let me look them up."

I waited, hoping there would be some record of that sixth book.

"Yes, here they are."

"Great. I'm interested in the one that was $39.95."

"'Inside the Camps', by Dr. Gerhard Wolff?"

"Yes," I said, faking excited recognition. "That's the one! Could I order one of those also?"

She chuckled. "Well, it's funny that you say that. When that professor bought so many, I thought they might be for a course at the university, so I ordered three of each, just in case. The rest have been sitting here since then. I was about to box them up to return them to the distributor."

"You mean you have a copy of it there right now?"

"That's right. I'll get it for you. Come on down."

"I'm on my way."

At Fabulous Beast, I handed over forty dollars that was technically rent money. I figured I was covered for browsing there for the next six months. The woman, swathed in a purple paisley caftan today, disappeared into the back of the store and emerged in a minute with a very thick book.

She handed me "Inside the Camps" with a big smile and said, "Enjoy!"

Thirty-eight

On any other fall Sunday afternoon, I would have been lounging in Ben and Stan's dorm room watching football and goofing on the announcers. Not today. I wondered what they would make of my absence. I hadn't actually seen any of my friends since the dance Friday night. Life was taking one of those weird detours that add zest. Or leave you dead.

I had brought the other five books with me from Jackson's office, don't ask me why, and I hauled everything up to the apartment.

I called Rachel at the police station again, but she still wasn't around. It occurred to me that I did not have her home phone number. I didn't even know where she lived. A little searching showed that she was not listed in the phone book. That seemed odd, but maybe cops don't list their home phone numbers to avoid harassment. Especially the beautiful single ones.

I stashed the books in my room and had a terrific lunch that featured waffle cuisine. I felt relieved that I was almost certainly getting my full daily requirement of vitamin W.

I was just spacing out thinking about what to do next when there was a knock at the door. I hesitated. This could be one of Eli's legion of near-sighted girlfriends. Or it could be Rachel. Now that would be something. Or it could be a Nazi assassin. It was that kind of day.

Throwing caution to the winds, I got up and opened the door. I was stunned to see Lisa standing there. Stunned, because people rarely came to visit me here. It was too far out of the way from campus. I always went there, or we met someplace else. Lisa, for one, had never been here. This was unprecedented, and I guess I stood there goggling a little too long for her taste.

"Thanks, don't mind if I do," she said brightly and left me gaping at the door while she strolled into the living room.

I shut the door and turned around. "Hi," I said.

"Hi," she said, as if she came here to visit me all the time. She shed her coat and scarf onto the couch and relaxed gracefully into the best armchair. She ran her eyes around our dingy living room.

"Are those real goat tails?" she wondered, pointing.

I followed her glance to the alleged decorations on the wall and winced. "I'm not really sure," I said. "I'm not brave enough to examine them that closely."

She nodded understandingly and continued looking around.

"Can I get you something? A Coke?" I felt unaccountably awkward with her here.

"Just the thing for a snowy day," she declared, her head coquettishly on one side. "I'd love a Coke."

I kept a small supply of soda and beer for just such unlikely events. I washed off the dusty can and called out, "Glass? Ice?"

"Au naturel is fine," she called back. I knew just enough French for that phrase to make me uncomfortable. I walked back into the living room and handed her the can. She popped it open and sipped. I sat down.

"To what do I owe the honor?" I asked, genuinely puzzled.

She smiled impishly at me and said, "Oh I thought we could have a little talk. And then maybe do something together."

She obviously had some hidden agenda behind this. "Okay. Talk. About what?"

She regarded me from over the can. "Your love life."

I was shocked. This was a little forward even for Lisa, who was a non-shrinking violet from way back. "That shouldn't take long," I commented.

"And about Lee," she added.

I made a face. "Ick. Must we?"

She nodded solemnly. "I think so. A little. How long has it been since you saw her now?"

I considered. "Not counting nightmares, about eleven months."

"Have you dated anyone since then?" She was being relentlessly forward, I could see, but in a way, I didn't mind it. In fact, I rather welcomed having all this out in the open for once. Stiff upper lips only get you so far in life.

"No." I considered telling her about Saturday night with Rachel, but the more I thought about an evening spent primarily at a murder scene, the less date-like it seemed.

"Slept with anyone?"

"Lisa!" I blurted, genuinely shocked.

She shrugged. "I'm not going to tell anyone," she said, a little defensively. "I'll put you down as a 'No'. And why is this?"

I looked down. "You know why."

She bobbed her head. "Yes. The Perfect Woman Theory. A woman will come along who will see beyond your outward appearance to the real you, the inner you, and you will have a perfect relationship together."

"Very well put," I said, and I meant it. I had told her of my aspirations one evening when we had both been drunk enough to talk about such things.

"And what about Lee? Was she the perfect woman?"

I sighed heavily. "I thought so. At the beginning. We had something, a bond. I can't describe it."

"And now?"

I looked away. "I guess not. It obviously didn't work out."

"So now what, Mark?"

I shrugged. "Keep looking, I suppose."

"And go through all that with another Lee again?"

"I don't know." I was getting very depressed by this. "I hope not."

"Me, too. 'Cause that nearly killed you last winter. I was worried about you. So was Ben. So was Stan. We all were, and there was nothing we could do. You kept saying everything was fine, but it really wasn't. You can't keep going through this."

I couldn't reply to that. I was stuck on something else. "Stan was?"

She looked at me sincerely. "Stan cares about you. He admires you more than he'll ever admit."

"Admires *me*?" I was dumbfounded.

"Very much so. You remember last year when you were helping him through different equations? Or whatever they were?" I nodded. Stan had just squeaked through his last required math course. I had helped him practically daily, but low-level differential equations are triv. "At one point he said to me, 'Mark is the smartest person I'll ever know.' He admires how easily you learn and know things."

I found this hard to fathom. It was true that I could learn things easily, and I knew he struggled with his schoolwork. It always amazed me that he could remember entire albums, like "Thick as a Brick", verbatim but couldn't remember how to perform integration by parts correctly. If Jethro Tull had ever put out an album about calculus, Stan would have been the next Isaac Newton.

"But that's nothing," I replied. "He has a lot of things easier than I do. He doesn't stew about things, women, life, like I do. He doesn't worry about things like I do. He doesn't get stuck on stuff like—like dancing with some woman. I would trade with him in a minute." He was also tall and handsome and athletic, and I would never be any of those things. And he had Lisa. But I didn't mention any of that. It seemed petty, as true feelings so often do.

She laughed. "You dope! He admires you about that, too. He admires how you know right and wrong and you *will not* do something you think is wrong. You will not compromise. You will not justify yourself. He sees that as a kind of strength you have and he's not sure he does."

This boggled my mind. The constant stream of pain and doubt that seemed to constitute "my life" seemed utterly unwantable, never mind admirable. That someone might admire those very qualities that I found agonizing burdens was incomprehensible.

"I don't know what to say."

"Look, the point is that we care about you, we want your life to be better, we don't want you going through that again."

I gave a laugh. "Sounds good to me. Any ideas?"

"Well, first, I do like your theory. I'm as romantic as the next ten people put together. But, Mark, it isn't working. Shouldn't a good theory work?"

"I don't know. Of course it should. Maybe I just have to give it more time."

"More Lees?"

I shuddered.

"Besides," she continued. "I don't think you really believe your own theory."

"What?"

"I mean it. You say that she's supposed to not notice your outward appearance. But you do notice outward appearances. That girl the other night was very pretty."

"You don't have to remind me. I have to avoid noticing it weekly."

"My point is that it may not be realistic to expect that. Maybe you *should* pay more attention to your outward appearance. Maybe that would get someone's attention, and something would happen from there."

"You mean compromise?" I said in mock horror.

"Let's call it an experiment," she said diplomatically.

I looked at her. "Maybe," I said. "And what else?" Because I felt that there had to be more going on here besides a "Neatness counts" lecture.

"And," she said with a meaningful look, "I have a theory of my own."

I smiled. "Oh, goody! What's your theory?"

"My theory is that, for you, Lee was like getting hit by an emotional truck. You've been recovering. But it's time to be out in the world again." She leaned forward making odd little gestures with her hands. "It's like you're in a batting slump. You can't just sit in the dugout all day. You have to go out and get your first hit."

I smiled more. "Somehow, this doesn't sound like your metaphor."

"Okay, how about this? Your horse threw you at the first jump. You have to brush yourself off and get back in the saddle again and clear the rest of the course."

Lisa had a wallful of trophies for horse-jumping competitions. "That sounds more like you."

I was beginning to see what was going on here. The Big Three had apparently held a summit conference—on me. I appreciated their concern: it was touching that they cared. Lisa had been chosen to speak with me. That was a smart move on their part. Ben I had been able to distract. Stan I had been able to rebuff. But Lisa was another story entirely. Lisa was unrebuffable. And, as I'm sure she well knew, but perhaps Ben and Stan did not, Lisa was also unrefuseable by me.

"You need to start dating some non-perfect women. You need to get out and have some fun. If the perfect woman does come along, great. We are, shall we say, increasing the probability of your success."

I always smiled when Lisa used mathematical terms for my benefit. Math and science were perhaps the only areas of human thought she had not conquered.

"I see. And how are we to accomplish this miracle?"

At this, she stood up elegantly and said, "I'm getting you back in the saddle again. Today. Now."

With that, she pulled her sweater up over her head in one smooth languid movement that suddenly reminded me of last summer. She and Stan had invited me along to the beach one day. Lisa had worn a simple white bikini that was rather modest as bikinis go, but I had still been startled to discover that, hidden under the long-sleeved turtlenecks and bulky wool sweaters she habitually wore, she had a body, and a female one at that. At the time, I had had to look away to keep from staring inappropriately. Since then, I did not bring that image of her to mind, because I did not like to think of Lisa that way. I thought of her more as a sister than anything. But as she stood there, I suddenly had that image again. I was uncomfortably aware that she was a woman and I was a man. I could feel my heart beat.

She was shaking her long blonde hair loose from the sweater now, and I found myself wondering what exactly she meant by "getting me back in the saddle again, today, now".

Then she looked up at me with a mischievous look and said, "So, where's your bedroom?"

That brought me up out of my chair like an ice-pick through the cushions. I automatically answered, "Through the kitchen, second left."

She gave me a wicked wink, said, "Okay, get ready!", and disappeared into the kitchen.

I was rooted to the spot. I gaped with astonishment. To me, her words could have only one meaning and I was pretty appalled at it.

Let's just calm down here, I told myself. Your always-tenuous grasp on reality is causing you to misinterpret what she is saying and doing. There is a perfectly simple, and a perfectly innocent, explanation for all this. Let's just wait and see what it is.

Then I heard the unmistakable sound of sheets being pulled back on my bed.

"Lisa, wait, no way," I called out. "No. Thanks, but no."

"I know what you're thinking," she called back from my bedroom. "You're thinking I won't be very good." I was aghast. I didn't know whether to reassure her or simply scream. "Stan thought the same thing, his first time. But I'm actually pretty good. I've had a lot of practice." This otherwise astonishing statement seemed to settle at least one question. I had always sort of wondered if Lisa and Stan were doing the deed. This seemed to indicate that they were.

I shook my head. "Look, I'm sure…," I began, then burst out, "Stan! That's right, what about Stan? What would Stan think about this, Lisa? What if he found out?"

"He already knows," she laughed gaily. "I told him. He thinks it's a great idea. And he's promised me not to say anything when he sees you."

"He…you…he…" This was simply unbelievable. We were seriously entering the Twilight Zone, and we were not stopping to ask for directions.

I had managed to take a paralytic stagger toward the kitchen, just in time to see her exit briskly from my bedroom, her arms full of my sheets. I winced.

"You're going to like this," she was saying, an impish look on her face. "It doesn't hurt, you know. Or don't you remember?"

"I know it doesn't hurt," I said. "That's not the point. The point is…"

I never got to tell her what the point was because at that moment she shook out one of the sheets and spread it on the kitchen linoleum tiles.

This was too much.

"On the floor?" I exclaimed.

"You don't want us to make a mess, do you?" she inquired sweetly.

"No, I don't want to make a mess," I said, skipping over the "us" part. "I don't want to, to, to do this at all. And what if Eli were to come in?"

She shrugged. "Big deal. We're not doing anything to be ashamed of. Let him watch."

I was preparing to swoon at this appalling notion, when she picked up one of our three kitchen chairs and set it in the center of the sheet on the floor.

This was a new one on me. I had no doubt that I had led too sheltered a life. But still—a chair?

I took a deep breath, looked her straight in the eye, and said calmly and clearly, "No, Lisa. Thank you very much. It is a generous offer, an unbelievable offer. But, no. Absolutely not. Thank you, but no."

Her response was to lean onto the back of the chair and give me a grin that was absolutely devilish. From her purse, she slowly withdrew a pair of hair scissors and snipped them in the air twice.

"One chair," she said. "No waiting."

Thirty-nine

She was right. It didn't hurt.

However, it did feel distinctly eerie to sit there watching large clumps of my hair and beard cascading onto the sheet. She had draped the second sheet over my upper body like a big loose bib. I shrieked a few times and clutched wildly at my head when extra-large clumps appeared on the floor. She told me not to be a baby.

While cutting, she called me every synonym of scaredy-cat she could think of, muttering occasionally about birds' nests and hedge clippers, while I gave her a hard time about snipping off certain bodily appendages I valued. In short, a splendid time was had by all.

In the end, I had to admit that she had done a good job. Nobody was going to mistake me for a Marine. But I did look like a fairly conservative rock musician. And my hair was approximately the same length on both sides of my head, which was my only true criterion for a good haircut. She had also lopped about a foot off my beard, so that it actually conformed to the contours of my face. I could now be reasonably described as "a guy", rather than "a guy with a beard".

She had extracted from me a sacred promise to trim my beard myself periodically, and to get a haircut at least every couple of months. I vowed solemnly.

And, finally, she made me agree to only wear my glasses for seeing. My eyes are not really that bad. I only need glasses for driving or seeing the blackboard. I just wear them all the time out of laziness and habit. She seemed to think I would look better without them. When someone like Lisa makes a suggestion like that, you tend to take it seriously.

When she was leaving, she berated me for putting up such a fuss. Her parting words were, "Well, what did you *think* I meant?"

Forty

After she left, I cleaned up the kitchen, grateful now for the sheet. Then I took a long hot shower to remove the clippings that had fallen on me. When I looked in the mirror afterwards I was surprised to notice that I had a face, something that I had previously gone to great lengths to conceal.

I wondered idly what Rachel would make of my new appearance. But that got me thinking about German spies, and eventually I found myself sitting on the corner of my denuded bed, brooding over the pile of books on my dresser. I dreaded the prospect of looking through them, especially when I didn't know what I was looking for.

Okay, I thought, don't think of the pictures. Don't think of the topic. Think of it as information. As a list of names.

A list of names. I felt that I could deal with that.

The books were a list of names. One of the names was possibly a spy, and a murderer, and the one who had nearly killed Jackson. And who might actually try to kill me.

And with that name, there was a face. Perhaps the face of someone I saw every day.

But which name?

As I thought about it, it occurred to me that only the names in the sixth book mattered. It was in the sixth book that Speen had presumably found the spy. The other five books were irrelevant.

But which name in the sixth book?

There must be hundreds of names. One was the name of the murderer. The others were irrelevant. Just like the other five books. Too bad the irrelevant names couldn't be subtracted from the sixth book as simply as the other five books could.

Suddenly my eyes popped open. Wait a second. The sixth book was a list of names. The other five books were another list of names. Any name in the other five books was irrelevant.

What if some of the sixth-book names were in the five-book names? Any name on both lists is not the murderer. Could it be that some of the names in the sixth book were actually in the other five? As I thought, it seemed more likely. How many grim pictures could there be? There must be some overlap.

Then I slumped. This would take a lot of work. I would have to read a name in the sixth book, then look through the other five for that name.

Wait. A better way. Read all the names in the sixth book. Then read the other five. If a name looked familiar, check it against the sixth book, then toss it out.

Or, an even better way. What if there was already a list of names in the sixth book? I looked in the back of the book, praying for an index. No such luck. I mean, it had an index, but it was mainly of topics and places, not people. That figured.

So, write out a list of all the names in the sixth book myself. Then read the other five.

I paused. It would be even better if the list were alphabetized, easier to locate the names. But that would be a major pain to do by hand.

So, don't do it by hand. Use the computer. This was one of those times I wished there really were such things as computers in houses. I mean, you always read science fiction stories where there are computers in the den and in the kitchen and in the bathroom. I wondered if any of those science fiction writers had ever seen a real computer. The ones at the university were the size of large refrigerators, about ten of them. The chances of anyone ever having a computer in their house seemed miniscule at best. I had to bite the bullet.

I grabbed the sixth book and headed for the computer center.

Forty-one

Each semester I was given 5 or 6 different computer accounts, one for each course I took and one for each course I taught. I generally didn't use them much. Sometimes a homework assignment required a complicated calculation that I would whip up in a BASIC or Fortran program. I also occasionally dropped by the computer center to check out if there were any new games to play.

I sat down in front of a vacant paper terminal and typed in one of my account numbers, AGC101, and my password, MERLIN. I liked Merlin. I think I would have made a good wizard, back in the days when any kind of scientific knowledge was stupefying to people. The terminal clattered to life before me.

These terminals were a new phenomenon for me. Used to be, you had to type out your programs on punched cards, then hand your deck of cards to the person behind the counter downstairs. I had actually had that job when I was a senior. It had the grandiose title of "computer laboratory assistant", but basically involved taking people's decks, throwing them into a bin for the computer operator to run, then matching the output— double-wide sheets of green-lined computer paper—with each deck and filing them alphabetically to be picked up. It took like fifteen to twenty minutes to run a deck of cards, and even then, you had probably forgotten a comma on card two so your run died there.

It's funny how, when you're used to doing things one way, you can't imagine how it could be done better. But somebody had, thank heavens. These new terminals were amazing. You could type in your program, save it in your own user area, edit it to get out the mistakes, and run it as many times as you liked, all without leaving your chair. There were paper termi-nals, where computer paper fed continuously through a big electric-type-writer kind of apparatus, and monitor terminals, where everything appeared on a TV-like screen. The monitor terminals were good for playing games, because you could do graphics tricks, and also left no tangible proof if you were doing something you shouldn't. Since I was trying to make a printed list of names, though, I used one of the paper terminals.

I wrote a quick and dirty program in BASIC to read in names I typed, alphabetize them, and store them in a file. I ran it and it died. I examined it and changed something egregiously wrong. I ran it and it ran, but didn't alphabetize properly. I examined it some more, and corrected a subtle logic error. I ran it and it worked.

I began typing names in from the sixth book. I typed as quickly and as carefully as I could. Spelling definitely counted here. To make it easier, I used all small letters. My pinkies miss the shift keys most of the time anyway. There were a lot of pictures of buildings and so forth, which I just skipped over. The photographs in the book were meticulously captioned, giving locations, dates, and names of people in every photograph. This Wolff guy had put a lot of work into this.

There were not many people in the computer center on Sunday night, which I did not find surprising, and I had taken care to sit far from the main aisles. Still, occasionally someone would pass by where I was working, glance at the open book of pictures, and shoot me a horrified look. I would glance up and say, "Research project," with a resigned shrug. They would nod with a shudder and withdraw, usually rapidly.

It took me nearly three hours to type in all the names. I wrote another little program to print the list of names, and the total number of names. There were 236 of them, and it took almost 5 pages to print the whole list. I tore the list off, turned the terminal off and headed home again.

Forty-two

At home, I took a break for a sumptuous dinner, with a main course of waffles.

Then I sat in an armchair in the living room, the list in my lap, the five books in a pile on the floor. I picked up a book, the one that seemed to have the most pictures with names in it, and started reading the names. I have a good memory, and when a name seemed familiar from my typing, I checked the name against the list. If the name matched, I crossed it off the list with a pen. And so I went through the first book. No. No. No. Yes. No. No. Yes. Yes. Yes. Some of the photographs were exact duplicates, so I could cross off five or six names at a time.

I finished going through the first book in about forty-five minutes, and I estimated I had crossed off over a hundred names. This was working beyond my wildest expectations.

I did the second book. After about a half hour I had eliminated about fifty more names.

The third book. Thirty more names. I started getting confused between names that were on the list and names I had seen in the first two books.

The fourth book. It took a long time, because I had to check the list more and more often. Another twenty names or so.

The fifth book. Thank heavens. I was extra careful, because my mind was now a blur of names. I crossed off about a dozen names.

When I finished, I let out a deep breath and rubbed my eyes deeply. I went to the bathroom and splashed water on my face. I felt like I had been dragged through a real-life house of horrors for, try as I might, I couldn't really pretend these books were merely a list of names.

Forty-three

I went back to the living room and looked at the list. There were still eleven names left. Much better than 236. But I still didn't know which of these eleven—if any—was the murderer. For all I knew, these eleven people could all be dead now.

How could I find out? Who would know about these people?

I looked at the cover of the sixth book. Inside the Camps, by Dr. Gerhard Wolff. I opened it and looked at the inside back cover. The author photograph showed an elderly man with a serious face, which was not surprising. It said he was a professor of history at the University of Nebraska at Omaha.

I got up and found the phone directory. I located the area code for Omaha, and dialed information. There was only one Gerhard Wolff and I wrote down his number on the back cover under his picture.

Was I really going to do this?

I sighed. I could always hang up. That was the beauty of the telephone.

I dialed the number, feeling more relieved after every unanswered ring.

After six rings, someone picked up the phone. "Hello?" said a high male voice that did not like being disturbed on a Sunday night.

"Hello. I'm trying to reach Dr. Gerhard Wolff."

"Speaking," he said in a clipped, precise voice. He had a vaguely European accent. Speakink.

"Hello, Dr. Wolff. My name is," I began, then became more cautious. "Well, actually I'm not going to tell you my name right now." I felt suddenly secretive, without really knowing why.

"Oh, really?" His tone made it clear that he did not take any crap from anybody. "I do not like anonymous callers. You will tell me your name now or this conversation is ended."

"Wait, wait, wait," I pleaded. "Please bear with me, Dr. Wolff. I have a problem I'm trying to solve, and it involves your book. Inside the Camps."

"What kind of problem?" He sounded annoyed, but also a little curious. Here we go.

"I'm a college student, a graduate student actually, and one of my professors was murdered last week." I hated using the word "my" in connection with Speen, but it seemed like a shorthand way to express my interest in the affair. I didn't want to get into all the Rachel-Katanga-physics dimensions of the thing.

"How terrible," he stated. There was a subtle change to his tone. He was trying to sound detached, but he seemed even more curious. Maybe even distressed. Of course, he hadn't known Speen.

"Yes. And I have reason to believe that one of the people mentioned in your book may have been involved. I was wondering if you had any information on them now, whether they're alive, where they are, and so forth."

"Young man," he began in exasperation. "This is unacceptable. You are tossing around these wild thoughts. With what basis? How am I to know that this is real, and what your interest in it may be?"

I shrugged, which didn't help him any. "Okay. I see your point. Let me tell you as much as I know and see if that helps. But I'm not telling you any of the actual names. I—for some reason, I feel that I need to keep that confidential."

There was a pause, and I started wondering what all this was costing me in long distance. "Very well," he allowed. "Tell me."

I told him. Speen became Professor A. Jackson became Mister B. The unknown spy was Mister C. I explained about the books: Speen's getting rid of them, their being disturbed, and my examination of them all. "You see what I'm getting at," I concluded. "This may all be imaginary, but it may also be real. If you can give me any information about the names that are still on my list, it might help catch the murderer." I took a deep breath as he thought it over.

He sighed. "You are making a very grave mistake here," he stated. "You should turn this material over to the proper authorities immediately for their investigation. It is far too dangerous for an amateur to handle."

"But, Dr. Wolff, I can't do that. It all seems so—so ridiculous, so unbelievable. There's no proof at all, just a chain of connections. But if I could narrow it down to one person, or one picture, then they might take it seriously."

He was insistent. "If you will not do that, then you must bring in outside experts. There are people whose job it is to track down these Nazis and bring them to justice. They will take you seriously."

"I can't do that either. This guy, this spy, he's on the campus somewhere. He may be in my own department. He knows the campus. If strangers started showing up asking questions, he'd be gone. The only chance is if someone who's already here can find out what's going on. And I guess that's me for now."

I heard a discontented sigh and some muttering that I couldn't make out. "This is most unsatisfactory. Yet, I believe what you are saying, and I can understand the reasons for your actions. I will try to help you if I can. But if the information is at all useful, you must immediately bring it to the attention of the police. However, I genuinely doubt if it will be of any use in what you are trying to accomplish. What is it that you want to know?"

For a moment, I couldn't believe that he was actually going along with this. He seemed dead against it. "Well, thank you," I said. "Like I told you, I have narrowed down the names to a few who it might be. What I need to know is if any of these people are still alive and could actually be the killer. Would you know about stuff like that?"

He snorted. "Young man, it happens that I am a member of an organization that gathers material about such people, and assists in their capture and prosecution if possible. I did not write that book as an academic exercise, but to make available material that might assist in their identification and capture. I may well have information that is helpful to you. Who is it that you are interested in?" There was something in his voice that gave me the strong impression that he was not telling me everything about this organization. I felt even more justified in being secretive about myself.

"Well, that's actually the problem. I'm not sure which one. I've narrowed it down to eleven names. Could I read you the names and maybe you could tell if you know anything about them?"

"Just so," he said, with the apparent effort of trying to seem patient. "Let us try."

"Gerhard S. Axel."

"Is now dead." I crossed him off.

"Dieter Bunt."

"Ach! That one. Unknown. Let us set him aside for the moment." I marked him with a question mark.

"Wolfgang M. Franckel."

"Is dead also." Crossed off.

And so we passed a merry two minutes. At the end, there were four names with question marks.

"Hmmm," I said. "I'm not sure how to proceed now."

"Could you possibly tell me any further details about what happened to your professor?" he inquired with perhaps just a hint of sarcasm.

I considered this cautiously. Then I pouted and shook my head, which was useless for him of course. "No one is really sure. It looks like someone threw him out a window. And the same person may have dropped a cinder-block onto Mister B. Missed his head, but broke his collarbone."

"Mein Gott," he exclaimed. "It is Bunt, most certainly. Dieter Bunt, from your list."

I didn't know who he meant at first. He pronounced the "u" in "Bunt" like the "oo" in "hood". Boont. I had been pronouncing it as "bunt", like in baseball. My eyes snapped to that name on my list. "Really? What makes you think so?"

"This Bunt had a mania, an obsession with falling, with death by falling. He had been first a soldier in the war, a—what is the word?—paratrooper. On his first jump, parachuting into Russia, both his legs were broken in the fall, crushed really. He was captured by the Russians, but given no medical care apparently. He was then recaptured by the Germans and joined the Gestapo. He rose quickly through the ranks because of his cruelty and willingness to perform any act, no matter how heinous. His legs never did heal correctly. Always obsessed with falling he was."

My heart was pounding. Falling. "That sounds like it could be him," I said. Then, very apologetically, "Dr. Wolff, please excuse my ignorance here. I know the Gestapo were terrible, and all of this was grim beyond words, but what is this guy supposed to have done?"

"I suppose it is difficult for most people to comprehend the enormity of the crimes of these people. I understand. The purpose of the Gestapo was to maintain order and loyalty in Germany and in the occupied countries. They did this through fear and intimidation, through torture and murder. It was the Gestapo and SS who ran the death camps. They held a terrible power over everyone. Even in such evil, some were better than others. But some, like this Bunt, were very much worse. In the hands of a twisted and evil man, such power is a horror no one should have to endure. Let me tell you what this Bunt is known to have done himself."

He told me.

I cannot bring myself to repeat, let alone set down on paper, the horrifying acts he related to me in a few minutes. You, as a civilized person, could not even imagine such things, as I could not before hearing them. But, if you will imagine the most dreadful crimes against a person that you can conceive, and then imagine that these things could be done at whim, to the weakest and most defenseless innocent, with no hope of escape or rescue or mercy whatever for the victim, over and over, by men who laughed and took delight in their own bestial cruelty, and that these things could be done to hundreds or thousands or millions of such victims, you might approximate a fraction of what I heard.

At several points, I wanted to stop him and say, "Wait. You must be mistaken. No one would ever do such a thing to another human being."

But I didn't. Because that was the whole point: they would, they could, and they did.

Finally, I did interrupt him, after an account I found utterly incomprehensible. "He did what?"

Dr. Wolff explained patiently. "There was a four or five story building at the edge of the camp. When a prisoner was too sick or weak to continue, Bunt would make him walk to this building, saying he would get special medical treatment. The prisoner would never be seen again. Some chose to believe they really did get medical treatment, perhaps were even transferred somewhere else. The rest suspected the truth. Only after the camp was liberated, was the full truth known. This building had been gutted by fire—no floors to the rooms in it at all, just a metal staircase up the outside. Bunt would make the sick prisoner climb the stairs to the top floor, then push them to their death. In the cellar were found over a hundred bodies."

I was sickened by this, but my brain was working. A man obsessed with pushing people to their deaths. A German. A Nazi. A war criminal. The piece fit the puzzle so perfectly it seemed impossible.

"Is he alive?" I asked carefully.

I could almost hear the shrug from the other end of the line. "That, no one knows," said Dr. Wolff wearily. "There have been several possible sightings of this one after the war, but nothing confirmed. Mexico, in 1956, I believe. Then in the United States, Texas, in 1964. Possibly Ohio, in 1969. After that, perhaps California. But, no proof. No one is sure."

"I see. Is there any way to identify this guy?"

"Do you have the book there with you? There is a photograph. Page 46." That he knew the page seemed astonishing, but it *was* his book. I did as he said.

This picture was a particularly gruesome one. Grainy and out of focus, it showed five Nazis in uniform standing smiling in front of the hanged body of a prisoner in a striped uniform. The caption read, "16 March 1945-Execution of Grigori Austikanis. Sergeant Hans Tell, Sergeant

Leopold Dreth, Captain Friedrich Kriger, Lieutenant Willi Stanz, Major Dieter Bunt."

I stared intently at the right-hand figure. Dieter Bunt looked like anybody, and nobody. He had a vaguely smiling face and light (or possibly just short) hair and a somewhat stocky body, but that could have been the winter clothes. I'm no good with faces anyway, but this was as generic and ordinary a face as I'd ever seen. No disfiguring scars. No eye patch. There was nothing distinctive about him at all. I could have walked right past him today for all I knew.

"He could be anybody," I said. "Do you have any idea how old he is now?"

"That is one of the things we do *not* know," said Dr. Wolff regretfully. "Any birth certificate or enlistment papers were destroyed in the war, perhaps by his own hand. He may have been a teenager in 1945 or he may have been in his thirties. He may be in his fifties now, or in his seventies. We do not know."

I stared at the picture again. He was right. This could almost be a teenager. Or it could be a guy in his thirties. There was no way to tell. Thinking of a young person doing the things Bunt had done made my skin crawl.

I mused aloud. "Even if I found him, how could we ever positively identify him?"

"Ah," said Dr. Wolff. "As to that, positive identification is easy and absolute. While the Russians had him they did little else, but they did x-ray his legs. We have those x-rays. He cannot change the bones in his legs. If captured, there is no doubt he could be identified as Dieter Bunt."

"Okay." Again, I wondered who Wolff's "we" might be.

"But understand this," he continued urgently, "You must not even consider trying to capture him on your own. He is the most dangerous adversary you can imagine. He kills without hesitation. He is diabolically clever, and utterly desperate to remain free, for, if captured, he would almost certainly be extradited to Israel for trial, and he would almost certainly be condemned to death. The American federal police—pardon me, the FBI—actually investigated the possible sighting in Ohio, but two of them were killed when the house, if it was Bunt's house, exploded."

My eyes popped open. "He blew up his own house?"

"He had set some sort of trap. And even if *he* did not harm you, the others around him might."

"Others?" I had a sudden vision of gangs of elderly Nazis stalking around.

Again, I could sense a shrug. "There are those who help such people, I can never understand why. Sympathizers, perhaps. And there are others who seek him for their own revenge, or to bring him to justice. Unfortunately, if you are in their way they may not hesitate to eliminate you to get to him. Such is the nature of revenge." I felt a cold shiver pass down my spine as he said this. What was I getting myself into here? Then I realized: I already *was* in. That note I had left for Jackson had shoved me in deep. Now I had to get out again.

I looked at the picture again and shuddered. "This picture, this execution," I said. "This was Bunt's work, also?"

"Typical of Bunt, this was. This prisoner was a policeman, in his country, but rather than help the Gestapo round up Jews for the camps, this man had helped many to escape. So, they arrested him. This man was a kind of conscience in the camp. Bunt hated him, and seemed to suffer from this man's judgment. Finally Bunt had him hanged for some trumped-up charge."

"Gosh. That's awful."

"It is more awful than this. The camp was liberated by the Russians only three days later."

My mouth dropped open. "You mean, if this man had lived only three more days he would have been saved?"

Dr. Wolff spoke quietly. "More terrible than that. Bunt killed this man *because* the camp would be liberated soon. He knew the Russians were advancing and he wanted to make sure this man did not survive."

I could not speak. This twisted kind of thinking was beyond me.

Dr. Wolff went on. "Bunt himself disappeared before the camp could be taken. He has never been positively identified since."

I took a deep breath. "I want to thank you for your help."

"My help you are welcome to. But take my advice also, please. Turn over what you know to the authorities, now. If you like, you can tell me and I will notify the proper people immediately. There is a sizable reward for capturing Bunt, you know."

This was a new angle and, crass as it seems, I was curious. "Really? How much?"

"Sizable," he repeated dryly.

I shook my head. "Well, I'm getting ahead of myself anyway. First I have to find this guy. Then I'll see what to do next. I'm sorry I can't even tell you my name just yet. I want to look into this a little first."

"Be careful, young man. I urge you to be careful. If this one is Bunt, your life may well be in danger."

"I'll be careful," I promised.

It was a promise it would be no burden to keep.

Forty-four

I didn't sleep well that night. Falling down a well named Lee would have been a pleasant respite from these new dreams.

Names kept echoing through my brain, an endless twisting litany of names, like a thrashing printed snake. I was still falling down the well, but now I was accompanied in my fall by Dieter Bunt. He wore the same bland expression on his face as in the photograph, but he was a dark, winged creature, like the evil angel I had seen in that Bible. He loomed near me, close enough to threaten and frighten me, too far to touch or push away.

Who are you? I kept asking, but he never spoke. He just kept falling down the well with me, his face unmoving, his tumbling motions insanely matching my own.

Through all this, I was trying to write. I had a large unwieldy book in my hands, and I was trying to write on its blank pages the myriad names flowing incessantly through my brain. I was struggling furiously, trying to get it all down on paper. Every buffet of the well knocked my pen from the page, so that I never wrote a single name.

And I fell endlessly onward and down.

Monday

▼

Forty-five

The phone rang, disturbing a delicate breakfast experiment involving peanut butter and waffles.

"Hello," I said, more brightly than I felt.

"Hi, Mark." It was Rachel, and my heart fluttered.

"Hi," I replied cleverly. "How are you?"

"I'm fine, thank you. Listen, an FBI agent is coming today to handle the espionage aspect of this case. His name is Payne Stickney. He's some big expert they're flying in. I was wondering if you could meet with him and with me to go over what you had found out from Jackson Katanga before he speaks with Katanga himself."

I thought of all that I had learned just last night that I had not shared with her yet. Boy, was she going to be impressed. And wait until she saw my newly shorn hair and beard.

"That sounds great," I said enthusiastically. I thought over my schedule a moment. "How about one o'clock?"

"That would be fine. At my office?"

"I'll see you then," I said meaningfully.

"See you then," she said, without meaning, then clicked off.

Forty-six

She leaped two steps towards me, lunged forward, and stabbed me square in the chest. I looked down dully at the blade still quivering there.

She stepped back and whipped off her mask. She was furious. "What is with you today? You didn't even try to block that."

I spent the night falling down a bottomless razor-lined hole, I didn't tell her. It's a little draining, I didn't add.

I took off my mask and lowered my own sword. "Sorry. Rough night. I'll try to pay attention."

"Well, I hope so." She put her mask back on, retreated to the end of the gym mat and dropped into en garde position.

Kim was a good foot shorter than me, but made up for her slight stature with a ferocity of competition found only in phys ed majors. She wore her blonde hair cropped short, the better to dry after frequent showers, and she was very cute. A ring on the fourth finger of her left hand exerted a powerful repelling force that kept me from thinking about her except as a fencing partner.

I put my mask on also. Around us, the other fencers in the class leaped back and forth, foils flashing and clashing, with grunts and exclamations and the occasional cry of "Touché!"

Although I saw these people every week, Kim was the only one in the class whose name I knew. I thought of the others only by nicknames.

The Marine was a muscular guy with a crew-cut who wore USMC shorts to every class. He was a hacker, slashing madly with his foil, always getting finessed by anyone he couldn't unnerve.

The Stork was tall, with at least a foot more arm reach than anyone else in class. He was slow, though, often seeming two moves behind anyone he faced.

"The Ballerina" was even smaller than Kim, with short dark hair and a pixie face. She was no menace with a foil, but her graceful footwork and artistic balance were breath-taking. It was a pleasure just watching her walk into position.

I wondered what they called me, the bearded long-haired guy, awkward as hell, but occasionally pulling off a clever move. I *thought* about fencing, you see. I couldn't always perform what I had thought up, but when I could it usually worked.

I dropped into en garde position. Kim immediately advanced, the point of her blade spiraling in toward my chest. I still hurt from that last jab. This time I stood my ground, batting her advancing blade aside, sliding my point upward, forcing her to draw back. I took a step forward, quick, but none too graceful. She turned her wrist awkwardly to parry my point and I slid my foil sideways, grazing her shoulder.

"One," she said. "Damn."

We en garded again. This time she advanced, I defended the same way, she dropped back quickly, I got excited and advanced too roughly, and she put one under my hand, waist high. "One-one," she said in an intense monotone, dropping immediately into en garde. I could see her eyes gleaming behind the wire mask.

I dropped into en garde and she advanced slowly. I advanced slowly also, and soon we were very close, our foils whizzing between us. I started bouncing my torso forward and backward, slowly and rhythmically at first, then faster and more unpredictably. As I hoped, it threw her off. She couldn't tell whether I was advancing, retreating, or just moving my upper body. She had to look down at my feet to tell, and when she did, I bashed her blade sideways and struck her solidly in the side.

"Two-one," I said.

"You pain in the ass." I grinned behind my mask. I knew I was going to lose to her eventually—I almost always did—but at least I had made two hits. And I had tried out one of the new moves I had dreamed up.

When we started again, she stomped one foot forward, which startled me. I lost a beat, she advanced and stomped again. I was expecting it this time, but the expectation itself made me lose another beat. I was a tiny fraction of a second behind her blade, racing to catch up, but I couldn't. I felt like someone dangling from a rope, watching it unravel strand by strand. Her blade was whirring now, I was falling farther and farther behind, when suddenly she moved her blade up into mine, clang, down onto mine, clang, then straight forward. She hit me smack in the heart and I just nodded.

"Good one. Really, very good. Two-two." This would be the deciding point.

She was already in position, ready to go, her chest heaving. "Come on."

This was it. I settled into position. I was relaxed. I somehow felt that I was going to win this time, that my calm control would beat her intensity. I took a slow, oddly graceful step forward. And she bounded forward twice, lunged, and stabbed me full in the chest, just as before.

And just as before, I looked down at the quivering blade. "Wow."

She pulled her mask free, all smiles now. "Good three," she gushed, holding out her hand. I shook it.

"You *are* getting better," I said. "I can tell."

"You too," she said automatically, bending over, catching her breath.

I shook my head. "No, I'm not getting better. I think about it too much. And I'm no athlete." She shook her head breathlessly. I couldn't tell if she were agreeing with me or disagreeing.

Since she was in gracious-winner mode, I decided to try something. "I did think of another new move to show you though. Lunge at me the way you just did, I want to try it."

Our teacher was passing us. "Dr. Mueller," I said. "Would you please watch this for a second?"

She stopped near us. A woman in her mid-thirties, she was coach of the fencing team and took fencing *very* seriously. The class lived and died by her judgment, advice, and encouragement. She turned and watched us steadily. The rest of the class had stopped to watch us, and Dr. Mueller's reaction.

Kim got into position. I got into en garde but immediately lowered my blade. I was now defenseless, nothing protecting me from Kim's advance. She bounded, lunged, and stabbed at me, just as before. At the last moment, I stepped swiftly to my right. Her blade slid harmlessly past my left side and I reached out and grabbed it with my left hand. Astonished, Kim turned toward me and I brought my blade up and tap-tap-tapped her gently on the stomach.

Kim exploded, ripping her mask off and throwing it to the mat. "That's not legal! Is that legal? No way that's legal!" She demanded satisfaction from Dr. Mueller. The others in class were already loudly debating with each other about the legality, and morality, of what I had done.

Dr. Mueller only looked at me, raised her eyes to heaven, shook her head in mock-profound disappointment, and walked away.

Forty-seven

After fencing, I was walking dripping from the shower to the locker room when a voice behind me said, "Hey, hippie."

Great. I usually got this kind of thing in dimly lit bars, somebody compelled to make a comment about my hair and beard. I hated getting into fights, mainly because I had not the slightest clue about what to do in one. Besides getting the crap beat out of me, I mean. I generally found that the longer I could keep them talking, the less likely it would get physical. Running fast helped, too. Still, it was a nuisance and a threat I didn't need. And I had *never* had to face it at school before. I didn't relish running around campus naked and dripping. Streaking was no longer the in thing to do, especially in November.

So I turned to face…The Marine. Swell. Naked, he was even more muscular than I remembered. His hands were big and powerful, with bony knuckles I could imagine would hurt. He brought one of his hands up towards me quickly and I stopped myself from flinching, but I did say, "Uh."

"That was a great move you did in class today." He was smiling. His hand was waiting to be shaken. I shook it. He had a powerful and convincing, but not bone-crushing, handshake.

It slowly dawned on me that he wasn't going to beat me up for having a beard and long hair. He actually seemed to like me.

"Dr. Mueller didn't think much of it," I said, coming pretty close to sounding casual.

He snorted and dismissed her with a wave of his hand. "Yeah, well, it may not be legal in fencing, but take my word for it: a move like that could save your life in a real fight."

I shrugged. "You're prob'ly right. But I so rarely find myself in sword fights these days."

He laughed. "Right."

I laughed, too.

I suddenly had an image of us, two wet guys laughing with our hoohas hanging out. It felt strange.

I fiddled with my towel. "Anyway, thanks."

"Yeah, see you around." He got his towel down from the rack.

I turned to go, then turned back. Don't ask me why, I just can't leave this kind of thing alone. "By the way, my name is actually Mark."

"Oh, yeah?" He sounded surprised. "So is mine."

I was surprised, too. We shook hands again.

"See you around."

I walked away, shaking my head. You just never know about some people.

Forty-eight

I taught a one-hour lab on Monday mornings, a strange time for a lab, and I didn't know who to feel more sorry for, myself or my students.

It was a long way from the gym to the physics building. Dashing into the building that morning, my eye had fallen on the glass-enclosed directory of the building. I noticed certain names for the first time and stopped dead. Dr. Axalt, Dr. Berger, Dr. Petz, Dr. Wilhelm. Even Peter Schultz. German names. Any one of these professors was old enough to be Bunt. Dr. Petz hobbled around like he might have fallen out of an airplane in World War II. Dr. Wilhelm had a strange antagonistic streak. Heck, Peter Schultz might be Bunt's grandson. Or the grandson of one of Bunt's victims.

There was even Dr. Mueller, my fencing instructor. The world suddenly seemed to be lined with Germans. And not the ones who wrote symphonies and made medical breakthroughs, either. The bad kind. The real bad kind.

I shook my head. I was getting irrational about this. Then I reminded myself what had been going on around here lately, and what had gone on thirty years ago. Irrational was not so out of place in this situation. In fact, irrational might keep me alive. Until I could figure out Dieter Bunt's current identity—somehow—everyone was deservedly under my suspicion. I was going to be careful, as Dr. Wolff had advised.

Mr. Andersson was prowling the halls, no big surprise. I regarded him warily. He was old enough to be Bunt, too. And he didn't walk so good. Not only that, but he was already involved in this. He supposedly had seen Dr. Speen get pushed off the roof. Or something. Or so he said. What if he had done it himself, then tried to blame Jackson? It was so bone-headed though: his testimony had been so easily discredited, not just by me, but by mounting medical and lab evidence. Wouldn't a Nazi spy be a little more clever? Still. Maybe he wasn't so Danish after all. Or so loony.

He turned and saw I was looking at him. This was always a mistake, and I braced myself for the result. He gave me a dirty look and muttered, "I know all about you," in his silly voice before he stalked out of the building.

A menacing enough comment. But you could say that to *anybody* and they would feel uncomfortable about *something*. Still, I would keep my eye on him.

The lab proceeded uneventfully. It involved little toy carts, pulleys, springs, and inclined planes. Nothing very dangerous, nor especially challenging for either students or instructor.

Then Mrs. Arden walked in, and everything changed.

Forty-nine

The very fact that Mrs. Arden was entering a classroom was unprecedented. I could not easily remember seeing her outside the main office before. How did she get in and out of the building? A vast system of hidden and hitherto-secret tunnels whose very existence I was only now becoming dimly aware of? Whoa, boy. Down, big fella.

She walked over to me and said in a low voice that Dr. Axalt wanted to see me. Now. I was to leave my class and go to his office. This, too, was unprecedented. I had never been summoned out of class to see him before. And there was an urgency to her message that did not escape me.

My heart began to pound. Axalt was a German name. In fact, I remembered that his middle name was Gunther, which seemed significant somehow.

Mrs. Arden preceded me down the stairs and into the office. She sat down at her desk, restoring some balance to the cosmos, and I continued on into Dr. Axalt's office. I automatically began registering anything in sight that might conceivably be used as a weapon.

He looked up from his desk and smiled genially at me. "Come in, Mark, come in," he said, half rising. "Close the door. Have a seat."

I did as he said. He seemed a little too chummy to be a psychopath, but you never really know with psychopaths, do you? He sat down again. He had his hands folded in front of him on his desk. I couldn't see how he could hurt me from that position and began to relax slightly.

"Mark, we have a problem in the physics department," he began. I tensed up again. My mind began to range wildly over various negative possibilities. No money to pay my salary anymore: I had been fired! My grades were too low: I was expelled! I was spending too much time with the police! (How did he know?!) Speen had left a note fingering me for the espionage!

He went on, unaware of my mental tortures. "Since the tragic and unexpected death of Dr. Speen, we have been trying to find replacements to cover the courses he taught." They were eliminating Electromagnetic Theory! I would never be able to graduate!

"We had already been rather short-handed this semester before this tragedy occurred. Unfortunately, what with covering his other three courses, and assuming supervision of his graduate students, none of the other professors has the free time to cover his electromagnetic theory course this semester. It just can't be done." That was it! They were canceling the course! We would all have to become English majors! I would have to read *Billy Budd* again!

"That's why I would like you to assume responsibility for teaching the course for the remainder of the semester."

I sat speechless. I opened my mouth, but only little "abba abba" sounds came out. I swallowed hard and managed to squeak out, "But I'm *taking* that course." And floundering in it, I didn't add.

He nodded. "I know that. And I would not ask it of another person, nor would I ask it of you unless we were in such a desperate situation. You are by far the most conscientious student in the class, and I think you can handle it."

They wanted *me* to teach the course? I felt like screaming at him, But I'm hopelessly *lost* in this course! Luckily, I had just enough good sense to realize that that would not be a good thing to scream, or even say, to the department chairman.

I also thought about the rest of the class. It seemed unlikely that any of the Four Asian Students could handle this. For all I knew, they were all E+M gods with a perfect command of the English language. But I rather doubted it. I also doubted if Peter would be able to keep himself awake long enough to teach it. He was probably a pro-Nazi, or anti-Nazi, assassin himself anyway.

I found myself saying, somewhat dazedly, "Are you sure about this?"

Dr. Axalt assured me had every confidence in me. He also said, "Naturally there will be an adjustment in your salary appropriate to your additional duties."

Adjustment in your salary? He meant money. I would get paid more money. That clinched it. It might be utter lunacy for me to teach a class I was currently blowing in a big way, but the prospect of more money somehow gave it a very reasonable air.

Of course, the whole idea was absolutely wacko, and it was somehow typical of a physicist to even consider as a possible solution, but I sure couldn't see an alternative. If I didn't do it, they would almost certainly cancel the course. If I could somehow get through it with any success, it would be a tremendous accomplishment. Even if I screwed up big time, nobody could reasonably blame me. Plus they would pay me more to try.

It was utterly preposterous. "Okay. I'll try it."

He smiled and stuck out his hand, and I flinched. He still wasn't off my short list of suspected murderers. I shook his hand and approximated a smile.

He walked me to the door, assuring me of this and promising me that. I kept trying to twist around to see if he was slipping a dagger of Oriental design between my vertebrae.

Outside his office door, Mrs. Arden smiled at me. She, knowing all and seeing all as she did, must have been in on this.

"Congratulations, Herr Professor," she said.

That stopped me cold.

"I beg your pardon," I managed to get out. "I didn't know you spoke German."

"Well, I *am* German," she explained. "At least, I was German. I was born in Germany and lived there until I was 12."

A cold shiver slid down my spine, and I felt a little sick. Not Mrs. Arden, too!

"I didn't know that," I stated, trying to keep up my end of the conversation through a hailstorm of thoughts and suspicions. "'Margaret' doesn't sound very German."

She laughed lightly and I thought I'd scream. "My real name was Greta. Greta Held. Mother and I thought it better to Americanize it when we moved here."

"Makes sense," I said, wondering if anything did. At least she hadn't said "Greta Bunt". The sick feeling eased somewhat. "Just you and your mother."

"Yes, well, I never knew my father. Mother had divorced him when I was an infant. In fact, I never even knew his name, mother hated him so. We used her maiden name, Held."

So, her father could be anybody. The sick feeling was back. "You left Germany in…"

She thought. "I forget now exactly. 1933, 1934. When all the trouble started. Mother said my father was mixed up in it all."

"Was he?" I said automatically. I felt like puzzle pieces were caught in a windstorm in my mind, and I was trying to assemble them through mental effort alone.

She nodded. "Mother said he was not a nice man. He died in the war."

"I see," I said. Well, of course that's what her mother would tell her! She wouldn't tell her daughter that her father was a Nazi war criminal! She would say he was "not a nice man". "So you speak German."

"Yes. I hardly ever get a chance to use it. Sometimes it comes in handy, though. You'd be surprised."

"I'm sure I would," I said.

"Well, anyway, congratulations again. I'm sure you'll do fine." She was beaming in my direction.

"Thanks," I said. "I'll try."

I left the office in a major daze. It took me a few seconds to remember that I was still teaching a lab, and couldn't just go home and hide under my bed as I so desperately wanted.

What was going on here?

Could Mrs. Arden really be Dieter Bunt's daughter? Yes, it was possible. If so, Bunt would have to be in his seventies now, at least. But if she was, she was totally unaware of the fact. She didn't even know his name. Or, at least, claimed she didn't. But why tell me all that if she really did know who he was? Therefore, she didn't. But what if *he* knew she was his daughter? That might explain why he would hang around here. Engaging in espionage. Murdering professors. No, that didn't make sense either. If he really wanted to stay around her, he would probably try to behave himself. And he had not been behaving himself. Therefore, that's not why he was here. Therefore, she wasn't his daughter.

Which made far more sense, if you thought about it. Millions of women must divorce jerk husbands. The husbands don't *have to* be Nazis to make them jerks. And shielding your daughter from knowledge of a jerk father seems sort of reasonable, although I would imagine the daughter would always kind of wonder. But Mrs. Arden didn't seem to wonder. That part of her life was closed, it seemed.

I shook my head to clear it before entering the lab. So, this was just a red herring. A weird coincidence. Mrs. Arden was not Dieter Bunt's daughter. I had nothing to fear from that quarter. I could just put the whole thing out of my mind. It had nothing to do with this situation. I had nothing to worry about. I had no reason for concern at all.

I grimly resolved to keep an eye on Mrs. Arden. And any seventy-year-old men who seemed to be hanging around her.

Fifty

The rest of the morning passed in a haze, as I tried to accustom myself to this new situation and figure out how to handle teaching a course I was taking and not doing well in. I got through the lab, and managed to sit upright through Soper's class.

At an early lunch, Stan was true to Lisa's word and did not razz me about my new haircut and beardcut. It was eerie.

Lisa smiled at me, admiring her own handiwork, and said, "You look good."

Ben said, "I remember you. Welcome back."

To Stan I said, "Guess who's replacing Speen teaching my course."

He narrowed his eyes suspiciously and shook his head. "Who?"

"Me," I said. This went over big.

"You?" Stan said. "But you're *taking* the course."

I nodded. "That's what I told Axalt."

Stan sat back in his chair, grasping the implications. "Well, I know at least one person who's going to get an A in this course."

"You forget who you're talking about," Ben pointed out.

Stan smiled as it dawned on him. "Oh, right. Mark will probably only give himself a C. He might not even pass."

We all laughed.

Lisa said, "And remember: no dancing with yourself either."

Fifty-one

When I got back to the physics department, Mrs. Arden held out a key to me. "Dr. Axalt wanted you to have this."

I took the key and looked at it. It resembled my office key. "What is it?"

"That's a key to Professor Speen's office." My head came up with a jerk. "Dr. Axalt thought it would help you to have access to his class notes and books."

"Good idea," I said, simulating indifference. I was trying not to betray my excitement. With a key to Speen's office, I might be able to turn up something connecting him with Bunt, or a clue to who Bunt really was. Again feigning disinterest I asked, "When do you want this back?"

She shook her head. "No hurry. There aren't any plans for his office yet. Just use it as you need it."

I frowned as if the key were another burden I was shouldering. "Oh. Okay." I left the office, shoving the key in my pocket.

When I was out of her sight, I sprinted up the stairs. As I came to the fifth floor landing, I was a little winded and paused for a bit at the corner. My timing could not have been better. Directly in front of me, Dr. Wilhelm was fitting a key into the lock of Speen's door, twisting the door-knob, and disappearing inside.

I stood there breathing heavily for a bit, then moved cautiously forward. I decided to scout out the terrain before doing anything else. I walked swiftly and noisily down the hall. As I passed Speen's door, I flicked my head sideways for a quick glance and kept going. At the end of the hallway, I imitated Mr. Andersson and perused a dusty bulletin board.

I mentally reviewed what I had seen. Speen's door was shut all the way. There was no light showing through the frosted glass window or under the door itself. There had been no sound or motion from inside. I remembered Speen's office as being very dark with the lights off. If Wilhelm was in there with the lights off, it could only be because he didn't want to attract attention to himself.

I waited five minutes at the bulletin board. Ten. At fifteen minutes, I gave up and started down the hall. As I reached the stairwell, I heard a sound behind me. I forced myself not to look around. I started down the stairs, then whirled around to scrutinize a shiny steel trash receptacle at the top of the stairs. In its surface, I could see a distorted reflection of Dr. Wilhelm looking up and down the corridor as he shut and locked the door behind him. I noticed that he was empty-handed.

I continued down the stairs, turning things over in my mind. He had also been empty-handed when he went in, I remembered. He had the lights off, so his presence wouldn't be noticed. Clearly, he must be looking for something in Speen's office. Something he didn't want anyone to know about. But he hadn't found whatever it was. Would he be back again? If so, I aimed to get in there before his next try.

Fifty-two

One o'clock found me chez Maybelle once more. The sun was out and it was actually warm enough for me to remove my battered old coat as I walked from my car. The snow had melted and saturated the ground so that the whole world squished with each step.

I was somewhat curious to meet FBI agent Payne Stickney. I knew about these birds with two last names. I could picture this white-bread WASP preppie already. Tall and somewhat stooped, receding sandy hair, horsey nose, liquid eyes, spectacles if not an actual monocle, a pipe, no chin, and a wife named Buffy. I suspected that his forebears had arrived in America on different boats than mine had.

When I knocked at Rachel's door, Sgt. McKinnock wished me good afternoon, let me in, and vanished. My eyes were on Rachel anyway, and my heart was doing flip-flops. I couldn't wait for her reaction to my newly trimmed hair and beard. I was even contemplating asking her on a date—one that didn't involve blood stains.

"Hi, Mark," she said. "Thanks for coming down. Please have a seat."

"Hi, Rachel," I said, sitting at her table.

"Agent Stickney will be right back," she said.

I nodded. I was in no hurry to have a third person join us. In fact, I was trying to summon my courage to ask her out. It was at that moment that she looked up and said, "Ah, Agent Stickney, this is Mark Napoli. Mark, this is Payne Stickney."

I looked up to see a large man glowering at me. Although we both had our hands out for shaking, he did not seem especially enthusiastic about the prospect. I had never met a man who seemed to dislike me on sight before, and I couldn't help wondering why. He grasped my hand in a crushing grip that was mercifully brief. Then he reached into the breast pocket of his suit coat and handed me a business card that said "G. Payne

Stickney II, Special Agent, Federal Bureau of Investigation," and an out-of-state phone number. No smiley face.

G. Payne Stickney II. Welcome to WASP World.

Payne Stickney had a sneer like a barracuda. Well over six feet tall, with straight dark hair combed sleekly back in a streamlined pattern that said, "Predator." He was wearing a suit that would have cost me a month's salary. He exuded arrogance and belligerence. I guessed he was in his late thirties. He had dark eyes and a nose I was pleased to see had once been broken, probably in a polo accident. He had a short dark mustache trimmed fastidiously. His build was large and muscular, and I had no doubt he could easily toss me around the room if he wanted to. And I had the feeling he wanted to. I had a hunch we were not going to be pals.

Still, there was something about him that dinged a little bell in my head. I didn't know what the bell meant. Something about G. Payne Stickney II's face reminded me more of Stan than of a signer of the Declaration of Independence. It didn't fit, somehow.

He sat down at the table aggressively. "Let's get to it," he growled.

Rachel said, "Yes, well, Mark has been kind enough to assist us in our investigation into the death of Dr. Speen at the university, and the assault on Dr. Speen's graduate assistant, Jackson Katanga."

I nodded and opened my mouth, but before I could say anything, Stickney interrupted with, "That's the guy who confessed to espionage."

I shot a look at Rachel. "Has Jackson confessed to anything?" I wondered. I had rather hoped Jackson would have kept his mouth shut for at least a brief period after our little chat.

"No," said Rachel, directing an inquiring look at Stickney. "He hasn't. Katanga gave Mark certain information which Mark shared with me. Katanga has not been arrested or charged with anything. He has made no statement to the police."

Stickney cut her off with a curt gesture. "Means nothing," he said gruffly. "We've got him by the balls. He's going down for this. Now we need to find his contact."

I stared at this baboon. He didn't talk like a proper WASP. I rather doubted if any of his Puritan forebears had ever used the word "balls" in quite this way, for example. "What do you mean, 'He's going down for this'? At first, Jackson didn't even know he was doing anything wrong. And then he was coerced into continuing by Speen."

"This guy," said Stickney, raising his voice further, "admits to transporting classified documents to person or persons unknown. Right?"

I hesitated, but I couldn't see an alternative to answering his question. "Right."

"Espionage," Stickney pronounced. "He goes down."

I raised a hand. "Excuse me," I said. "Now, I'm no lawyer, but isn't there some kind of formality involving a trial before he's found guilty?"

You may be surprised at my taking on this rather large and belligerent jerk like this. All I can say is that I was emboldened by the wide table between us, as well as my knowledge that the also-immense Sgt. McKinnock was hovering somewhere off-stage, hopefully with his night-stick ready.

Stickney looked at me as if he'd just bitten into an apple and struck worm.

"Oh, a funny guy. I love funny guys," he said, the way you might say, "I love oral surgery." He dismissed me and turned to Rachel. "I don't know what your plans are regarding this suspect, Lieutenant, but I can assure you that we will be prosecuting him for espionage. Ten separate counts, as I understand it."

My eyes popped open. Ten counts! "With what proof?" I demanded. "You don't have the documents. Speen is dead. You don't know who received the documents. And all you have is my word on what Jackson said, which is hearsay. Why don't you arrest him for the Kennedy assassination while you're at it?"

Rachel was looking at me, a little shocked. Stickney just smiled widely, which was repulsive. He looked even more like a particularly well-groomed shark. "Hey, I don't mind a little hearsay between friends.

Besides, your story is just giving me the lay of the land before the main event. Just let me talk to your little pal," he said in a low dangerous voice. "I think he'll make a very full and complete statement about his involvement in this situation."

I thought of Jackson alone with this man-eater. I had no doubt that Stickney could scare Jackson into admitting he had shoplifted Fort Knox. Stickney would go through Jackson like a buzz saw. I felt I'd better warn Jackson, fast, and make sure he had connected with a lawyer.

To Stickney I said, "I think there's a concept you're not too clear on here. There are what are called good guys and bad guys. For example, Speen was a bad guy. Whoever killed Speen is a bad guy. Your job is to catch the bad guys. Now, Jackson is not a bad guy. Jackson is a good guy. You see the difference?"

Stickney was unfazed by this. "Thank you, professor, for your enlightening lecture. But I'm not in *Who's Who in Law Enforcement* for nothing. Bad is as bad does. Katanga did bad, ergo Katanga goes down. You stick to your blackboards, and leave the espionage investigation to me."

I stood up. "I see no point in continuing this," I said. I headed for the door. Stickney was grinning broadly. Rachel was out of her chair.

"Wait a second, Mark," she called and I stopped. No one but Rachel could have kept me there.

She then addressed Stickney. "Agent Stickney, I think you are as interested as we are in identifying the third person involved in this. I think you'll agree that finding and arresting that person is probably more important than pursuing a possibly questionable charge against Mr. Katanga. Now, Mr. Napoli has already provided information to us that has been helpful in our investigation, and I believe he may have further information that may assist us in apprehending this third person. I'm sure you would be interested in receiving any assistance possible in clarifying this situation. I suggest that we all cooperate in this investigation." She shot Stickney a look like she was ready to throw a choke-hold on him if necessary.

Stickney spread his hands magnanimously. "I am always interested in input from the civilian sector. And, as an aside, I am entirely willing to forgo certain prosecutions in the interests of higher justice."

It sounded like he was reading off the pedestal of some statue, but at least it seemed conciliatory. I sat down again.

Rachel sat down also and folded her hands before us. She would have made one hell of a junior high principal. "Perhaps we should confine ourselves to any further information Mark has at this time." Stickney made a face but was silent. "Mark?" she prompted.

I let out a breath. This was going to be a tough audience.

"Okay. Jackson does not know who the third person is. He said that Speen referred to this third person as "he" and as "German". Jackson said that Speen had found material to blackmail this third person, so that he would release his hold on Speen. Speen intended to confront him on that Thursday afternoon."

Rachel was nodding at all this. She had heard it before. Stickney was doing his best to act like someone who is totally bored, pretending to be mildly interested. Time to start dropping bombshells.

"That same afternoon, Speen gave me a bag of books he wanted me to put in Jackson's office. When I checked that bag yesterday, I saw that it contained books about Nazis and the Gestapo. Also, it had been moved from where I had left it. And one book was missing from the bag."

Rachel was looking very interested in this. So was Stickney, in a grudging, scowling way. I plunged on.

"I believe that Speen found something in those books to link this third person with the Gestapo. I also believe that this third person, whoever he is, took the missing book after murdering Speen. I bought another copy of the same book yesterday. Since that was the only book missing, it was probably the only one containing the evidence against this third person. Out of two hundred and thirty six names in that book, two hundred and twenty five were duplicated in the other five books. Of the remaining eleven names, seven are dead. Of the other four names, the author of the book identified one as a person who was obsessed with death by falling, and was known to push people to their deaths. His name is Dieter Bunt. Here is his picture."

I pulled out the book and showed them the grisly picture of the hanging. Rachel was gazing at me as if I had just taken a stroll across the Sea of Galilee. Stickney was sitting with a sullen, skeptical look.

Rachel was trying to put words together. "So this, this Bunt was Speen's contact, the one Speen was passing secrets to via Katanga. And Speen found out about his past and attempted to blackmail him about it. But Bunt knocked Speen out and pushed him out the window. Then took this book to hide the evidence."

"Yes," I said, nodding, and looked at Stickney.

He was still staring at the picture. Then he looked up at me and said, "What a crock!"

I regarded him with marked disinterest. I had learned something from Speen, anyway. "You seem to have some objection to this theory," I said.

"Theory," he sneered. "First of all, you're going by what an admitted spy is telling you, no doubt to lessen his own guilt. All this stuff about Germans and Nazis may be pure horsehockey. Even if he is telling the truth, which this guy doesn't seem to have a good track record of doing, he's repeating what Speen told him, and Speen could have been lying, too. Or he could have meant "Nazi" figuratively."

"Figuratively," I repeated. "My."

Stickney looked an "Up yours" at me and continued. "Now, even if—if, I'm saying—Mr. Reliable Katanga is telling the truth and Speen is telling the truth, how do you get to this one guy? *Maybe* the third person took that book. Maybe not. Maybe, *if* they took it, it was because it contained evidence. Maybe not. Even if it was, eliminating most of the names just because they *are* in the other books may not make sense. Who knows what that third person knew about those other books? And then to narrow it down to one name on the say-so of some guy in," he looked at the back cover of the book, "Nebraska, a real hot-bed of Nazi investigation. I say it's baloney."

I saw no point in refuting each point he had made. But I did object to the final one. "This Bunt has a history of killing people in this way. And he may well be alive, and if he is, he would certainly do anything to avoid being caught. Like killing Speen."

Stickney leaned forward and gestured aggressively. "Listen to what you're saying: that the most likely suspect in this murder is a Nazi war criminal. Take my word for it, a lot of crimes happen every day, and a lot of them are just like things people might have done thirty-forty years ago. That does not mean that Nazi war criminals are responsible for them all. Or suspects in them all. I've caught a lot of criminals, bad guys as you call them, and none of them have been Nazi war criminals. They're just ordinary scumbags, and that's what this one is. He's just some scumbag, and this Nazi crap is only clouding up the issue. It's a dead end."

I could see what he was saying. I had certainly felt that it was far-fetched myself. It certainly did seem outrageous that the solution to this murder lay in some shadowy figure from thirty years ago. Rachel looked like she was trying to decide who was right.

"Okay," I said. "I see your point. This seems like a tremendous long-shot. I have no real evidence, just a chain of related circumstances. If any of them are wrong, the whole thing falls apart." Stickney was nodding vigorously. "But. But. There is no other line of investigation right now. All we have is Jackson's information, which seems to lead here. But this idea fits the puzzle perfectly. And if what I'm saying *is* true, there is a tremendously dangerous man out there whom nobody suspects, and who may try to kill somebody else." Like me, I didn't add.

Everyone was silent for a moment. Then Rachel cleared her throat and said, "I think we should consider the possibility that what you suspect may be true. It really does not seem like the most likely possibility. But I also think we'd be foolish to ignore it, given that the murderer is still at large and is quite obviously dangerous, and also given that we have no other lines of inquiry at the moment."

She looked over at me, "Thank you, Mark."

Stickney gave me a look too, but his was not saying, "Thank you."

We all stood up. Stickney excused himself and marched out of the room, rather than shake hands again.

"Him I like," I said, indicating the door Stickney had just slammed.

Rachel was shaking her head. "Wow, I don't get him at all. I had asked some of my colleagues about him, too."

"Did they mention if he'd had his rabies shot?"

She smirked. "Everyone who had worked with him described him as competent, professional, and easy to get along with."

I was having a hard time pinning any of those words to Stickney. "Maybe this is his evil twin," I suggested.

"I just don't get it," she said, frowning. "He seems very antagonistic, but I don't know why."

I needed to change the subject here, so I shrugged and made dismissive gestures toward the door. "Maybe he's just having a bad day. Jet lag or something."

"Maybe."

I faced Rachel and, aware I was blushing vividly, said, "You know, not to change the subject, but there's a Beatles movie festival tomorrow night on campus. I was wondering if you'd want to go with me." I said this in a way that even I thought sounded casual, but it had actually cost me a good deal of effort. My insides were churning, and I was buttressing myself for rejection.

She seemed to be considering. "Tomorrow night," she said speculatively. "No, I can't."

Though I felt terribly disappointed inside, my understanding look and comment were all ready. Then she suddenly said, "Oh!" and I thought she had changed her mind. I felt excited and happy as she continued, saying, "We got more lab results. Dr. Speen's blood stains were on one of the carts, and there was a small one on the floor of the room near the window, so your idea was correct. Isn't that great?"

"Terrific," I said, utterly dejected. Blood stains again. The moment seemed to be gone. I let it be.

As I was leaving, Rachel was studying me closely. I stood motionless to allow her to thoroughly take in my new hair- and beard-style.

Finally, she said, "New shirt?"

Fifty-three

Back on campus, I risked being late for my two o'clock class so that I could make a detour to the library. I pulled out a card catalog drawer in the W's and was surprised to find that the library had a recent copy. After a quick dash up to the third floor, I was turning the pages of *Who's Who in Law Enforcement* to S.

Now, what made me so interested in checking on this extraneous human being? Besides what was so obviously wrong with him, there was something not right about him. I didn't know what that was, but thought if I rooted around enough I'd either find something out or get bored with the topic and take up stamp collecting.

Gregory Payne Stickney Jr. I made a mental note to call him "Greg" the next time I saw him. No birthday, so no card from me. *Mother: Alana.* Didn't sound WASPish. Beginning to look like old GPS Sr. had strayed from the fold there. But here were all the WASP credentials I had fully expected. *Greenwich, Connecticut. Choate Academy*, the prep school. *Yale pre-law.* Joined FBI on graduation, probably some favor from the family Senator. "Hank, Junior needs a job. What have you got in DC that would be suitable?" Postings in Dallas, Cleveland, and, most recently, San Diego. Now, you wouldn't think New England was in the San Diego jurisdiction. But Rachel did say that he was some expert brought in for this purpose. Lots of commendations. Probably for browbeating lots of people like Jackson into prison. The picture showed a much nicer person than the one I had met today, with a worse haircut.

Although acutely aware of the time, I couldn't help flipping to the T's. And there she was. *Rachel Trask. Daughter of Ralph and Edna.* My future in-laws, God willing. I'd have to send them a nice thank-you note on her birthday. Local girl. I saw with a shock that she had been a police officer for less than five years. But in that time, she had racked up some pretty impressive credentials. Undercover work. Drug rings. Smugglers. Swift promotion. Medals and commendations. No wonder she was already a Lieutenant.

I snapped the book shut and sprinted across the squishy Quadrangle to my lab.

One minute late, and no one complained.

Fifty-four

The afternoon lab passed in an uneventful repeat of the morning session. Carts rolled, springs sprang, planes inclined. There are times when I think that physics was developed primarily as an excuse to keep playing with toys well into adulthood.

By the time the last student had left at five o'clock, I was tired and hungry. Mondays are long days for me. Fencing class. The stay-awake Olympics with Soper. The morning lab. Mid-afternoon arguments with brain-dead FBI agents. They all take their toll on a growing boy.

Unfortunately, I couldn't leave immediately. All the equipment had to be packed up and trucked down to the first-floor lab for tomorrow morning's class, thanks to the miracle of anti-common-sense university scheduling.

I picked up three large cardboard boxes full of equipment, one on top of the other, determined to move them all in one trip. As I neared the stairs, however, the topmost box began coasting sideways and, wiggle as I might to stabilize it, it slid off and crashed to the floor.

I was treated to the sight of a hundred and sixty-two springs all springing madly in every direction. It was like a cartoon show. For a moment, I actually enjoyed this as a wonderful demonstration of random motion, until I realized that I had to pick them all up again. And then I made my discovery.

One of the springs was bouncing and flipping crazily—but not on the ground. As I watched with astonishment, I saw that it was performing its antics hovering in mid-air about five inches above the floor, near the top stair. My God, I thought, I've discovered anti-gravity. It involves springs.

The spring's motion dampened and stopped, and it just hung there suspended in space. I could not believe it. I was mentally rehearsing my Nobel Prize acceptance speech when I almost involuntarily reached out to touch the spring. When I did, I noticed it resisted my touch. Almost as if it were attached to something. It was only then that I saw the thread.

A nearly-invisible black thread was stretched tautly across the top step, tied to a banister post of the staircase at one end and to a small eye-bolt screwed into the wall at the other end. I touched the thread and was surprised to find that it was incredibly strong and nearly unbreakable.

I thought, Wow, it's a good thing I noticed that before I tripped over it.

And fell down the stairs to my death.

Well, maybe not to my death. But falling headlong down a flight of stone and metal steps would definitely have caused—what? Broken arm? Collarbone? Concussion? It would surely have taken me out of action for the rest of the physics season.

And then it all slowly dawned on me. Somebody *put* this thread here. Deliberately. After all the students had gone. In this building which was pretty much empty except for me. Precisely *to* trip someone—me?—down the stairs and injure them, perhaps kill them.

By falling.

An icy finger traced down my spine. Dieter Bunt. Dieter Bunt had been here. Dieter Bunt might still be here, somewhere. In fact, Dieter Bunt might be waiting at the bottom of the stairs, waiting for me to trip and fall so he could finish me off with his golf club. If so, I now had a golden opportunity to try and catch him.

I didn't hesitate. I flung the other two boxes to the side, producing a hell of a crash. At the same time, I yelled as if in pain, vaulted over the thread, and descended the stairs to the half-way landing as quickly as possible. I glimpsed a figure on the floor below emerge from the shadows and then draw back again. He was there. But he had seen I had not really fallen. He was escaping.

I leaped down the stairs to the bottom then but, not being Stan, tripped and fell sprawling onto the floor. Ignoring my own injury, I twisted my head sideways to see down the corridor. But I only caught an impression of someone rounding the corner at the far end of the hall, toward the other stairway. I had no doubt that this had been the murderer. But I had seen no details of him whatever.

I got to my feet and limped down the hall in a sorry imitation of pursuit. I looked down over the edge of the other stairway, but I could see no one. He was not stupid enough to look up to see if I was following him, unfortunately. I heard the front door of the building bang shut.

Had he left? Or was that someone else? There was no way to tell.

When I was satisfied there was nothing more to see, I turned my attention to myself. I was not hurt badly. My ankle felt a little twisted, but not badly. As I was brushing myself off, I looked up to see Dr. Wilhelm turning the corner toward me.

He almost never spoke to me at all, and this time was no exception, giving me only a brief nod of acknowledgment as he passed. I watched him closely as he continued on down the corridor. Dr. Wilhelm was in his 60s, tall and gaunt, with a light frosting of gray hair. He seemed to have a slight limp.

Dr. Wilhelm?

Part of me immediately thought it was ridiculous. Dr. Wilhelm a Nazi war criminal? A spy? A murderer? No way.

Then another part of me thought, *Someone* was a murderer. That is the whole nature of mysteries, after all. *Someone* is not what they seem. *Someone* has done something, and no one knows that they have. Dismissing suspects on the grounds that you don't know if they have done the crime makes no sense.

And he had been arguing with Speen that afternoon, before I interrupted. What was that about?

And poking around Speen's office with the lights off today. Where did that fit in?

Dr. Wilhelm.

Maybe.

Maybe he had set that little trap for me. Waiting in the corridor would seem very natural to anyone coming by. He could have run down the corridor, then walked back slowly. Easy.

I would have to keep my eye on him. And Axalt. And Mr. Andersson. And Mrs. Arden. Good thing I wore glasses.

I walked back upstairs. The equipment from the boxes was all over the floor. As I repacked the boxes I was both triumphant when I realized there actually was a murderer still present and still trying to get people to fall— confirming my Dieter Bunt theory— and dejected that I had missed an opportunity to capture, or at least see, him.

After removing the thread, and moving the boxes downstairs without further incident, I called Rachel. She was astonished and gratifyingly concerned at my story. She agreed that this gave new urgency to finding the murderer. She also seemed to think that this confirmed the existence of Dieter Bunt. But she seemed most interested in me and my well-being. Her concern warmed me considerably, but I did try to down-play the incident to seem brave to her.

"Take care of yourself," she admonished me when we were done speaking. I hung up the phone with a sweet feeling for her.

The feeling was erased a moment later.

Someone was trying to kill me.

Fifty-five

After dinner, I went to the library to prepare for my professorial debut tomorrow afternoon. I felt both excited and blasé about this. I still figured that I had nothing to lose. And I even had an idea about how we might all salvage this semester from the dumpster.

My near-fall this afternoon was very much with me. Besides the mild ache in my ankle, I found myself constantly aware of things above me and below me. I scanned the roofs of buildings and the overhanging branches of trees. I examined staircases minutely, above, below, and on each step. Every time someone walked past me, my head snapped up.

As I walked home around eleven, I remembered my conversation with Dr. Wolff. This Bunt was dangerous. I was tempted to call him back, to tell him everything. I had the feeling that he was part of some organization of dedicated Nazi hunters. Maybe they could parachute into Kingstown and scour it clean of Bunts and any other nasties.

But I was hesitant. Partly because I wanted to solve this myself. Something to do with Rachel maybe, but more to do with me. This was a problem, not a physics problem, but like a physics problem. Finding the unknown. Uncovering the hidden. It was, I had to admit, exciting. Like the delicious thrill of discovery, of finding the answer, of *knowing*.

It was also partly because I was afraid they would mess it up. Here was this guy on the run for thirty years. He's on his guard anyway, because he's just had to kill somebody to hide his tracks. And suddenly here come all these strangers swooping in on the campus, poking around, asking questions. He would be gone. Again. And no justice would get done.

But I was a known quantity to him. I was no stranger to the campus. Maybe he felt like he could handle me, that he might be able to salvage his cover.

In any event, I decided not to call Dr. Wolff. Yet.

But I would definitely follow his advice. When I reached my apartment building, I examined the upper landings for looming cinder-blocks very carefully before I ventured inside.

Fifty-six

Before dropping off to sleep, I had an odd thought. Today was Monday. That wasn't the odd part. The murder had occurred on last Thursday evening. That wasn't the odd part either. What was odd was that it had taken this long for somebody to make a try for me.

Think about it. The murder had happened Thursday afternoon. The murderer had realized from the books in Jackson's office that Jackson might be a threat, and had struck again on Friday night. He had pretty nearly succeeded, too.

But the murderer had learned about my involvement at the same time. There had been plenty of time to set up something against me since then. I had been in and around the physics department and other campus buildings on Friday, Saturday, and Sunday. Why wait until Monday? What was special about today?

I couldn't think of anything. My schedule had been pretty much the same as always. Indeed, my schedule was so predictable that it was farcically simple to set booby traps like the thread-at-the-top-of-the-stairs trick.

The only difference I could see had been my meeting with Rachel. But I had met with her on Saturday and Sunday too, so that couldn't be it.

Except today Stickney had been there. Did that make a difference? I half sat up in bed. Here was an interesting sequence of events. I get involved with a murderer on Thursday. Nothing whatever happens to me. The day that Stickney arrives, a low-level attempt is made on me. Post hoc, ergo propter hoc? After Stickney, therefore because of Stickney?

I had had a strange feeling about him since we met. Could he be one of those people Dr. Wolff had warned about? People who actually help Nazis escape? I had pretty much given the game away today, telling him all my suspicions about Bunt. I had even told him about Bunt's obsession with falling, if he didn't know it already.

How difficult would it be to follow me back to the department and rig that trap? It's not like this required major special effects—an eye-bolt and a thread. Finding out my schedule would take about twelve seconds at the bulletin board.

I lay back again. Maybe I was getting ahead of myself, here. All I really had to go on was my negative feeling about Stickney. Not much. Especially given that my feelings about people were usually so off-base. The whole problem here was that it was too easy to get paranoid about things like murder attempts.

I closed my eyes. Ready to drop off to sleep. Or whatever.

I snapped my eyes open again. Feeling or no feeling, I'd been attacked the very day that Stickney arrived.

Tuesday

Fifty-seven

On Tuesday afternoon, I was sitting in my usual seat in our now Speenless electromagnetic theory class. At two o'clock, I stood up and walked to the front of the class.

"I've been asked to continue the course since the death of Dr. Speen," I began.

Peter smiled. "Cool," he said. I had never heard him speak in class before.

The Four Asian Students looked alarmed. They may have been thinking that they were all in fairly deep dung with me because they had denounced me to the police as Speen's murderer. Now here I was, their new instructor. Not a good position to be in. I hoped it would teach them a lesson, although exactly what that lesson might be I couldn't say.

I continued. "Obviously I don't know any more about this subject than you do, and I may well know less. I also feel that we've all been lost pretty much from the beginning of the semester."

Peter nodded vigorously. The Four seemed to give grudging assent.

"I'd just as soon give everyone A's and bag the course altogether. Unfortunately Dr. Axalt is going to administer a final exam to us from a previous year, based on the whole course."

Everyone looked demoralized at the prospect. I wasn't too thrilled myself.

"So, here's what I think we should do. There are twelve classes left until the end of the semester. The whole course covers twenty-four chapters, of which we've supposedly covered fifteen by now. I say we start over again from the beginning, and cover two chapters per class until we're done."

They sat there stunned. I didn't blame them. We had been covering less than a chapter a day so far, with minimal comprehension.

I went on. "Everyone will share whatever notes, books, information or insights they have. Everyone will share their homework. No one is going to be left behind. Either we all make it together, or we all blow it together."

I turned to the blackboard and wrote, "From each according to their abilities, to each according to their needs." It seemed appropriate.

I turned back to them. "So, what do you think? Are we going to do this together, or are we going to give up?"

Peter shook his head. "We have to go for it. We have no other choice."

I addressed the Four Asian Students directly. "What do you think? Yes or no?"

Astonishingly, they answered one by one. They each said, "Yes."

"All right," I said, looking at each person separately for a moment. "Let's do it."

Peter was avidly turning the pages of his book. So were all of the Four, except one. She was looking at me in a way I found most interesting. I smiled at her.

I opened the textbook on the desk in front of me.

"Chapter One."

Fifty-eight

Class went 30 minutes over. We read the book. We gave interpretations. We argued over meanings. We found examples. We covered two chapters.

By the end, I was pretty wiped out from the strain of moderating the whole thing, and the sheer brainwork of trying to comprehend it all and share that understanding. We divided up all the homework for the two chapters, and agreed to photocopy all our work so everyone could have it. When I left, Peter was offering to buy beers for the Four at the Pub.

I would have joined him, except that I still had a heap of grading to complete for one of the professors. I decided to use one of the empty labs on the fifth floor, figuring I wouldn't be disturbed. I often used them for grading after hours since they were always quiet and unused.

I passed Dr. Berger on the way up, and gave him a surreptitious once-over. He was in his 50s, thin and athletic, like a runner. He always said hi to me, as he did now.

I didn't really suspect him. He was from Iowa, after all. Wilhelm was from New Jersey, supposedly. On the other hand, wouldn't Dieter Bunt cook up some plausible past to hide the truth? Wouldn't he claim to be from Iowa, too?

I decided to keep an eye on him just in case. Problem was, I was rapidly running out of eyes.

Up in the lab, I turned on the lights and shut the door. It was eerily still. Students abandoned the physics building as soon as humanly possible, leaving it a silent and empty shell. Just right for grading.

I had one hundred and twenty homework assignments that had been due a week ago. I began going through them as quickly as possible. You'd be surprised how efficiently you can do things like this. You just scan for certain key words or phrases or equations that indicate some grasp of the problem, check them and move on.

By five o'clock, I had already finished forty or so papers. I got up and stretched, then wandered out for a drink of water and a pee. Returning, I shut the door behind me again.

Around quarter of six, I looked up. I thought I had heard something outside the door. Janitors bumping around, probably. I noticed it was already full dark outside the two windows at the far end of the room.

I began grading again, then stopped. I smelled something strange. What was that? I took a deep sniff, but couldn't get anything meaningful. I started grading again.

I stopped. I smelled the something again, stronger. It was gas! Each of these labs had little spigots at each table for natural gas to run Bunsen burners. I rarely had occasion to use them myself. Could one of the gas jets be on? It didn't seem likely. I had been in this room for almost two hours. If one were open, I'd have noticed it before now. They couldn't just open on their own. I must be mistaken. I ignored the smell.

After a few more minutes, I couldn't ignore it. The smell was too obvious. There was definitely gas in the room. Somehow. I walked all around the room, checking every gas jet. None of them was open, but I opened and shut them all anyway. Then I sat down and waited for the smell to abate.

But it didn't abate. It just got worse. Gas was getting into the room, but not from the gas jets. Okay, genius, figure it out. Where was it coming from? And, more important, how to make it stop?

Maybe the pipe connecting to the gas jets had a leak. I traced it from where it rose up from the floor. I kept my head close to it, to smell or hear escaping gas. I followed it to the end of the lab benches. No leak that I could find.

The smell was getting quite strong now, and I was actually having a little trouble breathing. I couldn't find the source, I decided. I'd better just leave the room, and call the fire department or the police or somebody.

The door was locked.

No, not locked, for the doorknob rotated freely in my hand. But when I pushed against the door, it wouldn't open. I pulled. I pushed. I pulled and pushed. I stood back as far as my hand on the doorknob would allow, then slammed myself forward into the door. It hurt, and it rattled my vision a little, but the door didn't budge.

The gas was quite obvious by now, and was definitely interfering with my breathing. The fact floated into my head that natural gas is actually odorless. They add a special chemical called mercaptan to the gas so you can smell it. I didn't see how this would help me. It was just one of those useless pieces of information to which my brain busily devoted space that would be better used for storing alternate exits from rooms filling with gas.

I was calm. Or as calm as you can be when you're getting panicky and trying to reassure yourself that you're actually calm. There was, after all, another door to the room. I stepped to it and turned the handle. It turned easily and I relaxed. I pushed on the door. It moved perhaps a quarter of an inch, then hit something large and solid and stopped dead. With a lick of fear, I realized that the vacuum compressor was on the other side of the door. It shouldn't be, but it was. It was a large steel machine and must weigh four hundred pounds. It was mounted on wheels for easier transport, but the wheels could be retracted, so that it sat directly on the floor. A few whangs of the door into the machine satisfied me that it was not, in fact, moving in any perceptible way.

I was now feeling dizzy from the gas. Where was it coming from? Why? Why were the doors blocked? These questions skidded through my mind, but I didn't address them. As the Buddha said, when you get shot with an arrow, your first concern is not the color of the hair of the man who shot the arrow: first, you want to get the arrow out.

My eyes flicked around the room and rested with relief on the window marked "Fire Exit". A metal fire escape ran up this side of the building. I imagined climbing down a skeletal and probably shaky metal fire escape from five stories up. Probably slippery with ice, too. My palms began to sweat. I hate heights.

I clamped my teeth shut with resolution and determination. Better to be scared witless for the few minutes it would take for me to reach the ground safely, than to suffocate in here. Better, but not good. Like Jackson in the hospital.

I reached the window, undid the latch and pushed it open. At least, I pushed it. The "open" part didn't occur. Just stuck, I thought, and pushed harder, then struck it with my hand, hard. It didn't move.

It was only then that I noticed the shiny heads of nails all around the frame of the window.

My heart pounded as I realized someone had nailed the window shut.

I gazed wildly at the nails. Even if I had had a hammer, it would take me an hour to get all those nails out. I didn't have a hammer. I didn't have an hour, either. I knew that from the way the room was beginning to whirl around me.

Air. I needed air. I turned to the other window. I saw with relief that it was not nailed shut. I undid the latch and threw it open. It only opened about a foot, but I didn't care. I stuck my head and shoulders out the window and drank in the clear frigid air. I coughed out gas and kept breathing in great heaves until I felt myself returning to normal again.

I looked down from this window and immediately regretted it. It was a sheer five-story drop to the same sidewalk Speen had hit. I had to find another way to escape.

I tried to sort it all out. The two doors were blocked. The fire escape window was nailed shut. Now why had this window only opened a foot? I pulled my head out of the window and was immediately assaulted by the gas. I shut the window and looked around it minutely. There were two nails pounded halfway into the slot the window fit into. They prevented the window from being raised more than a foot. The nails looked just like the ones in the other window frame.

I opened the window again and stuck my head out so I could breathe while I thought. This was deliberate. Someone had blocked the doors. Someone had piped gas into the room, somehow. Someone had nailed the windows shut some time recently, but allowed this one to stay open. A little.

Who had done it was obvious. Only one person was actively trying to kill me, as far as I knew. Dieter Bunt, or whatever he was calling himself now. The fact that I often used this lab for grading seemed to confirm the idea that he was someone in the physics department who knew my habits. But this didn't seem like his style, if I could contemplate such niceties as style in a room rapidly filling with flammable gas. He liked to kill people by falling.

And then I understood.

The gas. The doors. The windows.

He was trying to get me to jump.

This slightly open window was my only means of escape. If dropping five stories to one's squashing could be considered escape. I couldn't open it enough to dissipate the gas in the room, only enough to squeeze my body through. He wanted me to panic to the extent that I would be desperate enough to try dropping from that window.

I immediately resolved that that was not an option. I might die up here anyway, but I wasn't going to satisfy his demented program in the process.

As I thought about it, I began to think there might not be any urgency to this after all. I could see only three possible dangers from the gas. First was suffocation. Well, as long as I could stick my head out this window I could breathe just fine. It was a little awkward, but not as awkward as, say, falling to your death. Second was fire. I had no personal plans to light a fire in this room anytime soon. Since the doors and windows were shut tight, I didn't see how anybody else would have the opportunity either. Third was explosion. If an electrical spark, say, were to ignite the gas it might well explode. Not good. But again, I didn't see any danger to me. I had no electrical devices running in the room. The lights were on, it was true, but unless they were turned off and on and produced a spark that way, I had nothing to worry about. I certainly wasn't about to start flicking them off and on myself. And again, since no one else could get into the room, I had nothing to fear from that contingency.

I calmed down considerably. I would just wait here until someone opened the door. Or until someone saw me from the street. It would be dull. It would be uncomfortable. But I would survive. I would not jump out the window. Dieter Bunt would be defeated.

I took some pride in the fact that my ability to reason logically about the situation had removed the possibility of panic and danger to myself. He had not counted on dealing with someone like me. I had outwitted Dieter Bunt, I thought smugly.

The lights went out. And, a second later, flicked back on again.

My heart stopped.

He was turning the lights off and on from outside the room!

The fuse box in the basement. He must be pulling and replacing the fuse for the room lights.

He was going to detonate the gas himself.

My calm shattered. I had to get out of here. Now.

My first thought was for that fire escape window. I saw a metal rod near the door. I left the window and grabbed it. I ran with it to the window. The lights flicked off again as I ran, and I collided painfully with the corner of a lab bench.

At the window, I took aim, swung the rod back, and smashed it directly into one of the panes of glass.

Nothing happened.

My brain did not register this immediately, as I was already on the backswing again, striking the same pane a crashing blow.

Nothing.

This was not happening.

I dropped the rod helplessly and examined the window. It was Plexiglas. Reinforced with wire mesh. I suddenly remembered talk of concern a few years ago about break-ins at the physics building, and the measures taken to fortify the building against intruders.

I examined the other window and saw that it was the same indestructible stuff. I would never get through them.

I was staggering from the gas now. I stuck my head out the open window again for a few hits of oxygen. The lights flashed off and on behind me.

In a moment of perception, I could see Mr. Andersson's house very clearly across the street. It was dark except for the dancing bluish images from a television. I thought I could even make out his form seated on a couch. "Mr. Andersson," I tried to yell, but I had no voice. If only he would come out of his house, I might get his attention somehow. How ironic if this scourge of humanity were able to help me! I ruefully thought that here was one suspect I could eliminate from my list. If I weren't eliminated first.

But he didn't come out. And I did not think I could dally waiting for him.

The door, I thought. It was my only hope. If I could get that door open. But how? What was keeping it closed in the first place?

I took four big breaths, then inhaled as much as I could and held it. I went and picked up the rod again. I walked to the door and whacked it for all I was worth. Nothing. It was solid wood. It wasn't going anywhere. I dropped the rod helplessly.

As I bent to pick it up again, I had a sudden inspiration. I sprawled on my face and tried to look under the door. Something was beneath the door.

I stood up. How could I see better?

The lights flashed on and off again. I knew I was living on borrowed time. At any moment one of these light bulbs would blow out, make a spark, and that would be it. The room would go boom—and me with it.

I took a quick breath at the window, then crossed to a metal storage cabinet, which I wrenched open. When the lights flicked on I saw what I wanted, in with the optics equipment: a mirror. I grabbed it and knelt in front of the door.

I placed one edge of the mirror on the floor, and angled it so that I could see under the door. There were five or six dark rectangles and four or five dark circles under the door. The gas was choking me again, and stinging my eyes, too. I gently laid the mirror down and dashed to the window.

I gulped in air as I thought. Circles and rectangles. Circles and rectangles. A hose. Hoses. The circles were almost certainly hoses, pumping gas into the room. And the rectangles? Doorstops! Rubber doorstops! No wonder I couldn't push the door open. Every push only wedged it tighter.

I left the window. I pulled the door tightly closed, hoping to loosen it from some of the doorstops. I picked up the rod and the mirror. Holding the mirror with my left hand and the rod with my right, I tried to poke at the hoses and the doorstops. It was hopelessly clumsy. Being right-handed, I could not control the mirror well with my left hand. It was hard to look down into the mirror and poke sideways along the floor with the rod. And everything in the mirror was backwards. It was oddly like playing a strange video game, with demented controls and a deadly outcome.

I finally was able to line up the rod on one of the circles. I jammed it hard. Nothing happened. I lined it up again, and thrust it hard. It hit, and popped away from the door. In the mirror, I could see I had dislodged one of the hoses. But I had to stop to breathe.

I crawled on hands and knees to the window, then back again. I quickly set up my equipment and repeated my actions. I dislodged another hose. The lights were flicking on and off continuously now, and the effect made me even more dizzy and disoriented. I persisted, and got another hose loose before I had to lunge for the window.

Back again, I worked on a doorstop. They were harder, wedged in, their sloping surface throwing the rod off again and again. I was getting used to seeing things backwards in the mirror, though, and hit repeatedly until I pounded one loose.

Another gulp of air and I got the last hose out. The room was still full of gas, but at least no more could enter.

I worked on the doorstops continuously now. Four left. The lights flashed. I drooped dizzily over the mirror. I thrust back and forth unceasingly. Three left. Two. I wiped sweat from my forehead. One. One left. I heard an ominous sizzling noise coming from one of the lights above me. I didn't dare to stop and look.

Done! The last doorstop disappeared. I stood up groggily, but forced myself to open the door slowly, not wanting to jam it again.

It opened an inch, two, four. I jammed my face against the opening to breathe. Air never tasted so sweet. Six inches. Nine. I jammed my arm, shoulder, head, and body through the space.

I collapsed onto the floor, doing nothing but breathe for several minutes. At one point, I stretched out a foot and shut the door. Just in case.

When I felt slightly recovered, I got to my feet. It was quite an undertaking. I felt drunk and my legs were no longer cooperating. I saw that five black rubber hoses stretched from the next lab. When I went into that lab, I saw that they were connected to gas jets turned full on. I turned them all off and pulled the hoses loose.

I opened the door of my lab wide, then scampered around the corner to the men's room where I doused my face with cold water. I looked at myself in the mirror. Two lives down, pal, I told myself. How many more have you got?

When I eventually and hesitantly returned to the room, I noticed the lights were full on. He had stopped. He had given up. He knew that I had escaped. He was gone.

I sniffed deeply. The gas smell was gone now, dissipated by the draft from the door and window. I sat down in a chair and glanced around the lab, which now seemed utterly normal.

A light bulb overhead popped and blew out.

Fifty-nine

So, what do *you* do after surviving yet another murder attempt on your life?

Myself, I notified a certain police lieutenant I was in love with, then went to the movies.

Rachel was even more astonished and concerned than she had been before. Quite gratifying. I assured her that, other than having developed a sudden and intense determination to always use electric stoves, I was fine. She informed me that she would have police investigators at the physics building immediately, and I should stay there.

I balked at this. I didn't want the police crawling all over me, especially if she wasn't among them. Besides, I doubted if this guy had left any fingerprints anywhere. She relented, and I gave her a very full statement of what had occurred.

She didn't really understand—a very common occurrence in my life— but she agreed to go along with my wishes—a very unusual occurrence in my life. She would pass my information to the investigators, who would provide her with their results, which she could then piece together with my account.

I dearly wanted to ask her if she knew Stickney's whereabouts during my ordeal, but I held off asking her. I didn't want to push my luck with my theories.

When we were done with the official stuff she wished me goodnight and urged me to be careful, but didn't give me any details about what alleged commitment was keeping her from accompanying me to the movies. Drat.

Sixty

After dinner, during which I kept my recent adventures secret from my friends also, I decided to go to the movies anyway. Why not? I wasn't going to call off the rest of my life just because of this espionage-Nazi-murder stuff. Besides, it was right on campus, in Edgar Auditorium, and only a buck.

Finding people to go to the movies was always problematic for a gentleman of my description. Ben was usually broke. Stan preferred Clint Eastwood movies with high body counts. I had once talked Lisa into joining me, but when she later learned that the movie we had watched was rated R she said she felt like a tainted woman. Lee had always preferred movies with subtitles: she often argued with the translations. As for the other 2 billion women on earth, the less said the better.

Thus, I found myself attending the 9 o'clock showing of "Let It Be" solo.

While leaving the lobby to enter the theater itself, I was surprised to see the Four Asian Students lined up to buy tickets. I somehow didn't picture them as Beatles fans. I was even more surprised when that same female of the crew gave me a surreptitious wave, out of sight of the others. She was cute. I had always supposed her to be going with one of the male associates of the troupe (or the other female one, for that matter), so I had expended no effort regarding her. Her recent friendliness to me indicated some possible interest on her part. Her name, I suspected strongly, was Xiao Xia. Even if I were certain, however, I would not have tried to pronounce it without professional assistance.

I made my way up to the balcony. Not only did I prefer watching movies from up here, but, life being what it was these days, I also felt that it was safer than sitting *below* the balcony, cinder-block-wise. To keep from being hurled from the balcony itself, I sat in the middle of a row that was eight rows back from the edge. I kept one hand gripped on the arm-rest, too, just in case.

The lights lowered and the movie began. Soon immersed in the day-to-day life of the Beatles completing one of their last albums, I hardly noticed my darkened surroundings.

Suddenly someone climbed over the back of the seat to my right, and dropped down abruptly beside me. I leapt a foot, and raised my hands to fend off an attack by Dieter Bunt, but was even more startled to see by the flickering screen light that it was the female Asian student who had waved to me.

She leaned toward me in a vivacious way and whispered, "Hi."

"Hi," I managed to whisper back.

I relaxed somewhat. Though still surprised, I did not seem to be in any immediate danger. No matter how wild my imaginings, I did not suspect her of being Dieter Bunt. She was one of the few.

We both watched the movie for a few seconds. Then she leaned toward me again and whispered, "I like the Beatles."

I was startled by this, too, then realized that I would be startled by almost anything she said. The whole situation was startling. "Me, too," I replied.

We watched the movie some more. Her English was perfect, and I was beginning to wonder if she might not be from Des Moines, rather than Kowloon as I had imagined. I was seized by a new curiosity, and found a diplomatic way to satisfy it.

"I've never really introduced myself," I whispered to her, extending my right hand. "I'm Mark Napoli."

She took my right hand in her left hand and settled both our elbows onto the arm-rest. We were now officially holding hands. Her hand was light and warm and dry. I liked holding it.

"I'm Xiao Xia," she whispered back.

If I had to spell out what she said to me, I would say it was "show" (to rhyme with "how") "sha" (to rhyme with "ha"). But the sound she made in my ear was like that of a satin slipper stepping gracefully along an exquisite marble hall, rich in mystery and enticement.

We talked in low whispers about the Beatles for a bit, then just watched the movie in silence. Between her hand and her whispers and her very female presence itself, I felt a delicious thrill. And she had come to me. She had sought me out and boldly, almost outrageously, dropped in on me. It was all almost unbearably exciting.

Finally, she turned to me and whispered, "I have to go back to the others now. They think I'm in the ladies room." She giggled mischievously at the trick she was playing, and I joined her.

Then she suddenly lifted her face to mine and kissed me lightly on the cheek. She squeezed my hand, let go, and walked smoothly down the row and was gone in the darkness.

I sat back in my seat. I was positively vibrating from the experience. My hand, my ear, my cheek were glowing from my contact with her. What could it mean? I found her tremendously attractive and exciting. Perhaps most exciting was that she had approached me. Why now, all of a sudden? A thought popped into my head. Back in the saddle again. My gosh, could all this be due to a haircut and a trimmed beard? If so, Lisa deserved a Nobel Prize in Male-Female Relationships.

I slouched down, hardly noticing the movie, so intent was I in spinning out the possibilities of something happening with Xiao Xia. Xiao Xia. What a strange and mysterious name. XX. Two unknowns. Doubly unknown. And to think that only this afternoon we had been virtual strangers to each other, in the same classroom for months, yet only now...

I lurched bolt upright in my seat.

She was my student now!

I was her instructor!

I had been holding hands with a student!

Whispering and giggling with a student!

Kissed by a student!

I looked wildly around the balcony. Had anyone seen? Did anyone know? I could hardly make out a thing in the darkness. Vague suggestions of heads and shoulders. It seemed unlikely that anyone could have seen us, much less identified us.

My mind replayed the whole scene with her. Had I said anything suggestive to her? It all seemed pretty innocent. But the physical contact! I had hesitated at *dancing* with a student the other night. What about holding hands? Or kissing?

Suddenly the image of Stan loomed in my mind. What's the big deal, he wanted to know. She approached you. You were surprised by her actions. You did nothing to encourage her.

Right. And did nothing to *dis*courage her either. I shook my head. Sorry, Stan, you're not winning this one. I'm nipping this in the bud, as of now. I will be very much on my guard against Ms. Xia. I will be very much the detached and impartial instructor.

I relaxed a little. I had come to my senses in time. Nothing disastrous had yet occurred. I knew what was going on, and what I was doing about it.

Still, considering the last few days, between Stephanie, Rachel Trask, Lisa, and now Xiao Xia, I had had more action, or at least apparent action, in the past week than in the previous year.

I couldn't help but wonder if someone was slipping something into the Kingstown water supply.

Wednesday

▼

Sixty-one

Wednesday morning dawned sunny and warm.

Somewhere.

Here, it was grim. Some absurd snow-rain-wind-ice mixture was falling in sloppy bucketfuls and it was indescribably awful.

I couldn't start my car, and couldn't push-start it through the slush, so I had to hoof it to campus. My clothes were soaked and freezing within seconds, and I returned to the apartment for dry clothes. Not to wear, but to bring with me so that I could change when I got to the physics building. If I got to the physics building. It seemed more likely that they would find my frozen body in the spring, after the glaciers receded.

The cracks in the soles of my boots squirted about a pint of gelid liquid onto my feet with every step. I kept taking off and putting on my glasses. When I put them on, they quickly accumulated snow, ice and rain and it was impossible to see. When I took them off, the same crap hit my eyeballs, and it was impossible to see then, either. Icicles were forming in my beard.

When I finally slogged up the steps and stomped the snow from my boots in the warm dry entrance hall of the building, I felt like a visitor from another and more hostile planet. I directed a malevolent gaze at the goop currently glazing the outer regions, and wondered what on earth had ever induced people to settle here. Couldn't the Pilgrims take a hint? And what had been the big urge for anthropoids to leave Africa in the first place?

I squished down to Jackson's office, locked the door, and changed out of my wet things, hanging them to dry near the furnace, and trying not to befoul any of Jackson's belongings.

No matter what class I was in that day, I felt it was paradise compared to the arctic lunacy transpiring outside. True, I kept my eye very assiduously on anyone who came within six feet of me, and examined staircases closely before committing my toes to them. Still, I thought, even if someone attacks me today, at least I'll be warm.

Between classes, I visited Mrs. Arden in the office. I had a theory I wanted to test about our newly resident federal ape, Payne Stickney. Something else strange about him to add to my file.

He had arrived on Monday, in time to possibly lay a trap for me at the top of a staircase, as you recall. Since then, I hadn't seen one atom of the guy. Not that I was complaining, exactly. It just seemed odd to me that this FBI agent, supposedly here expressly to investigate espionage within the physics department, had not yet set foot inside the building.

At least, that's what I thought. Mrs. Arden, the all-knowing and all-seeing, would have the facts.

After a few opening pleasantries, I got down to cases. "Anybody from the FBI been around here since Dr. Speen's murder?" I wondered.

She squinted her eyes and tipped her head on one side. "The FBI? What for?"

I shrugged casually. "Well, I thought that Dr. Speen did government work of some kind. I thought they might send someone to get his papers or something."

She shook her head emphatically. "No, no one like that. The police were here when it first happened, and then later when they interviewed everyone. But no one's been by since then."

"Maybe they wouldn't let on they were with the FBI," I suggested. "Maybe someone poking around, or asking questions."

"No," she stated flatly. "I would have noticed."

"Just curious," I smiled, and left her.

I walked out of her office with satisfaction. Just as I thought. Some big expert. He doesn't even check out the scene of the crime. What has he been doing here, then? Maybe getting in touch with Dieter Bunt some-how? Maybe arranging a little gas attack last night?

Something was rotten in the state of Kingstown, and its name was Stickney.

Sixty-two

The weather was such that I was extremely reluctant even to go to lunch, and only the prospect of eating a meal that did not involve waffles pried me out that door.

The dining hall was nearly deserted, not many souls being as hardy as I. Stan was present, dutifully shoveling it in. The rest of his classes had been canceled for the day, so he was in high spirits. I ate as many warming dishes as I could, then trudged back up the hill to the lab I had to teach. I switched clothes with the now-dry ones near the furnace.

Attendance was low, and I resolved not to penalize anybody who had shown more sense than I and stayed home. I abbreviated the lab considerably for those present, and we all got out a good hour earlier than usual.

Since this day seemed to be a total waste of my time, my thoughts naturally turned to Speen. I still hadn't gone to his office to see if he might have had anything that would actually be useful to the students in his electromagnetic theory class. It seemed a long shot, but I didn't have any better way of spending the afternoon.

I trudged up the stairs to his office and used the key Mrs. Arden had given me to unlock the door. I felt a little thrill about this, something to do with violating his space, but being perfectly justified in doing so. It was like being given a license to steal.

The thrill evaporated quickly, however. Staring around the crammed disorder of his office, I felt dispirited. Somewhere in this mess there might be something of value, but it was clearly going to involve more effort than I had hoped.

I figured that any material for the classes he was teaching he would keep close to hand, on or around his desk. I sat in his desk chair and felt prickles of unease as I did so. I wanted to get this over with.

There were some scattered piles of papers and file folders on his desk. After skimming through them, I concluded there was nothing of value for me. The desk drawers held the usual litter of office life and I slammed them all shut. The bookshelves nearest my head seemed more promising. I found a copy of our textbook right off, and next to it, the fabled Landau. Pulling Landau loose dislodged an accordion file that I just managed to catch in my lap before it spilled onto the floor. It was labeled "E+M 2".

Grail.

I took the file and stood up. I didn't want to keep sitting in his seat. I also didn't want to do this in my office, in case I needed more of Speen's stuff. I turned a slow circle in the middle of his office and finally spotted another chair behind the open door, buried in back issues of the Physical Review. I moved these into piles around the floor of his office, slammed the door shut, and sat down.

Speen actually had good handwriting when he wasn't writing for students. I could read through his lecture notes for the course with no trouble at all. As I had suspected, he had complete references to Landau and other sources sprinkled throughout his own notes. He just didn't see fit to share this information with his class. One might wonder why on earth a man would create detailed notes for teaching students, and then not actually give that material to the students. I didn't wonder, though. I had known Speen.

I was making little arrow notations in the margins of his notes to mark items to point out to the class, when I heard a key being inserted in the office door. There was a click, the doorknob turned, and the door swung inwards. It was beginning to look a lot like other people shared my thrill at breaking into Speen's office.

The chair I was in was behind the opened door, so whoever came in didn't see me. As he absentmindedly shoved the door closed with one hand while making a beeline for Speen's filing cabinets on the opposite side of the room, he didn't see me then either. But I had a fine view of his back as he grabbed the top drawer of the first filing cabinet and pulled it open.

It was Dr. Wilhelm. Wilhelm, who had argued with Speen just before the murder. Wilhelm, who had been sneaking out of Speen's office only a few days ago. Wilhelm, who had been present and accounted for, when I had almost been offed the other evening. Wilhelm, who had broken out of the pack and was now emerging as the candidate most likely to be Dieter Bunt.

Whatever he was looking for, he was certainly searching intently for it. What else could it be, but some incriminating document that had been overlooked somehow? Some ace in the hole that Speen had been keeping, but never had a chance to use. Finding, say, a single piece of paper in this mess of an office was worse than looking for a needle in a haystack. But I was willing to watch Wilhelm do it anyway.

You see, if he really was looking for something incriminating, it made more sense for me to let him find it than to stop him. After all, he had a better idea of what he was looking for than I did. All I had to do was keep my breathing quiet and wait.

As I sat watching him, I did sketch out a Plan B. After all, this guy had clubbed Speen into unconsciousness, then dumped him out a window. If he made any move toward me, I would be up and out that door before he could catch me.

He soon finished with the first drawer and started on the second. There were four drawers in that filing cabinet, and two more filing cabinets. I settled myself more comfortably in my seat. I would have given ten bucks to clear my throat.

So the long day wore on, so to speak. Drawer number two eventually gave way to drawer number three. That drawer seemed sparse from my angle, and Wilhelm finished it off fairly rapidly. The bottom drawer was empty. He slammed it shut with his foot and gave a long stretch during which I was sure he would look around and spot me.

He didn't, though, but instead started on the top drawer of the second file cabinet. I'm afraid I must have let my attention wander for a bit. You know how it is when you have to sit in the same position for a long time, looking at nothing much. I found myself glancing around the office, guessing at what this or that might be. In any event, I wasn't watching when Wilhelm gave a little grunt and stopped searching.

That got my attention. With a contented sigh, he drew a thickish wad of papers out of the file cabinet. He was not facing me when he pulled them out, but now he turned to the side to examine them more closely. He would notice me at any moment, and I began wondering if I could grab the papers out of his hands before executing Plan B.

The papers looked like a very long report, typewritten on ordinary white paper. He was paging through it carefully. Every now and then, he would shake his head, as if in disbelief. I was growing very curious as to what it could be. I don't know just what I had been expecting. Something like a photograph, or a birth certificate, or some single official-looking document. Something showing Wilhelm had once been Dieter Bunt. But this looked more like a typed paper than anything. It didn't fit my theory.

Eventually, Wilhelm lowered himself into Speen's desk chair, still absorbed in whatever he was reading. He was actually facing me now, and if he hadn't been so rapt in his attention, would have spied me sitting there in front of him.

I was just toying with the idea of leaping up, grabbing the papers, and making a break for it, when he looked up and saw me.

"Hi," I said.

His eyes bulged and his mouth fell open. He dropped the papers onto the desk and actually tried covering them with his forearms. Talk about being caught red-handed. I wished that I had a camera to capture his expression.

His discomfiture at being nabbed soon turned into professorial outrage, however. "What are you doing here?" he demanded.

I didn't mind his demands. After all, I had a police detective lieutenant in my corner and an approved key in my pocket. I had all the trumps in this hand. I waggled Speen's class notes in the air. "I'm preparing my next E and M lecture," I replied smoothly. "And you?"

He scowled at me. "That is none of your business," he shot back.

I raised my eyebrows. "Gee, I'd have to say that that's a matter of opinion," I continued, still smooth. "I've been working with the police lately to find out who might have wanted to kill Speen. I think that they would be very interested to hear about people secretly searching his office. Especially people who were seen arguing with him shortly before he was murdered."

"This has nothing to do with that," he asserted.

I was somehow unconvinced. I could see the big finish coming up, with me and Marshall Trask riding off into the sunset together. I indicated the papers he was huddling under his arms. "May I see that, please?"

He hugged them closer to his body. It really was comical to see him like this. "No," he answered.

"Suit yourself," I said, rising from my chair. "If you'll excuse me, I have to go call Detective Lieutenant Trask now."

He jumped up. "No!" he shouted.

I spread my hands. "I'm sorry, Dr. Wilhelm. You can't have it both ways. I think the police should see this. If you're not going to hand it over, I'm calling them."

He held out one hand. "No," he said, a little calmer. "Just, just sit down for a second."

"You first."

He heaved a sigh and sat down. I sat down, too.

He gestured toward the papers. "This is a private and sensitive matter," he said. "It doesn't concern you and it doesn't concern the police. It has nothing to do with the murder."

I heaved a sigh, too. He seemed very sincere. Of course, if he was selling me a lie, he would try to sound sincere, wouldn't he? I tried another approach.

"Is this what you were arguing with Speen about that day?"

He seemed to consider this, like a player before taking his hand off the chess piece. "Yes," he conceded.

"And it doesn't have to do with espionage?"

He looked confused. "Espionage?"

I nodded.

"No." He shook his head, as though this seemed a bizarre idea. "No, nothing like that."

"This have to do with you?" I asked.

He shook his head again. "No."

"Katanga?"

Again, he seemed confused. "No."

Now I was confused. If it didn't have to do with murder or espionage, and it didn't have to do with him or Jackson, I was stumped. "Well, who does it have to do with?" I said in exasperation.

He glanced furtively around the office, then seemed to make a decision. He looked me in the eye. "This goes no farther than this room."

I shook my head. "I can't promise that. What if it turns out to be relevant?"

He shook his head. "It isn't. Look, if it's not relevant to the murder or to whatever you mean by espionage, can you keep this a secret?"

I felt like I was being set up. Hell, this was Dieter Bunt, wasn't it? Sitting across from me. Trying to save his miserable hide by cooking up some smokescreen. So, why did I feel like that wasn't true? Why did I feel like there was something else going on here?

I crossed my arms. "Yeah, okay. I promise. So who does this have to do with?"

He swallowed and said, "Emily Whitney."

I squinted at him. "Emily Whitney?" I repeated. This was nothing like what I had imagined, and sounded even more cockeyed than anything that I had imagined. "What does Speen have to do with Emily Whitney?"

"He's—he was—on her dissertation committee."

I was still fogged. Okay, Emily was getting near to graduation. Okay, she had probably written or was writing a dissertation. Okay, she had the poor judgment to include a jerk like Speen on her committee to review her dissertation. That was as far as I went. "So what?" was all I could come up with to say.

He suddenly pushed the papers toward me. "Read this," he said.

I leaned forward and picked up the papers. I tried not to take my eyes off him. He was still my number-one pick for Dieter Bunt, but I was also curious about what was going on.

I glanced at the top page. The title was about a yard long, but I got the gist. This was Emily's doctoral dissertation, about the superconductor research she had been doing with Wilhelm. I started flipping through it. Pretty soon, I struck comments in Speen's handwriting. On nearly every page. I started reading them, and nearly dropped the whole thing.

He was blasting her out of the water. Everything he wrote was phrased very matter-of-factly, but there was no doubt that he was tearing her research to shreds. But there was something else, too. I didn't catch on until I was almost twenty pages into the thing. As I read what she wrote, it seemed very sound, even important. But his comments made it seem as if she had avoided doing additional work. The thing is, it was the kind of commentary you could make on any research by any scientist. Not attacking what she had said or done, but what she hadn't said or done.

There was no defense against an attack like that. No one can find out everything, study every aspect of a problem, read every book and paper, examine every nuance and connotation of the ideas. Especially for a dissertation, where you want to bite off something reasonably chewable. Speen had to know that. But he was making it sound as if she hadn't done anything. It was a slick and sneaky hatchet job.

"He's torpedoing her," I commented to Wilhelm.

"Yes," he agreed. "You can see it, can't you?"

I shrugged. "But if you can see it, and I can see it, isn't it obvious what he's doing?"

Wilhelm pointed at the dissertation. "It doesn't matter. He could take this and use it to force her to do more research. Years more. She might never get her doctorate."

"But why?"

He looked down. "This is the private part," he said in a low voice. "He was blackmailing Emily."

This I didn't get. Speen already had Jackson blackmailed into doing his dirty work for him. What did he need Emily Whitney for? Blackmailing graduate students is not the road to riches. "For what? Is she independently wealthy or something?"

He tipped his head to one side and looked at me. "He wanted her to sleep with him."

"Oh, yuck!"

Now it made sense. Now it all fit. This was vintage Speen. This was so Speenlike it made me sick.

I set the dissertation down so I could gesture more freely. "So Speen was holding this over Emily's head. So, Emily doesn't know what to do, of course. So, she told you. So, you had an argument with Speen. Naturally, he refused to surrender. So after he died you had to search his office to get it before someone else found it."

"Yes," said Wilhelm nodding.

"Well," I said, nodding also. "That certainly makes sense. He's just the kind of dirt-bag to do that, too. And, really, the only problem I can see now is that this makes a terrific motive for murder."

He stopped nodding.

"You see how this looks, Dr. Wilhelm," I continued. "Sure, Speen is a jerk. But that could prompt you or Emily or some other public-spirited citizen to kill Speen to stop him."

He glared mightily at me, as if I'd tricked him. "I certainly did not have anything to do with Professor Speen's death, and I'm sure Emily didn't either. Who are you to accuse me?"

I put my hands up placatingly. "I didn't say you did it. I just said it makes a great motive. And I have a personal interest in this."

He scowled. He was reminding me more and more of Payne Stickney. "What personal interest?"

I smiled crookedly. "I've been attacked twice myself."

"By who?"

It should have been "whom", but this was only the physics department, so I let it go. "That's the question. I didn't see them either time." I briefly described the string trick and the gas attack.

"Those are strange ways to attack someone," he remarked thoughtfully.

"Yes, aren't they."

I was turning something over in my mind. Describing the two attacks to Wilhelm had reminded me of the one I was looking for: a Nazi war criminal and spy who had murdered Speen to stay safe. Somehow, this did not fit with a professor who was trying to save the honor of a young woman. Would Dieter Bunt care so much? It seemed wildly out of character.

But if Bunt wouldn't act that way, and Wilhelm had acted that way, then Wilhelm couldn't be Bunt. Neither could Emily, of course, but I'd never really thought of her as a suspect. She was more in the Jackson category.

Instinctively, then, I felt that Wilhelm was not Bunt. But I wanted something more than a warm feeling. Some proof that he could not have done the murder. An alibi would be nice, but even those could be tricky. I was groping for something else to convince me.

Wilhelm had been waiting for me to continue as I thought this all out. "Look, I'm inclined to believe you on this, and I really don't think you or Emily are involved in Speen's death."

"Thank you for your vote of confidence," he said, voice dripping with scorn.

"But," I continued, "I'd just like to satisfy myself about this situation."

He frowned. "How?"

"I want to talk to Emily Whitney about this. Get it from her own lips."

He shook his head furiously. "Absolutely not. That girl has suffered enough through this. I won't allow it."

I stood up. "I'm afraid you have no control over this. I'm going to speak with her, in a very respectful way, about this painful topic. I'd like you to be there, too. But even if you don't come, I'll still do it myself."

He glared at me again, then looked away and stared at stray nitrogen atoms for a while. "All right," he relented at last. "But I'll come with you."

"Fine," I said. I picked up the dissertation and waved him to the door. "After you."

He left the room. I took Speen's E and M notes, shut the door, and followed him.

Sixty-three

At the stairwell, he headed up. I stopped. "Where are we going?"

He turned to face me. "Emily's office is on the sixth floor."

"I thought it was in the basement."

He shook his head. "No, the lab is in the basement, and my office. Hers is on the sixth floor."

He turned and started climbing stairs again. I shrugged and followed him.

Something seemed odd. Then I noticed that we were on the wrong side of the stairs. I usually walk on the right side of staircases. It's less likely you'll bump into anyone. Except, I reminded myself, on steep staircases. Disliking heights as I do, I tend to walk on the side away from the center of the staircase, so I can't see down the space in the middle. When going up, that means the left side.

I stopped and watched Wilhelm climbing stairs on the wrong side. Something occurred to me, something that, if it worked out, would eliminate Wilhelm as a suspect in my mind. When he got to the halfway landing I said, "Dr. Wilhelm, before we see Emily, there's something I'd like to show you."

He grunted. "What now, Napoli? Can't we just get this over with?"

I held out the dissertation. "You do this for me, and I'll give you this, without us talking to Emily."

He blinked. "All right," he agreed readily, and started down the stairs again, still on the side away from the open center.

I led him to the room Rachel and I had been in last Saturday night, the room Speen had actually been dropped from. I walked over to the window and lifted it all the way open. An icy gust swept in.

Wilhelm stopped in the doorway. "What do you want to show me?" he asked in irritation.

I watched him carefully. "The place where Speen's body was found."
Something happened in his face. "I've seen it," he said.
"I'd like you to look at it again for me," I replied in an even voice.
"Fine," he said, turning away. "Let's go down and look at it."
"No," I persisted. "I want you to see it from this angle."
He looked from me to the window and wet his lips. "All right," he said in a hearty voice.

He strode halfway across the room, then stopped as if he'd hit an invisible wall.

"Just right over here," I encouraged him, indicating the window with my hand.

He took half a step forward and stopped again, paralyzed. His mouth was open and he was breathing rapidly.

"Only a few steps more, Dr. Wilhelm," I said mildly.

He gritted his teeth. He seemed to be willing one leg to move, but it wasn't budging. Although the room was freezing from the open window, perspiration stood out on his forehead.

I held out the dissertation. "Here it is," I said. "You can have it if you come here and take it."

He tried to fix his eyes on the dissertation, but they kept sliding off to the window. He managed to take one step, then another, then collapsed on the floor in front of me, heaving for breath and weeping. His hands writhed convulsively on the linoleum tiles.

I looked down at him for a moment, then turned and closed the window. I reached down, hooked my hands under his arms, and heaved him up and into a desk chair facing away from the window. My face burned with shame. "I don't like heights either," I said.

He raised his head and gazed at me through eyes that wouldn't focus. He was shivering, his hands grasping the desk before him tightly.

I thought of what I knew about Dieter Bunt. He had lured prisoners up open metal staircases to the top of burned-out buildings with no floors. He had opened this window, shoved Speen off a cart and over the sill, and closed the window again. He wouldn't keep his lab in the dingy basement. He wouldn't avoid the upper floors of the physics building. He wouldn't keep away from the edge of a staircase. He was not afraid of heights.

Wilhelm seemed recovered. He was breathing normally now.

"I'm sorry about that," I said. "The person I'm looking for would have no trouble with a window on the fifth floor. I had to find out. I hope you can see it from my point of view. I'm a little touchy about being bumped off."

An odd expression developed on Wilhelm's face, which I took to be his version of a smile. "I think I can see that," he said huskily. He cleared his throat and then extended his hand toward the copy of Emily's dissertation—covered with Speen's blackmail campaign—that I was still holding.

I handed it over.

"I never saw it," I said. "And I never heard anything about Emily and Speen."

I definitely felt relieved that Wilhelm was not the murderer. But it also reminded me that the real killer was still out there, and still after me.

Sixty-four

Needless to say, after this encounter with Wilhelm I wanted to put as much distance between us as possible. Given the weather outside, that would be difficult. I had no immediate desire to leave the building and get involved with that muck again, so I ensconced myself in the small department library on the first floor, in one of the few sittable chairs in the building. There I read physics magazines and watched cars slide unsteadily down the road outside the window.

That was where Mr. Andersson found me late that afternoon.

"I know about you," he started in on me, before I had even registered his presence. As always, his Danish accent amused me no matter what he was actually saying. Form over content.

He was wearing three or four coats and a scarf about twelve yards long wrapped around his neck, face, ears and upper body generally. A black hat with a brim was stuck down flat on his head. A little blob of ice was inching its way down his cane. I envied him his rubbers.

"You been talking to the police. Telling them not to listen to me."

I was taken aback. First, that he knew about my involvement, somehow. Second, that he had somehow twisted it into some kind of persecution fantasy against himself. Third, that he was that worked up about it. Still, he didn't seem to have any cinder-blocks concealed about his person, so I just looked at him mildly and let him continue.

"I saw what I saw. I know who killed the professor. And you better watch out, or something happen to you, too."

I was able to watch his face and eyes, muffled as he was. His eyes seemed to be operating independently of each other, roving erratically around the room. His mouth worked in a stiff diagonal action that I found truly bizarre.

I didn't know what to make of him. Was he warning me? Did he know who was threatening me? Had he really seen what had happened? Did he see Jackson? Did he see someone else, but say it was Jackson? Had he even told the police it was Jackson? Rachel had indicated so, but maybe that wasn't true. What *had* he told them? Was he merely angry with me for some perceived slight? Or was he trying to help me?

He seemed crazy. Maybe he was crazy. But maybe he had some useful information, too. I found it impossible to sort out.

I started to speak, but he interrupted me. "You'll see. You'll all see. I told you what happened. You'll see. It not over yet. You'll see."

With that, he pointed his cane at me meaningfully, causing him to nearly topple over, and stalked out. I could hear the door slam as he left the building into the gale.

I was thoughtful for a moment.

Then I burst into laughter. Not at him. Not exactly. At me. For ever thinking that he could be Dieter Bunt. For imagining he was some kind of espionage mastermind who had set up those subtle attempts on my life. What could I have been thinking of? Hadn't I myself told Rachel he was a lunatic?

Out the window, I could see Andersson on the sidewalk, preparing to cross the road to his house. A young woman walked past him, then suddenly whirled back, startled by some harangue I could not hear. He was gesticulating wildly with his cane. She hurried away from him.

I wiped tears of laughter from my eyes. I took a few deep breaths, still giggling a little.

My list of suspects was dwindling rapidly today. There was still much that I didn't understand about what was going on in this case, much that was confusing and unclear. But, at least, and finally, and despite whatever else might be going on, I did know something.

At that moment, I was absolutely certain that Mr. Andersson was not Dieter Bunt.

Sixty-five

In the next moment, I was absolutely certain that Mr. Andersson was Dieter Bunt.

Sixty-six

I mean, think about it. Suppose you are a Nazi war criminal on the run. You have to avoid being recognized. But you're not hiding in a cave. You're still out in the world. You're among people. How do you live among people without them seeing you and noticing you and recognizing you?

By being an unpleasant lunatic, that's how. By being someone everyone flees from and avoids at all costs.

Not by being friendly and nice. Then people would want to get close to you. They would be interested in you, want to know about you.

But by being nasty, so that no one wants to get close, no one is interested, no one wants to know about you.

Not by being reclusive, mind you. Reclusiveness invites curiosity, even scrutiny.

But by being very public, very obvious, but repugnant. Obnoxious. Someone people shun.

Not in a criminal way of course. You avoid anything that's actually criminal. But that still leaves a lot of leeway to be repellent in the personal realm.

Mr. Andersson was the ideal cover for Dieter Bunt. Everyone saw him. Everyone avoided him. Nobody showed him the least amount of interest. He attacked, personally and not criminally, anyone who came near him.

And yet, he was out in the world. He could go anywhere. Be anywhere. No one was ever surprised to run into him. He had an astonishing amount of freedom, with no interest or curiosity attached to him.

It was perfect.

I resolved from that point on to focus my scrutiny exclusively on Mr. Andersson. I was going to watch him and keep tabs on him.

And, at the first opportunity, break into and search his house.

What choice did I have? I couldn't go to Rachel, much less Stickney, and say, "I've found Dieter Bunt. It's Mr. Andersson." What proof could I offer? All I had were my surmises, my feeling that this made a good fit. Stickney would never go along with it. Rachel might, to be nice to me, but she would be foolish to do so. Yet if I could find something, anything, to indicate that Andersson was not who he claimed to be, then that would be another story.

The only way to do that was to burgle his house.

Obnoxious. Now who else did that remind me of?

Stickney, G. Whatta Payne. He was the poster child for Obnoxious. Given that being obnoxious was a good cover. And given that Rachel's contacts had indicated that Stickney was usually okay to get along with. And given that on this case he was not okay to get along with, to put it mildly. And given that he seemed to be doing everything possible to steer us away from Dieter Bunt, and toward Jackson and other dead ends.

What was the conclusion?

Dr. Wolff had warned me about sympathizers, people who, for whatever twisted reason, might actually try to help escaped Nazis. They might be even more dangerous than Bunt himself, he had indicated.

Could Stickney already know who Bunt was? Could Stickney be trying to help Bunt? Could I be in danger from Stickney too?

That was scary.

The idea that an FBI agent, who could, after all, carry and use a gun and justify himself afterwards, might be a threat was very scary.

I had to get out of this. I had to finish it off as soon as possible. Before Andersson and/or Stickney finished me off.

Tonight.

Sixty-seven

Reasoning that successful burglaries depend on proper nourishment, I ventured from the physics building to the dining hall. After a very quick dinner, I was back at the physics building, which seemed like an ideal vantage point for staking out Andersson's house almost directly across the street. The building was warm and dry, an important consideration on a night like this. That snow-rain-ice mix had slackened off, but the wind was bitterly cold, and the temperature was plunging. By tomorrow, everything would be sealed under a hard and frozen glaze.

I started my vigil in the department library. I turned out all the lights, and pulled a semi-comfortable chair over to a window that had a view of Bunt's house. As on the previous night, I could see the flickering light of a television, and what looked like a figure sitting on the couch. I was not going to be taken in by that, though. It might be some kind of dummy or decoy, while Andersson, or Bunt, or whoever he was, left the house on whatever his rounds might be. Another shot at me, probably.

It was dull work. I suspected after the first hour that I would never make a good detective, and after the second hour, I was sure of it. Too much sitting. Too much looking at the same monotonous thing. I kept changing my view of the outside, just to have something else to look at and keep my attention fresh, but it didn't help much. Try sitting and staring out a window at a single object for a few hours sometime. I'm sure you'll be able to compile quite a list of things you'd much rather be doing.

Around eight-thirty, I also began thinking that I hadn't selected a very good observation spot. From the department library, I had to look off at an angle to see his house, which was annoying. It would be better to see it straight on. I decided to change locations. But to where?

At the end of the first floor hallway was one of the warrens of graduate student offices. This was a big room separated by eight-foot-high wooden dividers into little cubbyholes for grad students. There was not much room, but this was compensated for by the utter lack of privacy. You could hear other people scratch themselves. Still, it did face in the right direction. At this time, on such a night, I thought there was a good chance no one would be around.

I took one last look out the window, assured myself that nothing remarkable was happening, then dashed down the hallway. I opened the outer door silently, so as not to attract attention if anyone happened to be there. I heard nothing, and figured I was in luck. I walked around to the right, toward where a window should be facing the house. I discovered that this was Peter Schultz's office. Even if he were in, he would probably be asleep.

I turned the doorknob quietly, the door swung open, and I entered. Nobody home. Pleased with myself, I sat in his chair, leaned back and drank in the view of the house yet again.

I gradually became aware of a soft noise in the background somewhere. It sounded like someone breathing loudly. Maybe someone really was in one of the other offices. I resolved to be as quiet as possible, to avoid attracting their attention and having to answer questions that I could not answer. I watched some more.

The tone of the noise changed. It now sounded like a sob, which I found alarming. Could someone be in pain here? Could someone be *causing* someone pain here? Bunt was on the loose, after all. I stood up, trying to locate the sound. I couldn't, really. I couldn't ignore it either, though, so I decided to investigate.

This made me uncomfortable. It would be embarrassing to break in on someone who was just crying, for example, or doing something else ordinary and private. I would just have to try to be as quiet and unobtrusive as possible. Luckily, the wind outside made a good white noise background to mask the small sounds of my movements.

I walked around on tiptoe until I thought I had found the office. It belonged to one of the male Asian students. I suddenly had a vision of him hurting Xiao Xia because he had found out that she had approached me in the movie. Jealousy. That made me angry, and leant an urgency to my investigation.

I put my hand on the doorknob. I took a deep breath and turned the knob. The door swung silently inwards and I entered.

I was right. It was one of the male Asian students—and Xiao Xia. They were not, however, fighting.

Their jeans were down around their ankles. Xiao Xia was half-standing, half-sitting back on the desk. He was half-standing, half-leaning over her. It looked like a very uncomfortable position for him, but he was not complaining. He was instead making little grunting noises I had not noticed before. I couldn't really blame him.

Xiao Xia did not appear to be in any pain either. She was actually facing me, and if her eyes had been open, she would have been looking right at me. As it happened, her eyes were not open, and her face bore a look of concentration and intense bliss. It was she who was making the little noises I had heard which, I now realized, were not so much sobs as little exclamations of pleasure.

I know that you'll think me hopelessly cynical, but as I stood watching her for a moment, I could not help but wonder if her romantic interest of the previous night was genuine and sincere. In fact, and again please excuse my cynicism, the possibility began to emerge that she might have actually been trying to get a good grade from her new instructor. I, of course, would never let private matters such as those I had just witnessed influence my judgment or actions in any way and as I backed out of the room, silently closed the door, returned to the corridor, and gave the outer door the most horrific slam imaginable, I considered that I had behaved sensibly.

After the echoes of the slam died away, I heard muffled exclamations in Chinese slowly subside into the same little sounds I had originally heard. I had an inkling that Xiao Xia's own office on the third floor might well be vacant for the next one to thirty minutes, depending on the stamina of her friend.

I found that her office commanded a perfect view of the house. I sat down and leaned my arms onto the window-sill, the better to gaze downwards at it. And I suppose my mind must still have been mulling over the intimate scene I had just witnessed, because it took me nearly fifteen minutes to realize that the tracks in the snow leading away from the house's front door must mean that Andersson had gone out. The great detective.

I stood up. If he was gone, I could try breaking into his house. Better wait a few minutes, though, just to see if he was coming right back. I sat down again.

In five more minutes, he had still not returned. In fact, nobody had passed at all, either on foot or in a car. Only we lunatics were about on a night like this.

I didn't leave immediately, but composed my plans. Get into his house somehow. Look around. Don't touch anything. In fact, wear my gloves so as not to leave any fingerprints. If I found anything damning, either take it, or report it to Rachel. That would be a tricky call. I supposed I would take something if it were merely suggestive, but not actually incriminating. Better to leave any incriminating evidence for the police to find, so that it would be admissible in court.

I was really going to do this. I was really going to break into somebody's house. How my lifestyle was expanding these days.

No time like the present, I thought. I stood again, stretched my muscles, and opened the door.

The first thing I saw was the gun.

Next, I saw the one holding it.

Mr. Andersson.

Dieter Bunt.

Sixty-eight

I don't know if you've ever been held at gunpoint by a homicidal lunatic Nazi war criminal who has already murdered thousands (and one quite recently), and you happen to be the only obstacle to his escaping certain death by hanging? Perhaps not. Allow me to save you the trouble by assuring you that it is an unnerving experience. In my own case, I found that I was unnerved to the extent that I couldn't think, speak, move, breathe, or perform any of the other activities normally associated with life.

You'll scarcely believe me, in these modern times, when I tell you that my life had so arranged itself that until that moment I had never been held at gunpoint by anyone. I had never even *seen* a real handgun before. This one was a black metal ugly thing, obviously built to cause death. It didn't look that big, but I had no doubt that it could launch a projectile fast enough to create a hole in my heart or my brain quite large enough to kill me.

Looking at him and looking at the gun, the only thing I could say was "Guh" or words to that effect.

His speech was unencumbered however. "Come this way," he said. The Danish accent was gone. He spoke in German-accented English, and with a nasty rasping intensity I found almost more frightening than the gun.

Despite his instructions, I found myself still unable to move. I was horrified into paralysis.

He flashed up his cane and jabbed me in the chest, right in the heart. It reminded me of Kim, my fencing partner, for a moment, and the contrast between my former life as a comparatively carefree graduate student and my current life as a potential murder victim would have made a good topic for a thoughtful essay.

"Move," he barked.

I somehow did as he commanded and shuffled out into the corridor. He was going to kill me, I knew. With the gun? It would make a hell of a noise, maybe too loud to be risked. Maybe it was a threat, to get me to go somewhere, do something else which would kill me.

"This way," he ordered and we walked down the corridor, me in front, him in back, the gun leveled at my spine, the cane jabbing me occasionally in the back, and always expertly aimed at the heart. I had no doubts: if he shot me, it would be straight through the heart. I wished I kept a Bible or a cigarette case or a block of titanium in my breast pocket like the detectives and spies in the movies always do. Just not dissipated or religious enough, that was my whole problem.

"Stop," he commanded and I stopped. We were standing next to the elevator. I realized we must be going to the roof. He was going to drop me out a window just as he had done Speen. The obsession with falling again.

He pressed the button and we waited for the elevator. It was absurdly ordinary, the quiet way we waited. We stood there like strangers in an office building. Except for his gun in my back.

My mind was slowly thawing after the initial shock. I began thinking. I have to find a way out of this. I have to either escape or convince him not to kill me.

I regretted now that I had never taken some courses in martial arts. They would come in useful right about now. To just lash out with a kick, knocking his gun down, then a quick throw and he would be unconscious on the floor. Instead, I had taken fencing. Sailing. Badminton. Somehow, I didn't see my skill with a rudder or a racquet getting me out of this.

The elevator doors slid open, a thing I had never found ominous before, but which filled me with dread now.

"In," he said and we both stepped in. He pushed "6", the doors closed and we began to move upwards.

I spoke. "You are Dieter Bunt, a former major in the Gestapo. You are wanted for murder and war crimes in Israel and other countries."

Dieter Bunt, the man pointing the gun at my heart, said, "I don't know what you're talking about."

I was astonished. He was insane. There was no way around it. Or maybe it was mere prudence on his part. Who knew whether we could be overheard or not? Living a life of evasion and deceit as he had, he might naturally and automatically deny everything. I had seen way too many movies where the villain freely describes his crimes and motivations in tremendous detail for the hero's benefit. Reality clearly didn't work like that.

Still, I persisted.

"You broke both your legs parachuting into Russia. You were captured by the Russians and given inadequate medical care. Your legs never healed properly." No response. In fact, I had noticed that he wasn't using the cane at all. He could walk perfectly fine. "You were later freed, and joined the Gestapo."

"I still don't know what you are talking about," he reiterated mildly. Then his voice switched to the Danish accent again as he said, "My name is Vitus Andersson. I am Danish schoolteacher. I never fought in the war. I fled the Nazis." It was eerie to hear him change identities in front of me like that.

I continued. "You used to take prisoners to the top floor of a gutted building and make them fall to their deaths." I thought I saw a glimmer of something in his eyes then, but his face was impassive.

The elevator doors opened on the sixth floor. "Out," he said. We stepped out of the elevator. The doors closed behind us. "This way," he commanded. We started walking, but away from the attic entrance that led to the roof. I was totally confused now. How was he going to kill me?

I went on. "You escaped after the war. You went to South America." We had now reached the staircase.

"Down," he said. What the hell was he doing? First, we had gone to the sixth floor, now we were going down the stairs? Why? Why not just go directly to the fifth floor? Was this some strange torture: death by elevator and staircase? I was baffled, but I kept talking.

"Later you went to Mexico, then to the United States. You lived in Texas and Ohio. You killed two FBI agents in Ohio."

He said, "I think you must have me confused with someone else."

I continued slowly down the stairs and kept speaking. "You moved here. You got secret information from Professor Speen and passed it to spies. Then Speen found out who you were and you killed him. You tried to frame Katanga for that murder but that didn't work. When that didn't work, you tried to kill him too, but you blew it. You're making a lot of mistakes. You tried killing me twice, but you couldn't. You're losing, you know. They're closing in on you, and you're losing."

You see, it had occurred to me to try to tick him off. With him already pointing a gun at my back and sure to kill me anyway, it was hard to see how provoking him could have a negative effect. I wanted him to make some error, something I could capitalize on and use to my advantage. It was, in fact, very much like fencing, where you try to provoke your opponent into making mistakes that you can use against them.

We had reached the fifth floor landing. I paused. "Left," he ordered, jabbing me again, and we went left. I was growing peeved at the jabs from his cane, but I had not yet decided to point this out to him.

The building was totally quiet except for our movement. No one else was here, which was tremendously disappointing. In detective stories, someone is always there to help the hero in spots like this. Maybe someone he asked to follow him around. But no one knew I was here. There was no one in the building. Well, maybe two others, but I had a feeling that they were either still busy or had left. No one else could help me. I had to do it myself.

I spoke again. "I have written down all my information about you. I have left it in a safe place. Even if you kill me, the police and FBI will know all about you. Who you are. What you look like. What you've done. You can't escape."

"Stop," he said. I stopped.

We were now next to the elevator doors on the fifth floor. Not the elevator again, I thought. Are we going to keep riding the elevator all night? I was totally mystified by what we were doing, and a little surprised that a former Gestapo major couldn't come up with something more directly lethal. Still, if he could stand it, I could.

He stepped around me carefully, so that he faced me.

"You're wrong," he said. A deviation! Maybe what I said was working. Maybe I *was* provoking him. Was that good?

He went on. "You have left no information. I have been watching you carefully. Even if you have, it makes no difference. I will escape. Tonight." He moved near the elevator doors.

"You're wrong," I said, copping his line. "Unless we go and collect that information"—where could I take him?—"you will be captured and executed."

He smiled a ghastly smile. "I know about such tricks, you see. I tell you, I know you have not left any information, and I don't care even if you have. For you, all will soon be done."

I didn't like the Germanic syntax of his last sentence. I felt true panic then. My only gambit had failed. This guy hadn't survived being hunted for thirty years by falling for tricks by amateurs. I still had no idea what he was going to do, but I knew that he was *not* going to travel with me to retrieve some mythical information.

He suddenly raised his cane vertically above his head, and for a moment I had the bizarre notion he was going to dance a jig. Instead, he poked his cane up through a small notch I had never noticed at the top of the elevator doors. He twisted his cane and there was a metallic snap. The doors unlatched and slid slowly open.

He stepped back away from the doors. I could see the underside of the elevator on the floor above and I could see the empty darkness of the elevator shaft below.

Uh oh.

He motioned toward the opening with his cane. He meant to push me
down that shaft, five stories and more, to the basement. My palms were
suddenly wet.

"Go," he said.

I took a baby step forward.

He moved around behind me. I felt the tip of his cane touch my back
and I stiffened. He pushed me forward a little, toward the shaft. I could
see a ways down the shaft now. If I fell, I would surely be killed. You
couldn't survive a fall down an elevator shaft, could you? I felt dizzy and
sick and frightened, but knew I must keep my balance.

He drew back the cane and then jabbed me again from behind. I took
another small step forward. The touch of the cane reminded me again of
fencing. Except, I thought, in fencing you face the other person. And you
get to carry a sword, too. And nobody dies.

Again he drew back the cane and prodded me forward. I was now a foot
from the opening, but I almost didn't notice. Something interesting had
occurred to me. Even more interesting than falling down an elevator shaft.
It was like a solution to an equation hanging in space before me.

I knew what to do. I saw a way out.

I cleared my throat. "I just have two questions," I said with difficulty.

He said nothing. The cane was still pressing into my back.

I went on. "In that building, did you ever have the guts to push them,
or did you make them jump?"

There was a long silence. Then he whispered, "*I pushed them all,*" in an
obscene tone that made me want to vomit.

He drew the cane back and touched me again, lightly, teasingly. I slid
my feet forward gingerly. I was now only a few inches from the edge of the
shaft. I could see down several floors now. My hands were damp with perspiration.

I managed to speak once more. "And did you ever have the guts to look
them in the eyes when you pushed them?"

There was a longer silence. I was almost vibrating with anxiety now. Then I felt the cane removed from my back.

"Turn around," he commanded gruffly.

I turned around *very* carefully, as you may imagine, and faced him. His face was an indescribable mix of wildness and control, of hatred and fear.

He drew the cane back, still pointed directly at my heart. I looked straight into his eyes. Looking at him explained everything about the Nazis to me. Everything.

"Like bugs, they was," he spat out. "We stomped them out, like bugs." With each word, he gave me a little jab. "Like. Bugs."

He suddenly lunged the cane forward at my heart. I stepped swiftly to my right and the cane slid past me. I turned slightly and grabbed it with my left hand as it came past. I yanked it violently toward the shaft. He stumbled and cried out. I pulled the cane hard and, as he was pulled *toward* the shaft, I was pushed *away*, in accordance with the third law of motion of Sir Isaac Newton, praise be to his name.

There was a moment when we were directly next to each other at the lip of the open door. His eyes were wide with astonishment and terror as he saw the empty shaft before him.

I stumbled forward and hit the wall on the opposite side of the corridor from the shaft. I twisted around to see:

His feet were on the very edge of the shaft, and his body was over the edge, teetering slowly outward. His arms were windmilling helplessly to try to restore his balance. The cane was ricocheting uselessly off the walls of the shaft. He was looking backwards and caught sight of me and suddenly twisted and brought the gun up to point at me.

I hurled myself sideways, which was a smart move, as it happened, because he fired then and blew a two-foot hole in the plaster wall where my head had been.

The kick from the gun gave him the final push over and he fell backwards off the edge into blackness. He didn't scream, depriving me of the pleasure of the Doppler effect. I heard only a sickening muffled whump as he hit the bottom of the elevator shaft, finally completing a fall that had started years before. And then all was silence.

I was sprawled along the floor, covered with plaster dust and splinters, trying to breathe again. I rolled onto my back. As sometimes happens after a near-collision in a car, I was overcome by a wave of adrenaline trembling. That son-of-a-bitch had almost killed me! I could hardly see for the released fear flowing through my body.

Another thought came to me: I had just killed a man. My God, what had I done?

Then I thought about who it was I had killed—and why—and my feelings changed rapidly. I finally settled on the opinion: Not a bad night's work.

The wave of trembling slowly subsided. My labored breathing gradually calmed. Without the pounding beat in my ears, I could once again hear the silent building.

But not completely silent. From far below me I unmistakably heard a rasping moan. The bastard was still alive!

I've said it before and I'll say it again: they build assholes to last. Look at your Mafia bosses and third-world dictators. Same principle: they live forever, too.

I was simultaneously fascinated, appalled, and, yes, a little relieved that he was still alive. I crawled toward the shaft, keeping my distance. It would be a long time before I would use an elevator willingly again. I stood up quite carefully and looked a little down the shaft very very carefully.

I now had a problem in etiquette, of all things. How to inquire about his health, while still sending the clear message that I was disappointed he wasn't dead?

I finally said, "So, you're alive."

I was answered first with a groan of intense suffering, his voice echoing weirdly in the shaft. Then he said, pain straining every word, "My legs are broken."

"Good," I said, and left him there.

Sixty-nine

I wasted no time. Anyone might have heard that gunshot. The police might be on their way over right now. If I wanted a try at Bunt's house before they arrived, it had to be now.

I went directly to my office, pulled on my coat and hat, and tugged on my gloves. I walked down the stairs and out the front door.

It was drizzling out now, turning the whole snow-blanketed world to slush. I squished my way across the street. The frigid night air helped clear the fear and tension out of me. Not a soul was to be seen in either direction. All the lights in the physics building were out, even the one in the first floor office. Xiao Xia and her playmate must have left.

Bunt's house was isolated from any others in the neighborhood, I could see, surrounded by empty lots with scraggly trees. No witnesses to my breaking and entering. I went directly to the front door of the house, but it was locked. I walked around the back, through a gate in a high stockade fence that I closed behind me again, leaving ruts in the slush.

The back door was unlocked. I pushed it open without hesitation and went in.

My face fell as I saw the inside. It was the cleanest, neatest house I had ever seen in my life. It looked like Donna Reed lived there. Any hope I may have had of finding incriminating evidence lying around was gone.

Still, as long as I was breaking and entering, I decided to give it the old college try. I pushed the door shut with my back and swept my gaze around. To the left of the door was a kitchen chair with a grocery bag on it. Beyond that was a small bathroom. Then the living room area. A couch with a coat and pants draped on it gave the impression of someone sitting there. Fooled me. The couch rested on a cheap thin carpet. The front door. A small bookcase with what looked like volumes of an encyclopedia. The television, playing with the sound turned low. A door to the only bedroom. Another door that might go to the basement. The kitchen counter and cabinets. Refrigerator. Sink. Kitchen table and three more chairs. The back door again.

That was it.

I don't know what I had expected to find. A framed photo of Hitler signed, "Dieter, Keep up the good work, Yours, Adolf." A team banner reading, "Go, Gestapo." File cabinet with drawers labeled, "Espionage", "Victims", and "Miscellaneous". There was nothing like that.

I looked in the bathroom. It looked uncannily like every other bathroom on earth. Dieter used Right Guard. Call the feds.

I started getting a creepy feeling. Like I had forgotten something. Or like Dieter Bunt was still watching me from somewhere. Unlikely. Dieter Bunt was lying at the bottom of an elevator shaft, hoping nobody wanted to go to the basement. Maybe one of his little helpers, though. I wondered where Stickney was right now. I tried to shrug the feeling off.

I crossed to the bedroom. I opened the drawers of a dresser. I was looking at socks and underwear belonging to an old man. I dumped the contents onto the bed. Nothing under the socks, or behind the socks, or in the socks. Nothing under the drawers, or behind the drawers. All I had to show after a thorough search was lint.

Wait a second. This guy had to be putting secret documents somewhere. Money. Weapons. Even if not here, where were bankbooks, keys, something?

I left the bedroom. I looked at the bookcase. Feeling I was wasting my time, I started pulling out volumes of the encyclopedia. They were, in fact, volumes of an encyclopedia. They did not have holes carved out in their centers holding guns, money, or passports in different names. I put them all back.

This was getting frustrating. Here I had a Nazi war criminal safely at the bottom of an elevator shaft, with absolutely no evidence of his activities whatsoever. I couldn't help feeling that I was wasting my time in a big way.

I opened his kitchen cabinets. I was building up a picture of this guy and his lifestyle now. Forensics. The mind of the criminal. He apparently ate on plates, and drank out of glasses. How had no one spotted this before?

Wheaties. Prince spaghetti. Oreos. He ate better than I did.

The basement. Good idea. See exactly what kind of lawnmower he uses. That should crack this case wide open. Boy, will Rachel be proud.

I flicked on the light and opened the door despondently. I've always found basements a little creepy, even if they weren't owned by war criminals.

I stepped carefully down the basement stairs, alert for anything. My senses seemed to reach around corners. At the bottom, a quick survey showed a trash barrel, a snow shovel, a bag of sand, a washer and dryer, and, in the far corner, the predicted lawnmower. Sears. I sighed with depression.

In the middle of the floor was a furnace. For no particular reason, I started walking towards it. Gas heat, I noticed, and smiled a little. Any leaks I should know about? I spotted where the gas pipe came into the basement from outside. I followed the pipe with my eyes. About halfway to the furnace I saw it.

A small bundle of wires, four long rectangular tubes, and a digital clock, all bound to the gas pipe with duct tape. As I squinted at the clock, the luminous red numbers changed from 18 to 17.

I turned and bounded up the stairs three at a time. Seventeen seconds would not be long. I must have tripped some hidden switch when I entered the house, starting the timer.

I streaked across the kitchen to the back door. As I was passing through the door, I saw, out of the corner of my eye, it. Somehow I knew—*knew*—that it was important, somehow the key to understanding what was going on. I knew I should take it with me. I also knew that if I stopped to take it I would soon be a dead person. I didn't pause for a moment. I hit the door and kept going.

In the yard, I was stopped by the wooden gate. I lifted the latch. Nothing happened. Down. Nothing happened. Left. Nothing. Right. Nothing. I jangled it randomly. Nothing.

I then did the bravest thing I've ever done in my life. I dropped my hands. I shut my eyes. I took a deep breath, held it an instant, then let it out. I opened my eyes, reached out my hand, and undid the latch.

Then I crashed the gate open and was sprinting toward the street. There were no cars driving there, which was a good thing, because I didn't even look. I crossed the street in three strides and hit the quad running flat out.

I've never been much of a runner, but I easily surpassed all previous personal records, despite the poor track conditions. I raced across the empty quad. My shoes slipped and slid in the slush, but I never lost my footing. My breath came in heaving puffs. It suddenly occurred to me that I should veer toward the right to get the physics building between myself and the house. I started to veer, but began slewing sideways in the snow. Forget that, I thought, and straightened out again.

By then, it was too late anyway.

I saw the flash first, as the buildings around the quad were suddenly brilliantly illuminated yellow and red.

"Suck a duck," I said, and sincerely hoped that those would not be my last words.

The *poom* of the explosion hit me in the back like a two-by-four, lifting me completely off my feet. I fell sprawling onto my face and skidded about six yards on my left cheek. I later learned that the blast shattered every window for blocks in every direction.

I lay dazed and aching in the snow, slowly lifting and shaking my head. I heard several smaller explosions and the low roar and brittle crackle of fire.

The scientist in me demanded that I observe this phenomenon personally, and I tried to turn over, without much effect. Stabs of pain shot up my right leg. Instead, I push-upped myself with my arms, flipped onto my side, and sat.

It was worth the effort.

The whole area, the quad, the surrounding buildings, the distant trees, were lit with a bright golden light that danced and jiggled and made all these solid things seem to dance and jiggle, too. I looked up just in time to witness Bunt's roof tumbling slowly, over and over, some one hundred feet up in the air. Sparks streamed from the corners and edges. It broke up into beams and shingles that rained into the snow in the empty street.

A column of flame surged from the center of the former house, with sparks speeding and skidding through the night air. The walls of the house were gone. I couldn't even see debris to indicate what had become of them. Unidentifiable objects on fire floated and cascaded to the ground. Half of a green plastic cereal bowl fell near me, smoking and sizzling.

I looked at it and thought, This is the second time he's almost killed me tonight!

Correction. It was actually the third time tonight. Fifth time this week.

I could hear sirens wailing in the distance. With all this going on, I thought, it would be quite a long time before they found Bunt and his broken legs at the bottom of the elevator shaft.

I smiled at that, and then, for some reason, I lost consciousness.

Seventy

I awoke in an alien spacecraft.

Every surface I could see was a sterile smooth shiny white. It was utterly silent. Through a small rubber-edged porthole, I could see stars going by outside, and the occasional comet.

I lay back on the thin cushion. There was writing on the ceiling above my head. It was black, and in some alien alphabet. It said:

LN3WLdIVcI3CI 3dIIJ
NMC)LSi)NI>I
JC) hLdI3cIC)dIcI

or words to that effect.

I realized that my aching ankle had been bandaged. That was kind of them. Perhaps our two races could one day become friends.

Through the porthole, I saw a face. A human face. A man's face. A, not to beat around the bush, fireman's face. I was glad I wasn't the only one to be abducted. But why a fireman?

He looked through the window at me, then turned away and I heard him call out, "He's coming around again, Lieutenant."

The smooth shiny white door opened and Rachel stepped in. Behind her, I could see flashing lights, a tangle of hoses, and people huddled in bathrobes pointing.

Even at this time of the night, she looked wonderful. Dressed in her jeans-and-jacket outfit, she crouched near me and said, "Are you all right?" with a wide-eyed concern that instantly healed whatever trifling pain I was feeling.

I turned to face her and told her what had been happening. She listened quietly, even though it took a while.

When I was done, she opened the door and briefly issued orders to people I couldn't see. Police were dispatched to the elevator shaft to arrest

Andersson for (at least) attempted murder. He was to be held at the local hospital until they could figure out what to do with him next.

She talked with the fire chief. He had the local arson experts examining the ex-house for the remains of the bomb. I thought he had about as much chance as a popsicle on the sun of finding anything, but he assured me that it wasn't unusual. I'd have to work out the physics on that.

Finally, I told her about what I had seen when I was so impatient to leave the house. It had been at the bottom of a brown paper grocery bag on a chair near the back door. I had only had a single glance at it, but I had memorized exactly what it looked like.

It was about the size and shape of a shoe box, made of black plastic, with rounded edges. In the top were two circular holes, padded, which looked the perfect size and shape to hold two styrofoam cups of coffee. Except the coffee would spill, because the holes were angled outward away from each other slightly. From the bottom ran three or four strands of colored wire.

I had no idea what it was. Neither did Rachel.

"Could this be some kind of safe-cracking machine?" I asked her.

She smiled quizzically. "I've never heard of such a thing," she said. "Why do you think so?"

I shrugged. "It just occurred to me that with Speen dead, maybe Bunt would want to break into his safe. Besides, on top of this thing in the bag was a slip of paper that said 'KLB126'. I thought that might be a safe combination."

Her face contracted in thought. "It could be. It all seems rather James Bondish, though, doesn't it?"

"Maybe, but these are real spies. Who knows what kind of equipment they might have?"

She nodded and shrugged. "I'll look into it," she promised. "We have a lot to do here. In the meantime…thanks."

The look in her eyes was enough to last a man the rest of his life.

"You're welcome," I said.

"You did it," she said with admiration.

"I guess so," I said sheepishly. This was kind of embarrassing. But it was kind of nice, too. There's nothing like having the woman you love thinking you're the greatest guy on the planet, even if only for a few moments.

She reached out and touched my cheek. I thought I would burst. She smiled at me one more time, then left.

I lay back, cradling my head on my crossed arms and grinning the biggest grin of all time. I twisted my head around and read the ceiling again. Now it said, in block stenciled letters:

PROPERTY OF
KINGSTOWN
FIRE DEPARTMENT

Thursday

▼

Seventy-one

I was stiff as hell when I woke up the next day. A brown plastic bottle of souped-up aspirin pills was on my dresser. I had a splitting headache anyway. When I moved my right leg, it felt like I had been stabbed there.

But I didn't mind.

I was, after all, alive. That's something I tend to take for granted, but after the events of last night, it was a state of affairs I could definitely appreciate.

I lay back in bed and contemplated last night. Had I really captured a Nazi war criminal last night? Dropped him, in fact, down an elevator shaft? Been shot at? Survived an explosion?

Apparently. It didn't seem real. It didn't even seem as real as a lot of my nightmares do.

And surpassing all these mere events, these comparative trifles, was Rachel. My mind still sang with her presence last night, her concern, her admiration. I closed my eyes and basked in the echoing glow of those moments.

She had returned to the rescue squad after they found Bunt, alive, where I had left him. We had had a quiet talk. This story was about to hit the news big, but she had promised me sincerely that she would keep my name out of police and press reports to the best of her ability.

Most important to me, we had arranged to meet for a celebration lunch today. I was already thinking ahead to it.

As it happened, my only injuries were a lightly sprained right ankle and the normal bumps and bruises one comes to expect when fleeing exploding houses. The guys in the rescue squad dropped me off at home in the early hours of the morning.

After I actually got out of bed, I padded over to the phone to check out a suspicion I had.

"Physics department," Mrs. Arden answered brightly.

"Hi, this is Mark Napoli."

"Oh, hi, Mark."

"I heard a rumor that classes were canceled again today. Any truth to that?" I tried to sound off-hand about it.

"Yes, that's right. All the windows on one side of the building are broken. Mr. Andersson's house exploded last night! And he seems to have been mixed up in Dr. Speen's death."

I sprinkled "Really"s and "Wow"s and "Golly"s through this, for verisimilitude.

"The workmen are putting up plywood now," she continued. "I'm sitting here in my coat and gloves. I would say just take the day off, Mark."

"Thanks, Mrs. Arden. I may just do that."

I smiled the smile of those released from the bonds of day-to-day-dom, even if only temporarily.

I turned the TV on. Coverage of the explosion was on every local channel, preempting the usual chats with celebrities about their new diet books. It had been a very photogenic explosion, starkly black and sinister against the dazzling white background. The sun was apparently out. From an aerial shot, it was eerie to retrace my footsteps—mentally, as all physical traces had been obliterated—up to, and away from, the wreckage. A few seconds difference and I would have been a charcoal-colored stain on the snow. Like those FBI agents in Ohio. I shivered.

I snapped the TV off, showered, and treated myself to a feast of waffles.

Then began the long and complex process of suiting up for lunch with Rachel.

Seventy-two

I was resplendent in my sports jacket, tie, and lone dress shirt as I arrived once again at Maybelle. My beard was carefully trimmed. I had the rest of the rent money in my pocket. I intended to take Rachel to Le Chateau. This was a famous, and famously expensive, restaurant by the sea-cliffs in Newport. Spectacular food. Spectacular views. Spectacular prices. Very romantic.

I felt like one of those Roman generals returning in triumph. I had come, I had seen, I had kicked serious hiney. Granted, there were no thronging multitudes jostling for a better view of the young hero leading his fallen enemies in chains. In fact, given that I wanted no publicity, there couldn't be. Yet, it still felt like a triumphal entrance. Perhaps Russell Mercer would donate a commemorative arch to the police station. They could call it the Arc de Mark.

Within, I inquired after Rachel in a spirit of exultation. The cop pointed with his thumb to the back, as usual.

I walked back toward her office, beaming at everyone.

Rachel was waiting for me in the corridor. She was probably wearing something, probably something pretty, but I didn't notice. She was beautiful and my whole attention, my whole being was centered on her.

"Hi, Mark," she said.

"Hi, Rachel," I said.

"Mark, this is my husband, Russell. Russell, this is Mark Napoli."

I gradually became aware of a man standing behind Rachel. So taken was I with her, I had not noticed him at all until now, even though he was taller than she was, large and athletic-looking, handsome, well-dressed, smiling, and, at present, extending his right hand to shake mine.

I don't know if you've ever met face-to-face with someone you had previously only seen on TV, or in magazines, or in the newspaper. It kind of takes you a few seconds to wrap your eyes around them, to realize that this is a real person, and not just a two-dimensional image. They expand before your eyes into full 3-D reality.

That's what it was like meeting Russell Mercer.

Husband? Russell? My eyes shot to her left hand. No ring. No jewelry at all, on either hand.

She was married to Russell Mercer?

I was so astonished and embarrassed that I let slip out exactly what I was thinking, something I make it a point never to do.

"I didn't know you were married," I blurted.

Something about my words, or my tone, or my expression seemed to click in Rachel. She opened her mouth, but it was Russell who spoke.

"Honey," he began with amused mock-reproof.

"Russell, we've discussed this," she replied, in a snuggling and flirtatious way that made me nauseous. "My rings interfere with my gun if I need to use it. Besides, I always *wear* them."

With this, she pulled her gold chain into view. Dangling from it in plain view were a wide gold wedding band and an engagement ring with a fairly immense diamond. My heart pounded.

Russell gave me a wistful smile and shrugged, as if to say, "What can you do when the woman you love drives you crazy sometimes?"

I couldn't answer that one.

Rachel Trask was married to Russell Mercer. He was tall and strong and good-looking and rich. I was, in a word, not. And Rachel was married to him. I couldn't even bring myself to dislike him. He seemed like a genuinely nice guy. If we had met in other circumstances (for instance, had I not been in love with his wife), we might have become friends. As it was, I thought probably not.

I found that Rachel was apparently speaking, apparently to me. "Russell's going to take us to lunch at Le Chateau, in Newport."

"I hope you don't mind me tagging along with you two," said Russell earnestly. "Rachel's been telling me just a little about what you've done,

Mark, and I just had to hear all about it in your own words. You are a real hero. It sounds like an unbelievable adventure."

Unbelievable. That about summed it up for me. I suddenly envisioned the prospect of trying to get through a meal with these two.

No way. I would far rather get a sharp stick in the eye than have to sit at table with Rachel and her husband (her husband!) and try to form coherent sentences for the next few hours.

I shook my head in mock sadness. "Actually, I was coming here to explain that I can't come to lunch today at all. Something's come up." I was hearing myself talking, but I had no idea what I was saying. I was kind of curious to see what I would say next.

Rachel looked at my jacket and tie quizzically. How could I explain the obviously-special way I was dressed?

I spread my hands. "Job interview," I said, which seemed plausible. Her face seemed to brighten. "Yes. I guess one of the science teachers at the high school is ill, so they called the university and my chairman suggested I apply." I tried to look embarrassed, not a difficult feat under the circumstances. "I can really use the money."

"Oh, of course," Rachel blurted hurriedly.

"I'm really sorry about lunch," I offered. "It's a last-minute thing."

"That's too bad, but maybe we can all do it another time," Russell suggested brightly.

"Another time. What a great idea," I said.

"Well, good luck," said Russell.

I looked at him blankly.

"On your interview. Good luck on your interview."

"Right. Sure. Thanks," I said rolling my eyes in mock-confusion. "A lot's been going on lately." I shrugged.

"Of course it has. Well, I'll see you," Rachel said. She was looking at me, I think beginning to understand a little about what was happening.

"Yeah, be seeing you," I said.

And with a few more hurried exchanges, I escaped.

Seventy-three

My dentist had once used some anesthetic on me that had rendered me totally unaware of the existence of my mouth and lower jaw. I felt that way now, about my entire body. I still don't know how, with unfeeling hands and limbs, I managed to walk to my car, start it, and drive the few blocks I was able to before I started weeping and had to pull over because I couldn't see.

Out of the supernova of surprise, disappointment, anger, betrayal, confusion, embarrassment, vulnerability, fury, shame, outrage, depression, and hopelessness that I had felt only a few moments ago, only a hard, dense and featureless sphere remained:

Why?

Why did this keep happening? Immediately, a chorus of inner voices rose to argue that this was different, there was nothing that "kept happening". But the question silenced them. Why? It went far beyond the simple whys. Why hadn't I realized those were wedding rings on that pendant? Why didn't I assume she was married until it was proved differently? Why did I misinterpret everything that had gone between us? Why had I learned nothing from my devastating experience with Lee? Why could I not recognize reality when I saw it? Why did I think that someone like Rachel would ever be interested in someone like me? Why did I think life would ever turn out differently? Why continue struggling? Why was the world like this? Why was I like this?

Why?

I found myself at home somehow. I didn't even remember restarting the car. That was kind of disturbing.

I sat down in the living room, something I rarely did. It was too exposed to Eli. But Eli was apparently not home. Thank heaven.

I felt like I was slipping down a hole, like I was half-in, half-out of a hole filled with sticky pulling tar. I had fallen in when Lee had left. In a year, I had managed to crawl half-way out, agonizingly, inch by inch. But now I was slipping back in again.

I was slipping.

I could feel it.

I could feel it.

My mind was slewing sideways, trying to escape the explosion, slipping, sliding, futilely struggling for a toe-hold that wasn't there.

My eyes rested on my box of records. The first record was by Bread. It was full of depressing songs about loss and sadness and pain. I had played it over and over after Lee. I could not go through this again. I just couldn't. Slipping. Slipping.

I found myself on my knees on the floor before the record box. I didn't remember walking, or crawling, over. I had the album in my hand. I took the record from its sleeve. It was black and round, shiny. I flexed it in my hand. It bent and bent. I exerted more and more force. It bent and bent and. Snapped!

I exhaled the breath I didn't know I'd been holding. I breathed a few times. That felt good. I dropped the shattered pieces to the floor. I pulled out another album. America. Depressing. I pulled out the record and flexed it, flexed it, flexed it. Snap! I dropped it on the floor.

The Moody Blues. Snap! Carole King. Snap! Bread again. Snap! Neil Diamond. Snap! Neil Young. Snap! Cat Stevens. Snap!

Snap. Snap. Snap. Snap. Snap.

Elton John.

Elton John. Lee had liked Elton John. I hesitated a good three seconds before I snapped it.

Elton John again. A song about a madman. A madman.

I looked at the broken records all over the floor.

What the hell was I doing?

I was snapping.

I had snapped.

I sat back on the floor. I felt much better. And much much worse.

I heaped together the pieces and threw them into the trash. I went to my room and fell on the bed. I could not cry anymore. As I lay there, my cheek pressed against the unknowing sheet I had a thought. A thought of clarity. Forget Why? That's too big a question. Here's the question on today's quiz:

Problem 1:

Mark and the world make a terrible combination. Given that you can't change the world, what *can* you do?

I knew what I could do. I walked to the bathroom, filled my hands with water at the sink, and splashed my face.

I looked up in the mirror.

I knew the answer.

I knew what to do.

It was so obvious. So simple. Why hadn't I thought of this after Lee? Why had I dragged myself through the last year trying to survive in this tar pit? Well, I knew the answer now. I knew what to do. How to stop the cycle of Why?

I went to my room and opened the top bureau drawer. Near the back, I found it: my razor, long unused. I brought it to the bathroom. I touched the edge of the blade with my finger, not hesitating at all to bring forth blood. Too dull. Far too dull for this job. Dull from time and disuse. I couldn't remember the last time I had used it. Well, I had a very special job for it now. Very special.

I opened the medicine cabinet and stole one of Eli's razor blades. Let him find out. What would I care? I touched the edge. Oh yes. Very sharp. Just right. Just what I would need for this job.

I looked at myself in the mirror and noticed my clothes. I still had the tie and jacket on. That was no good. Blood all over them. What a mess.

I walked back to my room and undressed to my underwear. I hung up the jacket, and tie, and shirt and pants. I would not be needing them for a while.

Back in the bathroom, I noticed the shower. Should I do this in the tub? Nice hot water. Not so messy to clean up. I remembered that's how the Romans would commit suicide. A nice hot bath, some nice slits along the veins, and then a nice cup of wine while you wait. I could use a cup of wine. I knew we didn't have any in the house, though. Too bad. A cup of wine would have been good. Ah, well.

I decided against the tub. I was in too much of a hurry. I knew what to do, and I wanted to do it, now. I could feel myself getting second thoughts. Do it now, before you start questioning your decision.

Now.

I washed my face with good hot water. I looked at the mirror. I looked into my eyes for a long time. Long enough.

So long, I said to my reflection. So long.

I took a deep breath and raised the blade to the taut skin of my throat.

Seventy-four

Stan was eating lunch alone in the dining hall when I sat down in the seat opposite him. He said, "It's taken," automatically and only then looked up from his plate.

"Holy Moses!" he exclaimed and dropped his fork. I heard it bounce onto the floor.

"A common mistake," I said, nodding. "He's always getting mistaken for me, too. However," I pointed out, "he has a beard, and I don't."

Seventy-five

I couldn't resist viewing the wreckage at the physics building. The large window in the main office was covered entirely by a sheet of raw plywood.

Mrs. Arden looked up at me and her mouth popped open, but she was too polite to comment on my appearance directly.

"Well," she said finally. "I have a package from a young woman who was looking for 'someone who works in the physics department with long hair, a big beard and glasses', but I'm not so sure I should give it to you now."

I smiled. "Kind of a shock, huh?" I ran my fingers along my newly-smooth cheek and chin. It was so strange to feel them, and for them to feel the air. It seemed like they could detect every molecule that struck them, especially in the wintry outside air.

"I should say so," she agreed heartily. "You know, Mark, you have a nice face when it's not all hidden by a beard."

I stood there and we looked at each other for a moment. "Thank you," I said finally.

She held a small package out to me, smiling. "Here you go."

I took it from her, mystified. It was about the size of a book, wrapped in plain white paper, taped closed, neatly and simply. There was nothing written on the outside.

"Who brought it?" I wondered.

"She didn't give her name," said Mrs. Arden. "And she didn't know yours either. She just described you to me." She was obviously full of curiosity about the package, about the girl, and about me.

Well, I was baffled. It couldn't be (shudder) Rachel. Admittedly, she knew my name, if precious little else about me. I tore open the package and saw the back of a book. I turned it over. It was a collection of essays by Albert Einstein. I was delighted.

I riffled the pages and a small envelope fell to the floor. I picked it up. It too had nothing written on the outside. I opened it. There was a small folded note inside. The note read:

> Dear Sherlock, [I smiled]
>
> Thank you for your help on the road to Kingstown. I took your advice and that very day I found a pretty good job waitressing at Steve's Restaurant. I made friends with Carol, one of the other waitresses and so now I'm living with her and her family. I signed up to take my high school equivalency test in January. If I pass I'll try to start at Kingston University in the fall.
>
> You really helped me and I wanted to get you a present. I thought someone in the physics department would like Einstein so…
>
> Thank you again,
> Love,
> Harriet

My first thought was, Good for her. Steve's was a great place for her to work, an unpretentious restaurant serving mainly breakfast and lunch, with Steve himself (although his name was actually Frank) cooking away in perpetual motion at the grill. You felt like part of a family there, not like a customer. You thought nothing of getting up and borrowing a bottle of ketchup or something if you needed it. And the friendly atmosphere would mean a safe environment for her. Good tips, too.

My second thought was, Damn, now I can't go to Steve's anymore. I occasionally treated myself to a modest Sunday omelet at Steve's, but I wouldn't want to run into her there.

My third thought was, She didn't look like a Harriet.

My fourth thought was, She shouldn't be wasting her money on presents for me. It said $4.95 on the spine. Too much. Almost what I gave her. I frowned and examined the book closely, especially the inside front cover.

I realized that she had bought it used, for 50 cents, at Fabulous Beast. I grinned. A perfect present: an Einstein book for a physicist, prudently purchased. What a wonderful woman!

My final thought was, "Love"? How many times in my life had I gotten *that* in writing?

I looked up. Mrs. Arden was waiting patiently. I couldn't explain to her who the book was really from without admitting what I had done, which I was unwilling to do. I equivocated.

"Friend of a friend," I said. "Met her at a friend's house. I helped her with some calculus homework. Never did get her name. I guess I mentioned I worked at the physics department." I hefted the book. "Nice of her."

Mrs. Arden wasn't buying it, any of it. "A very pretty girl," she remarked meaningfully.

I nodded. "Yes." I screwed my face up and regarded the ceiling theatrically. "Engaged to somebody in, I think she said, the English department."

She wasn't buying that either, but she let it go. "Thoughtful," she concluded.

"Yes," I agreed. I replaced the envelope in the book as casually as I could, knowing I would treasure this present always. I slipped her book in an inside pocket of my coat, near my heart.

I made to go, but she stopped me. "You had another message," she said, extending a slip of paper to me. "A Sergeant McKinnock."

My hand stopped in mid-air on its way to the paper. McKinnock? What was this about? This afternoon seemed like a mil'ion years ago. I wanted very much to be done with this particular group of law enforcement officers.

I took and read the note: Please call immediately. And the number.

Swell. Whatever good feelings Harriet's present had produced were extinguished like hot coals splashed by a bucket of water.

"Parking ticket," I said shortly to Mrs. Arden, then stomped up to my office to get it over with.

Seventy-six

Ten minutes later, I was reluctantly driving back to the hospital. McKinnock would say nothing, except that Lt. Trask had asked him to contact me about an urgent meeting with Payne Stickney. Urgent, he had urged urgently.

I was not looking forward enthusiastically to this particular tête-à-tête. I liked meeting with Stickney about as much as surgery without anesthesia, but I would rather meet with a thousand Stickneys than one Trask at this point. I could not be sure that I wouldn't strangle her when I saw her next, and my understanding was that the courts were cracking down on that sort of thing.

At the hospital, I found Payne Stickney readily enough, in a musty conference room on the second floor that smelled like people used it to sneak smokes. We exhibited all our usual camaraderie, which is to say he looked up from his legal pad when I entered, did a mild double-take at my clean-shaven face and developed a pained expression, while I slumped into a chair and stared pointedly out the window.

I felt like I was justified in doing so. I mean, think about it. Here I risk my neck to capture a spy, murderer and all around bad citizen, and this slab of beef doesn't even mention it. There was something distinctly odd about his behavior. I didn't for a moment expect him to say, "Good job," or anything like that. But to not say anything? Something was up with this bird. Something I didn't quite have a handle on yet.

"Where's Lt. Trask?" I asked eventually.

"'Lt. Trask', eh?" smirked Stickney. "What happened, you two have a spat?"

I looked lasers at him. "Drop dead, Payne."

He shrugged and went back to scribbling on his pad. "She'll be along shortly," he said absently.

I looked out the window at him some more.

Presently, I heard the tap-tap of shoes outside and Rachel entered. I turned from the window, looked at her and exhaled noisily. She was still beautiful and I would have married her on the spot if I didn't hate her so much.

She seemed angry with Stickney and ignored him. She smiled at me and said, "Hi, Mark. How'd the interview go?" Stickney looked up at this.

I had no idea what she was talking about. I was enraged with her. How dare she even speak to me? I realized that she was probably completely unaware that she had recently ruined my life, but that only enraged me more. How dare she not know what I had never told her? Besides, I was starting to have the sneaking suspicion that perhaps my own woman-related lunacy had played the starring role in the debacle of our relationship. Swell: I felt like crap and I didn't even get to blame somebody else for it. What kind of world was that?

Interview?

It slowly dawned on me that she was asking about the saving lie I had told her and (shudder) Russell to get out of lunch.

"Oh," I said morosely. "They've already filled the position."

Stickney seemed pleased with this and returned to his scribbling again.

"I'm sorry," she said. She seemed to be studying my appearance closely. Given that she was married, I didn't care if my new look swayed her one way or the other. Still, I was curious about her reaction. "New shirt?" she wondered.

I shook my head distantly and looked back out the window. It was torture being around her. Either she had done something mean to me, in which case I hated her, or I had been stupid with a woman again, in which case I was mortified around her. Take your pick, I was not a comfy character. What was I doing here?

Stickney stood and smoothed his tie and jacket. "If," he bellowed, "we can suspend the mutual admiration society for a moment, we have some things to discuss."

"There's nothing to discuss," Rachel countered hotly.

Despite myself, I began wondering what was going on. Rachel was usually at least polite to Stickney, but now her hostility toward him was matched only by, well, mine toward her, or mine toward myself, mine toward him, and maybe his toward me. We were lucky there were no flammable liquids present.

"Oh, but I think there is," Stickney said smoothly. He seated himself on the conference table and pulled a paper from his vest pocket. "This arrived this afternoon."

I looked at Rachel. She said, "I've read it," turned her back on Stickney and walked to the far end of the room. I watched her in disbelief. Hey, *I'm* supposed to be the angry one here.

I reached up and snatched the paper from Payne's hand. I unfolded it and saw that it was a telegram. I had never actually seen a real telegram before, so I found it interesting and examined it minutely. When Stickney started making impatient noises, I finally got around to actually reading it. It was phrased in some strange police-type dialect of English, but in essence it said that, not that it was anybody's business, but they happened to know beyond a doubt that Dieter Bunt had died in 1964, never mind the details, and thanks for asking. It was signed by someone who identified himself as the Assistant Director, and "they" apparently were a branch of Special Intelligence, State of Israel.

I reread it four times.

When I saw no point in rereading it further, I held it out rather limply. Stickney grabbed it from me, refolded it, and replaced it in his vest pocket.

He leaned forward from the waist and kicked his feet back and forth slightly as he began talking.

"So, fellow crime-fighters, apparently the old man YOU," he indicated me with a bob of his head, "threw down the elevator shaft and whose house YOU," another bob, "blew up, is not, in fact, a Nazi war criminal at all. MY guess, and I admit I'm only a Special Agent for the FBI and not a graduate student like you, is that this old man is probably one Mr. Vitus Andersson, a retired Danish schoolmaster."

I refused to be goaded by him. "Who is this guy?" I asked, indicating the telegram in his pocket.

"'This guy', as you refer to him, is a friend of mine in the Mossad. We FBI Special Agents occasionally make contacts with members of agencies of other governments. Rather than go through official channels right off the bat, I thought I would check this out unofficially. After your little hoe-down last night, I sent my friend a simple question, with no details about what's been going on, or your questionable theories about it. Just: Do you know if Bunt is alive? My contact is, shall we say, in the know there. This," he patted his pocket, "is his reply."

I wasn't satisfied. "Why would they think that Bunt is dead when no one else on earth seems to think so?"

"Well, let's think about that," he mused theatrically. "Suppose that you are the Israeli secret service department charged with tracking down and capturing Nazi war criminals. Suppose that you play rough sometimes, and maybe you don't dot every i and cross every t when it comes to crossing national borders and kidnapping foreign citizens and so forth. And let's suppose that in the process of tracking down and capturing a certain major dirtbag named Bunt that you somehow, inadvertently, make him dead. And let's say, for the sake of argument, that all this occurs in a country we shall, for the heck of it, choose to call Texas. What would you do? Would you, in fact, announce to the world, The Bunt is dead, and we should know because we killed him in, as it turns out, Texas? Or would you, perhaps, sit on that information, and quietly close the file, and be content with the fact that the world was down one dirtbag? Your call, doc. What do you say?"

I could see it. I could easily see it. And I could even believe it. All except for the fact that I had faced Dieter Bunt late last night, and that he was now presumably in a bed on one of the floors above me. "Is that what happened?" I asked.

Stickney looked at me earnestly, which made me want to barf. "It goes no further than this room," he said. "But yes, that is what happened."

I looked out the window again. What was going on here? What was this guy trying to pull, and why?

Stickney went on. "This simple fact leads to several conclusions. First, since this guy upstairs is not a Nazi war criminal, there is no good reason to hold him on that charge, or try to extradite him to Israel. Second, since this guy is not Bunt, he obviously could not give a whiz if your man Speen tried to blackmail him by threatening to expose him. Therefore, this guy has no motive to murder Speen, so there's no reason to hold him for the murder, either. Third, since this guy is not the Nazi your pal Katanga claims was the spy working with Speen, he is not the spy I am interested in. I have no reason to hold him for espionage, either. Three, two, one, blastoff!"

Rachel, silent until now, exploded. "Mark, he wants to set him free!" she raged.

Stickney held up a finger. "Not immediately. He has to stay in the hospital anyway. I see no reason not to watch him lightly while he's here."

"But after..." she began.

"Your whole case," Stickney thundered, "depends on him being Bunt. He isn't. There's nothing to charge him with."

I interrupted. "He tried to kill me last night," I said. "Thrice."

"You say," countered Payne. "We only have your word on that. There is no other evidence."

"The gun," I said. "A big hole in a fifth floor wall."

"Yes, he held the gun. Fingerprints. Yes, the gun shot the wall. Ballistics. But him threatening to shoot you? No, nothing."

"So why did he end up down the elevator shaft?"

"You tell me, doc. Why? This guy was not a Nazi, but you convinced her that he was. Then some attacks—unprovable attacks—supposedly occurred against you. Then he ends up down an elevator shaft, almost dead, and his house blows up. No evidence. All evidence destroyed. Just your accusation. So why would you do that?"

I felt a thrill of fear in my bowels. "What are you getting at?"

"Let's make up a story. Very hypothetical. Speen and Katanga are spies. But there is somebody else. Somebody in the physics department. Katanga is the messenger between Speen and this somebody. Speen drops little hints to Katanga that the spy is a German, maybe a Nazi, to put him off the scent. Speen and the somebody never meet. Even though they're in the same building, they never meet. Katanga is the go-between."

"You're crazy. I hated Speen."

"Of course you would *pretend* to! That would be the perfect cover. It would be too suspicious, if anything went wrong, for you to be pals with Speen. No, there would be no connection between you two. You would even organize a little in-class confrontation, to show how much you hated him, to endure his humiliation. You and Speen acting together on anything? How absurd!"

I couldn't speak. My mind was awhirl with his concoction.

"Then something goes wrong. Maybe Speen was acting up. Maybe Katanga. So, you decide to get them both. Kill Speen and pin it on Katanga. Two birds with one stone. Andersson happens to be on the scene, and you get a wonderful idea. To muddy the waters even more, you build on Speen's fable to Katanga. A Nazi war criminal in our very midst! How perfect: now Katanga can be a witness for you. Everything Katanga says now has a basis in reality that lets you out."

"This has a million holes in it," I burst out. "What about Speen's books? What about the gun?"

"Of course it has holes! So what? Don't you see how it could be presented to a jury? It makes at least as much sense as your version. And the fact is you did put him down the elevator shaft and you did blow up his house."

Rachel was livid. "We will never prosecute him for any of that, Payne. Never."

Stickney raised and lowered his hands, palms down. "Let's everybody calm down now, shall we? I said hypothetical, didn't I? I'm just trying to show that there are alternate ways of explaining everything. Given that our friend upstairs is not Bunt, your way is not very convincing. There may be some things we can't actually explain. Let's see if we can come to some understanding of what we can explain."

Rachel sat in a chair, her arms crossed over her chest, still seething, but willing to listen. I slumped in my chair, weak and boneless. I felt like I had just narrowly escaped charges of espionage, assault, murder, and leaving an exploding house without a license.

Stickney started ticking off points on his hand. "Speen was obviously spying. Katanga says that, and I believe him. But he's dead, so there's nothing there. Katanga was helping Speen, however unwillingly. So, he's spying, too. I'm pursuing that."

Rachel looked at me, but I was in no shape to object, and she let it go.

"There is at least one other spy. It's not Bunt, 'cause he's dead. It's not Andersson, 'cause he's not Bunt. We have no other suspect. We can't go any further on that. Speen is murdered. I'll buy that Katanga didn't do it. That's really your investigation."

"We are not arresting Katanga again," Rachel declared flatly.

"Fine. Your prerogative. It's the other spy again, so we can't go any further on that either. So, we have Speen dead, Katanga spying, and the unknown spy murdering Speen. I think that's it."

Rachel turned to me. "You're not really going to let Katanga take the blame, are you? You're not going to let Bunt escape after what he did to you, are you?"

I looked at her, into her big blue eyes, and finally heard the bell. She had actually been using me all along. I won't flatter myself by claiming to be any detective, but I do have, shall we say, certain abilities, and she had been using them ever since I walked into her office. She had solicited my physics opinion about how the murder had been done. She had encouraged me in my search for Bunt, a long-shot that it would have been difficult for her to justify as part of her police investigation. I was the one who had tracked Andersson, when she couldn't. I was the one who had faced down Bunt, alone, when the police had nothing to charge him with. I was the one who had broken into his house for information, nearly getting myself killed in the process. All along I had done whatever she needed doing, and whatever she and the police could not do.

And why had I done it? There was, ultimately, only one reason. For Rachel Trask. She must have known that. She must have realized the effect that she was having on me. To call me out of the blue like that, not to come to police headquarters, but to go out for coffee together on a Saturday night. Like a date. And on campus. Convenient to the scene of the crime. Never wearing a ring. Never mentioning a husband or any other men. "Pick me up." She knew what she had been doing. She had been around the block. She wasn't some wide-eyed innocent. She knew precisely the right bait to use. She had hooked me and reeled me in, and I had enjoyed every minute of it. Just to be near her. Just to be close. Maybe I was a dope around women. All right, no maybes: I was a dope around women. But maybe some women use dopes for their own purposes. And maybe I wasn't the same dope I had been.

I stood up. "Yes, I am," I said.

She was speechless, which was kind of enjoyable.

To Stickney I said, "You're right. If the Israelis aren't interested in this guy, he can't be Bunt. I'm not apologizing for what I did to him though: he did come after me with a gun, and he did wire his house to blow up, for whatever reason. I don't know who the other spy is, and I don't know who killed Speen. Katanga did commit a crime, so I guess he has to be tried."

Stickney was floored. He actually stammered, "I'm not saying we have a great case against him. All we really have is his own story. The U. S. Attorney may even decline to prosecute."

"That would be good." I shrugged. "Whatever. I'm sorry if I've gotten in your way. I was trying to help. No hard feelings."

I stuck out my hand.

"None here," he said, shaking it limply.

"So long," I said.

"So long," he repeated, still in shock.

"Goodbye, Lt. Trask," I said, and left without waiting for her reply.

She caught up with me in the hall, breathless and incredulous.

"What are you doing?" she demanded.

"I'm going back to campus," I replied simply. I couldn't look at her. I was too confused, both embarrassed and furious.

"I don't understand," she said, shaking her head helplessly.

"I think you understand a lot of it." She stepped back as if I'd slapped her. "As for the rest, I'm not the cop. I'm a physicist, or I'm trying to be. You're the cop. If you want to catch the bad guys, you go ahead. I'm done with it."

I turned and left her there, and she was too surprised to say goodbye.

Seventy-seven

As I drove back to the physics department, I did a little catechism in my mind of my current beliefs:

Is Andersson really Dieter Bunt? Yes, there is no doubt in my mind. Did Andersson kill Speen? Yes again. Did it make any sense whatsoever that Israel would maintain that Bunt was dead when I knew he was alive? No, it did not. Had Rachel Trask played me for a major sucker in this entire investigation? Why, yes, she had. Was it entirely her fault? No, I guessed not: I had to admit I was an utter moron around women, and pretty much bound to shoot myself in the foot, emotionally speaking, sooner or later. And lastly, did I have any idea whatsoever how to prove that Bunt was a spy, that Bunt was a murderer, or even that Bunt was Bunt? No, these things are mysteries to us and we must just take them on faith.

But I was done with all that now. It felt as if an immense weight had lifted from my shoulders. Someone else would catch the Nazis now, or not, but it was out of my hands. Someone else would be threatened at gunpoint, and pushed down elevator shafts, and blown up by houses. I had done my share. I was out of it. I heaved a sigh of relief.

What I needed now was physics, lots of physics, big heaping bowls-full of physics, and keep them coming. I had tried dealing with reality and it hadn't worked out. I had learned my lesson. I was homesick for things that didn't exist except in the minds of scientists, and that 99% of the planet didn't understand or care about. I wanted to find a beautiful equation to call my own and a build a life with. When I mounted the steps to the physics department, I felt like I was finally coming home.

Seventy-eight

"Back again?" asked Mrs. Arden, as I passed her office on the way to mine.

Back to stay, I felt. "Yes, I am."

She brightened. "Would you feel like running a quick errand for me?" she asked. "I'd go myself, but I'm waiting for a phone call here."

I stepped into the office. "Sure," I said. "What is it?"

She handed me what looked like an invoice. "The new cable for the computer terminal came in. Would you please walk over to the computer lab and get it for me? It won't take you five minutes."

"Sure," I said again and left.

That's just what I need, I thought. The end of a simple mystery. A new cable. A simple task to perform. Nothing strange or bizarre. No crime. No Nazis. Just walking. Holding a piece of paper. Carrying a cable. Going and coming back again. This I could handle. This was the kind of life I wanted to lead now.

At the computer lab, I handed the invoice to a student clerk at the counter who glanced at it and called out, "Art!"

It didn't seem particularly artistic to me, but a few seconds later the manager of the computer lab appeared, wearing a name badge that said, "Art". He was a burly bear of a man, with ginger hair and beard. The clerk handed the invoice over. Art glanced at me and said, "Okay, come around."

This I can handle, I thought, passing through a flap in the counter.

"It's in my office," Art said over his shoulder, as I trotted behind.

He passed through the office door, then swung around and said, "Hey, are you all right?"

He said that because, rather than catching the spring-loaded door as he passed it to me, I had let it smack me right in the face. I could neither move nor speak.

Art opened the door and I tottered against a filing cabinet. I managed to raise my arm and point, saying dazedly, "What...what is *that*?"

He followed my pointing arm, hand, and finger to an object on his desk.

It was about the size and shape of a shoe box, made of black plastic, with rounded edges. In the top were two circular holes, padded, which looked the perfect size and shape to hold two styrofoam cups of coffee. Except the coffee would spill, because the holes were angled outward away from each other slightly. From the bottom ran three or four strands of colored wire. I had no idea what it was.

Art looked from it back to me. "It's a modem," he said.

I was massaging my forehead. "What's a modem?" I asked. It sounded vaguely middle eastern.

"Same as an acoustic coupler," he explained unhelpfully.

"Acoustic what?"

"Acoustic coupler," he repeated. "It lets you connect terminals to the computer using phone lines. We use them for off-campus locations where we haven't laid cable yet."

Computer? Phone?

"How does it work?" I blurted.

"Very simple," he said. "You connect those wires to your terminal and turn it on. Then you dial the phone our computer is connected to." He lifted the receiver from the phone on his desk and mimed dialing. "When you hear the tone, you put the phone in the cradle." Before my wondering eyes, he placed the ends of the phone into the two padded holes in the modem. They fit perfectly. "Your terminal then communicates with our computer through the phone lines."

I was breathing heavily. "Do it," I urged. "Call the computer."

He looked at me as if I were crazy—a pretty accurate assessment. He looked up a number from a list on his wall, then dialed the phone for real. After a few moments, he held out the phone to me.

I listened, my heart pounding. I heard a high-pitched squeal, as if he had dialed a number that was out of order. I hung up the phone and pointed to the modem.

"Can I borrow this for a little while?" I asked.

Seventy-nine

Art was quite amenable to my borrowing his modem, especially after I turned over my keys, driver's license, and all my other ID cards. He let me keep my shoes, luckily, and I trotted back to the physics department with the modem under my arm.

I burst into Mrs. Arden's office out of breath. "What's the matter?" she asked. "Where's the cable? What's that?"

I had forgotten the cable. I shook my head. "Never mind that," I puffed. "Do you still have that phone number? The long-distance one. The German one."

She nodded slowly. I crooked my finger at her. "Come with me," I said.

We went upstairs and she unlocked the door to the room with the terminal. "Watch this," I said. I connected the modem wires to the broken wires protruding from the back of the terminal, as Art had shown me. I turned on the terminal. It sat there and hummed. I took the number from Mrs. Arden and dialed the phone. When it rang, I held it up to her ear.

Her eyes widened. "That's the same sound I heard before."

I nodded and fitted the phone receiver into the modem holes. Her eyes widened further. The terminal leaped into life, swiftly typing rows of text in German.

I waved a hand at the paper. "Please decipher," I requested.

She bent down to look at the paper spewing from the terminal. "'Welcome to the University of Esel Center for Computers'," she read. She turned to me, her eyes gleaming. "Mark, you figured this out? What does it mean?"

"Someone was breaking in here, pulling the cable out of the back of the terminal, then using their modem to call this computer in Germany."

She shook her head. "But who? Why?"

I couldn't think of any easy way of explaining. "Dr. Speen was killed by a German spy. The spy did this."

I spent the next couple of minutes giving her a rough sketch of recent events in and around the physics department. It was an odd feeling for me to be the one in the know for once. She kept saying, "That's unbelievable," which was right on the money.

When I had finished she said, "Now what?"

"Now we see what is on this university computer. Do you want to try it?"

"Absolutely," she said, flexing her fingers eagerly. "This is like the movies. What do we do first?"

"We have to figure out how to log on. What does all this say?"

She gave me a quick summary of the typing. Welcome to…Date…Time…Please enter your six-character user code.

"Six character user code," I mused. Modem. "Try 'KLB126'," I suggested.

She complied, wondering, "Where'd you get that?"

I shook my head. I really didn't feel like going into the whole exploding house saga. "Long story. What's it saying?"

"'Password?'" she translated.

"Try 'Andersson'." I spelled it. She looked at me quizzically, then did so.

"It says, 'Passwords more than eight characters long are forbidden.'"

"Try 'Bunt'." I spelled that too, and she typed it without any reaction.

"'Passwords must have more than five characters.'"

"Try 'Dieter'." She typed it and pressed Return. There was a moment's silence, then the terminal erupted with about a page full of text.

"What's it saying?" I wondered.

"'Good evening. Last login October 21. Notices about University events. You have 7 messages waiting. Read them now?'"

I sat back. "This is how they communicated," I mused. "They could leave messages for Bunt, and he could leave messages for them. Even if their phones were tapped, who would figure all this out?"

Mrs. Arden was wiggling in her seat. "Aren't we going to read their messages?" she said hopefully.

"Absolutely. Let's do it."

She entered a J for Ja and a columned list scrolled out. She pointed. "This is date, time, length, and from who."

Under the column headed "Von:" it said Uncle Franz seven times.

"Uncle Franz," I muttered. "That must be Bunt's contact. Let's see what Uncle Franz has to say."

She began to read the messages, and translate them to me.

Uncle Franz started out very happy with the toys his nephew had sent, and assured him that the candy was on its way, and please be sure to share the candy with his friend at school. In other words, the spies had received the information that Bunt had sent, and that they had then sent payment for it, to be distributed to Speen.

Next Uncle Franz was concerned that his nephew's friend was not playing nicely. Perhaps his nephew could give him more candy? In any case, the nephew must be a good boy. Namely, Speen was beginning to give Bunt a hard time: Bunt should offer more money, but not do anything drastic.

Then Uncle Franz was shocked at how naughty his nephew's friend was acting. The nephew must teach him some manners, but not turn naughty himself. This must have been when Speen started threatening Bunt. Bunt must deal with Speen forcefully, but not kill him.

Uncle Franz heard that his nephew had been very naughty, and must apologize at once. They must have learned somehow that Speen had been murdered, knew that Bunt must have done it, and demanded an explanation.

Uncle Franz was growing impatient with his nephew for being so long in writing. Obviously, Bunt had found it too hot to get near the computer terminal both before and after he had murdered Speen. In fact, he had probably not even seen any of the previous messages, and had tried to handle things on his own without consulting his own bosses, with not very admirable results. They would not like that, I suspected.

I was right. Uncle Franz was giving a very stern warning that he must apologize immediately. Bunt was being given an ultimatum to communicate with his contacts.

Finally, Uncle Franz hinted darkly that some boys might be mean to his nephew unless he heard from him soon. Maybe they were putting the spy equivalent of a contract out on Bunt. I wondered how safe he would be in that hospital. Not very, one hoped.

"Wow," Mrs. Arden said when we were finished. "That's the most excitement I've ever had in my life. Now what?"

I sat back in my chair. How could I use this material for the best? If the Israelis said no, there was no way that I could prove that Andersson was Bunt. But maybe I could still prove that Andersson was a spy. That would supply the motive for murdering Speen right there. Might get Katanga off, too.

I shook my head. Oh no. I was back in it again.

To Mrs. Arden, I said, "I think that now we do a little creative writing. Please hang up the phone."

With the link to the computer severed, the terminal was just an electric typewriter, at which Mrs. Arden was a virtuoso. Her typing skills were never put to such a demanding test. Duplicating the format of a computer printout is no mean feat, especially when taking my dictation in English and translating it into German at the same time. But, within a half hour, we were finished.

After Mrs. Arden and I were done at the terminal, I said good night to her. I promised to let her know the outcome of her work. She was all excited. I could imagine that this would be all over the building by the morning. With any luck, it wouldn't matter by then.

I went to my office and called Payne Stickney. It took three different numbers before I found him, back at the hospital again. I asked him if he had any "friends" in Germany like he had in Israel, and if he was any good at tracing phone calls.

He said yes to those two questions. And to the next seventeen that followed.

Eighty

I called Jackson Katanga's twin sister Lillian and explained what I needed. She agreed readily. After a quick detour to the computer lab to swap the modem for my ID and keys, I drove by her apartment building. She met me at the door and handed me an envelope.

"I'll take good care of it," I assured her.

She shook her head. "It is yours to do with as you wish," she stated. "I know that you will do the right thing."

I met Stickney at the hospital. Rachel was there too, but I couldn't look at her and think straight.

Stickney was getting cranky. "I want what you have and I want it now," he demanded.

"Now, Payne," I said. "Play nice. You let me play first, then I share with you. We will have fun." I was starting to sound like Uncle Franz.

"I'm liking this less and less," he muttered.

"It will all be over in a few minutes. Are we set to go?"

He nodded. "We're set on this end. Let me check with Rolf."

"Rolf?" I wondered aloud as he gabbed in what even I could tell was lousy German on one of eight telephones labeled with masking tape. Guys with neat haircuts, white shirts, and headphones were milling around drinking coffee. Stickney must have yanked every free FBI agent from Providence, Boston, and Hartford to get all this arranged so fast. Maybe he really was secretly competent. Nurses kept passing in the corridor outside, shooting dirty looks through the open door at the noise and commotion in their hospital.

Stickney came back. "Okay, we're ready," he said. "But he has to talk for at least two minutes for this to work."

"Don't worry," I assured him. "These old pals are going to have a lot to talk about."

Eighty-one

I nodded at the police officer outside Bunt's door. He nodded back. He had been told to let me in, per my instructions. I took a deep breath, pushed open one of the swinging double doors, and went into Bunt's room.

"Hi, Dieter," I called cheerily.

He looked up with profound hatred. I noted the phone on the table by his bed. When I had called Stickney before, I had instructed him to get a pretty nurse to go to Bunt's room, say, "Haven't they installed your phone *yet*, sir?", install a phone, fluff Bunt's pillow, and leave. I didn't check his pillow, but it looked like the rest had happened.

"What are you doing here?" Bunt demanded. "Get out! Officer!"

I pulled a chair up close to his bed and plopped down into it. "Forget about it, Dieter," I said. "I'm friends with the cops. They're not going to throw me out on your say-so."

"Stop calling me that. My name is Andersson."

"Not for long," I replied gaily. "And I really can't stay long myself. I just wanted to drop by and say goodbye and thanks."

Bunt looked baffled. "Goodbye? Thanks?" he repeated mechanically.

"Yes, goodbye," I went on merrily. "Because you, Dieter Bunt, have won an all-expense paid trip to Israel!"

"Israel," he said. "That will never happen. Extradition takes…"

I interrupted him and continued in the same jovial game-show-host vein. "Yes, you and an armed guard escort will soon be winging your way to lovely Israel, home to the world's Jews, many the survivors of your very own death camps. While in Israel, you'll enjoy accommodations in the most maximum security prisons on the planet, and feast on kosher delicacies like matzo and water. Your cell will be luxuriantly decorated with stars of David. And all under the watchful eyes of Jews! All supervised by Jews 24 hours a day! All at the mercy of Jews!"

During this spiel, Bunt had been growing steadily more agitated. His hands began to move on the sheets, clenching, unclenching. I could see his mind imagining the whole scene.

"And what a time you'll have. Imagine reliving tender moments from your past, with people you probably haven't seen in thirty years. Ah, what memories they'll bring back. I hear that the Russians have some charming snapshots of your leg bones that prove conclusively that you are Dieter Bunt. And what better hands to have your fate in than twelve conscientious Jews who will give your future well-being all the consideration it deserves. Imagine how happy everyone will be when you're led out to the scaffold, and the cheers as your neck snaps at the end of a rope. And have no fear: your ashes will be respectfully scattered in the sewers of Tel Aviv until the end of time."

By this time, two hunted eyes had joined that ferocious scowl on his face. He looked about the room anxiously. For help? For escape? The phone, Dieter, the telephone.

"But enough about you," I proceeded in the same convivial manner. "Let's talk about me. I'm mighty grateful to you, Dieter. Mighty grateful, indeed."

He stared at me as if I were mad. "What?" he managed to say.

I sighed. "You know, we graduate students don't earn a lot of money. That's why it's so terrific and generous of you to give me the opportunity to make a little extra cash."

He was speechless. I saw that I was going to have to carry this conversation myself.

"I've been speaking to Uncle Franz," I confided.

His eyes widened and his whole body stiffened. If he had been concerned before, he was terrified now. It warmed my heart.

"You lie," he grunted through clenched teeth.

I pulled a sheaf of computer paper out of my coat. "Oh no," I assured him. "This is the straight stuff, Dieter. Why, did you think you were the only person on earth who could figure out how to use a modem? You see, Dieter, that's the mistake you master race types always make. You think you're the only ones with brains. This just goes to show what happens when you try to tangle with a non-Aryan genius. I took the liberty of lifting your modem just before I blew up your house. Figured it might come in handy. Didn't tell the police, of course. None of their business, really. I dialed up your alma mater, old Esel U., said the magic words 'KLB126' and 'Dieter' and voila: a mailbox crammed with postcards from Uncle Franz. He's been very upset with you."

I showed him some of Uncle Franz's more strident messages. He could hardly hold them, his hands had started to shake so badly.

"Yes, he was very upset. Until he finally heard from you, that is."

His head whipped up to me. "But I have not..." he began.

"Dieter, Dieter, that is, after all, the beauty of using the computer for messages rather than the telephone. Perfect anonymity. All I had to do was type messages to Uncle Franz, pretending I was you. Oh, he was so relieved to hear from you again. Especially with the good news you had for him."

His mouth was hanging open. He was out of control now, and knew it. There was no attempt at pretense any more. "Good news," he repeated.

"Sure, about how you had cracked Speen's safe, and now had reams of lovely toys to send him. But, of course, you would need more candy." He cringed at my use of their little code words. "You were very insistent with him, though, and he finally gave in."

Here I showed him a torn-off sheet of computer paper. It looked just like any of the other messages, but Mrs. Arden had typed it on the terminal from my dictation.

"Two hundred thousand dollars!" Bunt erupted.

"A fair price, don't you think?" I queried. "For all the lovely secrets you promised him?"

A little of the old Bunt emerged. He sneered, "They will never pay so much."

"On the contrary, Dieter. He's so anxious for delivery he's already wired me ten thousand dollars to grease the wheels."

At this, I pulled out the envelope Lillian had entrusted to me, and fanned a hundred $100 bills in Bunt's face. His eyes bulged.

"This is a year's salary for me," I admitted to him. "But not any more. Because I'm going to get another hundred thousand up front, before I disappear later tonight."

"Disappear?" he said weakly.

"Well, of course, disappear," I chided him. "I don't have any secret papers to deliver to him. I'm going to take the hundred grand down payment and vanish."

"But they will track you down," Bunt eagerly informed me. "They are tireless in tracking down betrayers. And they will be merciless when they find you."

I laughed in his face. "Dieter, baby, you still don't get it. They won't be looking for me. They'll be looking for *you*! *You're* the one who sent them those messages. *You're* the one who promised them secret material. *You're* the one who demanded the money. *You're* the one they're sending the hundred grand to. Why would they look for me?"

He had turned a shade of green that didn't do anything for him. He was paralyzed. He stared straight ahead. His breathing was hoarse.

I stood up and stretched. "Well, gotta go," I said amiably. "I can see you have a lot on your mind." I glanced at the wall clock. "Is that the time? You'll excuse me, Dieter, but I have some packing to do. You know how it is." I glanced at the guarded door meaningfully. "Or maybe you don't."

I strolled to the door and paused. "I doubt we'll be seeing each other again, Dieter, so this is probably goodbye." He looked up at me with unseeing eyes. "Have a nice trip to the end of that rope. And if you run into Hitler in hell, tell him I said, 'Heil.'"

I smiled, waved, and stepped out the door.

Eighty-two

Outside, I took in and let out a deep breath. Wow, did that suck. I felt like chowing down on a bar of laundry soap.

I walked directly across the hall to a darkened empty room. Standing on a chair, I could see Bunt through his door's window, but he couldn't see me.

The phone, Dieter, the phone.

His hands were still clenching and unclenching on the bed. I sincerely hoped he wasn't going to have a coronary on me. He looked at the window. The window, the window. No way could he get through those narrow vertical panes. He examined the ceiling. Not with two legs in casts, Dieter. He looked at the door. The door, the door. Overpower the guard? He looked around the room. No cinder-blocks. No elevator shafts. How inconvenient. His eyes rested on the phone by his bed.

The phone.

The phone.

He picked up the whole phone and set it in his lap on the bed.

He seemed to be considering, his hand on the receiver. You must have a number, I thought at him. You must have a number where you can reach Uncle Franz in emergencies. If you don't call them, they will come and kill you. If they don't kill you, then you will be tried and executed in Israel. Only one way out, Dieter. Call Uncle Franz now.

He picked up the receiver.

He hesitated, then put the receiver to his ear. He would get the switchboard automatically. They had my instructions to dial any number he wanted, anywhere on earth, with no questions.

His face lit up in a smile that turned my stomach. He was speaking now, sweet-talking the operator. Nodding his head. Laughing. What a charming guy. A model patient.

Serious now. Saying the phone number, very carefully. His eyes wandered as the connection went through. His face was very serious now. Getting ready to talk to Uncle Franz.

After a few moments, he began talking. I glanced at the wall clock in my room and noted the minute and second hand. Two minute warning. Of course, once Bunt gave her the phone number, that should supposedly give the location of his contacts in Germany. But, as Stickney had pointed out during the conversation where we set this whole deal up, that phone could well be a cut-out, its only purpose to relay phone calls to a second location where the bad guys actually hung out. Hence the need for Stickney's pal Rolf to check out the location in person. I had thought this uncharacteristically astute of Stickney, but maybe this was his non-evil double.

I turned back to Bunt. Some preliminary responses. Passwords. I am the egg-man, you are the walrus. Talk, I thought, talk.

And suddenly he began talking. Fast. What would he say first? Disclaim the messages that I'd sent. What messages? They would go and check. He was talking, obviously explaining, warning them against my alleged deception. Listening. Talking again, insisting. I glanced at the clock. Thirty seconds past.

He seemed confused. They didn't know what he was talking about. What messages? Where had he been? He began explaining. His face was earnest, almost cajoling. What a week I've had, he was telling them. First I had to kill Speen, then a few graduate students, one threw me down an elevator shaft, then my house blew up. One minute past.

He was now gesturing to himself in the bed. I'm in the hospital, I'm under guard. He was shaking his head and pointing. No, you have to come and get me. Arguing. Insisting. Demanding. A minute and a half.

He stopped. He looked at the phone. My heart skipped a beat. They didn't hang up! They didn't hang up! He put his mouth to the receiver and spoke again. It's okay. He was just surprised. What did they say? Why are you calling us? What do you mean, some student has access to your computer messages? He was defending himself now. He looked wild. He was shouting into the phone. He was pouring a torrent of words down the receiver. He was realizing I had tricked him into calling them, but he had no choice now. He had no other way to escape. I looked at the clock.

Two minutes!

He was pleading now. Begging. Promising anything, everything. Come get me. Don't kill me. You're all I have. You can't do this to me.

Two and a half minutes.

Threatening now. The old Bunt. Yelling. I could almost hear his voice through the doors. Shaking his fist at the phone. Ranting. Just ranting. Fury. And suddenly nothing. He looked shocked. He looked at the phone. He spoke a word. They had hung up.

Three minutes.

I sincerely hoped that the FBI had not screwed up. The stuff was seriously hitting the fan now.

I looked through the window and saw something unbelievable. Bunt was getting out of bed and struggling to stand on his two broken legs.

I got down from the chair and stepped into the corridor. The cop looked up. From inside his room we both heard a crash. The cop half-turned to the door. The door banged open, and there was Bunt, fighting to stand up. "Hey!" yelled the cop and twisted to grab him.

Bunt saw me and went berserk. He lunged at me, his fingers claws, his face a snarl. The cop had him by the waist but couldn't stop him. "Backup!" he called. "Security! Orderly! Help here!"

I stood immobile, transfixed by the spectacle of Bunt. There were already long cracks along his two casts. He dove forward again, and would have snagged me if the cop hadn't dragged him down. His face smacked against the floor, but he reared up at me again.

A second cop leaped from the left against Bunt, knocking him back to the floor. Bunt was striking at him with the phone receiver he still held. Two burly orderlies waded in from the right and flattened Bunt to the floor. They were followed by a nurse hurrying with a hypodermic. She swiped his hip with a cotton ball and popped him with the needle. He screamed. A second nurse brought a second hypodermic. The first nurse tossed the first hypo aside and popped him with the second needle.

After a couple of minutes, the cops and the orderlies stood up and hoisted Bunt by his limbs. His body was already going limp from the sedatives. Before he disappeared through the doors again, our eyes met once.

He transmitted fury and fear at me.

For some reason, my own eyes were wet.

"Mazel tov, Dieter," I said as the doors slammed shut.

Eighty-three

Downstairs, it looked like Times Square on New Years Eve. All the white shirts were whooping and slapping each other on the back.

Stickney was jubilant, his face red, a huge grin beaming.

"I guess it worked," I said to him.

"You son of a bitch," he addressed me, then gave me a sweaty bear hug I found repulsive. "Yes, by hell, it worked." He was fairly incoherent, but I gathered that at this moment West German state police were barrel-assing down on Uncle Franz's neck. Apparently, Uncle Franz was a major collection point for espionage material from agents like Bunt and Speen all over the world. They anticipated dozens of arrests, rounding up spies in Europe and America. It was big, a major touchdown.

Hospital officials were now giving the room's inhabitants some serious guff about the noise and goings-on.

Stickney raised his head and bellowed. "To the bars. I'm buying."

There was a ragged cheer and they all streamed out of the room and down the corridor, like a kindergarten recess. I grabbed Stickney by the arm as he went past me.

"What about guarding him?" I flicked my eyes upwards.

He scowled at me. "The locals can handle that," he said belligerently. He shook my hand loose and joined the others. Nobody said thank you that I noticed.

After the tumult and the shouting died, I made my own way out. It had been a day-and-a-half. I wanted to cruise home and hit the sheets.

Rachel was waiting in the corridor.

"You did it again," she said simply. She gave me a look that surpassed the one from the night before, but it only felt painful this time. I couldn't look at her.

"I guess," I managed to say.

"Now what?"

I shrugged. "Life."

She nodded.

"I'll see you around, Rachel," I said.

She nodded again. "See you, Mark. Take care. Thank you."

I drove directly to a liquor store. I bought a small bottle of wine, took it home and drank the whole thing. Some time after that I got sick and threw up everything, the whole day, the whole week, the last thirty years or so. I felt better then, and fell asleep at last.

Eighty-four

At the sound of the telephone ringing, I sat straight up out of my usual Lee nightmare. I looked at the clock.

Two a.m.

Oh no.

No one ever calls with good news at two a.m. I had had my share of two a.m. calls. Someone had died. Someone was dying. Someone would die.

I got out of bed with reluctance, a spinning head, and anticipatory distaste. The apartment was hermetically silent. Eli must be at her place. Whichever "her" it was tonight.

A column of icy moonlight pierced the living room window and flowed onto the linoleum and the carpet. I sat down in the chair near the phone. As I picked up the phone, I suddenly knew who was calling, and why, and I was more frightened than I had ever been before. I didn't mind death nearly as much as losing my mind and my reason.

I was cold sober as I held the receiver to my ear, and heard the hollowness of long distance and the half-heard whispers of electronic ghosts. The phone line was like a tunnel opening beneath me and I felt myself falling into the echoing electric stillness.

"Hello, Lee," I said.

"Hi, Mark," her voice sailed over the distance. "Sorry I woke you up."

I know a little too much about science to believe in telepathy, but it had always been this way with us. After a year of nothing, I knew it was her calling, and she knew she had awakened me. She had somehow known the number, too, because the phone was listed under Eli's name, not mine. We knew each other, you see, maybe more than was healthy. We would have made a wonderful couple, except for the fact that I loved her and she did not love me.

"That's okay," I said. "How are you doing?" In Seattle, I almost added, because I was now sure that's where she and her fiancé were. They wouldn't have much money, living on his internship stipend, and she would wait until after eleven her time, 2 a.m. my time, to call.

"Fine," she said, and I knew it was not so. Something was wrong between her and John. I felt like I was underwater trying to breathe. I looked down and saw that I was standing. I didn't remember getting up.

"How are you?" she continued. Do you still love me? Do you still hate me for what I did?

"I'm okay," I said. I am wracked by unending nightmares and my personal life is a shambles.

"I may be coming east for a while," she said, and I stopped breathing altogether. "I thought we might," she continued and the floor tipped under me and I nearly passed out.

Cold moonlight was spilling onto the floor. I moved my toe into it as she talked. I could almost feel it, like a thin and silvery liquid flowing along my skin. The moon is a sphere of rock and dust a quarter of a million miles away, I knew. It has no light of its own, but shines by reflecting light from the sun.

I felt a strange motion within me. A year ago, she had shattered the world beneath me, and I had been falling ever since. I now felt the jagged shards of that world falling upwards, coming together again, not slicing and torturing me as they had, but joining into a solid mass below my feet again.

I felt the earth balance beneath me.

"No, Lee," I heard myself say softly into the receiver.

She was silent for a moment. "I don't understand," she said quietly. "I only want to—"

"No," I said. "I can't know about you." Was this me speaking now?

"I'm sorry, Mark," she said presently. "You know I didn't mean to. You know how I feel about you."

I knew then that she loved me, had loved me, and could be mine now if I gave her the chance. As I had wanted. As I had wanted since the first moment I saw her. As I had wanted continuously in the desolate shadow of the year since she had left me.

Do it, I told myself. Don't be so foolish that you reject her just because she rejected you. Let yourself have what you want. For once, do the wrong thing.

I had a sudden image of our relationship: as a binary star system, two stars orbiting around each other forever, while the titanic gravitational forces between the two bodies tear them both to pieces, locked in an eternal dance of death.

I cleared my throat as best I could. "Listen, Lee," I said tenderly. "I love you. And I know you love me. But we can't be together. It just hurts too much. There's nothing wrong with me, and there's nothing wrong with you. It's our being together. It would destroy us. It would destroy us both."

I heard the silence on the line that meant she was crying, her silent tearless crying.

"Everything will be okay," I said. "It will work out. You'll be okay."

I heard a shudder of acknowledgment tumbling down the wire.

There was a space of silence.

"Goodbye, Lee," I said. "I'm going now. Goodnight."

"Okay," she said, calmly, resolutely. "Goodbye, Mark."

I went back to sleep, a mercifully dreamless sleep.

Friday

▼

Eighty-five

The phone rang again at 6 a.m., and I figured it had to be the Pope. I mean, who *hadn't* called me in the past 24 hours to tangle my life in knots?

It was Rachel, and I was instantly awake.

She gave no preamble. "Mark, please come down to the hospital immediately." ·

"What's going on?"

"He's gone."

Oh no, I thought. All that trouble, and the bastard died after all. Then it occurred to me that there were several meanings for "gone". And for "he", for that matter. I didn't want a repeat of the Jackson mixup.

"Time out. *Who* is *what?*" I asked calmly.

"Bunt. Andersson. He's escaped. He's gone."

My mouth opened and closed, but nothing came out.

"Come down here. Now. Please."

She hung up. I hung up automatically, in a serious daze. I looked at the clock again. Six hours ago, he was sedated and surrounded by police!

This was impossible. No wonder she needed me.

Eighty-six

After a rapid shower and shave (!) I careened to the hospital once again. The roads and woods were filled with morning mist. The world seemed totally silent. This changed markedly when I entered the conference room on the second floor.

"You!" Stickney thundered when he saw me. He lunged at me. Two of the nameless FBI guys seized him and held him away from me.

"You're gonna die!" he yelled from between them.

"Who isn't?" I retorted, trying to back away without seeming to back away. "What are you mad at me for?"

"It was *your* idea," he growled, jumping up and pointing at me. "*Your* idea to have him call his German buddies. Well, they came and helped him escape."

I smiled a crooked smile. "What did they use, that new Concorde? You can't get from there to here in less than six hours."

He was briefly silent, apparently appreciating my point. "I don't know how they did it, but they did it."

Rachel came into the room behind me, followed by Sergeant McKinnock. I felt relieved. He, at least, could probably take Stickney. I wouldn't have minded having Jackson in my corner, too. Rachel looked relieved to see me. Despite my feelings toward—or against—her, I felt for her.

"What happened?" I asked her.

She shook her head. "We're not sure. We were just about to make a complete examination of his room. Would you care to join us?"

I nodded and began to follow her. Stickney started to follow, too. The FBI guys still held him. He pushed at them. "I'm okay," he declared belligerently. They let him go and I gave them a look. They looked sheepish, exchanged a look between themselves, then followed Stickney closely. We all trooped upstairs.

There was a small group outside Bunt's room. Rachel indicated a cop with his arms crossed. "Officer Petri was on duty last night."

"You lousy traitor," Stickney began. "They got right past you, you hick flatfoot. You coward."

Petri lifted his chin and gave him a look, but otherwise ignored him. I liked Petri right off.

"Nobody got past me, Lieutenant," he addressed Rachel alone.

Rachel nodded. "Thank you, officer."

"I believe you," I said. I did. He seemed naturally sincere.

Stickney made some noise, but didn't say anything.

We all filed into the room. On the bed was a pile of sheets rolled up under the covers to look like a person sleeping.

"Wow," I said. "Pretty clever. I haven't seen that since scout camp."

Rachel sighed. "Everyone assumed he'd still be asleep from the sedatives. We didn't know until the orderly came in to see about his breakfast. This is what he found."

I handled the sheets, turning them back and forth, over and over, until it was obvious I had found something wrong. I scrunched up my face and shook my head.

Rachel addressed the orderly. "Are these hospital sheets?"

The man came over and pulled the sheets out and turned them over and examined them himself. "I don't think so," he said slowly, surprised. "Ours have the hospital name stenciled on them so people don't steal them. These don't."

I nodded. There were some thick cloth strips lying on the bed.

"What are these?" I asked.

A nurse spoke up. "We restrained him after we sedated him, on Mr. Stickney's advice."

I nodded. "These go around his arms?"

"Yes. And those around his legs. He could move around, adjust his position, but he couldn't get out of bed."

Rachel came closer and I backed away. She examined the restraints carefully. "These have been cut," she commented.

I agreed. "Sliced would be a better word. Something very sharp." I turned to one of the crewcuts. "What are those really sharp knives they have in art supply stores?" I mused.

Crewcut One thought and said, "You mean like X-Acto knives?"

I nodded exaggeratedly. "That's what I was thinking of. Thanks." I turned to Stickney. "Bunt have a utility blade on him?"

He snorted. "Utility blade!"

"Then someone else must have cut him loose," Crewcut One deduced.

Stickney shot a look at Petri.

"No one got in here," Petri maintained.

"Gosh," I said theatrically. "If no one came in through the door, then how did they come in?"

Everyone began sweeping their eyes around the room.

The room had a dropped ceiling of acoustic panels. "So, like what would be above a ceiling like this?"

Another crewcut stepped onto the bed, then up on the headboard, then across to a box-like light fixture. It was good to see somebody taking action here. Everyone seemed too stunned to move. I, on the other hand, had nearly been shot, splattered, and blown up in the last few days, plus— or minus—my encounters with Rachel and with Lee. It's amazing how having your whole life ripped apart helps put things in perspective. I was way past being fazed by a mere escape.

Crewcut Two poked his head up against one of the ceiling tiles. It raised at an angle, and he ran his eyes around the room. "Not through there," he announced with a little pride. "Solid all the way around."

Several painted metal ventilation ducts passed through the room. Nobody larger than an infant could pass through one of them, though, especially not a man with two leg casts.

"I guess they must have come in through the windows," I stated naively.

This was manifestly impossible, and Stickney said as much, but more crudely. Some of the crewcuts laughed.

Only two parts of the windows opened, two vertical sections about eight inches wide, at each end of the room. Again, it was hard to imagine an adult getting through them, and impossible to imagine a man with leg casts doing it. Between the two narrow vertical panels were three large panes of glass, which did not open.

I strolled over to the windows, to the vast amusement of the agents. Rachel looked embarrassed. I cranked one of the panels as wide as it would open, then jammed my right arm and upper body into the opening. I looked down. There was a triangular hedge three stories down. I looked up. There were two blank stories above. I looked to the side.

I suddenly lunged sideways through the window. Rachel cried, "Mark!" and two policemen rushed forward. But I was fine, and struggled my way back through the window and into the room.

I held my index finger out to Stickney. There was a gray blob at the end of it. He held out his hand almost involuntarily, and I scraped the blob into his palm.

"Window putty," I said. "Fresh, soft window putty."

Two of the crewcuts advanced with astonished looks and examined the pane closely. "Somebody took out that center pane," Crewcut Three explained. "They came in through the window, took the guy, put the pane back in, and resealed it."

They all exchanged looks of astonishment, glancing from me to the putty in Stickney's hand, to the window. "Interesting hedge," I pointed out to Crewcut Four, then looked up toward the roof.

Crewcut Four looked down, then up. "They must have come from the roof," he said. He looked at Stickney, then headed out of the room. Everyone followed him like people in a trance.

We all banged up the stairwell to the roof door. One of the hospital security guards produced a ring of keys and unlocked the door.

It felt strange to be out in the open air, so high up. From up there, I could see the pond where I had first sailed with Lee. They should put up a plaque. I walked immediately to the edge and looked over. I hate heights, and was glad of the low wall that ran completely around the flat roof. I walked about thirty feet and looked over again. I could see the triangular hedge directly below.

"Hey, there's that same hedge," I remarked loudly.

Everyone came over, looked over the side, then glanced around randomly.

I walked around a brick chimney about seven feet high and four feet thick, running my fingers over the surface. Then I went to the edge and examined the metal facing. Another crewcut showed Stickney, "You can see the marks in the soot where ropes rubbed around the chimney. And the dirt's worn away from the metal edge of the roof."

"Wow," I exclaimed. "How many people would it take to do all this?"

Crewcut Five considered, then said, "Well, probably one up here tending the ropes. One to take out the window and hold it. Another to go in and get the guy."

I turned to Rachel. "These FBI guys are good," I said. "They have the whole thing figured out already."

She gave me a little smile. "They are professionals," she stated.

I furrowed my brow. "The thing I don't get is how they got Bunt up here, then down the stairs without anyone inside noticing."

The last crewcut looked over the edge. "Check it out," he offered. "Tire tracks in the snow right below the window. Looks like something backed up here. Maybe a pickup truck. They probably dropped right into it, waited for the guy up here, and drove away."

"Oh," I said. "That makes sense."

We all headed down to the parking lot, and found the triangular hedge below the window. We all examined the tire tracks in the snow, then gazed back up at the roof.

Stickney looked at the tracks, then at me, then at his men. When he spoke, it was with calmness and authority. "I want fingerprints. The room.

The window. The roof. Here. I want casts of these tire tracks. I want rope fibers from the roof. I want the type and make of window putty. I want the brand of sheets. And the type of utility blade that cut those restraints."

The FBI guys waited until they were sure he was done speaking, then looked at me. I nodded appreciatively at Stickney's orders, and they scattered in six different directions.

Stickney pointed at me and Rachel. "Come with me, please," he said. I was so surprised by the "please" that I did what he asked. Still, as I walked, I couldn't help wondering who, exactly, had grabbed Bunt.

Eighty-seven

As we followed Stickney to the far end of the parking lot, Rachel said in a low voice, not turning to face me, "I didn't know you were interested in puppetry."

I couldn't help a smile. In the same kind of low voice, I replied, "I only use my powers for good."

Rachel and I followed him to a nondescript late-model American car that screamed "cop". He unlocked the doors, and got into the driver's seat. Rachel got in the passenger's seat, and I slid into the back. It was inhumanly clean. He started the car and tuned the radio to an all-news station.

"You," he addressed me. He shook his head. "I can't decide whether to shake your hand or pound the crap out of you."

"Do I get a vote?"

"What's your problem, Payne?" asked Rachel.

"You want to know my problem? Here's my problem. The professor here is right. There's no way Bunt's pals could have got over here fast enough to grab him. Besides which, I think they're more likely to have greased him in his bed, than take him with them. So, who took him? And, more important, how did they know to take him? The way I see it, only us three knew, or even thought, that this was Dieter Bunt. I know I didn't tell anybody. I doubt if you told anybody," pointing at Rachel, "and you," pointing at me, "I don't know. I go back and forth."

Rachel said, "I have told no one. I would have no reason to tell anyone."

"Not your husband," said Stickney, and I winced.

"No. One." Rachel said.

Stickney nodded. "Leaves you, buckaroo," he said to me.

"Bull. You said yourself you sent a telegram to Israeli intelligence about Bunt."

Stickney held up a finger. "Saying nothing more than, Is Bunt alive? Even if they guessed we might have someone around here we thought might be Bunt, how would they know it was Andersson? How would they know we had him? How would they know he was in the hospital? Which hospital? Which floor? Which room? And how would they know in enough time to get over here and grab him? Israel's even farther away than Germany."

I shook my head. "I don't know."

"Well, it's not me, and it's not her. Who does that leave? Why can't you have called up the Israelis a week ago and said, Hey, we might have Dieter Bunt in a few days, stand by? Then last night, no two nights ago you call them and say, he's in such and such hospital, more to come. By this time, they're already here. Then last night you call and say he's on the third floor and there's a guard on the door."

I shrugged. "Why not is because I didn't. Why not you?"

"Come on, professor, figure it out: why would I give up my star suspect? As of last night, I had the biggest spy since Benedict Arnold in my hands and today I have dog turds. This is not advancing my career any, you know."

This made sense, in a crude sort of way. I looked at Rachel. Unthinkable. Whatever else might be going on between us, she was a straight arrow. No way it could be her.

"I don't know. There must be some other way."

"What way?"

"I don't know."

We chased around like that for almost an hour. Fact: One of us had to have done it. Fact: There was no reason for any of us to have done it. There was no way to resolve it.

Finally, I just gave up and left. Stickney promised he would be watching me. Rachel seemed not to know what to think.

I drove home with a bad taste of unfinished business in my mouth.

Would I never get myself untangled from this?

Eighty-eight

On my way up to the apartment, I automatically checked the mail. There was only one thing in the box, a large manila envelope with my name on it. I brought it up and tossed it on my bed.

I washed my face and ate lunch. I didn't have the energy to walk to the dining hall, so I had a waffle sandwich. You do not want the recipe.

As I passed by my bedroom, I noticed the envelope again. I was mildly curious. It seemed too big for junk mail, so it was probably from the university. That usually meant me paying some money for tuition or fees or some other bureaucratic synonym. Paying anybody anything would be a problem for a while. I was heavily into my rent money already. And my police consulting activities were not paying well at all. Add in the wear and tear on the soul, and I was a losing proposition.

There was something strange about the envelope itself, and I stared at it for a good minute before I realized what.

There was no address on it.

And no postage.

All that was on the outside of the envelope was my name.

This stunned me, and I'll tell you why. Only the mail carrier and the box owners have keys to the boxes. Obviously, Eli would not leave me an envelope in the mail box. If he wanted to leave me something, he'd put it on the kitchen table. But neither would the mail carrier be delivering anything without an address or stamps.

So, who had put this in my box?

And why?

I looked at the package suspiciously. I had heard of letter bombs, and while I would not ordinarily consider myself the likely target of one, the last few days had been rather unusual. For all I knew, I might be on a letter bomb mailing list.

I felt the envelope. It felt like it was full of paper.

I bent the envelope as far as it would bend, nearly double. It bent like paper.

I shook the envelope and listened to it. It sounded like paper.

I was going out on a limb here, but my theory was that it was paper.

I suddenly got impatient with caution, ripped the end off, and peeked inside.

It was paper.

I pulled out one of the papers and examined it. It was big and rectangular and looked like a stock certificate, all swirls and ornate writing and numbers in the corners.

Except it was all in German.

What on earth was this?

I could think of only one place to find out.

Eighty-nine

When I was a kid, the elementary school began a bank savings program. Each week my parents would put a few dollars into a special envelope and I'd carry it proudly to school. The school would pass all the envelopes on to the banks, which would deposit it in our names. The idea was to get us all started early in saving for college or, in the case of most of the kids in my neighborhood, bail.

There were two banks participating, and, at that juncture in my life, I did not know their names. But one bank had pink envelopes and one bank had green. Mine had pink, and I considered myself a member, a teammate, a partner, in the pink bank. Each week, we pinks and greens counted up to see how many envelopes there were of each. The pinks always won, a point I took considerable satisfaction in. Still, the greens maintained a resolute pride, which was admirable in itself.

I continued to be a pink until I went to college, where the only bank was the green bank. And so, I went over to the greens. Defecting was that easy.

It was to the green bank branch in Kingstown that I drove with the envelope. I took one of the papers with me and sat just outside the little rail separating the bank officers from the mere depositors.

At length, a big bald man looked at me from behind his desk and said, "Next?" I pushed through the little gate and sat before his desk.

He didn't like long hair. I could tell that right off. I considered telling him that until recently my hair had been much longer, but that I had seen the light and was now trimming down, little by little. He just frowned at me through big glasses and said, "May I help you?" in a tone that indicated that helping me was the last thing on earth he wanted to do.

"I hope so," I replied. I handed him the paper. "My uncle gave me this, oh it must be two years back now, and I just stuck it away in a drawer. Well, I happened to come across it, and I wondered if it might be worth anything."

Pleased with an excuse to ignore me, he examined the paper closely. Then he stood up and walked away. Uh-oh. I looked around to confirm the location of the exits. But he only walked over to another desk and showed it to a woman. He said something, then she said something, then he nodded and came back and sat down.

"This is a German bearer bond," he said. I daresay Ben would have known what he was talking about, and probably even knew a few good jokes about German bearer bonds, but as far as I was concerned, he might as well have said that it was a gathering spell for the Sixth Clan of Orn.

"I see," I said politely. "What's that?"

Glad to display his superiority over me in every way that did not involve hair, he leaned back and looked at me patiently. "You purchase these bonds. Then for the next few years they pay you interest on your money. Then at the end of the term, they send you your original money back again."

"I see," I said again. "Is it worth anything?"

He held the bond up so I could see it. He seemed reluctant to actually give it back to me, possibly because it had to do with money, which was clearly his department and not that of some scruffy college student. He pointed to the number that appeared in each corner. "This is the face value. That's the amount you get back after," he perused the paper briefly, "five years. And these are the coupons you send in each year to get," pointing to another number, "this amount in yearly interest. All in Deutschmarks, of course."

"Of course," I said. "How much would that be in dollars?"

He gave me a look of contempt, indicating his opinion of people who wanted to possess and use money, rather than leave it in banks where it belonged. Then he looked up a number in the newspaper, and did a calculation on a desk calculator.

Reading the result he said, "You would get about fifty dollars a year for five years, then two hundred and fifty dollars at the end."

I made my face fall, and he looked delighted.

"So, no Corvette," I said dully.

He tossed the bond back to me and smiled broadly. "Sorry, no."

"Thanks for your help," I said dejectedly.

"That's what we're here for," he said sincerely.

Outside I started my car and drove down an alley between two buildings, then looked around cautiously. When I was sure no one could observe me, I gave a whoop of delight and punched my fists in the air triumphantly.

"Yes!" I exclaimed.

You see, each bond might be worth only $50 per year, and $250 at the end of five years.

But I had two hundred of them.

I had just doubled my income.

Ninety

A quick visit to another bank gave me a safe deposit box in which to hold my new-found treasure.

It was something of a mystery to me, but not entirely.

I knew where the money had come from, of course. Dr. Wolff had mentioned a reward. A sizable reward. Well, I would call one hundred thousand dollars sizable. And I had no doubt that the same people who could spirit Bunt away through a window in a guarded hospital room could get an envelope into my mailbox.

That wasn't the mysterious part.

No, what was mysterious was: how did they know it was me?

Ninety-one

Sudden wealth made me feel good. I decided to celebrate with a richly deserved nap. After the early rigors of this morning, and the demands of dealing with the banker, I felt I owed myself a nice snooze. I retired forthwith.

When I woke up it was four o'clock. I idly cleaned up my room. The book of pictures was still on my dresser. I brought it to my closet. Before putting it away, I flipped to the photo of Dieter Bunt. We almost got you, you bastard. Almost. I pushed the book to the back of the closet shelf and went into the bathroom.

Ten seconds later I was back, cracking open the book with trembling hands, poring over the picture.

No.

No way.

No way, no way, no way.

I sat down heavily on the bed. I felt like a whole glacier was slithering down my spine.

I shut the book. The whole planet seemed to be lurching sideways, unstoppably and uncontrollably. Somehow, realizing that it was only my mind lurching sideways didn't help. Optical illusion, I thought, apropos of nothing, and everything. It looks like one thing, but is something else entirely.

Thirty years ago. Thirty years. A long time. A very long time. And yet, not so long for some things. For waiting. For searching. For killing.

Suddenly, a horrible thought occurred to me and I half-stood reflexively. I was in trouble, very personal trouble. Deep, vast, and deadly. I was in quite specific danger of my life.

And then another thought occurred, even more shocking in its implications: there was only one person I could go to about this.

My friendly neighborhood FBI agent.
I shut my eyes.
"Oh no."

Ninety-two

I sat stiffly at the kitchen table and, as if in a surreal dream, wrote a few sentences on a sheet of notebook paper. I signed and dated it and sealed it in an envelope. On the outside of this envelope, I wrote some simple instructions, then put that envelope into a larger one. On the larger envelope, I wrote "Rachel Trask" and the address of the police department. I stuck two stamps on it, and dropped it in the mailbox on my way to the car.

Before I left, I looked around the apartment. It wasn't much to come home to every day, but, with no exaggeration, I did not know if I would ever see it again.

Ninety-three

Stickney was staying at the Holiday Inn. I found his room on a perfectly quiet and still corridor and knocked on the door.

"Come in," I heard him say.

The door was unlocked (don't they lock automatically?) and I stepped in. It was like every other motel room in the known universe. A bathroom to the right, then two beds bolted to the floor (do people really steal *beds* from motel rooms?). On the left, a small dresser, wall mirror, TV and a tiny round table with uncomfortable armchairs. Stickney was sitting in one of the chairs, with some papers spread out in front of him on the tiny round table.

"You," he said, and it sounded like an accusation.

"Yes," I answered, correctly. I was shortly going to have to do something pretty unpleasant with this guy: I did not want his goading to make me like it.

"What are you doing here?" he demanded.

I pulled out the other chair and sat down. It was fully as uncomfortable as I had imagined. "Thanks, don't mind if I do," I replied.

"What do you want?" he said with annoyance.

"I want us to talk about a few things."

He leaned back in his chair, his hands clasped behind his head. His coat was on the back of his chair. His motion showed off a matching vest, an unwrinkled white shirt with no sweat marks, and the handle of a gun in its holster. It was mainly the gun that held my interest.

"What about?" he wanted to know.

Once, when I was watching Stan play hockey, an opponent had been crosschecking him relentlessly. Either the ref didn't know that crosschecking was illegal or hadn't noticed the miscreant. Finally, after the latest outrage and during the lull before a face-off, Stan dropped his gloves.

Now, every hockey player on earth knows what dropping your gloves means. Hockey gloves are too bulky and unwieldy in a fight. If you're going to throw punches, you need your fists free.

Sitting in the stands, I was surprised, because Stan is essentially a non-violent guy. He's big and can talk tough, but I've seen him simply walk away from many a potential bar-fight. Even on the ice, when others had dropped their gloves in preparation for instigating some mayhem, I had seen Stan just shove them away and ignore them.

But not this time. Stan had had just about enough of this guy's stick across his face. Stan's gloves hit the ice and he angled his body to the guy in a meaning manner. The guy turned abruptly and skated away, cursing a little under his breath. Stan calmly retrieved his gloves and lined up for the face-off. There was no more crosschecking.

I was feeling the same way about Stickney. I had taken just about enough of his heavy-handed bullying, and it was time for it to stop. I had mentally shucked my gloves. This goon was about to learn a lesson.

I took a deep breath and let it out. Show time, kids.

I leaned forward. "Katanga walks," I stated simply.

He smiled broadly at this, showing his teeth. More than ever, he looked like a well-dressed shark.

"'Katanga walks'," he repeated to himself with delight. "That's good. I like that." He suddenly lunged forward and slapped both hands on the table. "You've been watching too many detective movies, kid. Why the hell does Katanga walk?"

I studied him. He was making this extremely difficult.

I spoke patiently. "A couple of reasons. Katanga is innocent, in the best sense of the word. You don't need to try him. He isn't a bad guy."

Stickney snorted. "Bad is as bad does," he said, as he had before. I frowned, trying to puzzle out his meaning, as if from an abstract equation. "Katanga knew what he was doing. He transferred sensitive documents to unauthorized hands. He broke the law. He goes down."

I took another breath and let it out.

"Okay," I said calmly. "But that's only the first reason."

"What's the other reason?"

I looked straight at him. The room was very quiet. I thought about his gun again.

"If you don't let Katanga go, I'll turn you in for tipping off the Israelis."

He took my stab at extortion quite well. He threw back his head and laughed. I bring so much pleasure to his life. He sat back in the chair again, shaking with mirth. When he had composed himself somewhat, he said between giggles, "You'll turn me in, huh? That's funny." He gestured at the papers in front of him. "I'm in the process of turning *you* in for the very same thing."

I looked down at the papers. There seemed to be a lo of bureaucracy involved in framing me.

I nodded. "Yes, but the difference is that you actually did it."

He wiped some final tears of laughter from his eyes. "Why would you think *I* did it?" he asked, as a straight man might feed a line to a comedian.

I shifted in the chair a little. It really was grim. "It was something you said yourself. You said only you, me, and Lieutenant Trask knew about Bunt, and you trusted Lieutenant Trask. I agree with your reasoning. The leak had to be one of us three. I know I didn't do it, and I trust Lieutenant Trask too, so…" I spread my hands in a helpless gesture.

He smirked. "Still 'Lieutenant Trask', huh? I could have told you she was married, kid."

I glared at him, unable to speak.

He went on. "But it was more fun to watch you follow her around like a puppy dog," he said with glee.

I scowled at him. I did not like this man.

"Be that as it may," I said word by word, when I could speak. "It had to be you."

He spread his hands in a magnanimous gesture. "Well, then, we have a difference of opinion. I believe you did it, and you believe I did it. Of course, you were the one who knew Speen and Katanga, not me. And you were the one who blew up Bunt's house, destroying any evidence, not me. And you," he said, dropping his voice, leaning forward, closing one eye and aiming at me along his pointing finger, "you were the one who knew how to contact the German spies, not me."

My jaw dropped. The way he told it, it implied very strongly that I was involved somehow with Speen and Katanga, and that I did turn Bunt in.

None of this was true. This isn't *The Murder of Roger Akroyd*. I didn't do it.

But I *was* speechless.

He lowered his finger from my face and sat back in his chair. "Besides which, why on earth would I give away my only real suspect in this case? And why on earth would I give up the biggest world criminal captured since Eichmann? Some FBI agent that would make me."

I had calmed sufficiently to be able to respond. "Yes, some FBI agent. You've done nothing on this case at all, except try to cut me out of it. You've talked to no one, you haven't even gone to where the crimes were committed."

He chuckled. "Are you following *me* around now? How do you know where I've been and who I've talked to?"

Whom, I thought. What do they teach at Yale, anyhow? "You've never been interested in the espionage at all. You've always been perfectly happy to let Katanga take the full rap, as long as it meant Bunt would stay clear of the charges."

"My investigation has proceeded in a reasonable fashion," he countered. "I have one of the espionage ring in custody. Another is dead. The third has unfortunately escaped, thanks to you."

I shook my head. "You had a real problem there, didn't you? Thanks to me, Bunt was deeply implicated in both the espionage and the murder. You could do something about the espionage, since it was a federal crime and you're the federal investigator. But there was nothing you could do about the murder charge. I had established too well that Bunt was the murderer. And even if that didn't stick somehow, he had definitely attempted to murder me. Thanks to me, your man would certainly be convicted, either of murder or attempted murder. And you didn't want him convicted of anything."

He was shaking his head with a mock-bewildered look on his face. "Why?" he said. "Why wouldn't I want him to be convicted? I'm an FBI agent. We catch and convict criminals. It's sort of our thing. Why wouldn't I want Bunt convicted *if* he did those crimes?"

Now I leaned forward. "Because if he were in prison, he might never be extradited to Israel. And you wanted him to be extradited to Israel to stand trial for his war crimes, and be executed."

Again he spread his hands, with a still-bewildered-but-tolerant look on his face. "Again, why?" he asked. "I'll admit that, by rights, maybe Bunt should be tried for his war crimes at some point. But why should it make any difference to me if he rots in an American or an Israeli prison?"

"You know the reason," I stated.

He looked directly at me. "What reason?" he asked.

He was really going to make me say it. I thought of his gun for a moment, then thought, So what. I had sent the letter, hadn't I?

I sat back in my chair, regarding him for a moment. I looked down at the floor, then straight into his eyes.

"Because he murdered your father," I said.

The effect was instantaneous. He looked like the power had gone out at the main. His face drained completely of color. His hands, outstretched in braggadocio and bluster, sagged limply. His eyes seemed to be fixed on some small object ten parsecs away.

Since he was clearly in no condition to speak, I continued in a low voice. "On March 16, 1945, Dieter Bunt hanged your father, Grigori Austikanis. Three days later, the Russians liberated the camp and Bunt vanished. I'm not sure, but I believe your mother had already fled with you. You were just an infant, you probably never knew your father. She brought you to this country, changed your name to Stickney."

He stood up and ran his hands through his hair. He turned his back to me and looked out the window at the setting sun. He spoke as if in a dream. "My father had relatives who had come over earlier. The immigration agents had changed their name to Stickney. We lived with them. I grew up with them."

I nodded. When he didn't go on, I continued. "At some point, you found out about your father, how he had died. You became a cop to find Bunt."

He shook his head. "No, you've got it backwards. My father was a policeman. That's all my mother ever told me about him. She said he was a policeman, that he was a good man, that he died in the war. My other relatives told me how he had helped others to escape, before the Gestapo arrested them. He was supposed to be helping the Gestapo round people up to go to the camps. Instead, he warned them and they escaped. The Gestapo finally caught on and came for us. He managed to get my mother and me away safely, but he was arrested himself. I grew up wanting to be a policeman, to be like him."

"Then when did you find out about Bunt?"

He turned to face me, but his eyes were far away, like he was watching a movie unreel in his mind. "I had just become an FBI agent. There had been an incident in Texas, a possible sighting of Bunt, and I was one of the agents investigating. I read Bunt's file and saw that picture, the same one in the book. It was the first time I ever saw my father." His voice shook and I thought he would cry, but he continued. "And I saw Bunt. Standing there. Smiling. And I knew he was still alive, that I had to find him, and kill him."

I was thinking out loud now. "You followed him to Cleveland."

Stickney nodded. "We lost him in Dallas. But then he surfaced again in Ohio. I knew everything that anyone knew about him. When his pattern started appearing in Cleveland, I transferred there. We were close to him, so close."

I remembered something. "His house blew up! Killed two agents."

He nodded his head. "It was almost me. When I got the call that they had found his house, I told them to wait. But they were in a hurry. I was a block away when the house blew. They were friends of mine. We didn't know. They didn't know." He shook his head, lost in the past.

I prompted him. "Then this happened."

"Yeah. We lost him again, but I thought he had gone to California. That's why I was in San Diego all that time. When I heard the reports from here, I pulled every string I could to get this espionage case. All I had to do was find him, then get the Israelis." He looked at me earnestly. "I had come around to the idea that he should suffer as much as possible. He *had* to go to Israel, to be imprisoned by Jews, to be tried by Jews, to be hanged by Jews."

I nodded. "And that's where I screwed things up for you."

He let out a deep breath. "You. I don't know what to think about you. *You* found him. I was here. But *you* found him. And caught him. And I owe you for that."

I was stunned. I thought for a moment—madness, I know—that he might actually thank me. But he recovered.

"But then I couldn't shake him loose from the charges. You had done too much before I got here. Without you, I could have sweet-talked or bullied the local police into suspending the investigation until I was ready. But you had things locked up tight before I even got here. I didn't care about murder or espionage or Katanga or the German connection. But I had no choice, except to go along with what was happening. And the only reason I kept hanging onto Katanga was to have something to trade with. I thought if everything else failed, I might get you and Trask to swap Katanga's freedom for Bunt's custody somehow."

I was horrified. "That's the only reason you've been persecuting this poor guy? What is wrong with you, Stickney?"

"I needed Bunt," he said flatly. "He was in my hands. I was not going to lose him at this point. Thank heaven you broke his legs. The hospital was the perfect place to snatch him from. I contacted the Israelis days ago. They grabbed him the first chance they had."

He sat back down and we looked at each other. This man had been chasing his father's murderer for years. I had just stumbled into the middle of the hunt. This is indeed a strange little world.

"How did you know?" he finally asked.

I shrugged. "A lot of little pieces. Like your listing in *Who's Who in Law Enforcement.* Your full name is Gregory Payne Stickney, Junior. So, your father's name was Gregory, too. But he wasn't listed. Neither was your place of birth. Seemed strange. Like you were keeping your father and your birthplace secret. Why? And then it finally hit me. A father named Gregory, or Grigori. Stickney, Austikanis. I don't know where the Payne came from." I realized what I just said. Maybe I did. "And then it all fell into place. Your postings in Dallas and Cleveland. And right now, you're stationed in California, where Dr. Wolff told me Bunt was rumored to be. You've been following him half your life."

He nodded. "But it's over now. Finally. He'll show up in Israel soon. He may already be there."

"Your friend in the Mossad?"

"Yes. I actually sent him two telegrams. One was the plain query I told you about, to cover myself, in case I ever had to produce it. The second was very long, giving them all the information they would need to come and get Bunt. They already had their people here, waiting. All they needed was his location."

"So your friend answered that Bunt was dead, when all the while they were getting ready to grab him."

Stickney nodded. "So where does that leave us?"

I stood up. I leaned over his table, my hands resting on the papers. I put my face very close to his and said, "Katanga walks."

He sat back in his chair and regarded me. His old haughtiness was returning now. He seemed about to speak, but I spoke first and stopped him.

"You make sure. There will be no arrest or indictment or investigation of Katanga. His name will not appear in any report. You will never mention his involvement to anyone in any way." I paused. "Or I will give to the newspapers an amazing story of an FBI agent so intent on bringing his father's killer to justice that he subverts murder and espionage investigations, frees a suspected spy, and conspires with a foreign intelligence service to kidnap and deport the suspected killer. I think it would make good reading. And I know it would bring your career as a 'law enforcement officer' to an end. That's the deal. Katanga walks and I keep quiet. You lose nothing of importance to you."

"You seem pretty sure of yourself."

"That's the deal. That's the only way."

He looked at me levelly. I found myself thinking about that gun again. Then he said something I never really thought I'd hear him say.

"Okay."

I was fairly stunned. I was also wary. He was, after all, capable of doing almost anything to protect himself and bring Bunt to justice. If he thought I was getting in the way...

I stayed tough. "Don't try to intimidate me, either. I've written this whole thing down. If anything happens to me, it goes to Rachel Trask, who will know what to do with it."

He seemed to appreciate the truth of that. Rachel Trask would make a formidable avenger, and he knew it. "How can I trust you? When I do my part, what's to keep you from telling the newspapers anyway?"

"Payne, if you don't know by now that I'm someone to be trusted, you really are the worst judge of human nature I've ever met."

He considered that and nodded. "Deal."

We shook hands. I didn't trust him an inch.

"I'm sorry about your father."

He took a deep breath. "It was a long time ago. At least now, my life can go on again. I really owe you my thanks for helping to catch him."

I stood silent for a long moment, then went to the door and prepared to leave.

"One last thing," he said.

I turned back to him.

"What was it like?"

I knew what he meant. I felt like we were some secret knighthood taking a brief respite in the forever battle to save civilization from those who would rule by terror and preside over the slaughter of the weak and the innocent. Monsters still walked this earth, and we stood against them. This man's family, life and world had been savaged by Bunt and those like Bunt. He had spent his life seeking them out to do battle.

He was asking about a battle that I had fought, however unwillingly. I could feel him probing my mind, searching for that image: the look of horror as Bunt fell back into nothingness. Maybe that's all we can do, is remind the violent savages that they too are human, they too can suffer, and that whatever temporary power they may hold, they too can die.

I nodded slightly. "It was great."

The strain and anguish relaxed from his face. "Thank you," he said in a clipped voice.

"It was my pleasure."

Ninety-four

It was dark outside, and I took my time driving home. On the way, I changed radio stations to avoid yet another Bee Gees song, and heard an interesting news bulletin instead. Unconfirmed reports from Israel indicated that a long-sought Nazi war criminal had turned up under mysterious circumstances. This man was said to be personally responsible for the deaths of hundreds if not thousands of people. The trial promised to be an explosive one, as the man, long believed dead, seemed to have connections to spies around the world.

"I guess I was right," I thought, and changed to a different station.

Ninety-five

I returned to the apartment, and its dingy ordinariness seemed very special.

I sank into a chair in the living room, tired to my soul.

I had already asked Rachel to keep me out of any reports or news stories. She had agreed with great reluctance, seeming to think that I deserved some public recognition for what I had done. I felt exactly the opposite. I would have found it intensely embarrassing to have it generally known. I'm not sure why, but it would have been excruciatingly painful for me.

For the same reason, I had also determined never to tell any of my friends about this adventure. It just seemed too difficult. And where could I possibly begin? "Hey, guess what I did last week?" Too weird.

All I wanted to do now was live. Sleep. Go to school. Teach. Maybe try out Lisa's theory. Back in the saddle again. The semester would be over in a few weeks. Who knew what might happen? There might even be some other women, somewhere, who were not my students, who might find my new appearance acceptable. As the sportscasters say, I had my whole future in front of me.

The phone rang. Rachel? Lee? Stickney? Bunt? There was approximately one way to find out.

I picked up the phone and heard a familiar voice. "I'd like a large, no anchovies, please."

I smiled.

"Sorry, I spell my name Danger."

"Okay, now listen," Ben continued. "We haven't seen you in a week. You've probably been doing homework up the ying-yang, plus teaching that extra course. True?"

"You been following me around?"

"Just as I thought. Now hear this. Blick is having a house party tonight, and you are commanded to go."

"That sounds like Lisa talking."

"I'm not saying no. Anyway, you are coming to this party with us, no arguments. And don't make trouble, or we'll introduce you to some women there."

"That's cruel and unusual."

"Well, you've been asking for it. I know you: studying too hard and working too hard. You can't study all the time, you know. It's time for a little fun. A little excitement."

Excitement. I thought of the last week. Elevator shafts and exploding houses. Tormenting professors, insane war criminals, treacherous FBI agents. A shave and a haircut. Exorcising Lee and enduring Rachel. Meeting Harriet.

Harriet. Now there was a thought. I put my hand in my coat pocket and touched her book.

Maybe.

"When you're right, you're right," I said. "When's this party?"

THE END

About the Author

Edmund X. DeJesus was born in Providence and raised in Cranston, Rhode Island. He received a Bachelor of Science degree in mathematics from the University of Rhode Island, and Masters and Ph.D. degrees in theoretical physics, also from URI.

He has taught at Middle Tennessee State University and Boston University. He has been a programmer with IBM (writing software to help Navy subs not bump into things), a researcher at MIT's Lincoln Laboratory (analyzing data from Soviet missile tests), and an editor of BYTE Magazine (writing the cover story for BYTE's final issue).

He is currently a freelance writer who contributes articles to many technical publications. He lives in Massachusetts with his wife and two children. He enjoys reading humor (especially P.G. Wodehouse and Dave Barry), mysteries (including Agatha Christie and Dick Francis), and classic science fiction (such as Isaac Asimov and Philip K. Dick).

He has been published in *Alfred Hitchcock's Mystery Magazine*. This is his first novel.